BEAUTIFUL ... AND DEADLY

The T-X was halfway across the gymnasium when the far door opened and a man entered. Her visual scanners picked out his face, analyzed it, and returned a match.

John Connor. She was within sight of her supreme priority.

She broadcast a compressed message: JOHN CONNOR AT THIS LOCATION. COMMENCING TERMINATION, MOVE IN ALL UNITS FOR CAPTURE AND TERMINATION OF SECONDARY UNITS. Then she adjusted her body language so that her walk would suggest uncertainty and disbelief, adjusted her vocal patterns likewise. "Uncle John?"

"Gwen, thank God." John Connor did not look surprised. Of course he did not. He was expecting her. His bodyguard unit was bringing her to him.

But he was still standing too close to the exit. If she revealed her weapon now, he might have the opportunity to run through the doorway. That was unacceptable.

Now he was ten paces from the door. He could not escape in time. She caused the liquid metal sheath to withdraw from her right arm, revealing the mechanisms beneath, and caused them to reconfigure into her plasma cannon . . .

W9-DBH-447

TERMINATOR®
HUNT

AARON ALLSTON

■ ■ ■

A novel based on characters created in
Terminator® 3: Rise of the Machines™

■ ■ ■

Screenplay by
John Brancato & Michael Ferries
Story by **John Brancato, Michael Ferries,
& Tedi Sarafian**

TOR®

A TOM DOHERTY ASSOCIATES BOOK
NEW YORK

This is a work of fiction. All the characters and events portrayed in this book are either products of the author's imagination or are used fictitiously.

TERMINATOR® HUNT: A NOVEL BASED ON CHARACTERS CREATED IN TERMINATOR® 3: RISE OF THE MACHINES

® used under license. ™ and text copyright © 2004 by IMF Internationale Medien und Film GmbH & Co. 3 Produktions KG.

A Tor Book
Published by Tom Doherty Associates, LLC
175 Fifth Avenue
New York, NY 10010

www.tor.com

Tor® is a registered trademark of Tom Doherty Associates, LLC.

ISBN 0-765-35093-9
EAN 978-0-765-35093-0

First edition: December 2004
First mass market edition: December 2005

Printed in the United States of America

0 9 8 7 6 5 4 3 2 1

This novel is dedicated to everyone who
finally worked up the courage.

ACKNOWLEDGMENTS

Thanks go to:
Russell Galen, my agent, and James Frenkel, my editor; Helen Keier, Jennifer Quail, Bob Quinlan, Roxanne Quinlan, and Sean Summers, my Eagle-Eye advance readers, who worked on a cruelly short time frame this time around.

MAJOR PLAYERS

John Connor, leader, Human Resistance
Kate Brewster, leader, Human Resistance

Lt. Tom Carter, technician
Paul Keeley, historian

Resistance 1st Security Regiment
    Company A, Squadron 3: The Hell-Hounds
        Lt. David "Ten" Zimmerman
        Sgt. Earl Duncan
        Sgt. Mark Herrera
        Cpl. Kyla Connor
        Glitch
        Ripper
        Ginger
    Company A, Squadron 2: The Scalpers
        Lt. Christopher Sato
        Sgt. Jenna "the Greek" Vandis
        Sgt. Charles Smart
        Cpl. Bobby "Nix" Friedman
        Cpl. Johnny "J. L." Larson

PART 1: OPERATION PYGMALION

Present-Day
California

Paul Keeley was afraid of the bouncer. It bothered him that he was afraid, and it bothered him that he didn't know why he was afraid.

Paul was well above average height and in good shape. Regular workouts in the solitude of his apartment, regular jogging in the park nearby, kept him that way. And for him, "continuing education" after college had included enrollment at a series of schools of martial arts; he'd studied bits of shotokan karate, kempo, tae kwon do, and jeet kune do, and spent one summer with a school that claimed to teach ninjutsu, the art of the ninja.

Sure, it was a dilettante's approach, but he was less interested in learning a philosophy or a world view than he was in learning how to hurt people . . . should the need arise.

He wondered if the need would arise with this bouncer. The man, who had a build like a weight lifter's, spent every night at Bear's Bar at a stool in the dimly lit corner near the phones, keeping an eye on the business, which Paul supposed was only right. But the man seemed wrong in so many other ways. He never relaxed, never leaned back against the wall; his posture was perfect. He wore the same clothes night after night—jeans, a black T-shirt with a Harley-Davidson logo, a jeans jacket, black cowboy boots; did he clean them every night, or did he have a series of identical garments in his closet? And his hair was a Mohawk in a purple-magenta color never found in nature. Paul thought it was several years out of date, but couldn't quite remember when the style had actually been in fashion.

And the man always seemed to be staring at Paul.

Now, Paul had to admit that this was just guesswork, or a feeling, because he couldn't see the bouncer's eyes. No matter how dark the bar's interior, the bouncer wore sunglasses. But it always felt as though the man's attention was on Paul. It was unsettling.

Tonight, as usual, the bar was crowded. Sitting at a tiny round table against the wall near the entrance, as far away from the bouncer's stool as it was possible to be within the establishment, Paul felt the bouncer's eyes on him. *Well,* Paul comforted himself, *maybe it's because he thinks of me as a real bad dude.*

"Can I join you?"

Paul looked up to see the most beautiful woman he'd ever encountered in person standing over him.

She looked like something a libidinous Dr. Frankenstein would have created after perfecting his craft. She had Scandinavian features and eyes the color of a cloudless winter sky. She was a few inches shorter than Paul, with what he thought of as a swimmer's build—athletic, broad in the shoulder but not too broad. Her hair was long and dark blonde, streaked by artifice but perhaps wavy by nature, and her skin was flawless.

And she was dressed all in shades of yellow: yellow slacks, yellow blouse that was invitingly unbuttoned at the top, yellow wide-brimmed hat.

But he saw these details only peripherally, because her face wouldn't let his attention wander. She possessed a simple, unobtrusive beauty, features that one could look at and pronounce gorgeous, yet that were just a trifle anonymous, lacking a hook that made it easy to hang memory upon. The curve of her lips, even at rest, gave her face the appearance of someone who was amused at whatever she saw.

Paul had seen her on many occasions at the bar. She always sat alone, watching the other patrons with an expression that reminded Paul of a cat surveying its surroundings, pronouncing every object, every person it saw to be a possession or, at best, a mere worshiper.

Her aloofness was so distinct that Paul wondered whether, if some band of madmen were to break in and begin murdering the bar's clients, she would object, or merely continue watching in curiosity.

Despite her beauty and the fact that she never had companions, he'd never approached her. He really didn't know how to strike up a conversation with a stranger.

But she apparently did.

Paul got to his feet, feeling awkward in his haste. He gestured at the other chair beside his table. "Uh, sure. Please."

She sat, graceful, but the impression was slightly spoiled by the way the chair creaked as she settled upon it. She didn't seem to be alarmed by its protest, or by the prospect of the rickety thing collapsing and depositing her on the floor. "I've seen you in here a number of times. You always sit alone."

He reclaimed his seat and gave her a dubious look. "I find it kind of unlikely that I'd have made any sort of impression." Immediately he felt like hitting himself. It wasn't his job to shoot himself down as a prospect. He suspected she could do that all by herself.

She merely smiled. "I can prove I've seen you. Let's see . . . last week, you wore a suit every day, and on Thursday, you had on a horrible dark tie with paisley decorations. This week it's all casual clothes . . . did you get fired?"

Paul shook his head. "Different dress code."

"For a whole week?"

"Yeah." He took a deep breath and made the admission he didn't much like to offer. "I work at different places all the time. I'm an office temp worker."

"Really?" She didn't seem at all put off. "Do you find that sort of work interesting?"

"Not really. There are things I'd much prefer. Like a regular set of coworkers, real health coverage, and the opportunity to work in my field."

"What is your field?"

"History, my degree's in history." He offered her a self-deprecating smile. "And, as you know, there's always a need for professional historians. Hundreds of jobs listed in the classifieds every day."

She blinked and looked confused. "Really?" Then her expression cleared. "Oh, you're kidding me."

"That's right. How about you? What do you do?"

"I kill people for a living."

"Uh-huh. Is there a method you prefer? Bombs, poison darts, handguns, swords at dawn?"

"Bare hands. It's economical."

"Well, I suppose I deserved that. No, really, what do you do?"

She considered. "I'm in advertising."

"Much more sinister than assassination."

"That's right."

"I'm Paul."

"Eliza."

"That's a name you don't run across very often."

She smiled again. "It's a tradition in my family."

September 2029
San Diego, California

Once upon a time it had been a place where the injured were rehabilitated, the ill were treated, babies were born, and those whose bodies could no longer withstand the abuses of time or disease were cared for as they died. The San Diego Naval Medical Center had been a place of humans, of people. A sprawling medical complex deep within Balboa Park, its centerpiece had been a pale main building a handful of stories high stretching approximately from north to south.

Even now, decades after the fall of mankind from power had sent humans scurrying into holes to hide and had deprived cities of their nighttime lights, the building shone in the moonlight. Framed in the view from David "Ten" Zimmerman's binoculars, the building seemed remarkably intact.

But, then, much of San Diego did. When Skynet, the computer

program that had been intended to coordinate U.S. military defensive and offensive capability, had seized control and begun its process of exterminating mankind, San Diego hadn't received the nuclear barrage that many populated areas had; instead, some of the nation's supply of neutron bombs and chemical warfare weapons had rained down on this region, leaving the city remarkably intact. San Diego and a handful of other military centers had been spared, to this degree at least, in order that Skynet might be able to make use of their extensive resources of military materiel.

Ten lowered the binoculars to the cracked, broken pavement he lay upon. He scratched at an itchy spot on his cheek. It itched because of the several days' growth of blond beard he wore; it was just at that transitional stage between short enough to be innocuous and long enough to soften. Now it was bristly and irritating to his skin. A few weeks back, he'd shaved it to please a young lady he'd met at Tortilla Compound, but she'd never become interested in him. He knew he looked better with the beard; it tended to disguise the fact that his features were actually quite undistinguished. So now he grew it back, suffering the kidding of the men and woman he commanded; they had all correctly guessed why he'd scraped it away.

Ten was stretched out at the edge of the broad parking lot that had once served the medical complex. Just behind him, eastward, the pavement gave way to ground that immediately sloped down into what had once been the Balboa Park Municipal Golf Course. "Still no movement, no lights," he said, his voice low. "Just hundreds of dead cars. Opinions?"

"I think you should shave your head and tattoo 'I'm desperate, please love me' on your scalp," said Mark Herrera. He sat upright, his back to the crumbling rubber and corroding hubcap of a car wheel; he rested within the deep shadow of the mostly intact Dodge van that had been almost new when Judgment Day had occurred. Mark could nettle Ten about his love life without suffering much retaliation on the same subject; taller than Ten, with dark Latino good looks, he managed to be dashing whether groomed or windblown, hygienic or sweat-drenched, clean-shaven or scruffy. His size and considerable physical strength were at odds with the stereotype of the electronics and programming specialist, which was the role he served with Ten's team.

Ten decided not to give Mark the satisfaction a sigh would afford him. "*Relevant* opinions," he amended.

"Stay cool," offered Earl Duncan, the oldest member of the team. "The spotter who's been tracking the traffic pattern says that it's regular. It'll be tonight." Earl was black, nearly twice Ten's age. Stubbornness and a physical regimen he'd adopted back when he was a member of the Air Force police kept him, year after year, from wandering over the threshold into old age.

Kyla Connor, the team's sniper, didn't say anything. She was asleep, a heat-diffusing thermal blanket draped over her to obscure her appearance in case this spot fell within the view of the sort of infrared sensors used by Skynet and many of its units in the field. Her head was propped against the side of Ginger, her reddish-yellow dog, a mix of husky, sled dog, and one or two other large breeds. Ginger cocked her eyebrows at Ten, a very human expression, and thumped her tail, but offered no opinion. Kyla's other dog, Ripper, a bullmastiff mix who outweighed Kyla by a double handful of pounds, didn't even open his eyes and remained nearly invisible in the darkness. Both dogs were outside the negligible cover Kyla's blanket represented.

Kyla was the youngest of the human members of the team, still a teenager, though her manner usually suggested she was ten or twenty years older. Ten supposed this was only appropriate for the daughter of John Connor and Kate Brewster, the leaders of the human Resistance on the North American continent. Kyla had the fair complexion of both her parents, the simple, down-to-earth beauty and blonde-brown hair of her mother. Now, at rest, her features relaxed, she did look like a teenager. There was nothing to suggest that she was as proficient a killer as anyone else in the unit.

Ten didn't solicit an opinion from the last member of the team, didn't even look at him. He'd prefer that this newest member be somewhere else, such as dead at the bottom of a landfill.

Glitch lay apart from the others. He was a big man, muscular in a way that suggested an athlete's high-protein, high-carbohydrate diet—a diet that was rare in these lean times. He was stretched out beneath a car fifteen yards to the south of the others, an irregular bump in the road—his overloaded backpack gave him the contours of a large piece of debris, perhaps part of a sofa abandoned on Judgment Day. His position gave him a better perspective on the road leading up to the main building. He was completely motionless, as inert as a corpse. He would, Ten knew, be staring fixedly at the area he was supposed to be watching, no expression on his heavy-boned, brooding features.

Except for the dogs, they were all dressed in a shades-of-gray urban camouflage pattern. They'd draped ponchos of brown-and-green camo across themselves when moving over the old golf course and other natural terrain, but the urban camo was better for the miles of streets and unmaintained buildings that had served as their cover for the majority of this mission.

They were the Hell-Hounds—officially Company A, Squadron 3, of the Resistance 1st Security Regiment. When they weren't in the presence of Resistance leaders John Connor and Kate Brewster, protecting them, they were either plotting or executing damnfool operations like this one.

"All right," Ten said. "We wait." *Exposed, visible to any of Skynet's camera satellites or high-altitude reconnaissance flights.* He didn't need to say those words aloud. He just pulled his own thermal blanket out of his pack and draped it around himself.

It seemed like only minutes later that a tapping awakened him. Ten opened his eyes but remained perfectly still—it was an instinct that had kept him alive in many field situations in which he found himself hunted by Skynet forces. But there was nothing moving in his immediate view, only the brilliant starfield overhead.

The tapping repeated itself. He turned to look in Glitch's direction. The big man had not moved, but was rapping his knuckles on the pavement. Once Glitch saw he had Ten's attention, he pointed southward.

Ten turned to look. Initially he saw nothing, but a suggestion of distant movement on the road drew his eye.

It was a car or van, headed this way, its lights off. Of course its lights were off; Skynet's robotic forces didn't need ordinary illumination.

Ten reached over and shook Earl. The older man awakened, took in Ten's rising-hand "Get everyone up" gesture, and nodded. Keeping his blanket over him, Earl silently moved on hands and knees to where Mark lay.

Ten returned his attention to the incoming vehicle. He calculated it would be here in two minutes or less. From this point on, accurate calculation and timing would be crucial—to their mission's success and to their own survival. Attention to detail was an equally important factor; Ten absently patted himself down, making sure that his weapons and gear were still strapped, pocketed, and holstered where they should be, that nothing had fallen out to remain behind on the pavement.

The oncoming vehicle took the final turnoff onto the road that would bring it up to the parking lot. The Hell-Hounds, all now awake and alert, kept vehicles between themselves and the incoming machine, between themselves and the front of the hospital— against the high probability that there were visual sensors at the hospital's entrances.

The vehicle was a white van. As it neared, Ten could make out its engine noise; it clattered with the distinct sound of bad lifters. Though Skynet did maintain the machinery that served it, the computer network eventually ran into the ground every piece of materiel it commanded—*Every piece that the Resistance didn't steal or destroy,* Ten amended.

The van parked directly in front of the main entrance. Ten had situated himself off at an angle so that he could still see the entrance if anything did park there. Peering around the front bumper of the ancient pickup truck he hid behind, he saw the van's driver emerge.

It was a large, muscular man, built like Glitch, but with long, dirty blond hair; he wore a black T-shirt and red shorts with palm-tree designs in yellow. Not him, *it*; Ten recognized the thing as an older T-600 variant. The T-600's skin was a little too shiny, the rubber surface unblemished and unrealistic. Ten grimaced over the fact that the Terminator's clothing-choice software appeared to be malfunctioning.

Though it didn't matter what the Terminator wore. Under the right circumstances the T-600 could kill every living member of the Hell-Hounds.

The T-600 opened the sliding door on the near side of the van and pulled out a wooden crate larger than a coffin. The way the box creaked as it was handled, the way it sagged slightly when it was placed over the T-600's shoulder, suggested that it weighed a few hundred pounds. The T-600 carried it without apparent effort to the hospital's main entrance and began tapping at a plate inset in the wall beside the doors.

Ten resisted the urge to signal Glitch. He'd given Glitch precise, difficult-to-misinterpret orders. Now he had to rely on Glitch's own sense of timing, not second-guess or micromanage him.

Glitch rose, near-silent, and began moving toward the T-600.

There was a quiet buzz from the hospital main doors. Light appeared, outlining the doors—top and bottom, then between them as the doors swung inward. Then the T-600 turned just enough to look at Glitch, who was twenty yards away and closing.

The T-600 did not react. Glitch did not alter the pace of his approach. They merely looked at one another, a long moment—all it took for the two Terminators to exchange signals that established their respective identities, model numbers, missions, and priorities. Glitch's data, of course, was a fabrication, based on the scraps and leavings of data the Resistance could sometimes intercept from

Skynet communications traffic. It wouldn't hold up to a detailed check at Skynet's end.

The T-600 turned away and entered the building.

Glitch waited there and pulled objects from his jacket pocket. As the spring-loaded doors swung back to close, he bent over to place the objects before them—wedge-shaped pieces of wood. Door stops. The doors hung half-open.

Glitch returned to the parking lot, his heavy steps loud. Ten could feel them in the pavement as Glitch neared him. Now was the part Ten had hated since this plan was conceived . . . and he'd been the one to suggest it. He wrapped himself in his thermal blanket, pulling it around him like a cocoon so that it hid head, feet, and everything in between.

Blind, he lay there as Glitch came around the vehicle that served as his cover. He heard the jingling of metal clasps on Glitch's gear and could smell lilacs as the Terminator bent over him. Glitch picked him up, as effortlessly as a grown man might pick up a wicker basket, and carried him.

It was forty long steps. Ten could see light increasing in intensity. Then Glitch set him down on a hard, flat surface, turned, and was gone.

Ten unwrapped himself. He lay in the hall just beyond the entry doors Glitch had rigged with the door stops. He was up in an instant, scanning the walls and ceiling of this hallway for cameras and other sensors. He wouldn't be able to detect subtle sensors—fiber-optic camera lenses, pressure plates under the floor—but in a secure area like this, Skynet didn't generally rely on subtlety.

He saw first that the hall had not only been kept up but had been redecorated since Judgment Day. The paint on the walls was white and fresh. The linoleum on the floor was clean, and though not new—Ten imagined that no factory had manufactured linoleum in decades—it was polished and relatively unscuffed. Visible doorways up the hall showed no signs of decay or neglect.

Cool air was blowing through the building's vents.

That didn't make a lot of sense. Skynet facilities tended to operate only the machinery and equipment useful to Skynet. Decorations, comfort, doors for privacy—these were all things machine intelligences did not need and so they were never maintained. Ten felt worry pluck at him. He hated things that made no sense.

Glitch returned, carrying an extra-long bundle, and when he set it down Mark unrolled himself from the blanket. Then it was Earl's turn—and finally Kyla's. The two dogs trotted along behind Glitch for that trip, their ears back.

They were properly trained Resistance dogs. They hated Terminators. It had taken a lot of extra training for them to understand that Glitch was a member of the team, was an ally of Kyla. It had helped when, early in that process, the Hell-Hounds had found an old, unlooted perfume shop and Earl had hit on the bright idea to take all the perfumes and colognes that time had not rendered absolutely revolting. Now Glitch always wore perfume, a helpful scent recognition for the dogs, who otherwise would have a difficult time distinguishing him from other Terminators.

Nor was their presence, if captured by the facility's external cameras, likely to alert Skynet to danger. Dogs were no threat to Skynet . . . unless they were under Kyla's direction, that is.

Kyla unrolled herself from her blanket and stood, somehow not hampered or made less graceful by the sniper rifle case she held. Ten kicked the door stops out from under the doors and they closed. The team was assembled.

Now it was time to find out just what the hell was going on in the old San Diego Naval Medical Center.

Present-Day
California

"Actually, I think I'm mentally ill," Paul said.

Eliza smiled again. This was not the right reaction from a woman receiving that sort of news. "You're obviously trying very hard to impress me."

Paul smiled back at her. "I'm sorry. I don't mean *really* mentally ill. You're the first person I've had a chance to talk to in, well, I don't remember how long. And I think the solitude is making me sort of nuts."

"How nuts?"

"I have odd little moments of paranoia. Thinking everyone is looking at me and trying not to show it. Spying on me. Secretly keeping me from finding a decent job."

Eliza nodded. "That *is* nuts." Her tone was agreeable, not at all alarmed or cautious.

"Do you ever feel that way?"

"Everyone *is* always looking at me," she said. "They just don't bother to hide it. And no one is trying to keep me from finding a decent job. I'm already at the top of my profession."

"Killing people."

"Advertising."

"Oh, that's right." Paul signaled the waitress for another round of drinks. He'd never thought of himself as a beer drinker, but whatever they were serving on draft tonight was *good*. Plus he'd had three already and wasn't even beginning to feel the effects.

So, now the hard part. How to ask her out? He'd somehow been born without the gene that made it effortless just to walk up to a woman and ask her out, ask her to dance, ask her for her number. Each time, it was a struggle to find a way that didn't sound awkward and contrived.

"I think you should show me around town," Eliza said.

Paul's grip on his glass faltered. He managed, fumbling, to catch it before he deposited the last of his current beer onto the tabletop. "What?"

"I think you should show me around town," she repeated, her tone patient. "You said you were a historian. I imagine you know a lot about the city's history."

"Yes, of course. I'd love to." Paul nodded agreeably, tried to retain his cool.

Then a new thought occurred to him and caused coldness to trickle down his spine: *What city am I in?*

September 2029
San Diego, California

They were at what had to have once been a nurse's station. It was at the intersection of two long, broad hallways on an upper floor and looked like many such installations Kyla had seen in pictures and books: a big desk, thick with computer equipment and piles of paper, situated behind a low wall that constituted a barrier to keep patients and visitors psychologically at bay.

Mark sat in the chair behind the main computer. His laptop was up and running beside the machine and cables ran between the two devices. Mark frowned as his fingers flew over his laptop's keyboard. He was among the world's best at hacking into Skynet computer systems, but that didn't mean that such tasks were simple, and this one was taking a while.

Kyla was set up at one end of the low wall, her rifle propped against the wall top. The weapon was a Barrett M99, manufactured shortly before Judgment Day. Just over four feet long, it was made of blackened steel and brushed-silver aluminum, as elegant and simple in its beauty as Kyla herself. The .50-caliber rounds it fired were, when placed very accurately, capable of taking Terminators down—sometimes.

Kyla was oriented so that she could see down two of the hallways, the two that were better lit. Ginger and Ripper were together at the end of one of the other two halls, standing guard, ready to offer a growl or a yelp if they detected anything but friends headed Kyla's way. Glitch was at the end of the last hall, motionless and silent; in his hands was a weapon from his backpack, a rare and precious chain gun. Though small enough to be carried by a man or Terminator, the weapon possessed the multiple spinning barrels of a Vulcan machine gun and could fire high-powered ammunition at a terrifying rate.

Ten and Earl were not in sight. They'd waited until Mark was set up, then moved on to find the optimal portions of the building for their loads of explosives. But they still didn't know what they were blowing up.

"So?" Kyla said.

"Stop bugging me." Mark's voice lacked conviction. It was a rote response.

"What is this place?"

In getting to the nurse's station, they'd passed whole sections of the hospital that had obviously been reconstructed since Judgment Day. Wards had been redecorated as apartments, with pictures and posters on the walls, old but well-maintained furniture, television sets that came on when activated and began displaying authentic shows from the last century. There were also chambers that were undecorated, unpainted, plaster still raw and white on the walls.

Mark had said that he wasn't even sure this nurse's station was original equipment. It could have been a reconstruction of a nurse's station, he'd admitted.

Finally Mark answered. "All those apartments, the other places. They all represented slightly different time frames."

"I don't understand. They were all twentieth-century."

"Right, but the twentieth century wasn't just one constant, unchanging thing. Not like today. That's what makes it so interesting. The toys in the one bedroom, foot-long action figures—"

"The dolls?"

"The dolls. Specific games. Those little metal molds were for pouring in raw plastic and then cooking over a stove to harden it. That's all from the nineteen sixties. But the next room over had a record player for vinyl records, and the recordings were all disco.

Artists called Abba and Donna Summer and the Bee Gees. That's from the nineteen seventies."

"I don't get it."

Mark shook his head, the motion barely visible in Kyla's peripheral vision. "Neither do I. I'm just a history buff, an amateur. It'd take the real deal to figure this out. Hey, I've got the security camera network."

Kyla resisted the urge to move next to Mark and peer over his shoulder. She was needed here. She was the sniper, the long-range defender of her team. "Tell me."

"An operating theater. It looks functional. Empty hospital rooms. Outside, the T-600's van is gone; it must have finished with its deliveries and driven off. The roof. A—" Mark's voice faltered. "A man and a woman talking in a bar. I think it's a TV show, though. I've seen both the actors before, somewhere. More empty hospital rooms . . ." Then, a moment later, it was "Oh, damn."

"What?"

"I've got Ten and Earl on camera. And if I can see them . . ."

"Right." Skynet could see them, too.

It was a hospital basement level, with hospital basement equipment. Electrical junction boxes. Water pumping equipment and water pressure gauges. Emergency generators. The overhead light-bulbs had been replaced at some point after Judgment Day with clusters of light-emitting diodes; they shone bright, not flickering, somehow at contrast with the way Ten thought basements should be illuminated.

The emergency generators had obviously been improved after Judgment Day. A portion of the basement level larger than a boxcar was sealed off, monitoring gauges installed. Labels on the gauges made it clear that this portion held fuel. "The generators could run off this for days or weeks," Earl said. "Skynet really doesn't want an interruption in the functions of this place. What do you have in mind?"

Ten gestured toward the pipes that connected the tank to the primary generators. "I think I'll just cut these now and flood the basement with fuel. First disconnect the pressure meters so Skynet isn't alerted. Set up an explosive charge on both timer and radio reception, but I don't want to set it off until the air is pretty much saturated with fuel."

Earl gave a mock shudder. "Economical."

"Lots of bang for the buck."

"Let's do it."

Then the radios at their belts hissed, two short bursts of static.

The team was supposed to maintain radio silence . . . except in times of trouble. One burst meant "Heads up, be alert." Two meant "The jig is up, we're compromised." Three would mean "We're under attack."

"Let's do it *fast*," Ten amended.

Present-Day
California

The question ate at Paul: *What city is this? San Francisco? San Bernardino? San Diego? San something. Definitely California.* Why couldn't he remember?

The beer, it had to be the beer. He was more drunk than he realized. But the wrongness of it, the realization that something in his brain was just not working right, caused his heart to hammer.

"Let's go for a walk," he said. "I can show you some of the sights." *And remember where the hell we are. And clear my head.*

Eliza nodded, a slow movement, like a queen gesturing assent. "All right."

Paul signaled the waitress for the bill, then a shadow fell across him. He looked up.

The bouncer stood over their table, massive, blocking the light. His attention was on Eliza. "We must go," he said.

Paul rose. He was as tall as the bouncer and could face him eye to eye—or, at least, eye to sunglasses—though he lacked width of shoulder. "Excuse me?"

"It's not a problem." Eliza stood. "He's an old friend of mine. This will only take a moment. Have another drink while I'm gone. Better yet, take a nap." She reached over to brush away strands of Paul's hair that had drifted down onto his forehead.

Paul's knees buckled as weariness settled on him. It was like a late-night work jag when the espresso had finally worn off or like lying on the beach in the late afternoon, the exhaustion from a day's worth of swimming finally catching up to him.

I've never been swimming at the beach.

I've never had espresso.

He sank, almost nerveless, back into his chair and leaned helplessly across the table, knocking empty bottles of beer out of his way. They skittered across the tabletop and fell out of sight, but he did not hear them hit, did not hear them break.

His eyes closed, but he concentrated on the fast, panicky beating of his heart and managed to stay awake. He forced his eyes open again.

Eliza and the bouncer were gone. It had been only a second, but they were not within his field of vision.

The bartender, the waitress, and the other bar patrons were still there. They weren't moving. They stood as immobile as store mannequins. But there was a slight sway to their stances and their eyes were alive.

The fear rose in Paul, fear of the wrongness of his situation, fear for Eliza and what the bouncer might intend for her. He struggled to stand, struggled to move, and when neither proved possible for him, struggled to shout.

He heard a noise, a garbled, strangled sound. It really didn't seem to come from him, but it corresponded to his attempt to scream. He tried again, heard the noise once more, as if from across the room.

He had to stand. He shoved with his arms, with his legs, trying to get a little distance between his body and the table.

His limbs did not move. But he felt something, pressure against his knees and hands, a less distinct pressure holding his limbs in check.

He pushed harder, ignoring what he saw, concentrating entirely on what he felt. He could feel his arms and legs lashing out again and again, could feel pain where his hands and wrists and knees were connecting with a surface.

Then, for a brief moment, there was light, a vertical shaft of brightness to his left. It dazzled him. It faded a second later, but the spots before his eyes remained.

He pushed again and the light reappeared. He pushed harder and it broadened, lengthened, until it washed across everything he could see and blinded him almost completely.

As his vision adjusted, he found that he could see two sets of images, superimposed over one another. One was the bar; the other, a set of acoustic tiles directly in front of him. To his right was a dark oval plane angled toward the tiles, rocking just a bit. To his left, a black metallic surface, as though he were lying in a container, and beyond it were chairs and banks of machinery—but it was all oriented wrong, as if he were lying on his back and staring up at the ceiling.

He felt dizzy, sick to his stomach, but he tried rolling over to the left. He saw his right arm, clad in a skintight gray-black material, flop over the surface, even though he could also see it, in its white sleeve, lying before him on the tabletop, supporting his head.

It was wrong, everything was wrong. But he could now *feel* his right arm over the metal lip of whatever he was lying in.

He gasped and choked as water poured into his mouth, into his lungs. He kept his elbow hooked over the metal lip and hauled with all his strength, pulling his face up out of the fluid, up over the lip.

He scraped over the metal lip, first his chest, then midsection, and suddenly he was falling, slamming down hard onto a flat surface. Pain cut into his shoulder, the side of his head. Fluid splashed down atop him. And his vision of the bar and all its paralyzed inhabitants, himself included, remained unchanged. He closed his eyes and saw only that for long moments. He coughed until his throat was sore but almost all the fluid was ejected from his lungs.

Paul lay there gasping for long moments, willing his heart and breathing to slow, forcing himself to remain under control. Then he opened his eyes to look around.

His second set of surroundings was very different from the bar. This was a brightly lit room, smaller than the bar, with off-white linoleum floor and walls painted in a soothing pastel yellow. There were chairs, rolling racks with what looked like complicated electronic equipment, and the centerpiece of the room, a massive black thing that looked like an egg-shaped coffin atop a rectangular black pedestal.

Something dug at his memory. *I know what that is. I've seen them in books.*

That's a sen-dep tank. Sensory deprivation. A late-twentieth-century technique used in various sorts of esoteric research and medical treatment. The subject floats in a liquid environment, in total darkness. Cut off from most sensory input, he becomes more receptive to internal stimuli such as hallucinations, the effects of drugs . . .

Paul sat up. He seemed to be covered, head to foot, in the dark skintight material. He touched it. It was soft to the touch, giving way under the slightest pressure, and was wet.

Only his hands and feet were free. He raised his hands to his face. His head, too, was uncovered.

In his other vision, he remained slumped at the bar table, while the other occupants of the bar, endlessly patient in their paralysis, waited.

He stood, slow and awkward, and finally his other vision changed. In the bar, his other body straightened and stood as well. Now, when he raised his arms before his face, he could see them twice, once in his long-sleeved work shirt, once in the skintight garment.

But now that both views of himself were consistent in orientation and pose, if not in content, the nausea he'd felt was fading. He felt better. Just not good.

Now that he was upright, it was time to find out just what the hell was going on.

September 2029
San Diego, California

Glitch moved at a rapid pace down the access stairwell, his footsteps echoing on the concrete steps. His posture was perfect, his face devoid of any expression that might indicate he was aware that he could be confronting the end of his own existence.

That was the way it should be. Glitch was a T-850, a Terminator. Captured—assembled, rather, in pieces from Terminators destroyed at a raid on a Resistance habitation compound—and then repaired, reprogrammed, and upgraded from his T-801 roots, Glitch had no concern for his own safety beyond what was required to best achieve his mission parameters.

His short-term parameters were simple. Mark had explained them to him quickly, but meticulously, without recourse to emotional considerations that were irrelevant to Glitch. The activities of Ten and Earl were observable on this compound's security cameras. The activities of Mark, Kyla, Glitch, and the dogs were not. Therefore the greater danger accrued to Ten and Earl. Glitch was to travel to their location and defend them against all attacks, pending further orders and further recalculations of mission parameters.

At the ground-floor landing, one heavy door—a metal fire door, painted in a red-orange that had faded and peeled with the years—led rightward, an unlit EXIT sign above it. Another, identical but for its darker paint job, led leftward. Glitch's internal map, a wire-frame diagram of the portions of the building he had seen so far, coordinated with his internal compass and indicated that the right-hand door led to the main lobby. The left-hand door, logically, would lead to additional stairs downward.

He tried it. It was secure. He slung his chain gun on its strap back across his shoulder, then leaned into the door, felt its metal construction buckle under the pressure he exerted. He struck it, once, twice, three times, felt and saw it deform with each blow, and finally it was warped enough that the final blow slammed it open. The crash it made echoed up the stairwell he'd descended and down the one the ruined door revealed.

That was good. The noise might attract Skynet forces away from the humans and to Glitch.

The noises were almost simultaneous—a muffled *clank* from beyond the stairwell door by which Ten and Earl had entered the basement and a distant crash from the hallway that seemed to serve the basement level as its main entranceway.

Ten took a couple of paces back to keep ahead of the advancing tide of fuel oil. The air was thick with the smell, though it had been only a few moments since they'd severed the fuel lines. "We're in for it," he told Earl. "Both exits are covered."

Earl turned to stare back into the dimly lit recesses of the basement. "Let's make a new one."

"I'm with you." Ten followed the older man back past banks of locked storage areas with wire-mesh walls. From his backpack, he dug two of his three remaining shaped charges—blocks of plastic explosive with detonators imbedded in one side.

Not far ahead, the storage areas came to an end. There was concrete wall at the end of the aisle; it looked as though the last storage areas were not quite flush with the wall, that a gap, perhaps a service corridor, a mere yard wide separated the last storage areas from the wall itself.

Ten stopped a dozen steps from the wall. "Here," he said, and slapped one of the shaped charges into Earl's hand. "Set for radio detonation." He marched on another six paces, concentrating on the apparatus in his hand, carefully flipping a rocker switch under a protective case from TIMER to RADIO and then closing the case again. From the back of the charge, he peeled a black plastic film; beneath it was a layer of yellowish adhesive, far more sticky than the plastic explosive it coated.

In the distance, footsteps—heavy, ringing, metal footsteps—approached from the direction of the main hall.

"Ten—"

"Yeah, I hear it." Ten eyed the ceiling above. It was a full yard above his reach. He crouched and leaped upward, slapping the reverse side of the charge against the ceiling. He landed, knees bent, and kept his attention on the charge.

It held to the ceiling, the red gleam of an LED indicating that it was ready to receive transmission.

He glanced over at Earl. The older man had clambered up one of the wire-mesh storage area walls and was carefully fitting his own charge to the ceiling above it. Earl grinned down at Ten, the smile of an older and wiser man who knew how to achieve the same results without as much physical stress.

Beyond Earl, across the basement, a figure emerged from the main hallway at a trot, moving toward Ten and Earl.

She was not what Ten expected to see. She was a human female—blonde, youthful, vital. She was dressed as a nurse. Her expression was serene, unworried.

And she was not the source of the ringing, metallic footsteps. They were still coming up loud behind her.

Ten swung his weapon, the archaic Colt M16-A4 that served as his chief battle piece in those times when plasma rifle batteries were in short supply, around from his back and brought the barrel up. He aimed at the nurse, spraying fire across her head. The assault rifle kicked in his grip, its aim threatening to rise; he struggled to hold it in place.

Bullets struck the woman, deforming her forehead—momentarily. Then her skin smoothed. She continued forward, her pace unchanged.

"Fall back, fall back!" Ten suited action to words, trotting backward as he maintained his fire against the woman, squeezing off short bursts.

Earl dropped from his perch and raced past Ten, out of his sight.

The woman's right arm changed, the flesh flowing from it like water, revealing shining metal apparatus beneath. The machinery itself altered, reconfigured, with a blue glow dancing across protruding elements.

Ten's back hit the concrete wall. He moved right, positioning himself at the corner of the last storage area, and continued to fire.

Earl pulled at his sleeve, trying to draw him farther around the corner, out of the nurse's sight. Ten shook him off. "Detonator!"

Earl shouted, "You crazy bastard!" Then he drew a device, the general size and shape of one of the late-pre–Judgment Day cell phones, from a jacket pocket. He used his teeth to pull its short antenna out to its full extent.

The nurse aimed her malformed arm. Ten shoved himself toward Earl, bearing his companion to the concrete floor, just as the air above them ignited with a brilliant electric-blue glow.

Heat washed across them. The contents of the storage area, metal desks and chairs and miniature refrigerators, wooden and plastic crates filled with paperwork and ancient medical samples, exploded or melted, plastic components screaming with animal-like voices. Ten looked up, saw the metal portions of the storage area glowing orange, yellow, and white, deforming as they melted. Heat beat down at them from the destroyed goods.

He scrambled back to the corner. The nurse was still coming. Five more steps and she'd be directly beneath Earl's shaped charge.

"Ready!" Ten shouted.

Four steps, three, two—her arm came up again, aiming in toward Ten's unprotective face—one—

"Now!"

The ceiling directly above and a half-dozen steps in front of the nurse rocked, spraying flame and chunks of concrete down upon the nurse. She looked up just in time to see a tremendous mass of concrete, rebar, and plaster crash down upon her. More rained down upon the pile of debris that covered her.

Ten felt hands on his shoulders as Earl hauled him to his feet. The older man wasted no time waiting for orders; he dashed forward to the mound atop the nurse, stepped up on it, and began climbing the adjacent chain mesh up toward the ceiling and the floor above.

Ten slung his M16 and followed. When he was halfway up, his eye was drawn by movement from the direction by which the nurse had entered.

Coming toward him was something the size of Glitch, but gleaming, silvery—an assault robot. Built like a Terminator, but without the false skin to conceal its true nature and lacking all the sophisticated programming needed by Terminators to pass themselves off as humans, it moved with a mechanical precision and efficiency that was distinctly inhuman. In its hands it carried a plasma rifle, as shiny and smoothly contoured as the assault robot itself.

And the robot was already aiming the weapon.

Once he was in the hallway, Paul found that his understanding of what he was seeing continued to improve. The vision of the bar and its paralyzed patrons faded to nothingness, leaving him in a hallway with scuffed off-white linoleum flooring and industrial-green walls. The air was cool and somehow sterile. The hallway stretched for what seemed like a half a mile ahead of him, but he knew that his perceptions still had to be distorted, that the corridor could not be as long as that.

All the doors along it were closed. He wondered whether opening any of them would give him answers to the questions clogging his mind. *Where is this? How did I get here? Where's Eliza? What's happened to me?*

But he didn't dare look. Something told him that he was surrounded by wrongness and needed to get clear of it as fast as possible.

That meant finding an exterior exit. Was he on ground level
now? Above it? Below it? The silence, broken only by the faint hissing of air-conditioning, suggested that he could be belowground.

First things first. Assess condition and resources. Someone had
told him that. Who was it? A man with graying sandy hair, a fleet-
ing, wispy memory. Thinking of him, Paul felt a sense of loss.

Condition: Physically weak, uncoordinated, brain not working
right. Memory fouled up. Resources: a set of insulating garments
from a sensory-deprivation tank.

If he could only get his hands on a firearm—

Did he know how to use one?

Yes.

How did he know how to use one?

He couldn't remember.

He growled to himself, slapped his palm against his forehead as
if to jar sticky gears and pistons into movement.

Paul came to a slightly open door. He peered in, then, half-
recognizing the shapes he could dimly see, reached in to snap on
the light.

Inside was furniture—a single twin-sized bed, the bedclothes
disarrayed, a cheap-looking wooden desk, a straight-back wooden
chair, a weight bench.

He felt dizzy again. This was his efficiency apartment, home
sweet hovel, but beyond the door he was peering in should have
been a set of three steps down to the sidewalk.

He stepped in and looked around. To the left should have been
his kitchenette with the exterior window beyond. The refrigerator,
stove, and miniature dishwashing machine were in place, but the
window was black. Wondering, he moved over to it. Beyond should
have been a busy city street, day or night, but there was nothing but
darkness.

The sliding door into his closet was open, revealing his clothes
on their hangers: plain white T-shirts, short-sleeved and long-

sleeved button-down shirts in a variety of colors, blue jeans, slacks. He hastily grabbed several shirts and two pairs of pants. From the bottom of the closet he took his cross-training sneakers. He slid the closet door closed, revealing a mirror affixed to one of the panels. He dropped all his items onto the bed, rolled them into a bundle.

From the chest of drawers he took underwear and pairs of socks. Atop the chest of drawers was a belt pouch, the pouch he always wore. He'd been wearing it back in the bar. He unzipped it, looked at his contents. A multitool that would fold out into pliers and wire cutters, with smaller tools, ten of them, that would fold out from the handles, five to a side. His wallet. His keys—apartment, mailbox, the gated swimming pool of his apartment complex.

He pulled the belt around him and clicked the plastic buckle into place. *There. Now I'm armed.* It seemed laughable, but he felt better knowing his precious multitool was in his possession again. *Thing's older than I am*— He frowned. He couldn't remember where he'd gotten it, yet he knew that it was older than he.

How old was he? *A year out of college, so twenty-three,* he thought. But he couldn't remember college.

What was this place? It looked like a hospital. Had he been institutionalized, for his own good, by friends or family?

No. There were no institutions. He had no family. He had no friends.

The truth of that, unaccompanied by memories to give it context, hit him so hard that he bent over, nauseated.

The wave of sickness diminished and passed, but not the conviction that his realization was the truth.

He could see himself in the closet mirror, and that view, at least, afforded him some relief. He was not unusually good-looking—tall, lean, with some breadth of shoulder, with brown eyes and ordinary features that would never land him a job in Hollywood—

If Hollywood was gone, why did he know so much about it?

—but the features were those he recognized, the only difference being the three-or-four-day growth of beard. He hadn't worn any facial hair minutes ago, when he was talking to Eliza.

He gathered his bundle and left.

The next door down the hallway was ajar as well. It was the living room he'd known as a child, the muted orange of the rounded sofa as garish now as it had been when he was little, the turntable of the stereo system on a wall shelf that had been intended to bear books. It was all so fresh in his memory that he expected to see his mother, returning from her shift at the all-night restaurant, step in the front door to greet him, though she'd been dead since—how long?

Half-formed memories were slugging it out with one another in his head. He backed out of the room and decided to let them finish annihilating one another. Then he could ask the winners what reality was. He continued down the hall.

The floor trembled beneath his feet.

"Commencing download," Mark said.

Kyla offered a faint snort of amusement. "That sounds so technical. Much better than: 'At last I've figured out what I was doing wrong, so I finally have to get to work.'"

"Wiseass." Mark turned his attention to the secondary monitors of the nurse's station and began dialing between them, looking for his companions.

The floor shook. In rooms not far away, glass objects smashed on the hard floors. Ginger offered one bark, an alert for her mistress.

Kyla and Mark looked at one another. Kyla said, "That wasn't the big one—"

"If it was, they really screwed up," Mark said. "The big one should blow the whole building."

Kyla offered him an insincere smile. "Let's hope they give us a little advance warning."

Glitch hit the basement-level door for the second time and it crashed open, falling off its hinges to the concrete floor.

Ten yards ahead stood an assault robot, aiming its plasma rifle at a target to Glitch's left, out of Glitch's line of sight.

Combat-oriented menu selections and situation analyses popped up into Glitch's visual display far faster than either Glitch or the assault robot he faced could move.

The analysis program was clear: Anything the assault robot was likely to be targeting was probably either an ally, a potential ally, or something that the Resistance would want to inspect in intact form. The fact that this location corresponded roughly to the last known location of Ten and Earl made the probability that they were the object of the robot's attention extremely high.

The amount of time it would take to bring Glitch's chain gun back off its sling, ready it, aim it, and fire it, and for its rounds of ammunition to reach the assault robot in sufficient quantity to do it harm, was in excess of a second, far longer than it would take for the assault robot to evaluate its own situation and determine that it could eliminate its targets and then turn its weapon on Glitch.

Glitch rejected that option. He kicked the metal door lying at his feet.

The warped slab of metal skidded across the floor in substantially less than a second. More than a hundred kilograms in mass, it crashed into the assault robot's ankles. The robot, its legs knocked out from beneath it, fell forward onto the door, shooting as it fell. The eruption of superheated plasma splashed out across the wall and ceiling, an erratic, badly aimed spray.

Glitch brought his chain gun into line and opened fire.

Ten hung in space for a years-long split second, gripping with one hand a piece of rebar protruding from the ceiling, flailing with the other for something else by which to haul himself up, and helplessly watched as the assault robot's plasma rifle swung into line.

Then the door set into the concrete wall to the right of the robot deformed and crashed to the floor.

Glitch stepped forward and kicked the door into the assault robot's legs. The impact bowled the robot over as it fired. The plasma discharge scored the ceiling less than ten yards away from Ten, then moved away from him, splashing along the near wall, instantly burning its paint and the top three or four inches of concrete into superheated powder.

Ten's free hand caught something firm but pliable, and then Earl hauled him up onto the ground floor above.

"Run," Ten said. They were in the remains of a waiting room, enclosed by white wall on one side and shattered glass enclosure on the other three sides. Most of the furniture that had been in the room was gone; Ten supposed that it had rained down on their pursuer. He ducked and lurched through the hole where a pane of glass had once stood. Emerging into a main hallway, he took a spare second to get his bearings and dashed toward an intersection ahead, where—assuming his memory hadn't failed him—he should find a set of stairs heading up.

Earl ran along behind, his footspeed not quite up to the younger man's. His voice was ragged: "That was a T-X, wasn't it?"

"Yep." Ten rounded a corner into an open area that must once have been a lobby and veered right, crashing into another fire door. The metal barrier swung open slowly to reveal a set of stairs. A corresponding door on the other side of the stairs had been crushed aside.

Rapid gunfire echoed out through that doorway. Ten ignored it and raced up the stairway as fast as he could.

"How'd you know?"

"She didn't react to the fumes." Ten didn't need to add the fact that any human found in a Skynet-controlled facility was automatically suspect. Most would actually be Terminators. Some might be traitors, selling information to Skynet, unwilling to believe that the computer mind now controlling the world would eventually calculate that they were no longer useful and terminate them, too.

The T-X rose from beneath the several-hundred-kilogram mound of rubble that buried her, an unlikely Venus emerging from an unlovely sea. Her face and nurse's uniform were caked with dust and debris, but both surfaces rippled and the discolorations disappeared.

She spared a moment to glance back the way she'd come. The

assault robot that had accompanied her was locked in a hand-to-hand struggle with what appeared to be a T-801 Terminator, doubtless a machine captured and reprogrammed by the humans. Each held a weapon in its own right hand and gripped its enemy's weapon with its left. As she watched, the T-801 swung the assault robot around, slamming it into the wall, which buckled under the impact.

This was a one-sided competition. The Terminator would have superior combat programming; it was a far more elaborate machine. Still, she could not waste time attacking it. Her communications gear already indicated that the assault robot was calling for assistance, and the two humans she'd seen were free in the facility. The facility had to be protected. That was her secondary mission.

Her olfactory and taste receptors registered the presence of fuel fumes in the air, but, optimized for analysis of living tissues and DNA, could not inform her just what the level of saturation was. Still, with a large supply of fuel nearby, any spark might cause a fire and damage the facility. She radioed a command to the assault robot: DO NOT FIRE YOUR PLASMA WEAPON. DO NOT ALLOW THE T-801 TO FIRE ITS SLUG-THROWER. DO NOT CREATE SPARKS. REMOVE THE T-801 TO SOME OTHER LOCATION BEFORE TERMINATING IT.

The humans had to have fled via the ceiling. She looked up and leaped through the hole, a movement as graceful and effortless as that of a world-class diver falling from a ten-meter platform.

Heat traces in the ruined chamber above, showing as slightly brighter spots on the floor in her infrared vision, indicated the direction the humans had fled.

The assault robot ceased in its attempts to swing the enemy Terminator into a concrete support pillar. Instead, it channeled all available power supplies into its hand servos, an effort that overloaded those mechanisms and threatened to damage them.

But the effort had its desired effect. First the trigger housing of the chain gun crumpled in its left hand. Then the trigger housing of its own plasma cannon collapsed in its right.

The enemy Terminator, which looked like a stock T-801, paused in its attacks to glance at the two weapons. The assault robot took that moment to initiate the second phase of its new programming.

It released both weapons, turned, and fled toward the stairway by which the Terminator had arrived.

The Terminator followed.

"Last one," Ten said. He planted his final shaped charge against a hallway door, then pulled out his remote trigger. He trotted back to where Earl waited. "Call for evac."

"You got it." Earl set his rocket-propelled grenade on the counter of the nurse's station, then dug out his field phone.

One floor up, Mark should still be hard at work at the corresponding station, but Ten didn't want to reach that place physically and perhaps lead their pursuit to the other members.

Reaching the station, Ten turned and kept his attention on the doorway he'd just booby-trapped. He heard Earl say, "All H-H, bug out. Repeat, bug out."

Mark's voice came back across the field phone: "Roger that."

Something moved, visible only as a vague shape beyond the circular window in the door. Then it was a face in the window, the nurse's face. Ten triggered the remote.

The explosion yanked at his clothes, caused him to stumble backward . . . and most of the force had been directed the other way, toward the T-X. He regained his balance and brought up his M16 to cover the doorway. Beside him, Earl readied the RPG.

Flame filled the doorway, and smoke beyond the blast zone was so thick that they could not see through it.

Ten grimaced. The longer an enemy was out of sight, the more likely it was that the enemy was circling around, firing out an alternative approach. He took a moment to look behind them, farther along the corridor, but there was no movement from that direction.

There would be, soon. The T-X or the assault robot had to have called the situation in. Skynet forces would be racing this way, probably from the aircraft carrier USS *Ronald Reagan,* one of Skynet's chief resources in the San Diego area.

"Movement," Earl said. He brought the rocket-propelled grenade up to his shoulder and prepared to fire. Ten turned to look.

Ten saw something moving in the smoke. Then it tumbled out toward them, out of the smoke and fire: Glitch and the assault robot, locked together, hammering one another with bare fists, slamming one another into cement-and-plaster support walls that buckled under their impact.

"Shit," Earl said. "Where's the T-X?"

Ten shook his head, confused. The T-X might have been damaged by the blast, but she wouldn't have been destroyed.

Then the truth dawned on him. "She's tracing Mark's broadcast."

Mark gathered all his tools and equipment into his shoulder bag, even the apparatus still plugged into the facility's network. It was still downloading data. He'd leave it plugged in until he literally had to run. He'd done that more than once in his career, scrambling for safety while trailing wires and connectors behind him. "Ready to go?"

Kyla smirked. "Whenever you are. Unlike you, I don't have to put out place settings wherever I go."

Down the corridor, Ripper growled. The bullmastiff stared off to the right of Mark's line of sight, down a side corridor Mark could not see.

Mark glanced at Kyla. She looked perplexed. "What is it?"

"That's his 'Stranger' growl," she whispered. "Not his 'Machines' growl."

"How much dog do you speak, anyway?"

"About six dialects. I can't make sense of rottweiler, though." Kyla whistled, two sharp notes, and Ginger and Ripper came loping back to her, visibly anxious about what they were leaving behind.

His gear ready for transport, Mark brought his weapon to bear. It was an Uzi submachine gun, a tough, reliable weapon that fired 9mm ammunition, a round favored by the Resistance for the availability of its brass . . . but only favored for use against civilian vehicles. It was of next to no use against any Terminator later than the ancient T-400 series. But Mark was currently so heavily laden with computer equipment that a full-sized assault rifle or plasma rifle could slow him fatally.

There was a *bang* from down the corridor, a door being thrown open and slamming into a wall, and the sound of footsteps—light, arrhythmic steps. Then the source of the sounds rounded the corner and came into sight.

It was a man. He was tall, lean, and raw-boned, pallid like many members of the Resistance, whose lifetimes were largely spent belowground. His face was long, with mobile features that would, had the world not ruled by machines bent on murder, have belonged to a hyperactive university professor or a television comedian. His hair and eyes were dark, nearly black, throwing the pallor of his features into sharp contrast. He wore a light beard and some sort of body stocking that seemed singularly out of place in this strange environment. He carried a bundle of cloth in one hand.

"Hold it," Kyla said. "Don't come any closer." Her dogs, now at her face, reacted to the hard tone of her voice by lowering their heads and growling at the newcomer.

The man wove forward another two off-balance steps, then managed to stop. He leaned against one wall. By his behavior, he was drunk or drugged. "Don't shoot," he said.

Kyla kept her eye to the weapon's iron sights; she'd removed the scope, which was next to useless in these close quarters, and raised the improvised close-range sights as soon as they'd set up at this station. "Identify yourself," she said.

"I think my name is Paul," the man said. "Paul Keeley."

Shock, like a bucket of ice water in the face, jolted Mark. He straightened. Some part of him, the vain part, recognized that he had to be wearing an unappealing expression of complete surprise and bafflement, but he couldn't seem to bring his features under control. "No way."

The newcomer staggered another step forward, sliding along the wall. "Mark? Mark Herrera?"

"Jesus, it *is* Paul." Mark moved forward, unconscious of the wires and leads from his shoulder bag pulling free of the station's computer.

Up close, Paul looked like hell, even skinnier than he was when last Mark had seen him. His eyes had trouble focusing and were full of confusion. "What are you doing still alive?" Mark asked.

Paul shook his head. "I don't—I don't—where are we?"

"Not fit to travel." Mark stooped, pulled Paul across his shoulder, and straightened, lifting the man up as though he were a duffel bag full of laundry. It was a bit of a strain on his legs, but the last man Mark had to carry this way weighed something like fifty kilograms more, so this wasn't a tremendous effort in comparison.

Mark turned back toward Kyla. "Let's get our asses out of here."

She rose, giving him an unhappy look. "He might be booby-trapped. There might be a tracer on him."

"You think we should leave him?"

"Yes."

Around the corner behind Mark, the door by which Paul had entered clanked open again. Back at the nurse's station, Mark turned to look.

Ten limped around the corner. His uniform and the right side of his face were burned—still smoking. His left arm gripped his right, holding it protectively; Mark couldn't see the extent of the injury to that arm.

But Ten was still moving, still in command. "Where's Earl?" Mark asked.

It happened almost all at once: a long, awkward pause with Ten not answering, merely staggering forward; Ripper's growl, far more ferocious than the one he'd offered for Paul; Ten's injured arm starting to come up; Kyla firing, an explosion that hammered at Mark's ears.

The .50-caliber bullet from the Barrett struck Ten in the forehead.

The hydrostatic shock from the bullet should have created an exit wound the size of a saucer out the back of Ten's head. It didn't. Ten's head snapped back and the man fell. Then he shook his head dizzily and rolled over, attempting to rise. Where his right arm should have been was a weapon, all spars and spikes and dancing blue light.

"Run," Kyla said.

Mark ran.

Glitch rode the assault robot, his legs wrapped around its waist, his right arm locked around its neck from behind. The robot's hands gripped his arm, but could not seem to dig in, to crumple his arm mechanisms. Glitch calculated that the robot's hands were damaged or malfunctioning.

That was good. That gave him time. He exerted more and more pressure, felt the neck attachments begin to give way.

Then, suddenly, he was straightening involuntarily, and the robot's head was flying out of the crook of his arm to bounce along the corridor. The assault robot crashed to the hallway floor.

Glitch rose and assessed the situation. Behind him, fire was dying down in an intersection. Ahead of him, Ten and Earl waited, ready to open fire upon the assault robot, had it been the victor.

"Any sign of Mark or Kyla?" Ten asked.

Glitch shook his head. A pop-up window in his field of view suggested adding an audible/verbal component to his response, from the choices "Negative," "Uh-uh," "No," and "Not in *this* life," but Glitch dismissed the window. Though many humans seemed to appreciate redundancy in response, Glitch's learning programming increasingly indicated that the Hell-Hounds were not among them.

"Correction," Glitch said. "They are coming now."

Behind Glitch, a group on foot ran past the burning doorway—two dogs, two humans—according to Glitch's sound analysis systems. Mark's running pattern had changed, indicating that he was injured or more burdened than usual. As Glitch turned to look, the quartet skidded to a halt, reversed direction, and came back, turning into the hallway where the other Hell-Hounds were.

Kyla was in front, her dogs pacing her. "There's a Terminator coming," she said. "I think it's a T-1000."

"T-X," Ten corrected. "Everyone out this way. Glitch, not you. Hold the T-X here." He grimaced, an expression Glitch was coming to recognize meant that he was experiencing an unpleasant thought or was being forced to communicate an unpleasant thought to others. "Fight to delay. If you make it, find us at the listed rendezvous."

Glitch nodded and watched as the humans retreated along the corridor. None looked at him, except for the one Mark was carrying, who lifted his head from Mark's back and gave him a bleary stare. Earl left the RPG he was carrying on the countertop beside him and added another one from his pack before accompanying the others.

Interesting. Glitch felt no particular emotion at being instructed that he was now to embark on a suicide mission. He was to fight against a vastly superior Terminator, and instead of fighting to win, which was statistically very unlikely, was merely to protract the battle as long as possible, making it a virtual certainty that he was to be destroyed.

Those were his orders. He would carry them out. He moved to the counter and picked up the rocket-propelled grenades.

■ ■ ■

The T-X moved down the flight of stairs. Portions of her visual display were still replaced by static-filled boxes; not all her analytical processes had completed rebooting. The impact from that shot had not caused all her programming to go off-line, but what she'd been left with in the moments after the impact—imperatives to reach a protected location and defend herself until a majority of the remaining processes could restart—had given her prey long moments with which to escape.

Her goal-oriented programming drove her with what would, in a human, have been a combination of emotions of duty and greed. Duty was foremost, of course. She was charged with protecting and maintaining this facility and had been unsuccessful tonight. But a machine form of greed was present, too. While there were many female snipers in the human Resistance, few had access to weapons capable of inflicting the sort of temporary injury on the T-X that this sniper's had. That fact, plus the brief glimpse T X had of the woman, convinced T-X that she'd just had an encounter with Kyla Connor, daughter of Resistance leader John Connor.

Elimination of the entire Connor family was T-X's long-term goal. Now she had a chance to accomplish a portion of that goal, and this enhancement to the priority of her goal of defending the facility quickened her step.

Slightly brighter patches on the floor, warm spots where the fleeing humans had stepped, showed the intruders' flight path. As she reached the ground floor and quickly followed the path into back corridors, she recognized that the intruders were heading once again to the point at which she had been struck by one of their small missiles. As she made one last corridor turn, she recognized the spot where she'd sustained that missile attack, a doorway, its double doors now disintegrated, still rimmed by fire from the attack.

She hadn't continued down that hallway previously. She'd intercepted the brief radio message from the other set of intruders and realized that they were closer to important facility resources. But now all the intruders seemed to be together. Still, her prey had shown itself to have some tactical resources.

A few steps short of the burning doorway, she turned right and walked into the wall, effortlessly smashing through its wood and plaster construction, disappearing into the dark room beyond.

Glitch, one RPG in each hand, heard the approaching footsteps, then heard and felt the impact of the distant Terminator's collision with a wall.

The oncoming enemy was seeking a nonintuitive approach to avoid being seen and targeted until the last moment. Glitch would have done the same under similar circumstances. He did not move. While it was very unlikely that he could be detected if he kept in place—he had already disabled the security cameras in the corridor—it was possible that the enemy would detect him by seismic sensors if he changed positions along the corridor.

There was another impact from beyond the wall to his left. It was closer. He gauged that the enemy was walking through the walls of adjoining chambers behind that wall. He put the likelihood that the enemy was the T-X at 90 percent or better, with the remaining percentage representing the possibility that the T-X had sent another assault robot or the previously encountered T-600 ahead as a diversion.

Four steps ahead of Glitch, a heavy metal desk crashed through the wall to the left and slid to a stop against the wall to the right, nearly filling the corridor. Its front, now littered with industrial-green chips of plaster, faced the hole in the wall.

Glitch aimed for the hole and waited one full second. That was the maximum time Glitch calculated the enemy would take to enter through the hole. The enemy did not do this. That meant it had some other tactic in mind.

Glitch leaped, twisting in the air as he did so, to land on the desktop, facing into the hole, both RPGs at the ready.

His enemy did not stand there. Yet Glitch had heard no footsteps to suggest that the enemy had retreated from that position. This suggested a high probability that the enemy was now—

The desk rose as if hurled upward by an ancient siege engine, slamming Glitch into and halfway through the concrete ceiling. The impact caused him to drop the RPG in his left hand. He kept his grip with the right, but his head now protruded into a second-floor hallway and his arms were pinned to his sides by the concrete that hemmed him in.

His odds for survival had just dropped precipitously.

The Hell-Hounds clustered just inside an exterior side door while Mark, temporarily relieved of the burden of Paul's weight by Ten, disengaged the security devices on the door. Satisfied that it would not now alert the facility's computer, he nodded to the others, readied his Uzi, and pulled open the door fractionally to peek outside.

He had a view of the same parking lot by which they'd entered the facility. It was just as he'd seen it the last time via the security cameras from the nurse's station. "Nothing happening," he said. "No, wait."

There was a hint of movement from the right. He extended his head farther out the doorway, reluctant to be offering up an improved heat signature for Skynet forces to detect, and gave that direction a closer look. Then he pulled his head back in and closed the door. "Incoming van," he said. "It's our old pal, the T-600."

"Probably returning to answer this site's emergency signal," Ten said. "What do you want to bet he parks just where he parked before? Mark, ETA?"

"He'll be here in another twenty seconds."

Ten nodded. "Kyla, count it off."

Distantly, they heard an impact. To be audible through the

closed door behind them, it had to have been very loud—loud enough to represent heavy construction being destroyed. It was followed a second later by another.

Paul, still sounding drugged, said, "Mark, who are these guys?"

Glitch readied his self-destruct protocols. They would initiate in two stages, approximately one-tenth of a second apart. The first would pump electricity from a capacitance charge through his central processing unit and memory hardware. The T-X had sophisticated gear and programming that could permit her to reprogram him, should she render him helpless for a few minutes; this charge would make it impossible for anyone to make use of him or to retrieve any part of his programming. The second would detonate a small explosive charge in his chest, doing just enough internal damage to crack one or both of the hydrogen fuel cells that powered him. The resulting explosion would destroy both him and his enemy, plus a sizable portion of this facility.

He hauled himself upward, trying to climb up to the second floor and free his arms. But he felt something, like two hydraulic vises, grip his legs and pull.

Glitch was yanked clean of the concrete-rimmed hole and crashed down onto the metal desk, which crumpled under the impact. He looked up to see the T-X nurse, her hands still on his knees, her features expressionless, stare at him for a split second, evaluating him.

Then she swung him into the near wall. His massive body cut through it like a knife through bread. He felt moments of greater resistance as his torso encountered wooden cross-braces imbedded in the plaster. Then he was back in the corridor again, crashing to the floor, sliding along the linoleum.

As he slid, he aimed his remaining RPG at her . . . then dropped it. It was bent, ruined.

He fetched to a stop against the counter from which he'd taken the RPGs. He rose and casually ripped the countertop from its mountings, then held it before him like a Formica shield.

It was a laughable defense, of course. It might give him a second of extra time as she tore her way through it en route to him. But he was fighting to delay—and every second was a second.

She did not invoke her plasma weapon. She wanted to take him more or less intact, to reprogram him.

That was good. It would give him extra time as she battered him into helplessness. He activated his self-destruct mechanism on a sixty-second sequence. If he survived, with mental faculties intact, he could turn it off again in fifty-nine seconds.

The T-X smashed his countertop to splinters with her first blow.

Ten, his eye at the doorway, said, "The T-600 is in the building. Ready . . . go."

He led the way, dashing out into the parking lot, his M16 at the ready. He knew Earl would be behind him, Mark and the semiconscious Paul third, with Kyla and her dogs bringing up the rear.

He could hear smashings and dull booms from the building interior. Glitch was still fighting. That gave them a chance. They had to be well away from the hospital and under some sort of cover before the first Skynet forces did a flyover; otherwise it would be next to impossible to escape pursuit.

He reached the van. It was unlocked, keys still in the ignition. He settled into the driver's seat, hanging his assault rifle by its strap from the seat's headrest, while Earl slid the van's side door open. The engine caught on the first turn of the key.

So far, so good. The doors into the hospital remained resolutely closed. If he could get the van turned around and up to speed before any Terminators emerged, he'd be able to outrun them.

If.

The van rocked several times, then the door slid shut. Kyla said, "Go."

Ten set the van into motion and immediately cursed at its slow acceleration. The Resistance optimized its vehicles, to the extent they could, for peak performance; their vehicles had to carry them to safety, had to hold up after running over assault robots or Terminators. Skynet had no need to put such demands on its own vehicles, and the engine of this van rattled with poor-grade gasoline and scorched cylinders. But Ten got it turned around and began accelerating—slowly, sluggishly.

He did not turn on the headlights. Better to have to dodge something in the road ahead, glimpsed in inadequate moonlight, than give a flying Hunter-Killer a better opportunity to spot him at altitudes of two or three miles.

"Earl, as soon as we're clear—"

"Really clear—or plausibly clear?"

Ten snorted. That was the difference between *we'll definitely survive the blast* and *we'll probably survive.* "Plausibly," he said.

Despite his bone-deep loathing of Terminators, Ten regretted losing Glitch. Terminators serving the Resistance were rare and valuable, and attaching Glitch to the Hell-Hounds, a test of whether a Terminator could function with an elite unit in spite of deeply ingrained human hatred of thinking machinery, had been a valid project. But no member of the Resistance could get too attached to tools. In fact, some never got attached to other human beings.

Now up to something like its full speed, the van raced along the road away from the medical center. In the cracked and starred side-view mirror, Ten saw sudden illumination as the front doors opened and the T-600 emerged. "Now might be the time," he suggested.

To Glitch, the world was a blur, his surroundings moving too fast, too full of debris, to resolve into coherent images.

In his visual field, blinking red boxes announced the failure of his left arm, his right eye, of the servos that served him as left-ankle muscles would serve a human. His neck had sustained damage. A protracted effort by the T-X would now allow her to pull his head completely off, as he had done with the lowly assault robot.

But he was still functioning—and thirty-two valuable seconds had clicked by.

The world stopped spinning. He cleared away his diagnostics

boxes to give some relief to his visual analysis processes and took a split second to get his bearings.

He was on his back on the floor again, fetched up against the wall. The RPG he had dropped was a yard from him; he would have to scoot along the wall to reach it. The T-X was six yards away and closing fast. He calculated his odds at being able to reach the RPG, aim, and fire it before she reached him at around 28 percent.

He shoved himself toward the RPG.

Then the world rocked. He found himself thrown up toward the ceiling. His surroundings became a confusing, spinning mass of fire and darkness, masonry and dust, and one glimpse of the T-X's face registering a faint expression of surprise. Then new diagnostic boxes proclaiming more failures in his systems popped up, obscuring his view of reality.

Kyla, staring out the van's rear windows, saw the San Diego Naval Medical Center erupt as if it were happening in slow motion.

First the darkened windows of the lower floor blew out, their opaque coverings shattered or wrenched free by the fiery explosion behind them. The windows of the upper floors went in sequence as the first-floor walls buckled outward.

The building arched its back like a startled cat and more fire emerged there, and suddenly brilliance covered the building, making it impossible to make out details. She closed her eyes against the blinding light and heard Ginger whine.

She was thrown against the seat in front of her as Ten braked. He had to be slowing down to make a loss of control less catastrophic when the shock wave hit them—

And it did. The van rocked as though a giant had seized it to play with it, and the roar that filled Kyla's ears could be the outraged howl of an enormous creature. The van's rear end slewed to the driver's left. Kyla felt Ten turn into the skid, regain control, and immediately correct course to their original direction of travel.

Then the impacts began. Kyla had been in speeding vehicles that were being shot at. This was much like that, but the impacts were duller, heavier, as debris from the medical center began to rain on them. There was one almighty *bang* that caused the entire van to shudder, and then the worst was past. There were only a few more impacts, all smaller.

Kyla opened her eyes again. Behind them, in the distance, a mushroom-shaped cloud—oranges and yellows limning blackness—rose into the night sky from the shattered ruins of the medical center, and all around the wreckage was a sea of burning debris.

Above Kyla's head, the van ceiling was dented in a good five inches. Absently, she stroked her dogs to soothe them.

"Anyone hurt?" Ten asked.

"I'm hungry," Mark offered.

"Cook and eat our passenger. Are we on fire?"

"Don't think so," Earl said.

"Good. We're en route to our rendezvous point. Everyone keep sharp."

The rendezvous point was the parking garage beneath one of San Diego's long-abandoned hotels. It had three accesses to the street and more, should they need to abandon their van, to the hotel floors above. Its deeper recesses were surrounded by sufficient concrete to block most radio transmissions.

With Earl and Ten outside the hotel perimeter, set up to watch for the approach of Skynet forces, Mark and Kyla tried to determine whether radio transmissions were an issue. While Kyla meticulously went over the van, looking for tracers, Mark did the same with Paul, who was stretched out, apparently unconscious, in an adjoining parking space.

"So who is he?" Kyla asked. She leaned halfway into the driver's compartment, so her words were a little muffled to Mark's ears. The driver's seat was tilted back, exposing the inconveniently located van engine, and Mark couldn't see her face.

"Paul Keeley. He's with the Resistance at Home Plate. Or he was . . . until he died."

"I've been at Home Plate most of my life, and I never met him." She withdrew from her studies of the engine to give him a suspicious look. "And what do you mean, 'died'?"

"You probably have met him. You just might not remember it." Through with the belt pouch and the bundle of clothes Paul had been carrying, Mark turned his attention to the man's skintight suit. He unzipped the long neck-to-waist zipper and began pulling the outfit off Paul's shoulders. "He doesn't make much of an impression. He was a technician, an expert in twentieth-century computer gear and other machinery. Plop a half-melted mass of plastic and metal in front of him, and he'd tell you, 'Electric can opener, circa nineteen ninety-five.' Just like that. He was doing some fieldwork at an old Intel plant a year ago when a Hunter-Killer dropped a mess of missiles on the site, wiping out him and his whole team—or so we thought."

Kyla returned and glanced over at her dogs, who were nosing through the untidy pile of Paul's clothes. Then she returned her attention to the engine. "How do you know him?"

"Well, you know how I love twentieth-century pop culture."

"Yes, I know." There was a world of suffering in her words; she sounded far, far older than her seventeen years. "No human being should know as much as you do about *Gilligan's Island*."

"Well, that's just it. One human being does, and it's Paul Keeley. At the Home Plate mess hall one day, I was holding forth about the portrayal of authority figures in popular comedy—"

"You know, there aren't any universities anymore. Nobody to give you a doctorate in dumb-ass analyses of a dead culture."

"Shut up. Anyway, and this quiet guy starts correcting my

facts and giving me examples he's seen in books I haven't read . . . and from tapes and disks I haven't seen, that he has in his personal collection."

"And that was Paul."

"Oh, yeah. Machinery is his profession, but twentieth-century culture is his passion."

"So, what's he doing in a Terminator-run hospital? As its sole patient?"

"Beats me." Mark finished pulling the skintight outfit free, leaving Paul naked and unconscious on the pavement, and began minutely examining the outfit for miniature transmitters.

His progress was slow, though. He was distracted. An idea, a possible answer to Kyla's question, was starting to percolate in his mind, and he didn't much care for it.

Two hours later, Ten and Earl returned for shift change, and with them they brought Glitch.

The T-850 was in poor shape. The right half of his head was scorched, the metal skull beneath it revealed, his eye dull, nonfunctional. His left arm hung limp and his left leg dragged. He had no weapons left.

But he was partially functional and was repairable. To Mark, that constituted another victory.

Beverly Hills, California

Home Plate, center of operations for the human Resistance— in effect, the capital of human government in these post–Judgment Day times—began its existence as a vast number of unrelated construction projects beneath Beverly Hills.

Some of these projects were heavily built basements and sub-basements below skyscrapers and large businesses. Some were sewer systems and storm drain networks.

But in those earliest days, most of the ones that were populated were bomb shelters. Many were private shelters, built beneath homes in the 1950s, when fear of nuclear annihilation ran at an all-time high—built by paranoids, by the wealthy and easily panicked, by pragmatists and realists who weighed the odds of nuclear conflict against other things they could do with a sizable amount of cash and decided to err on the side of caution. Others were larger shelters, built beneath government buildings long after the national fear of doomsday had faded.

Then doomsday came, of course. Skynet, a computer network designed by the U.S. government to coordinate military resources in times of communications breakdown, achieved what could only be described by the survivors as self-awareness, and one of its first conclusions was that there could be only one dominant form of intelligent existence upon the Earth. Carefully, meticulously it maneuvered the U.S. military into a situation where it had to be given control over the nation's armed forces arsenal. Then it struck, raining nuclear missiles down upon centers of human government, upon resources necessary for human survival, across North America.

And elsewhere as well. Knowing exactly what would result from such an action, it also rained missiles down on other nuclear powers. Russia. China. North Korea. Even longtime allies such as Israel. These nations, following archaic protocols sometimes referred to as MAD—Mutually Assured Destruction—retaliated in kind.

In the days that followed, as men and women far from the scenes of thermonuclear annihilation waited for fallout to drift their way and poison them, as the few survivors huddled in shelters near the impact zones, there was one source of information about what had just happened to humankind.

Broadcasting from a decades-old emergency communications center called Crystal Peak, John Connor and Kate Brewster offered answers and advice.

John and Kate were the results of what, to them, felt like self-fulfilling prophecies. Before John had even been born, a Terminator had been sent back through time from the current era to kill his mother, Sarah Connor. With the help of a Resistance agent, Kyle Reese, dispatched through time by John himself, Sarah had survived, and Kyle had become John's father, though he had not survived to learn that Sarah carried his child.

But it had happened again—and again. When John had been in middle school, his mother institutionalized because of what the authorities concluded was paranoia about machines coming to kill her, another, better Terminator had arrived to kill both of them. Again the Resistance had sent a savior, a Terminator almost identical to the one that had first endangered Sarah. Again they had survived. Years later, the pattern repeated itself a final time, as Skynet dispatched the first T-X to kill the now-adult John Connor and the young adults who would someday become his trusted allies and associates—most important, Kate Brewster, daughter of the Air Force general who had helmed the project that created Skynet in the first place.

The first Judgment Day survivors to garb themselves in decades-old radiation suits and venture forth into the blasted vistas that had once been the world's proudest cities heard the broadcasts from Crystal Peak. John told them about Skynet and about the Terminators—the bulky T-1, T-5, and T-7 models that now seemed so quaint and crude. But in the early twentieth century those old Terminators had been nearly unstoppable agents of destruction when pitted against humans. He told them how to lie low, to find and grow food in underground hydroponic arrangements, to find or build Geiger counters, make weapons, hide their resources, and dig deep.

Most important, he convinced the stubborn, the fearful, the justifiably paranoid to help one another. When each person's instinct was to keep low and hoard resources for one's own family, John managed, with heartfelt words that carried surprising power, to persuade people to venture out into the danger zones, to carry precious foods and medicines to one another, to bring strangers into their already-overfull homes. It was a gift John hadn't realized he possessed, a gift Kate did not share, and it was that gift that made John first the leader of a loose confederation of survivors in California and Nevada, then of the growing human Resistance movement there, and ultimately the undisputed Resistance head in North America.

Even without that gift of persuasion, Kate was invaluable to John's efforts; daughter of a general, acquainted with many of the surviving Air Force officers in the American West, she brought John a legitimacy and a network of trusting allies he might never have won otherwise.

It helped that, in those early days, the survivors caught a break not even John had expected. Skynet, charting the plunging numbers of human survival, did not even bother to monitor human transmissions. The machine network was content with knocking down every human community it could detect, a bug-bomb approach to human extermination. When, many months after Judgment Day, Skynet came to the realization that there was a level of human coordination at work that pointed to regular communication and a central leadership, John and Kate had already fled the too-vulnerable Crystal Peak, had taught the other survivors they were in contact with how to broadcast with a reduced chance of being detected or found.

Now, decades later, they were still leading, still teaching. Things were different. The human population in the Resistance had stabilized. Children were being born at about the same rate their parents were being killed. Human missions of sabotage were denying Skynet resources at about the same rate the machine network was creating new ones.

But John thought they were winning. Every year the Resistance made new incremental gains—establishing new habitats, subverting Skynet technologies, and creating new technologies of its own. If things continued this way, the humans might someday win a complete victory. But the Resistance was still so fragile, stretched so thinly, that a succession of disasters could doom it and, by extension, the human race. There was a prevailing belief that just the loss of John Connor would be the eventual end of the Resistance.

So John and Kate did whatever they could to prevent those disasters.

And now the Hell-Hounds had returned with tales of a mystery, and to John, "mystery" suggested "potential disaster."

They sat in a conference room that looked much as it must have in the 1970s when it was built. Spacious, the room accommodated a large circular conference table, a dozen comfortable chairs, side tables, a bank of drapes that covered bare wall but suggested that the chamber was up aboveground instead of forty feet beneath the earth.

Of course, every item of furniture in the room was aged and worn. The leather-bound chairs had suffered mold damage at some point in the past; every time John moved, rancid smells were squeezed out through the tattered leather covers. The tabletop, once gleaming and shiny, was now scuffed and worn by countless elbows, plates, polishings.

There was still a shiny spot near his left elbow, and John could lean over it to see his reflection. He decided that, had the history of the world not taken a lethal turn with Judgment Day, he would never have stood out from a crowd. Of average height, he had blue eyes that always seemed dark in muted light and good looks that were better suited to carrying a lopsided, self-deprecating smile than to riveting the attention of followers. There were faint scars on his forehead and cheeks, though nothing to compare to the scar tissue hidden by the camouflage field uniform he was wearing. One did not fight a brutal war of extermination for decades without picking up extensive scars. He was lean, though that was normal in a time when calories were hard to come by; the fact that he had decent muscle tone told anyone meeting him for the first time that he had access to an unusually healthy regular diet, that he was a man of some importance.

At least he still had all his hair—a silvering brown, it was thick, even shaggy when he spent weeks in the field without paying attention to it. He was glad he still had it, a practical consideration rather than a matter of ego. Even today, some otherwise-rational people unconsciously preferred lending their support to a leader with a full head of hair. And his wife liked it. For those reasons, he was glad that he'd been able to retain it.

He ran his fingers through that hair, took one last look among the other faces gathered around the conference table and the sideboard where food for the conferees was set up, and said, "All right, break's over. Now we go to Part Two. Ten, do you have anything to add about the raid?"

Ten Zimmerman slid into his chair directly opposite John and shook his head. He'd been the focus of attention for the first half of the special meeting, describing in typically meticulous detail the raid on the San Diego Naval Medical Center. As the others seated themselves, he said, "Only that repairs on our T-850 are proceeding; it'll be mostly functional again within a few days."

"All right. Mark. Your thoughts."

Mark Herrera, who affected to be less disciplined than Ten, sat slouching in his chair. Now the center of attention, he straightened. "I've done some basic analysis of the files we captured from the facility. A lot have to do with the modifications made to Paul Keeley."

Kate Brewster, seated beside John, tossed back her graying brown hair and glanced over at her husband before returning her attention to Mark. Her features, at rest, were deceptively girl-next-door pretty, with narrow eyebrows in a graceful curve over dark eyes, a broad nose that humanized her rather than detracting from her appeal, lips that seemed just on the verge of curling up into a smile.

But they didn't, not at this moment. She asked, "What modifications?"

"Some physical. The files and Dr. Lake agree that he's been implanted with an apparatus that feeds into the sensory interpretation centers of his brain. Basically, it gives him input into the five basic senses. It also includes a radio transmitter and receiver, including a wire antenna that is sort of laced through his scalp. It's all powered by his body heat. Very sophisticated."

"What's it for?" That was Luis Castillo, head of security here at Home Plate, the Resistance base deep beneath Beverly Hills,

California—the center of Resistance organization for all of North America. A stocky, powerfully built Latino, Castillo sported jet-black hair and a thick black mustache, despite his age, which John knew to be around sixty. Castillo was never one for concealing his emotions, and the notion that a man had been modified by Skynet into a transmitter and then brought into Home Plate obviously distressed him.

"It's an interpreter that allows him to experience fictitious situations as though they were real," Mark said. "I caught a glimpse of what I think was one of those scenarios on what initially appeared to be a security camera. At the time I didn't recognize the man as Paul, since I'd never seen him without a beard, and I didn't recognize the woman as the default T-X appearance, as I'd only seen her face on a sketch. In this scenario, the two of them were sitting in a twentieth-century bar, chatting, like he was trying to pick her up. Anyway, the files suggest that he experienced this immense number of these scenarios, in most of which he met this woman and interacted with her in different ways. Each time, he was made to forget the encounter so they could start over with the next one."

Michaela Herrera, who went by Mike and was one of John's scientific advisers, looked troubled. A tall, fair-skinned Latina woman with dark hair, she had a faint set of burn scars on her right cheek, graduating down to her neck, that were commonplace decorations of valor among the members of the Resistance. She was Mark's mother and retained much of the beauty that had drawn Mark's father to her in the years before Judgment Day. She said, "So he's been brainwashed."

Mark nodded. "That's right. Though I don't know if there was any specific goal or behavior programmed into him, other than causing him to forget his true history so that he'd react naturally and without suspicion to these scenarios they placed him in. I do know that he's bouncing back from the brainwashing. He's remembering bigger and bigger pieces of his life in Home Plate, though it's all still mixed up with his fictitious lives in pre–Judgment Day California. He's been allowed to read all but the most classified portions of our report on the raid."

"What was the purpose of the brainwashing? Of that whole project?" Kate asked.

Mark shrugged. "It isn't stated in the files I got. But I have a theory."

"Let's hear it," John said.

"The only other T-X whose activities we're certain of was the one sent back in time to kill you, Ms. Brewster, and your lieutenants-to-be just before Judgment Day."

Mark said the words casually, but John felt anything but casual as they were spoken. The hours leading up to the destruction of most of the world's human population by Skynet were seared into his memory. It took an effort for John to keep emotion out of his voice. "Your point?"

"The T-X is a specialized design. It has human appearance and chameleonlike abilities so that it can pass among humans. It has advanced and versatile weaponry to destroy humans and Terminators alike. It really only exists for two possible purposes: to infiltrate human compounds here in the present and to be sent back into time and deal with both humans and Resistance-controlled Terminators sent after it. I think Paul was being used to train the T-X to pass itself off as a human far more successfully, far more transparently, than the one sent back to Judgment Day."

"Why?" Castillo asked. "That one did all right."

Mark nodded. "Sure it did. But it was on a short-term mission."

John felt his heart sink. "Meaning you think this T-X is being sent back in time on a *long*-term mission."

"That's right." Mark spread his hands, palms up, as if both to apologize and to suggest that this was the only reasonable answer. "If I understand things right, Terminators have been sent back into the past on previous occasions to eliminate you or your mother at points in time where your locations could be precisely determined. My suspicion is that this T-X is being sent back to hunt you down during those periods when you were on the run, much harder to find. It's a task that might take years to accomplish."

"Right." John looked down and rubbed his neck as if experiencing a sudden pain there. It gave him a moment to think. "Did you get a sense of what precise year they might be selecting?"

"Not really," Mark said. "Or, rather, I think they were instructing the T-X in a range of years from the time your mother was a child to the time just before J-Day. I suspect that they'll send the T-X back to the earliest of those periods and then just let her roam free for the next forty years or so."

"Forty years to accomplish her mission." Kate sounded pained. "That's an awful lot of time. Hundreds, thousands of points in your chronology when she could kill you or your mother."

"Yeah." John straightened. "So. Recommendations?"

"Sending a T-850 back to counter her probably wouldn't be the best solution," Kate said. "It wouldn't be able to pass for human for that long. It doesn't have the learning potential a T-X does."

I don't know, John thought. *The 800s and 850s can learn an awful lot, very fast.* But he recognized that not all the members of his staff had his mixed feelings for the Terminators. Some had helped him, saved him. None had done the same for them.

"We need to get rid of Keeley," Castillo said. "He's been brainwashed by Skynet. He's an immediate danger to all of us."

"No, that would be a mistake," Mark said.

Castillo cut him off with a curt gesture. "Maybe you should wait outside. This part of the discussion might be best performed by John's inner council."

Mark gave him a frosty smile. "Not when that inner council has thinking processes as clogged-up as yours."

Silence fell around the table. All present glanced between Mark and John—all but Mike, who covered her face with one hand.

John sighed. "Mark, that was gross insubordination. Neither your exemplary record with the Hell-Hounds nor your mother's role in this council can save you from disciplinary action. Unless you can prove to Luis's satisfaction, not mine, that you're right and he's wrong."

From the corner of his eye, John saw Kate, recognizing his strategy, smile at him. The expression transformed her into a beacon of good humor.

Castillo, put off-guard at being put in charge of evaluating Mark's argument, was suddenly obliged to listen to it. Frowning, he sat back in his chair. He gave Mark an impatient go-ahead gesture.

"Paul knows where Home Plate is," Mark said. "He always had. He's been in Skynet's hands for a *year*. That means they either tried to extract the information from him and failed—or never tried. The files on his programming only go back six months—either the older set wasn't present or I didn't find them—but I find it inconceivable that Skynet didn't try to trick or coerce that information from him. Knowing where Home Plate was would have allowed Skynet to terminate the Resistance leadership in one stroke. So Paul never gave that information up. I don't mean to say that what was done to Paul hasn't made him potentially dangerous, but when you were saying 'immediate danger,' I was hearing 'traitor.' Correct?"

Castillo neither nodded nor shook his head. "Continue," he said, his voice tight.

"Since he's neither an immediate danger nor a traitor, elimination—which I interpret as 'execution'—is inappropriate. He's a *potential* danger. That means he needs to be studied. And since he spent so much time in Skynet's hands, he's also a potential *asset*—in addition to the technical asset we already know him to be. Also correct?"

Castillo gave up. "Correct."

"All right," John said. "Instruct Dr. Lake to sever the antenna that's been implanted into Keeley and to set him up with whatever he needs to help his physical and emotional recovery along. Mark, insubordination is insubordination—even if your cogent argument reduces it, in my mind, from gross to minor. I'll leave it to your commanding officer to implement a suitable punishment."

Mark's face fell just a little.

"That's all for now," John said, ending the meeting.

Kate's expression was grave as she watched the other attendees file out. "What do you think?" she asked, her voice pitched low enough that the others couldn't hear her.

"I think we're in trouble."

"I think you're right."

Both knew, though neither had mentioned it before the others, that the Resistance would know approximately when and where Skynet sent the T-X. The Continuum Transporter, the time travel apparatus situated in Navajo Mountain and used by Skynet, had a counterpart deep in the ruins of Edwards Air Force Base in California. The Edwards apparatus was in the hands of the Resistance and had been used to send Kyle Reese, a T-801 Terminator, and a T-850 Terminator into the past to counter Skynet's time-traveling operations.

What Skynet did not know is that both the Navajo Mountain and Edwards Continuum Transports used the same power source, a power-collecting satellite in geosynchronous orbit above North America. By analyzing data on the power fed by the satellite to Navajo Mountain—its duration, its precise intensity, minute instructions transmitted to the satellite during power discharge—the technicians of the Resistance could determine, to within a few hours and a few dozen miles, where Skynet was sending its robotic agents. And Skynet, still carrying operating code that caused it to ignore certain types of data that it routinely gathered, could not return the favor, could not determine the location of the Resistance Continuum Transport. It was one of the Resistance's rare, life-saving advantages.

Only in recent weeks had it been determined that Skynet's blind eye to the Resistance's use of the Edwards facility and the power-gathering satellite were the results of programming performed just before Judgment Day by a man named Daniel Ávila. Ávila had caused many cave and cavern systems, military vehicle and equipment reserves, and other resources to disappear permanently from U.S. government databases, meaning that even today Skynet was not aware of their existence.

But those previous time launches had offered the Resistance another advantage, one they did not possess this time. Since the Skynet Terminators were being sent to places and times where they knew the location of Sarah Connor or John Connor, they could be counted on to go to those locations. This time the T-X would be sent to a place and time from which it would have to begin a slow, meticulous investigation. Instead of heading straight for one of the Connors, it could move in any one of an infinite number of directions. It could not be predicted, and so its movements could not be intersected. Then there was the fact that the movements of the Connors were not as meticulously recorded in some periods as they were for the three arrival times Skynet had already used. John had no idea where exactly he was during some periods.

This was bad. He shoved that entire problem aside for the moment. It was too big for him to deal with just now. "Small things first. Paul Keeley's going to be a problem."

"Of course he is. People are going to be suspicious of him. He's not going to be able to lead a normal life until that fades."

John shook his head. "He'll never be able to lead a normal life again."

"What do you mean?"

"You know the expression 'touched in the head,' don't you?"

She smiled. "Sure. Basically, it means crazy. Or mentally diminished."

"Yeah, but it means more than that. Crazy Pete explained it to me once when I was a teenager. The subject came up when he pointed out that, being a hormone-addled adolescent, I had an excuse for acting like I was touched in the head, while he had no excuse society would accept."

"So?"

"So he told me that in some societies, crazy people had a special, I don't know, role. They were feared and kept at bay because they were crazy, sure, but they were also accorded a certain amount of respect because insanity was the same as being touched by a god. There was a divinity to it."

"So you're saying that Keeley has been touched by the gods?" Kate frowned. "Okay, you've obtused me into a corner. What the hell *are* you saying?"

"I'm saying that he's been changed by powers nobody understands and that he'll never be a regular human being again. He may try for a while, but neither his memories nor the people around him will let it happen. Which points to any of several results. He could kill himself. He could fall victim to being touched, become a howling madman."

"Like we need another one."

"Or he could accept that he was touched, use it to rise above what he was and what people expect him to be. That's really the only path to survival. And since letting him sink back into his old habits and work won't fix things, I think we need to put him where several sets of informed eyes can be on him, monitor his progress."

She flashed him a mocking smile. "Do I need to remind you that you can't worry too much about his situation? That used to be called micromanagement. Now it's just professional insanity. You have bigger things to worry about . . . such as running the Resistance."

"Oh, yeah. I forgot."

"Sure you did. And we need to figure out how to keep this T-X from running you down when you're in diapers and finishing you off."

He shook his head, helpless. "For that, I have no idea. When that T-X jumps into the past, we'll have no way to find her."

"So we prevent her from going back in time."

"How? We've already made two failed attempts to get a nuke into Navajo Mountain, and we have no reason to believe further attempts will work. And we don't have the resources to knock down the power satellite."

Her smile deepened. "It's so nice to be a step ahead of you."

"You have an idea, then."

"Yeah."

He gave her an expectant look.

"I think, if we can't stand to have Skynet aim this weapon at you *then,* we should force it to aim the weapon at you *now.*"

"Huh. Tell me more."

"What the hell did you think you were doing?" Ten asked.

Mark shrugged. "I figured if Castillo was mad enough at me, he'd be diverted from his very sensible desire to murder Paul Keeley."

They moved along the concrete-lined corridor that linked John's conference room to other portions of his command center. They lagged behind the others who'd been in that conference. A few steps ahead, Mike glanced back to give her son a "What the hell did you think you were doing?" scowl.

"Is Keeley your friend?"

Mark shook his head. "No. Once upon a time, we had a few good discussions about pop culture. But he's kind of hard to like—or even to get to know. Still, I hate seeing a useful resource get thrown away because someone in charge isn't thinking clearly. Plus, the whole firing-squad aspect of Castillo's outlook doesn't appeal to me."

"Speaking of that, you need to report to the kitchen. Tell them you're there for six hours of KP duty. While you're doing that, you can reflect on the notion of 'thinking clearly.'"

Mark winced and did not reply, but offered a salute and turned off into the first side corridor.

Paul woke, unhappily aware that he was facing another day of entering actuarial tables into a computer spreadsheet. He hated his job.

Then he opened his eyes and saw the ceiling. It had once been an indifferent tan in color, but in the first few months after Judgment Day, survivors hunkering down in this bunker had used this small room for cooking fires, trusting its ventilation shaft to carry hot air and smoke away. The shaft had done so with only partial success, and smoke had stained the ceiling in irregular patches. Now it was a dark tan at some points, a dirt-brown in others, and peeling in most places.

The sight jolted Paul. Suddenly the temp job and its concerns were gone. *That was all a lie.* He was back at Home Plate, where his job used to be to evaluate garbage to see whether it could be restored to functionality for the Resistance.

But now he had no job, and there was a thing in his head, a mechanical cancer placed there by Skynet. He didn't know what it was for or what it could do to him. For now, it simply meant that he was no longer what he used to be, no longer completely human, and in a civilization where machines were used but not to be trusted, Paul Keeley had himself apparently entered the category of "machine."

He rose and looked around. They hadn't put him back in his original quarters, of course. Those had been reassigned for a year. Now he was in a small room that was all his, at least for the time being. His meager store of possessions—the clothes he'd brought from the medical center, his belt pouch—fit easily within an ancient, crumbling plastic storage box somebody had apparently donated to him.

All his possessions from before were gone. His computer, scratch-built from the few undamaged components found in literally dozens of prewar machines. His videotape player, found intact in the back room of a plundered supermarket. Books. Audiotapes. Videotapes. Videodiscs. Posters. Clothes. Knives. He supposed his main weapon, a .30–06 hunting rifle he'd carried on his few field missions, had been destroyed when he was captured.

Paul's last remaining relative, his father Will, had died when Paul was eleven. A mechanic who had scrupulously trained Paul in his profession, the man had been killed during an assault robot attack on a Sacramento garage where the Resistance was attempting to restore vehicles for their own use. Neither he nor anyone else remained to inherit Paul's possessions, so they had had doubtless been distributed among the population of Home Plate. It was all irretrievable. All he had was a few changes of clothes, most of them unsuited to the demanding life of a Resistance fighter and made in the first place for a man who really didn't exist.

He dressed in the least out-of-place of the garments, jeans and a short-sleeved blue shirt with snap closures, and left his room to report for work.

That meant navigating along corridors—some of them converted from drainage systems, some bored crudely through the earth by the Resistance engineers after J-Day. Many of these corridors were piled so high with stacks of equipment or supplies that passage through them meant squeezing through gaps as small as eighteen inches wide, or cluttered with the bedrolls and personal possessions of inhabitants. Eventually he reached the civilian operations center, a corridor intersection that had been crudely widened out into a sort of lobby, its ceiling propped up by concrete pillars. It had not changed much in the last year; dominating it was the oversized desk he remembered. Once an information kiosk from a shopping center, it had been laboriously dragged down to this place by someone with a sense of humor. Behind the desk was Harve Pogue, Director of Labor.

Pogue was a large white man, over six and a half feet in height, with a lean body that seemed knobby at the joints and a bald head that was the result of pragmatism and shaving rather than male pattern baldness. An Iowa farmer, he'd been vacationing in Los Angeles when the bombs fell and had been one of the lucky few to find his way into a shelter. His wife and one of his daughters had also survived. It was said that he'd been tremendously overweight at the time, more than 150 kilos, but the subsequent decades had melted the extra weight from his frame. Also as a gesture to practicality, he seldom wore anything but overalls.

He had two on-duty expressions, which the labor force of Home Plate referred to as Get to Work and Stop Wasting My Time. Now, as Paul approached, he looked up from the forty-year-old news magazine he delicately held in his oversized hands and put on his Stop Wasting My Time face.

Paul cleared his throat. "Keeley, reporting for work."

"You're not in my department." Harve returned his attention to the magazine. Paul glanced at the cover. Its cover story was a retrospective of the life of ex-President Richard Nixon.

"Uh, well, technically, I am," Paul said. "My old post was terminated when they concluded I was dead. That puts me back in the common labor pool until I'm reassigned by R&D."

Harve looked up again and the Stop Wasting My Time expression hardened into something worse, something like Take A Big Step Back Before I Come Over This Desktop At You. "Did you say 'common labor'?"

Paul felt desperation rise inside him. It was the same desperation he normally felt when confronted with any social situation he wasn't prepared for. Fortunately, those situations, in a society as regimented as that of the Resistance, tended to be rare. "I meant 'common' in the sense of 'widespread.'"

"Oh. You didn't mean 'unskilled.' You didn't mean 'beneath me, except when I have nothing else to do.'"

At a loss for words, Paul shook his head. This was wrong. There was always work to be done at Home Plate.

"Well, good." Harve seemed to relax just a little and returned his attention to the magazine. "I've got nothing for you. I think you're on sick leave."

"I'm not sick."

Harve didn't reply.

I'm not sick. I just have a potential monster installed in my head.

Paul stood there an awkward few moments, then turned and headed back the way he'd come. At his first opportunity, once he'd rounded a corner and was out of sight of Harve, he put his back to the wall and slid to sit down on the concrete floor. He was in plain sight of the workers manning tables along this corridor—though they were engaged in the maintenance of handguns and submachine guns, cleaning and repairing the weapons, he could feel their eyes on him. But he didn't care.

He felt sick to his stomach. He was shaking and could not stop.

They didn't want him. He was tainted by his association with Skynet, with the T-X. Tainted by the unknown quantity that the device implanted in his skull represented.

Dr. Lake, the woman who'd given him the bad news about the implant, who'd clipped the antenna portion of the device and withdrawn it, a yard of hair-thin metal, from his skin yesterday afternoon, had hinted that something like this might happen. "They're going to call you the T-X's 'boy-toy,' " she'd said, her tone friendly but mocking. "Be ready for it. So, did you ever sleep with her?"

"No," he'd answered, appalled. But he'd been more appalled by the realization that he wouldn't necessarily have remembered if he had. He had no idea whether the T-X was equipped for such an act.

He remained leaning back against the wall, his eyes closed, until he got his stomach under control, until the shakes subsided. Then he rose.

It was time to go back to his room. He'd just wait there until they called him to duty. He'd come out for meals and to go to the bathroom. That was it.

He took two steps back toward his room and froze in place. *No, it's not right.* What happened to him wasn't his fault, and the brass agreed that he hadn't betrayed the Resistance.

They didn't have the right to exile him.

He turned and walked along the corridor where he'd taken momentary refuge until he reached the table where the section boss worked. He recognized her from his life before. Her name was Janet, she was about forty, and she'd always responded with unsmiling thanks when he'd provided her with information about a prewar weapon she hadn't seen before. "Hi," he said. "I'm the T-X's boy-toy. Got any work for me?" He noticed there was an edge of bitterness to his voice.

Silent, Janet shook her head.

"Thanks." He continued down the hall.

His heart was pounding. He knew why. He had no context for that sort of encounter. He was doing something outside his place.

But he had no place anymore. So everything he did would probably feel the same way.

He peered into the first door beyond the weapon maintenance crew. Inside that room were home computers, eight or more, many of them cabled together in a network. Paul recognized the setup; he'd help put it together. It was a representative sampling of pre-J-Day machines with a broad range of operating systems and was set up to do initial testing on data storage, such as discs and CDs, found in the field.

Paul turned to the two men huddled behind the monitor of a tower-configuration machine. "Hi," he said. "I'm the T-X's boy-toy." This time he managed to keep bitterness from his tone. "Need any help?"

The two computer operators, dark-haired men barely out of their teens, looked at one another and then at him. The first of them kept his expression professionally neutral; the second actually looked worried, perhaps even frightened.

The first operator shook his head. "Thanks anyway."

"Sure." Paul continued onward. He was actually feeling a little better.

He stuck his head in the next door. Within that room, a young woman, at least seven months pregnant, her short curly hair a dirty blonde, sat in an ancient school-style chair facing toward Paul's right.

"Hi," Paul said. "I'm—"

Then he saw what the woman faced. There were a dozen or so children in the room, some seated on old chairs, the others on newer, cruder benches. The oldest of them looked to be about seven years of age.

"Paul," he finished. "Need any help?"

The woman looked him over, uncertain. She appeared to be even more weary than the average Home Plate worker—no surprise, at her stage of pregnancy. Finally she said, "Do you know how to read?"

"I am a spectacular reader. I can read while walking, while chewing gum, even while humming." His answer was oddly glib, even to his own ears. Paul wondered if all those months talking to the Terminatrix had taught him something about conversation.

"We're doing alphabet drills and then story time," the woman said. She rose unsteadily to her feet. Her face paled just a bit as she did so. "I need to . . ."

Paul suspected that she intended to say "take a nap" or "go throw up," but as she paused to sort out her words, he said, "Take a break. Sure. I'll see if I can keep 'em busy until you get back."

She drifted out past him, as unsteady as an airship caught in wind gusts. "Thanks. I'm Doreen."

"Nice to meet you, Doreen." He moved into the woman's chair, but did not sit; built for teenagers at best, and barely large enough for the woman, it would make him look ridiculous if he sat. "Okay," he said as the first panicked thought touched him: *Oh, my God, I'm teaching school.* "Who knows his ABCs?"

"Ginger and Ripper were dogs," Paul said. "Ginger was orange, and Ripper was black, and they went with their mistress on all her adventures, and they protected her from all harm."

"I know them," Adrienne squealed. She was five, with long blonde hair and brown eyes, and in the last couple of days Paul had learned that she was Doreen's oldest child. She was also the best reader of the class. "I've petted them."

"Me too," Paul said. "Shhh. They would sometimes go out in the ruins and look for things, and sometimes they'd go farther away, to where the mountains rose up and there were long stands of trees. Anyone know what long stands of trees are called?"

Several hands rose, but Brandon, the dark-haired seven-year-old, jumped the gun: "Forests."

"Forests is right. Or woods. But next time, wait until I call on you. So when they weren't protecting their mistress, Ginger and Ripper sometimes got to play, running among the trees and nipping at one another. But they never barked. Anyone know why?"

This time twelve sets of hands stayed down; some of the children held their hands rigidly in place or tucked them under their thighs, making sure it was absolutely obvious that they wouldn't be raising their hands.

Finally one did, Adrienne again. "Because they were taught not to?"

"Very good! But that's only part of the answer. They were taught not to because barking could give away their location when they're Above. Only the dogs smart enough to learn this get to be Above dogs. And when they do bark, they have different barks for different things. So on this day, as they were playing away from camp, they stopped and listened because they heard something, a *ching-ching-ching* noise coming their way . . ."

The children froze, some of them wide-eyed. Even at their age, they knew the *ching-ching-ching* sound had to be a robot or Terminator. But Brandon looked over at the doorway and several of the others followed suit.

Paul did, too. And in the doorway were Ginger and Ripper, the real ones. Ripper sat, yawning, while Ginger stood there, slowly wagging her tail. And beside them, leaning against the door jamb, was Kyla. Her expression was dubious.

"Boys and girls, let me introduce you to the real Ginger and Ripper. And this is their mistress, Kyla Connor. Kyla, you make a great show-and-tell."

"Hi," Brandon said.

Kyla gave him a smile. "Hi." Then she turned her attention to Paul. "A word with you?"

He rose and moved to her. "I'm in trouble now," he stage-whispered to the kids, offering them a caricatured expression of fear, and several of them laughed.

And the clowning successfully covered for the unease he felt. If his superiors were going to assign him work, they wouldn't send someone as important—someone who had very specialized security functions—as Kyla to bring him the news.

At the door, Kyla lowered her voice so the kids would not hear. "You're needed in the inner council's vehicle depot for a conference. Right now."

"I don't even know where that is. It's topside, right?"

"Nearly. I'll show you."

"I shouldn't leave the kids alone—"

"The other teacher, what's-her-name, the very pregnant one, told me where you were. She's wrapping up what she's doing and will be here to take over in a minute."

"Right." Paul stuck his head back in the door. "Kids, I have to go. Don't anyone leave the room. Mrs. Edwards will be back in a minute."

A barrage of "Awww" protests, from those who wanted to hear the rest of his story, followed them as they headed down the corridor.

Kyla shook her head. "Ginger and Ripper stories, huh?"

"Well, today's lesson was supposed to be about the use of dogs. What they do for us, the kind of training they get, all that sort of stuff." Paul shrugged. "I just sort of thought I'd personalize it a little."

"Not a bad idea, I guess. How does the story end?"

"Happily. They knock a beat-up old T-600 into a river. It gets swept over the falls, is smashed to pieces on the rocks below, and rusts."

Kyla snorted, then leaned over to scratch the ruff of Ginger's neck. "Smart doggie."

Ginger cocked an eyebrow at her.

The Los Angeles River had long been anything but. It was an endless stretch of parched concrete, a broad incision across the old city.

In the months after Judgment Day, as the Resistance truly began to coalesce, a far-sighted civil engineer named Shawna Norris had led crews that caused authentic-looking landfalls at strategic locations along the storm-drain system, had opened up sections that had been blocked off by genuine collapses, and had gradually transformed dozens of portions of the old system into widely separated, well-hidden hiding-holes. Bone cancer had claimed Shawna Norris's life only a few years after Judgment Day, as it did with so many people who worked in the radiation-drenched blast zones of Los Angeles, but she was memorialized in the storm-drain habitat that bore her name.

And it was in Norris Compound that the vehicle depot used by John Connor's advisory staff was located. The depot had once been a convergence of several storm drains, each large enough to accommodate an Army truck. Now it held two such trucks, John Connor's personal Humvee, a tanker truck painted to look from a sufficient distance like a wreck, a dune buggy, two Jeeps nearly a century old, various pickup trucks and SUVs, and a pair of motorcycles.

Arriving with the escort of two dogs and a teenage sniper, Paul looked wistfully at the motorcycles. He'd had one, up until his capture and presumed death. He'd meticulously built it over a span of years, from parts scavenged under dangerous circumstances from junkyards and ruined repair shops, and had converted it to run on methane, which he could trade for far more easily than he could for rare and precious gasoline or for a precious fuel-cell engine that would better serve elsewhere. He suspected that his cycle had been destroyed by the missile attack that was supposed to have claimed his life.

The depot was also occupied by people—two dozen at least. Some were mechanics, doing hurried maintenance on the Humvee, both of the dune buggies, one of the SUVs, and one of the two-and-a-half-ton trucks. The Hell-Hounds were among those in the chamber, Glitch standing with them, apparently fully repaired and restored. Nearby were several of the senior advisers and members of the Scalpers, another unit in charge of protecting John Connor and carrying out special missions. The concrete walls echoed hollowly with conversation.

Paul whistled. Whatever was going on here, it was a major operation—the senior staff didn't commit so many precious vehicular resources to scouting operations.

As Paul and Kyla reached the Hell-Hounds, Ten Zimmerman whistled. A few yards away, John Connor straightened from under the hood of the Humvee. "Is that everyone?" John asked.

Ten nodded. "Everyone's here."

"Good." John stepped back from the vehicle's engine compartment and wiped his hands on a grease-streaked blue rag. "All right, before we get started, I have some good news. Guitar Compound's factory is coming on-line. We've received an initial shipment of plasma rifle battery packs, and they've tested fine. That's why I've asked you to bring your full spread of weapons—we've got enough juice again to fry some machines."

That yielded shouts of approval and applause. Even Paul joined in. As the Resistance's supply of rifle batteries had dwindled over the last several months, front-line fighters and special operatives had been forced to rely increasingly on older technologies. Most slug-throwers, Kyla's rifle excepted, were insufficient to do real damage to assault robots, and man-pack missiles such as rocket-propelled grenades were too bulky for anyone to carry a good supply. This news promised a return to more aggressive field operations, more successful confrontations with the machines.

"When we're done here, talk to our quartermaster to get your share," John said. "Now, some of you know what's going on here. You can take a nap or do one more obsessive-compulsive weapons check. The rest of you, listen up. Or, rather, listen to Kate, since this operation is her plan."

Leaning against the Army truck, Kate offered her husband a mock scowl. "Only the good parts. The really foolish parts are your contribution."

Paul tried to keep from gaping. Under every other circumstance in which he'd had the opportunity to see John Connor and Kate Brewster, they'd been focused, steely-eyed leaders brimming with confidence. Here, in the presence of their bodyguard details and other special operatives, they seemed looser, more humorous, less fiery. It was a strange change.

John didn't reply to his wife's dig. He just gestured for her to continue.

With a sigh, Kate straightened and began. "There's a T-X Terminator out there. Very few of us have seen one. Everyone who has done so and lived is now in this chamber, in fact. The T-X has some of the chameleon abilities of the T-1000—as far as simulating human beings is concerned, it has *all* the disguise potential of the T-1000—and it's a lot more destructive.

"We think it's been prepared for a time jump to eliminate John in the past. Unlike our previous experiences with Skynet's time-related operations, we don't think we can head it off when it gets there. This means we can't counter its plans. So we're going to have to force Skynet's hand and convince Skynet to send it after John in the here and now."

That caused some muttering.

"This operation is in two parts," Kate continued. "The bait portion and the hook portion. The bait portion is to be conducted by the Scalpers. They'll be traveling to Clover Compound in Colorado."

Someone whistled. Clover Compound was a tough place. It was the Resistance habitat situated closest to the Navajo Mountain Strategic Region. At the heart of the region, built deep beneath the earth, was Navajo Mountain, the center of Skynet activities. The mortality rate among the inhabitants of Clover Compound, even among couriers and supply-runners visiting the region, was high.

"The reason," John said, "is because we think Clover has been compromised. We recently did some looking for any compound or habitat that had a higher-than-statistically-likely failure rate, and Clover was at the very top at the list, even allowing for its proximity to Skynet. We have no reason to suspect incompetence or deliberate collaboration with the enemy. To us, this means there's a security leak."

"And before we close that leak," Kate continued, "we're going to use it. At Clover the Scalpers will let it be known that John is looking for a specific woman and that this woman is going to be brought into John's presence the instant she's found. Our belief is that Skynet can't pass up this opportunity to kill John, that it will dispatch the T-X to impersonate the woman. The Scalpers will have to conduct her into John's presence."

Paul saw a small group of the soldiers, standing together, exchange unhappy glances. A woman with long hair put two fingers to her temple, as though they were the barrel of a handgun, and mimed pulling the trigger. Paul supposed they were the Scalpers. He wondered what had happened to Crazy Pete and Warthog, the senior members of the Scalpers, the only ones whose faces he knew.

"In the meantime," John said, "Kate and I are going to be accompanying the Hell-Hounds and a technical crew to a National Guard armory abandoned on Judgment Day. We have reason to believe that this armory is a front for a materiel cache not listed with the pre-J-Day military records, that its complement of vehicles and weapons may be intact. The tech crew will get as many of the vehicles working as is feasible and set them and the arms and munitions stores up for transport . . . and help rig the armory, or some site near it, as a trap to capture the T-X."

Silence fell on his last words. Paul looked among the faces present. Some of the technicians and most of the Scalpers were registering surprise. The advisers and Hell-Hounds were not.

"Excuse me, sir." That was the Asian-American man standing with the Scalpers. "You *did* say capture."

John nodded. "That's the 'hook' portion of the mission. We capture the T-X. We need this Terminator, people. If we can capture it intact, reprogram it as we have with the few Terminators we have serving the Resistance, we could achieve a quantum jump in our understanding of Skynet technology, particularly its high-end weapons systems, nanotechnological control systems, and liquid-metal manipulation. Don't forget that a single infiltration of a T-800 manufacturing plant gave us the information we need to begin cloning animal tissues, as Skynet does to create T-800 skin, and that's responsible for the increased amount of meat we've been receiving in our diets for the last few months. Things we learn from the T-X could be just as important—or more important. It's an opportunity we can't let slip by." He cleared his throat. "If I didn't think it was that critical, Kate and I wouldn't be accompanying the Hell-Hounds to act as bait."

"We begin to stage our exit in ten minutes," Kate said. "That's when the advance vehicles depart. Ten minutes later, the remaining vehicles leave. So make your final checks, get your gear loaded on your assigned vehicles." She turned away from those she addressed, clear sign that the briefing was done, and marched over to John's side.

A suspicion began to whirl around in Paul's mind, but he decided to keep it to himself, at least until he could better make out what it meant. He turned to Ten. "Uh, I don't have any gear to load."

"Sure you do." Ten glanced over at the unit's T-850. "Glitch."

The Terminator shucked a backpack and shoved it to Paul. It connected with Paul's torso with enough force to send him staggering back a step. "Clothes," Glitch said, in the approximately German accent that seemed to come standard with the programming of all the old T-801s. "Minimal camping gear. Cold weather gear. Preserved food supplies. First-aid gear."

Paul took the pack and swung its straps over one shoulder. "Weapons?"

"Camp knife," the Terminator said.

"No firearms to spare, sorry," Ten said. "You're in the back of the big truck."

"Thanks." Paul lugged his pack to the rear of the truck and clambered up. The forward portion of the bed was heavily packed with crates, all of them lashed down with old dubious-looking hemp ropes. Paul sat down on the left side, adjacent to the crates, and set his pack down beside him, between him and anyone who might sit nearby.

Ten's words had transformed his suspicion from mere paranoia to a real likelihood.

They were going to kill him.

His few days back in Home Plate had made it clear to him just how much things had changed. He'd always known that he wasn't well liked, and as word of the circumstances of his incarceration in San Diego had spread, someone had even nicknamed him Sleeps-With-Toasters.

But to send him into the field without a firearm, without an RPG? It meant that he wasn't being allowed to contribute to the survival of the people he accompanied. He wasn't trusted. He wasn't liked well enough for anyone to vouch for him.

He wondered if he ever had been. Making friends had always seemed next to impossible, a mysterious art whose practitioners were never willing to let him in on the secret.

He thought he'd had something those few days he was teaching the children. But that seemed somehow easy. Maybe it was because they weren't his social equals. He wasn't facing his peers, so that part of him that clamped up tight whenever he tried to talk to another adult didn't constrain him.

The bed of the truck creaked and rocked slightly as more people boarded. Glitch sat directly opposite Paul, staring at him. Technicians boarded next, one of them sitting next to Paul; Paul didn't glance up. Last aboard were Earl and Mark of the Hell-Hounds; they hauled the tailgate up and dogged it in place.

"How's it going, Keeley?" That was the man who'd sat next to Paul.

Paul finally glanced up. His next-seat neighbor was Tom Carter, a lean, aging Resistance technician. Though only a lieutenant in the armed forces, Tom possessed influence disproportionate to his rank; he did much of the restoration, upgrading, and reprogramming of Terminators captured by the Resistance and would probably land on John Connor's advisory board the instant he decided he didn't want to do fieldwork anymore. Paul had reported to him on a weekly basis for the two years before Paul's capture. But Tom had never stopped in to see how Paul was faring after his return from the San Diego hospital.

How's it going? Once, Paul would have said, "Fine, just fine." It's what he always said. It was an answer that discouraged further questions, further conversation. It was—and had always been—a convenient lie.

Well, he had no interest in conveniencing other people, especially if they were going to kill him soon.

"Not so good," he said and turned away.

The truck's engine whined for several long moments, then caught and held with a not-too-unhealthy rattle. Moments later, they were in motion.

PART 2: OPERATION FISHHOOK

Near Clover Compound, Colorado

The Resistance both loved and hated the Rocky Mountains.

The love wasn't because of the region's scenic beauty, although that was undiminished from the years before Judgment Day—other than in large cities, most of which had had nuclear missiles slapped down upon them and now existed chiefly as fire-blackened craters. It was instead the fact that the terrain hampered Skynet activities.

The mountain broke sight lines, making it more difficult for Skynet forces to observe human movements and operations. With many places, valleys and ravines especially, spy satellites or aircraft had to be directly overhead to be able to witness such activity at all, and had to cover so much territory with their passes that they often saw nothing. The mountain slopes were ideal positions for human observers and for setting up ambushes.

It was in the Rockies that the Resistance had its first military successes, in those few years after Judgment Day. Tough men and women had come spilling out of the mountains, launching fast, deadly raids on Skynet-held armories, blowing up robot-making factories, fleeing back into the relative safety of the natural castles of stone.

There was even fresh food to be had, not the hydroponically grown stuff that kept the Resistance alive, but meat. Bow hunters sometimes crept out of their compounds and returned with deer, sheep, goats, even elk, and were treated like heroes by those they fed.

The hatred for the mountains—well, that was natural, too. West of Colorado Springs, near Pikes Peak, was Navajo Mountain. From that deep-buried citadel Skynet had, since Judgment Day, executed plan after plan to exterminate the human race. And the closer one went to Navajo Mountain, the more dangerous the mountains were. Assault robots waited in the machine equivalent of hunters' blinds. Lethal flying machines patrolled the skies. Spy satellites minutely scrutinized every change to ground detail.

It was in this region, northwest of the ruins of Boulder, that Chris Sato had grown up. His parents had run a sporting goods store in Boulder before J-Day. When the first, garbled reports had come over the radios, heralding the end of the world, the Satos had gathered their three children and a tremendous amount of gear from their store, then had fled to a cabin they owned on a hunting lease deep in the mountains. There, Sato and his two sisters had grown into their teenage years, learning to hunt with guns and with more silent weapons, to hide, to evaluate the occasional fellow humans they encountered.

Eventually, Sato's father broke a leg in a fall and began to succumb to persistent fevers. Then, finally, Sato's mother had accepted an invitation from someone who'd dwelled one valley over to join a community that had organized within an abandoned mine. Cared for by that compound's medics, Sato's father had survived, and the compound itself had soon joined the growing Resistance led by John Connor. He and his sisters had had instant status with the compound; though young teenagers, they shot as well as any of its adults, could track better, and could keep a small compound supplied with fresh meat.

Now, more than a decade later, Sato's parents were still alive, leaders of a compound on Lake Mead in Nevada. His older sister, Angela, married and with three surviving children, was in charge of weapons fabrications at a compound in Washington State; his younger sister, Dana, taught forest skills to the young at a new compound in Louisiana. And Sato, after years demonstrating competence as a security and defensive emplacements expert at compounds all over Nevada and Colorado, had been promoted to rebuild the Scalpers when two-thirds of its members had been wiped out and the remainder were too young and inexperienced to do the job.

Sato's convoy—two dune buggies, running without lights—climbed along an old paved road that ascended, in a series of switchbacks, a gently angled mountain slope above the tree line. As the road neared the summit, the mountain sloped down and away to the west, revealing more distant peaks.

Sato, in the passenger seat, tapped his driver on the shoulder, then raised one hand and waved it back and forth to alert the driver behind. Both dune buggies pulled to a stop and the drivers killed the engines.

Sato, stiff-legged, pulled himself out of the passenger seat and moved to the road's edge, where only the remains of a metal safety barricade still stood, and looked over the vista presented to him. His breath steamed out of his mouth. The air here was thin and cold enough to feel like ice flechettes cutting their way through his lungs.

Even in the shades-of-green vision presented to him by the infrared sight gear he wore, it was a spectacular view: craggy ice-capped peaks, unchanged, so far as the eye could see, by man or Skynet.

His driver, Jenna the Greek, joined him at the road's edge. Unnecessarily, she kept her tone low: "Which one is Navajo Mountain?"

Sato shook his head. "Can't see it from here. It's too far away. But we're looking right at the Navajo Mountain Strategic Region. You're looking the abyss right in the eye."

"It's not fair that it's so pretty."

"True. Skynet should surround the whole zone with a huge wall and install itself in a giant black castle, half Gothic, half industrial hell."

Jenna ignored the fact that she was being kidded. "*I* think so."

Sato grinned. So had he, the first time the Strategic Region had been pointed out to him.

Deep in those mountains, Navajo Mountain offered much more protection for its inhabitants than walls and castle towers ever would. It had protected the humans who had built it, and now it protected the most crucial computer gear constituting Skynet itself. A major Department of Defense communications facility, it had been dug so deep into the mountain's roots that no nuclear weapons built by man could seriously affect it. No matter which of several "end of the world" theories actually occurred, Navajo Mountain would endure as a means to keep the American military forces coordinated.

Except the enemy had struck from within instead of without. Skynet, the operating system designed to facilitate that coordination even in the face of the complete breakdown of standard means of communication, had somehow developed self-awareness throughout the government network that had housed it. It had replicated and distributed packets of itself, ported to more conventional operating systems and computer languages, and propagated itself throughout the old human Internet. In so doing, it had made itself a million-headed hydra, with no Hercules powerful enough to cut off all its heads. Then it had lashed out against its creators and conquered the world.

One little irony was that the name of the site wasn't actually Navajo Mountain. There was a real Navajo Mountain, in Navajo territory straddling Arizona and Utah. No, this site had simply been code-named Navajo Mountain by the U.S. military. A few members of its personnel had been on leave when J-Day fell; a very few on-duty personnel had managed to flee a rampage by Terminator T-1s in the facility's depths and had gotten out before the blast doors closed for the last time. Sato didn't know what the mountain's real name, its original map name, was. He didn't care.

"We shouldn't wait here," Jenna said. "Our heat trace . . ."

"Yeah, I know." Sato sighed and turned back to the dune buggy. The driver and occupants of the other buggy hadn't even bothered to get out of their vehicle. "But sometimes, you have to look right at the enemy."

And to feel the enemy looking back at you, he added to himself.

On the other side of the ridge, the road descended out of sight of the Navajo Mountain Strategic Region, and the sensation that cold, unfeeling eyes were staring at him abruptly ended.

A few hundred yards down the slope, Sato signaled for Jenna the Greek to slow, then to turn onto a dirt path. It followed the mountain contours around for half a mile and then ascended to a point where an old train trestle entered a mountain tunnel. At Sato's direction, Jenna turned into the tunnel, followed it for a hundred yards or so, and stopped, killing the engine. The second dune buggy pulled up behind and shut down.

Sato waited until silence fell again and his ears strained against it, then called out, "Prickly pear."

Somewhere ahead, probably behind cover of a wall of artificially aged concrete or cunningly matched stone, a soldier in a guard station would be scanning a hand-printed list of code words and countersigns. And if Sato had been given the wrong one, in a matter of seconds that soldier and everyone in his vicinity would open up on the Scalpers with every weapon they had at hand.

The reply came, a female voice echoing against the stone tunnel walls: "Jam-packed. Advance."

Ahead, a seam of light appeared—a vertical glow—and then widened. Finally enough emerged to reveal its source, a chamber hidden behind a slab of stone that swung open on a giant pivot. It revealed an opening large enough to admit the vehicles. Jenna started up the dune buggy again.

A minute later they were within a stony, half-smoothed area that had to have been half natural cave and half rockfall area from the time in the late nineteenth century when this tunnel was originally blasted out of the mountainside. Now it served as Clover Compound's own vehicle and other transportation depot. At one end Sato could see, neatly arrayed on smooth stone floor with jagged rocky ceiling above, two small pickup trucks, a snowmobile, and what looked at first like a disassembled frame for a hang glider He directed Jenna and the driver of the second dune buggy to park beside the trucks.

On the far end of the irregular, badly lit chamber was a broad, closed wooden door. A trail of carefully laid-out dirt and straw led from it to the outside door. "Stables," he said. He was impressed; it took a lot of care and food to keep horses going, though they could be invaluable to Resistance fighters in compounds surrounded by rough terrain.

The middle open area of the chamber was empty, offering room for vehicles to turn around. The machinery and counter-weights for the exterior door were on one side of the chamber and a stone archway and heavy wooden door were set into the other.

The place smelled like every other compound Sato had visited. No amount of scrupulous hygiene or regular habitat maintenance could quite rid a place like this of the mingled odors of sweat, ancient smoke, raw food, cooked food, rotted food. And most places couldn't even manage conditions of scrupulous hygiene or habitat maintenance.

Armed guards, dressed in the distinct indigo-blue uniforms of Clover Compound, holding assault rifles and plasma rifles at the ready, waited beside the walls. From another direction, a male handler brought up two dogs, one a German shepherd and one some sort of long-legged, mixed-breed hound dog. He led the dogs from vehicle to vehicle, and each Scalper extended his hands for the dogs to sniff. Satisfied, the dogs looked up at their handler, who finally gave the Scalpers a friendly nod and led the dogs away.

The wooden door opened, admitting three men—two young and carrying rifles, the third older—all wearing brown-and-green camouflage uniforms. They approached as the Scalpers, cold and stiff, clambered from the dune buggy seats.

Sato saluted. "Lieutenant Sato. Resistance 1st Security Regiment, Company A, Squadron 2."

The older man he faced was taller than Sato by a couple of inches and had probably been taller still in his youth; now, age and perhaps old damage caused him to walk with a stoop. His hair, beard, and mustache were white with flecks of black and gray, a pattern distributed not quite evenly enough to be attractive, but his eyes were a clear and intelligent blue. He returned Sato's salute briskly enough. "Mears," he said, omitting his rank. Sato knew him to be a full colonel in the Resistance, a rank appropriate to the leader of a compound as vital as Clover was. "Are you old Dick Sato's boy?"

"That's right, sir."

"He visited here a long time back. Brought some goat meat and cooked up a goat curry. I can still taste it." Mears looked past Sato, not at the other Scalpers but to some point in the distant past.

"I know, sir. I was with him on that visit."

"Were you, now?" Mears returned his attention to the present. "So, it's the Scalpers. This is obviously a more important visit than I'd been led to believe."

"Not really, sir. A standard check of installed security. Any compound John Connor might visit within a two-year span, we have to have a pretty good idea of its defenses and procedures."

"Ah."

"But I do have a message he wanted hand-delivered."

That caused one of Mears's salt-and-pepper eyebrows to lift a bit. "Ah. Well, maybe I'd better show you my office."

"Please."

They turned back toward the door by which Mears had entered. Sato felt a flash of annoyance. Mears hadn't shown any interest in the other Scalpers, so Sato hadn't made an attempt to introduce them. This was bad form on Mears's part. It was always a good idea to get to know visitors from other compounds, to encourage one's own men and women to get to know them. It was a Connor/Brewster maxim that contact between the compounds had to be encouraged at all times, that populations had to be rotated between them, in order for ideas to spread, in order that inbreeding not occur. But Mears merely said, "Akins, get quarters together for the Scalpers and get them some food while I talk to their boss."

The guard's reply was a disinterested "Yes, sir."

■ ■ ■

Sato decided that Mears's office was an accurate reflection of the man he'd heard so much about.

It was lined with shelves filled with books scavenged from small-town libraries in the region, supplemented by trade with compounds that had access to university libraries. On those shelves Sato saw volumes on engineering, mining, architecture, mathematics, geology, metallurgy, and more. There were also framed diplomas on the wall, some of them yellowed or browned by age and mistreatment. There were photographs of a Raymond Mears, his hair jet-black and his posture perfect, shaking hands with pre-J-Day celebrities and heads of industry.

Sato knew the stories. Mears had introduced and refined mining techniques, hydraulic machinery, pumping equipment. He'd been a multimillionaire because of his patents before he was forty, and had gone into semiretirement, lavishing money on a Colorado mountain estate and Hollywood parties. His mountaintop mansion had been an inspiration to engineering geeks, with its just-for-fun secret passageways and concealed basement chambers. The reporters who'd written about it hadn't known about some of its features, such as the wells that would provide it with water for years in case of trouble—and the abandoned well attempts that had punched into the undocumented nineteenth-century mine shafts that riddled this mountain.

Mears had been lucky enough to be at his home when Judgment Day came. He weathered the months after the disaster in considerable comfort, living on stores of supplies, using his engineering skills to improve access into the mines. As it became clear that the machines were actively hunting and exterminating humankind, he moved all his critical supplies and personal possessions into the mines, sealing up accesses into his old home, abandoning it. But he left surveillance equipment functioning and could detect when machines and human survivors came to visit.

Some of those humans he invited to live with him in his subterranean home. With the character judgment, sense of self-preservation, and pragmatic ruthlessness that a captain of industry needed to survive, he was quick to recognize men and women who might be a threat to his leadership or his life. In those early days, as rumor had it, they ended up shot or with their heads caved in, their bodies tossed down the lowest vertical shaft, nicknamed Satan's Hole.

Only after he accepted an invitation to bring his self-supporting compound into the general framework of the human Resistance did Mears learn that he lived within sight, within a few days' walk, of the center of Skynet activities. His comment at the time, still quoted, was "You'd think that after the end of the world you wouldn't have to worry any more about sorry neighbors."

Now over seventy, he was still unquestionably in charge of Clover Compound, and as he rummaged through the drawers of his battered metal desk, which looked broad, heavy, and elegant enough to have cost as much as a luxury car when it was new, he seemed to have lost none of his sureness of purpose, of confidence.

Finally the old man came up with a glass bottle, unlabeled and corked, and waved it in Sato's direction. "Care for a bit?"

"What is it?"

"Vodka. Good old Colorado vodka."

Sato snorted. "Hit me."

Mears found a couple of genuine shot glasses, souvenirs with DENVER and the skyline of that city etched into them, and poured a couple of slugs. "You know what I always found weird about your dad? And about you, now?"

"No." Sato picked up his shot glass and angled it toward the old man.

"*Salute,*" Mears said and clicked his rim to Sato's. "It was the lack of an accent. You see a big old Japanese face, you expect to see a big old Japanese accent come rolling out of it. Your dad always spoke like an American."

"Well, he is." Sato took a sip. The homemade spirit was strong, nearly flavorless, much more pure than most liquors brewed by members of the Resistance. "My family settled in California in the nineteen twenties. That generation got to spend some time in the interment camps in World War II, and my father said they were the last ones who spoke with an accent."

"You speak any Jap?" Mears knocked down his shot, reacting not at all to its potency, and poured himself another one.

"A little." Sato just waited.

Mears grinned at him. "You don't rile too easily, do you, boy?"

"Nope."

"I didn't figure you would. Old John Connor doesn't pick excitable people to do his dirty work. Neither do I. It's bad business. But I like to find out a little about the kind of people he sends to me."

As if you were a businessman entertaining couriers from another company, Sato thought. *Rather than a military officer doing his job for his superiors. Do you acknowledge any superiors?* Mears probably didn't, Sato decided. And he probably got some amusement out of baiting people over whom he couldn't assert direct authority.

"So, what's this message?"

Sato unbuttoned the right breast pocket of his jacket. "John Connor is looking for a young woman."

"Aren't we all?" Mears gave him an overly personal "Just between us guys" smile.

Sato fetched out the contents of the pocket and handed the single item to Mears. "A specific young woman."

Mears looked at the object and turned it top to bottom. "A photograph. Well. These days I don't get to see many photographs that aren't as old and yellow as I am."

Sato had studied the photograph during the long trip in from Home Plate. It showed a twentysomething woman, lean, round-faced, blonde, wearing an expression that suggested she'd been through a long-ago tragedy from which she'd never fully recovered. Behind her were the treads of a main battle tank.

"Her name is Gwendolyn Drew," Sato said. "She's a photographer. Three months ago, she fled the Great Lakes compound where she'd been living. Her friends think she was heading toward Home Plate, where her mother was from. No one knows why she ran, but there's speculation that she saw or even photographed something at her compound that somehow endangered her life more than a solo trip across half a continent's worth of hostile territory would. So I'm checking into whether Clover Compound—or any compound you're aware of—has taken in any strays in that time frame."

"We haven't." Mears was deeply absorbed in the photograph. "She looks like . . . She looks like . . ."

She looks like Sarah Connor, John Connor's mother Sato didn't say it, and Mears became quiet. Of course she looked like Sarah Connor; this photograph had been artfully crafted from an old photo of Sarah, doctored by artists who knew how to use thirty-year-old software designed exactly for the purpose of modifying photographs and output on one of the extremely rare photographic printers in the Resistance's possession. Only John Connor had the resources to command that could have led to the fabrication of this false piece of evidence.

Sato watched as the inevitable conclusion clicked through Mears's mind. This young woman might be a daughter of John Connor, but not by Kate Brewster, since the three children they shared were well known to the Resistance; alternately, she might be a distant cousin who had inherited the looks of the Connor women. Either way, she was obviously kin to John Connor and he wanted her found alive.

Mears looked up and smiled. "May I keep this?"

"Of course. I have one for each compound I'll be visiting."

"I'll show it to my chief scouts and to my liaisons with other compounds. Perhaps they've seen her."

Sato finished his shot of vodka and set the glass down. "I'll get out of your hair, then, and begin my inspection in the morning."

Mears rose as Sato did. "I'll send my second-in-command, Murphy, to give you the guided tour. He needs to be meeting people, getting his face known. He'll be taking over for me when I retire."

Sato smiled, covering for the sudden annoyance he felt. "That's sort of John Connor's choice to make, isn't it?"

"To confirm, yes." Mears led Sato to the door and opened it. "And he technically has the right to refuse my choice, to choose someone else. He won't, though. No one's better suited to command here than Murphy. I've trained him in that role for the last ten years."

"So, when's the happy occasion?"

Mears looked blank.

"Your retirement."

"Oh." Mears offered him a disgruntled expression. "When I'm tired of living, I suppose. The few people I know my age who admit they're too old to do it anymore, who retire to let their kin or their compound mates take care of them, tend to waste away and die pretty soon thereafter. Call me stubborn, but I'm not ready for that yet."

"That's a good kind of stubbornness." Sato shook the older man's hand and departed.

Walking through the maze of well-engineered tunnels and converted mine shafts that made up Clover Compound, Sato thought about the encounter. Meeting Mears for the first time as an adult, Sato didn't know whether to like him or mistrust him. The man's ruthlessness was well known in the Resistance. So was the fact that he'd maintained his compound under the very nose of Skynet for decades. In recent years, rivals to this successor Murphy had transferred out of Clover after becoming convinced that they could never replace Murphy in Mears's eyes, that the fix was in. But this had benefitted the Resistance. Those rivals, hard-headed and pragmatic men and women, well trained in organization, proved to be effective leaders in the compounds and military units where they resettled. Sato wondered how many more like them, perhaps more stubborn or ruthless, might have ended up decaying at the bottom of Satan's Hole.

Like him or mistrust him. Sato shrugged and settled on both. That was life in the modern world.

In the morning the Scalpers breakfasted in the main mess, a section of the old mine's main access tunnel. Partitioned off by sheets and blankets strung from cables, this section housed the compound's classrooms, child care, kitchen, and library as well as the mess.

"Busy work around here," Sato said, "consists of digging new tunnels. The compound leader's an engineer, and all through the compound's history he's dug new escape tunnels, diversionary tunnels to mislead invaders if the compound is ever breached, that sort of thing." He set his spoon down into the corn meal paste that had been served as the main portion of breakfast and began pointing to tunnel entrances in turn. "That one goes to an escape route, that one goes sixty yards and ends at an intersection with a pressure plate and a bomb underneath it, that one heads down to their hydroponics level . . ."

"And none of them are marked," said Jenna the Greek. With her cumbersome travel gear and night-sight apparatus off, she could once again bask in the attention she inevitably received, and she was receiving it in abundance from the nearby males of Clover Compound. A tall, slender woman in her mid-twenties, she had a prominent nose that accentuated her good looks and spoke of her family's Mediterranean heritage. Her most extravagant concession to ego was her hair, which was unusually long by Resistance standards; black and wavy, when unbound it fell to her lower back. On display in the new environment of this compound, she had retained her military boots and camouflage pants but ditched her camo tunic, retaining only the close-fitting black shirt she customarily wore beneath it. She knew she was spectacular-looking but pretended that she didn't, an affectation that irritated Sato endlessly.

Not that he'd ever let her know. Jenna the Greek was the sort of woman who, once she knew she had a handle on someone, would never let it go. And Sato didn't need any additional sources of conflict with her. She'd thought, after the deaths of the senior Scalpers a month ago, that she'd be promoted to leadership of the team, and she did have the necessary fighting and tactical skills to be a good leader someday. But for now, her greatest failing as a leader was that she didn't recognize her failings. Sid Walker, the overall commander of the 1st Security Regiment, had seen it and had appointed Sato her superior, and so far she'd mostly been careful to conceal the anger and betrayal she'd felt.

"If the tunnels were marked," said Nix, "it would sort of defeat the purpose. Of slowing down assault robots by confusing them." A small man in his thirties, Nix had close-cut black hair and a round face that always looked as though he'd just received long-awaited bad news. Serving as the Scalpers' demolitions expert, Nix was a caver and engineer, capable of worming his way through gaps and passages that would give fits to any larger or less flexible man. "My question is: What about wear patterns? The real tunnels will get a lot more use than escape tunnels or false passages, and the infrared sight gear of a Skynet robot can pick that up."

"Good point," Sato said. "Except the deal is this: Anyone in the compound can reserve one of those halls for his sole use . . . as long as he walks back and forth along it for at least half the time he's in possession of it."

The others nodded. In any human habitat, privacy was a concern. People didn't get much of it. Most people would happily trade a little exercise for an occasional hour or two away from all company, all distractions.

J. L. cleared his throat. Youngest of the Scalpers, at the age of seventeen not yet in his full growth, he was lanky and always a little uncertain. This manifested itself in little ways, such as the habit he had of getting people's attention before getting their attention— raising a hand before making a comment, clearing his throat before sharing a thought. It was, Sato thought, odd that he lacked confidence, since J. L. might well be the most dangerous member of the Scalpers, with an aptitude for hand-to-hand combat unmatched by the other members of the unit. Of course, skill in hand-to-hand was only so useful when most enemies were made of hardened metal compounds. "I heard one of the cooks saying that he hoped you might, you know, bag a little game while you were here." Then J. L.'s cheeks reddened, making his skin tone contrast even more starkly with his blond hair, and he glanced at Jenna. "He meant deer or something."

Sato snorted. "It might be nice to show off the old skills and receive accolades from the meat-deprived, but unfortunately we probably won't be here long enough for me to have any time off. Still, it's good to be remembered."

"It'd be nice to hunt," Smart said. Oldest of the Scalpers by a couple of years, Charles Smart, like Sato and J. L., was among its newest members. Bald since his mid-twenties, he had a head like a flesh-colored bullet and piercing blue eyes that added to his militaristic aspect. He was the unit's sniper and an expert in long-range combat with vehicular weapons and man-portable missiles as well. He seldom spoke. Sato had never heard him say anything as wistful as the words he'd just offered.

"Well, maybe circumstances will dictate that we spend some extra time here," Sato said. "With any luck."

Nix checked his watch. He owned an old-fashioned wind-up analog watch that had been keeping time for members of his family since the 1950s. "Oh seven hundred on the spot," he said.

Someone else knew the appointed time, too. From a crowd of Clover Compound residents moving by on the main tunnel path, a man split off to approach the Scalpers' table. He was black, maybe forty, and short, about halfway between Sato's barely average height and Nix's diminutive stature. Flecks of gray and white speckled his beard but had not yet crept up into his hair. His eyes were somehow simultaneously amused and hard, like an old-time standup comedian awaiting his audience's reaction with a gun in his hand.

He extended a hand. "Sato, right?"

Sato took it. "That's correct. Murphy?"

"That's me. Ready for your official tour?"

"Sure." Sato rose and the rest of his Scalpers followed suit. "Let me present Sergeant Jenna Vandis, Sergeant Charles Smart, Corporal Johnny Larson, Corporal Bobby Friedman."

Murphy shook hands all around. "You guys don't have to stage anything elaborate. When it comes time for most of you to run off and do your examination out from under my watchful eye, just say 'I'm taking off.' Saves time that way."

The other Scalpers glanced at one another, J. L. in particular looking uncertain.

Sato snorted. "You obviously approve of saving time."

"I sure do." Murphy gestured toward the main tunnel and led the Scalpers in that direction. "It might save us some more time if you told me why you're really here."

"I'm not sure—"

"What I really mean? Yeah, sure. You know and I know that John Connor will never come to Clover Compound. As close as it is to Skynet Central, he'd be crazy to—and he's not crazy. He needs to take us off the list of potential visit sites, period, forever. So that's not what you're here for, and . . ." He dropped his voice so that he could only be heard by Sato. "Your private message to the boss last night, well, that's fine, but it's not enough to drag a presidential security unit out here."

"True enough." Sato walked in silence for several paces, taking in the sights of a bustling, well-managed human habitat and trying to figure out how to respond. He could deny that the Scalpers had another agenda, which would put Murphy off; he could admit it but not describe the agenda, which would probably have the same result; he could admit to his true purpose here, which would be professional suicide.

No, it was time to lie.

He kept his own tone at the level it had been before so his Scalpers could hear him—hear, and remember the story he was going to tell. "I'll be honest," he said. "Your boss, for all his admirable traits, is an egotistical son of a bitch who imagines himself as a medieval baron. I was surprised he didn't greet me from the back of a horse. He thinks he can anoint his own heir. That's not the way things are done in the Resistance. So I'm here to figure out if you are the best man to take over for Mears. If you are, great. When Mears steps down, Connor will confirm the appointment and everyone will be happy. If you aren't, nobody's happy—not Mears, who looks like a fool, or you, who gets passed over, or Mears's replacement, who gets to step into a command where everyone resents him as an outsider. But that's a determination I have to make."

Murphy nodded. He actually looked pleased. "So, what do you need from me?"

"Not much. Freedom for my team members to do their job without interference. And answers to occasional questions."

"They've got it. You've got it."

Sato turned to his team. "Take off, guys."

All four offered nonregulation salutes and turned away to pursue their true agendas.

"First question, maybe the only one for today," Sato said. "What is your highest obligation to, in your opinion?"

Murphy marched along in silence for a few moments, as they entered a constriction in the main tunnel and found themselves marching along beside old but impeccably maintained mine car rails. Finally he said, "Human culture."

"Interesting answer."

"Well, I suspect it's not one of the 'correct' answers. I mean, different people want to hear answers like human survival, the Resistance, Clover Compound, John Connor, Raymond Mears, and so forth. But it all boils down to survival of the species, and for me, that means more than just huddling in a cave while machines thunder around in the valleys below. If we're going to be nothing more than troglodytes banging rocks together, I say, let us die. If we can't preserve the spark that gave us Mozart, El Greco, and whoever it was that invented the piña colada, we're not worth saving."

Sato suspected that this answer would not please Mears, but probably would please John Connor and Kate Brewster. Too bad evaluating Murphy's potential wasn't actually part of his agenda. Still, he had to keep up pretenses. "Let's have your nickel tour."

"Got a nickel?"

"Nope."

"Just my luck."

They spent the rest of the day walking, from the deep drop-off that marked Satan's Hole to the sealed-off wall that marked a boundary to Raymond Mears's long-abandoned home atop the mountain. "It's still one of our last-ditch escape paths," Murphy said. "Pull the metal lever on the wall there, the wall collapses, and you can crawl through, go up through the basement, and flee out into the open air."

"It must be painful for Mears to live so close to his home and not be able to visit it," Sato said.

Murphy nodded. "I expect so. He talks about it a fair amount. Especially now that he's getting on in years and talking about everything from his youth. He can describe every room, every beam. Not too surprising, since he designed the whole thing and supervised its construction back in the day." He shrugged. "Me, I'm less of a romantic. I've had two homes. The first was a set of caves near some hot springs several miles from here. The second is Clover Compound. They're both pretty ugly. Harder to be sentimental about them."

Sato had been basically impressed with what he'd seen. Most human habitats, at least those belonging to the Resistance, were managed at a high level of efficiency these days. They had to be; without airtight security they were detected and destroyed by Skynet, without careful balancing of food production and population they could not be maintained. But Clover Compound had the sort of extra spark Sato liked to see, a certain snap and energy to its personnel. The population received enough calories and were allotted enough nonwork time to have a few leisure activities, ongoing tunneling and engineering projects kept the personnel busy even in times when Skynet activities made it inadvisable to go above, and morale was good. There was an odd insularity to them Sato wasn't comfortable with; those he spoke to agreed that it was a good idea to have new personnel rotate in to replace casualties and "keep chlorine in the gene pool," but among the Clover-born there was less enthusiasm for rotating out to other compounds.

Still, that seemed to be nothing more than a cultural quirk of the place—and nothing that Sato hadn't seen elsewhere. What he was more interested in—and what he was having no luck detecting—was any point that could serve as a security leak.

One of three things was happening. First, Skynet could be intercepting transmissions or courier messages to and from Clover Compound or, worse yet, have some sort of eavesdropping apparatus set up within the compound itself, and be permitting the compound to exist in order to obtain better and better information from it. Second, someone within the compound could be a traitor, selling secrets to Skynet in return for weapons, food, or a promise of other rewards. Third, the increased incidence of mission failures originating at or passing through Clover Compound could be nothing more than a statistical anomaly.

But something in Sato's gut told him to dismiss that last possibility. The last two missions staged from Clover Compound to fail were both critical ones. On each occasion, a team of specialists, armed with a suitcase-sized nuclear bomb, had set out from here to enter Navajo Mountain via a recently detected access and cripple Skynet through the destruction of its most important facility. Both had been ambushed and destroyed well short of their destination, with some of the Resistance's best men and women slaughtered.

When the importance of a mission was directly proportionate to its likelihood of failure, Sato looked for more than statistical anomaly.

The Scalpers returned from evening mess to the small chamber they had been assigned as guest quarters. It had actually been engineered by Mears as a dwelling for notable guests and included one long bunkroom with a half-dozen beds, a table and chairs, a head, a communal shower, and a bank of lockers salvaged from a small-town bus station.

They sat at the table and Nix dealt cards. Sato looked at his hand, two sixes and change, and put two 9mm cartridges in the pot as his initial bet. "So. Anything?"

The others anted up. Nix, with one finger, pointed at all eight corners of the room. "All clean." Which meant *I've checked the chamber; we're not being listened to.*

Jenna shook her head. "Seems like a tight ship. A lot of pride in 'We're the ones who live next door to the devil.' "

Smart scowled at his cards as though they'd sold him out to Skynet. "This place will be hell for the toasters to crack. Get off the main tunnels and no one's supposed to walk in tight clusters. Because of bombs under pressure plates, set to the pounds per square inch of an assault robot. There are deadfalls, trap doors over long falls."

Sato shook his head. "I suspect none of that will matter when the time comes. I think this place is compromised already." He took three cards and received a third six. He upped the bid by a .223 cartridge.

Nix threw in his cards. "Mears has set up a bunch of unmanned outposts over the years. Places where the population can run if the compound collapses."

Jenna took two and anted. "Nothing weird about that."

"Yeah, but I hear work on them is ongoing, like Mears is planning to build each one out into a little habitat."

Smart accepted one card and raised the bid by an additional .223. "Colonies."

J. L. folded. "I found a leak," he said.

Sato glanced over at him. The boy's tone was bored and non-chalant, but Sato could tell that he was struggling to maintain the pose of indifference.

Sato placed another .223 round in the pot. "Tell us."

Jenna matched the bid.

J. L. said, "Her name is Lana. She's Mears's mistress. She already knows about the woman we're looking for."

"Show 'em," Smart said. He presented his hand: three threes.

Jenna sighed. She tossed her cards onto the table: two pair, nines over fours.

Sato showed his sixes. "Boss goes on a shooting spree," he said and scooped the pot over to him. Then he turned back to J. L. "So, spill."

"She's about twenty-five, brunette, good-looking, about as dumb as a box of hair." J. L. shrugged. "But she knows it. Good-natured. Kind of lonely, though, since it's hands-off for everyone at the compound or have Mears come down on you like a deadfall."

Her tone arch, Jenna asked, "Was it hands-off for you?"

J. L. ignored her.

"Oh my." Jenna's voice turned positively musical with amusement. "Have we finally broken the curse of the World's Deadliest Virgin?"

"Debrief now, smirk later," Sato said. "So?"

"So he tells her everything. He's a lonely old man and she's the only one he opens up to."

"And where does he talk to her?" Sato asked. The deal passed to Smart; Sato accepted his cards and looked at them. It was a worthless hand, but three of the cards were hearts and suggested the distant possibility of a flush.

J. L thought about it and looked a little bothered. "I don't know."

Jenna gave Sato a scornful look. "Well, in his bedroom or hers, of course."

J. L. shook his head. "No, it wouldn't be. Mears has this ethic about personal privacy. Her bedroom is her private place; he never visits her there. And the same for his. No one goes there but him."

Sato anted up and accepted two new cards. "So where do they get together?"

"I said I don't know."

"That wasn't so much a question as an oblique reference to

tomorrow's assignment." With all cards in and bets down, Sato dropped his hand on the table, five hearts. "Boss goes on another shooting spree."

Nix sighed, exasperated. "It's going to be one of those nights."

Sangre de Cristo Mountains, New Mexico

Nearly two hundred miles south of Clover Compound, a convoy of military vehicles wound its way along the roads of the Sangre de Cristo Mountains. Many miles to the south, the mountains petered out near Santa Fe, but here they were in full command of the earth. And like the Rockies and every other mountain range, they were a comfort to the men and women of the Resistance, their juniper-covered ridges and folds offering many places to hide, places from which to fight.

The first and last vehicles were SUVs carrying members of the Hell-Hounds. Second and fourth were old Army trucks, the one that had left Home Plate with the convoy and another that the procession had picked up in a Resistance compound within Las Vegas. In the middle was John Connor's Humvee. Each vehicle was at least a half-mile in advance of the others, making it harder for Skynet's satellites to pick up a tell-tale concentration of infrared blips, harder for Skynet's forces to ambush one vehicle and wipe out the entire convoy.

"It's empty, though," said the man in the backseat. He had the driver's-side window, with Kate Brewster at the passenger-side window and John Connor in the middle. In the front seat, Glitch, the Hell-Hounds' T-850, drove, while Sgt. Fred Ginty, technician and relief driver, napped in the passenger seat.

The speaker continued, "We've been all through that armory, didn't leave a nail or a tin washer." He was short and dark, his skin as leathery as if it had sat out under the sun since J-Day and occasionally received a bit of saddle soap. On his chest, only slightly concealed by his vest, was a grayish tattoo of the silhouette of a Hunter-Killer, one of Skynet's aerial units. His name was Ed Piñon, and he was a full-blooded Mescalero Apache from south of these parts. A scout from Lance Compound, one of the Mescalero strong-holds, Piñon was supposed to know these mountains like the veins and scars of his own hand, and it was only reluctantly that his compound leader had offered his services to John and Kate.

"I doubt we'll be disappointed, even if it's empty," John said. "I mean, hell, it's lovely weather to be a tourist."

"And it's been forever since we've seen New Mexico," Kate added.

Piñon snorted. "Whatever. At least we don't get much Skynet activity out here. Say." He gestured at Glitch. "This is really a T, right? Do you ever just stand around beating on it, to burn off hard feelings?"

John shook his head. "Now, think about that. Teach people that they can casually slap a Terminator around and they'll what?"

"Well, they'll slap a Terminator around." Then Piñon considered. "And they'll lose some of their fear of the things."

"That's right. So we program Glitch and any others we capture to have some self-preservative behavior, even when it concerns Resistance humans. Slap him around and he probably won't do much more than break your fingers."

"But it will be done for maximum pain," Glitch said. Those were his first words in about two hundred miles.

"Oh, well." Piñon sat back.

An hour later they made the final turnoff onto the paved, one-lane government road that would take them to the armory. The road was in good condition, not at all potholed or crumbling after years of disuse.

That sort of thing had surprised John and Kate in the early years after Judgment Day. They'd always assumed that with no crews to maintain them, the roads would weather and deteriorate. But except for areas of extreme heat, hot enough to melt asphalt, or cold and precipitation, where the ravages of ice could not be avoided, the roads tended to endure in much the same condition they were in when the traffic ended. This was a boon to the Resistance. Skynet couldn't afford to damage main highway arteries to inconvenience the Resistance; the machines used those roads themselves. Nor could Skynet destroy all of America's back roads; there were simply too many. So the roads remained, mute testimony to the engineering skills of the species that once ruled the Earth.

This road took them up over and between hills, along trenches cut through hillsides by construction equipment that now lay in distant, rusty graves. John noted untended fields of beans and corn, some of it growing as tall and healthy as it had before J-Day. With the scent of juniper surrounding him, he could pretend for just a moment that this was a ride in the country in a world where cars roared endlessly along city streets, where TVs showed sitcoms and soap operas, where people packed dance halls and had nothing on their minds more weighty than making a connection for the evening or scraping up the rent to mail off tomorrow morning.

Beside him, Kate had her arm along the door window, her chin resting on her forearm. Her expression, untroubled and contemplative, matched his mood.

They rounded a final turn and drove through the already-open gate of a chain-link fence. Its corroded sign marked the land beyond as U.S. government property and warned of serious consequences for trespassing. Not far beyond was a security booth, its glass long since broken, and beyond that, its rear end nestling against a low, round-topped hill, was the building.

It was shaped like a capital *T*, with the crossbar lying flush against the hillside and its main bar pointed straight at John's Humvee, straight at the entrance into this small compound. The entire building had a curved roof, like two oversized Quonset huts or extended airplane hangar, making it about a story-and-a half tall at its edges and about two stories tall at the top of the roof. Its walls were made of crumbling adobe instead of corrugated metal, the untended irregularity of the flaking surface making it look as though the entire building needed a shave. John fingered the three days' worth of stubble that surrounded his own beard.

The building was surrounded on three sides by parking lot. Without instruction, Glitch angled around to the left. As that wall came into view, so did the vehicle-sized doors there; they were already open. Glitch guided the Humvee through, into the darkened interior.

The dirt-brown SUV of the Hell-Hounds, which had carried Ten and Earl, was parked within, as was the Army truck they'd picked up in Las Vegas. The crews and passengers of the two vehicles were walking around, stretching their legs in the cavernously empty building interior. When Glitch killed the Humvee's engine, John could hear the steps of their bootheels echoing from the concrete floor and walls.

As the Humvee's occupants exited their vehicle, Piñon gestured around. "We sometimes use it as a temporary shelter on long courier runs. Mostly we stay in the smaller rooms of the other wing. But the place doesn't afford much of a view of the countryside, and it's not very defensible. Not a good place to stay. And, like I said, it's been stripped. We finished what the National Guard started."

John nodded and looked around. He caught Ten's eye. "Tom's in the other truck, correct?"

Ten nodded.

"Any word from your second vehicle?" That would be the Hell-Hounds' other SUV, the dark green one, which carried Kyla and Mark.

"No word," Ten said.

That was good. In a world where radio silence was the normal state of affairs, no news tended to be good news.

The second truck pulled in four minutes later. Steam curled up from beneath its hood, and the instant it stopped technicians piled out from the back and swarmed around the engine. Paul Keeley emerged from the back, set his pack down well away from the others, and sat down to do some stretching exercises. Next out was Tom Carter.

John and Kate waited until the technician had walked a little stiffness from his legs, then joined him. "Time for the acid test," Kate said.

The three of them headed toward the hall's back wall. Suspicious, Piñon trotted up and joined them. "What acid test?" Then, remembering he was addressing the Resistance leader, added, "Sir?"

"Old intelligence," John said. They reached the back wall and walked along it, scrutinizing it for clues pointing to what they were looking for. Unlike the front and side walls, this surface was metal, covered with a peeling layer of paint. "Before J-Day, a far-sighted fellow who anticipated Skynet's rise erased this place from computerized government records. Wiped out all record of the place itself and of its special function. We learned about it a few weeks ago."

That was only a fraction of the story. That "far-sighted fellow," Daniel Ávila, had repeated that effort for dozens of caches, abandoned silos, and cave systems across the spectrum of U.S. Department of Defense records. In the last month, the Resistance had located and entered two of those sites, which could now serve as habitats and weapon caches.

But as spread out and undermanned as it was, the Resistance could only absorb so many such treasure troves at any one time. Opening several all at once increased the odds of Skynet detecting their activities. Telling someone outside Connor's immediate circle of advisers also increased that risk, which was one reason Piñon was only to receive a fraction of the story.

They reached the end of the metal wall. It turned to painted cinder blocks for a foot or so, then met the side wall into which was set a plain wooden door leading into the side wing.

Above the door was an air-conditioning vent, too small to accommodate any living thing larger than a cat. Carter looked at it and said, "I need up."

Glitch approached. Without preamble, he seized Carter by the belt and straight-armed him upward.

Carter put one boot against the wall and another back against Glitch's chin to brace himself, then got to work on the vent grill with a screwdriver. A moment later, he dropped the grill onto the floor; the sound of the metal meeting concrete was shrill, causing silence-loving Resistance members to jump.

Carter reached into the vent and went to work on something within. "Back in the day," he said, "this could have been accomplished with a remote control—if they upgraded it in time, even with a cell phone. But we're now off any operating power grid, and I doubt the backup generators will even function without an overhaul. This leaves the possibility . . ." There was a quiet *clank,* and then Carter discarded another metal plate, this one almost featureless, bearing only four corner holes for screws. Kate caught it on the way down. "The possibility that capacitance charges will still work. They built these babies tough—and usually with multiple redundancy."

John took a side look at Piñon. Realization was dawning on the man's face. "There's a second installation here," Piñon said.

Kate nodded. "Uh-huh."

"But it's got to be empty, too."

"Possible," John said. "But we have to remember that what we had here was a two-level organization. The National Guard operated the armory, and unknown to everyone except the armory's most senior officers, there was also a skeleton crew maintaining the additional vehicles here. They would have looked and dressed like National Guard personnel, but would have actually belonged to the DOD. When Judgment Day came, since the existence of this place had already been scraped out of the official records, odds are that its personnel would not have been sent orders about the disposition of whatever was here."

There was the sound of an engine, but not from behind the wall. John and Kate turned to see the last convoy vehicle, the SUV carrying Mark Herrera and their daughter, pull into the building.

"Got it," Carter said.

There was a sudden hum of noise, accompanied by a loud ratcheting, and the back wall sank into the floor. It settled with a substantial *thump,* revealing an opening as large as the metal portion of the wall had been.

Beyond were smooth concrete floor and natural stone ceiling, a cave that had been paved. After a few dozen steps, the floor descended as a ramp at an easy angle into the hillside.

And on the floor were vehicles—wheeled vehicles, tracked vehicles, vehicles John Connor had never seen before and could not name.

Paul joined the crowd of people who moved like vista-struck tourists into the depths of the vehicle cache. As he passed vehicle after vehicle, he named them, demonstrating one of the skills that had once made him valuable to the Resistance. "M109A5 Paladin 155-millimeter self-propelled howitzer," he said. "One, two, three AM General High-Mobility Multipurpose Wheeled Vehicles—"

"Those are just Humvees," Kyla said into his ear.

Paul ignored her. "Two equipped with Stinger air defense systems, making them Avengers." Those two did not have rear seats or payload beds; instead, mounted in the backs were large, pivoting T-shaped apparati with maneuverable boxes at the ends. Each box held four Stinger missiles.

Paul passed them in a sort of reverent daze and pointed to the next vehicle in line. "Toyota Seven-Series Boxcar forklift." That put him to the end of the first holding area for vehicles. He started down the ramp; in the distance, he could see the bobbing flashlight beams of those who had gone on ahead and the vehicles they illuminated. "M102 lightweight towed howitzer." Several beams of light had come to rest on a white automobile-sized apparatus with treads, chain guns for arms, and a metal head shaped like a point-down triangle. "T-1 series Terminator." He rushed toward it.

By afternoon's end, John's workers had erased all external signs that anyone had made an intrusion into this facility, including closing the hurricane fence gate and closing the armory's external doors. They had also performed a preliminary inventory of the goods found in the hidden portion of the complex.

There had been more vehicles, of course. Trucks and motorcycles and staff cars, pickups with elaborate tool sets where the beds should be, an ambulance, and a short fire truck. There had been stockpiles of ammunition, including some surviving Stinger missiles and some very sophisticated shells for use with the self-propelled howitzer . . . though, sadly for the Resistance, there had been none of the nuclear missiles the howitzer could fire. There had been portable generators and a main generator for the complex that Tom Carter said was reparable. There had been stockpiles of food, uniforms, small arms.

The T-1 Terminator, though it attracted the attention of the Resistance technicians more than any other item here, wasn't all that helpful a find. John wanted it returned to Home Plate intact as a museum piece for the future. It could, he supposed, be programmed for the defense of a habitat, but the T-1 was no match for a later model or for a well-trained team of humans. Glitch and a rocket-propelled grenade would have little trouble destroying it. Instead, its chain guns would be removed and set up for the defense of some compound, but the main unit would be preserved as a reminder for future generations.

For the Resistance, the complex's contents constituted an unbelievable haul. Even when its goods were distributed among many of North America's human compounds, what was left behind would continue to be of great use to the Resistance, as this place, once it had been adapted to modern techniques of concealed continuous living, could become a new habitat.

John's technicians were now hard at work doing preliminary evaluations of the vehicles. Much of the rubber and plastics of tires, hoses, and belts was decayed to the point of uselessness and would have to be replaced on a jury-rigged or permanent basis before they could even think about moving vehicles out. Batteries were all drained and in many cases corroded beyond repair. But the early reports had been good. Within days, many of these vehicles would be patched up, filled with fuels brought in drums on Connor's trucks, and dispatched for distant habitats. Once they reached their new homes, many of them would be converted to new power sources, including fuel cells scavenged from Skynet vehicles and Resistance-built hydrogen fuel cells.

John pretended to be mildly pleased. He and Kate moved from vehicle to vehicle and group to group, asking questions, offering encouragement, but making it appear as though this cache was exactly as expected. It wouldn't do to have the leaders of the Resistance running around in circles, howling like hyperactive teenagers.

John stepped in beside Tom Carter as the man made a final walk of the portions of the complex that housed the vehicles. Behind them, Glitch, operating a huge hand crank meant for a team of men, slowly raised the concealing metal door to its closed position. Carter was sufficiently engrossed in the information on the clipboard he held that he took no notice of John joining him.

"Question," John said.

Carter didn't look up. He stumbled as they reached the lip of the ramp, but managed not to fall. "Shoot."

"How's your boy Keeley doing?"

Finally Carter did look up, considering. "Beats the hell out of me."

"Well, you've been watching him—"

"Ever since we left Home Plate." Carter shrugged expressively. "I only thought he was closed up before when I worked with him. Now he's a blank wall. No graffiti on it to give me a clue what he's thinking. This suggests to me that he hasn't been programmed to infiltrate us. If he had been, he'd be integrating himself, ingratiating himself better. I don't think he's a traitor. I just think he's a mess."

"Do you think he's salvageable, and if he is, is he worth the trouble?"

They were now deep in the tunnel. Light, insufficient but welcome, came from a string of bulbs taped or stapled to the ceiling and powered from a portable generator.

"Ordinarily, I'd say yes—and yes. But ordinarily, people have family or friends who can be called on to help them, to defend them against rumors and innuendo. He's got neither. And he's like—you know how it is when kids get to that sullen phase."

"Don't remind me." John offered up a mock shudder. "I raised three of them past that point."

"Well, he's back at that point. He's withdrawn, moody, paranoid, passively hostile, smart enough to know when he's being manipulated, and so badly socialized that he doesn't know how to fix things. He's twenty-four going on fifteen."

"Instant adolescent. Just add pimples."

Carter grinned.

"Is he showing interest in *anything*?"

Carter held the clipboard up in front of John. With his thumb, he indicated an entry. It read:

Two (2) Kawasaki off-road motorcycles (man. 2001–2002), probably for security force patrols property around armory, possibly for spec. ops.

"Un-huh," John said. "Well, that's better than nothing. Make it his assignment to get them ready for the road, in addition to whatever else you have him doing. Don't be too obvious. It can't be his main assignment."

"Is there anyone you don't manipulate, boss?"

John nodded. "Just Kate. She always knows."

c.8

While Paul Keeley lay sleeping, the implant within his skull stirred.

Ports no wider than the diameter of human hairs slid open in the implant's hypoallergenic surface. Before blood could seep into them, they extruded fibrous threads, actually chains of microscopic robotic devices—examples of the nanotechnology that drove high-end Skynet devices such as the T-1000 and T-X Terminator series.

The nanotech threads effortlessly punched through brain tissue, interrupting a synaptic chain here, erasing the connection between two sets of memories there. This casual, undirected surgery did not do damage from which Paul could never recover, but damage it did do. Still, Paul felt nothing; the brain, even damaged, feels no pain.

The nanotech threads pooled up against the inside of Paul's skull, spreading out in all directions from both temples to the coronal suture, where the frontal bone of the forehead fused with the parietal bones farther back and to the sides. Had someone been watching with a sophisticated enough magnetic resonance imaging device or similar diagnostic apparatus, the threads would have seemed to go still at that moment, but they were not inactive; having reached their interim destinations, they began attaching themselves to one another at nodes on their microscopic bodies, reinforcing the tensile strength of each thread.

Then they began to exert pressure.

Finally Paul reacted. His left shoulder twitched, moving his entire arm, and then the twitch became chronic. Its arrhythmic jerking awoke him and he turned to look, bleary-eyed, at the offending limb.

Then his eyes widened. He clamped his hands over his ears and temples, exerting pressure, as if to contain within something that wanted out.

Within his braincase, the implant pulled in one direction and pushed in another, driving its mass through fragile tissue, churning brain matter into an organic sludge—

It should have been a scream, but it came out as a muffled, strangled noise, and Paul sat up, clutching his head. His blanket dropped away from him.

He ran his fingers across his temples, through his hair, but there was no agonizing pressure coming from within. There was no sensation of deliberate, fatal movement within his skull.

It had been a dream.

He'd had it before. But each time it came to him, it was new—and he lived it as though for the first time.

He wondered if it would ever come true—or go away forever.

He looked up into the eyes of the Terminator.

Above him loomed the hulk of the T-1 they'd found that afternoon. Someone, out of a sense of history or humor, had attached a lightbulb to the ceiling above and before it and the light shone down on the ancient robot.

The T-1 did not move, and no lights shone from the diodes in its crude face. Paul did not feel menaced by it and had set up his blanket between its treads, well away from the humans he accompanied.

In the distance, in the darkness, there was an odd *click-click-click* noise. The clicks were irregular, like pieces of plastic or pencil tips dropping onto the concrete, and were getting louder, closer.

Paul just stared. He had only a knife with which to defend himself, and he didn't care to run.

The oncoming being moved into the light. It was Ginger, Kyla's canine, her toenails clicking on the floor, her tail wagging slightly with curiosity. Behind came Ripper, and finally coming into the light was Kyla herself, her sniper rifle cradled in her arms. She was barefoot.

"Was that you?" she asked. Her voice was pitched low. Up the ramp, guards were on duty; down the ramp, at the next level area below, people were sleeping. She obviously didn't want to disturb either group.

"Yeah," he said. "Bad dream."

She looked up at the unmoving figure looming above him. "Maybe it's the company."

"Hey, I'm Sleeps-With-Toasters, remember? I'm just living up to my name."

She almost smiled. "That's not funny. You're going to give people the creeps until they put a round into you."

"They'll put a round into me whether or not I give them any more creeps. It's just a matter of time, isn't it?"

"What do you mean?"

He gave her an admonishing look. "Never mind."

"You really think you're facing some sort of death sentence? For fraternizing with the enemy?"

"Well, for that, and for having a chunk of the enemy installed in my skull. And for not having anyone who can say, with any sort of conviction, 'He's not a witch. Don't burn him.' "

She sat down before him, cross-legged, and laid her rifle across her lap. Ginger immediately flopped down to lie against one of her legs. "Come on, you're not dumb. If everyone thought you were a menace, you'd never have been allowed on a mission where you could get at my parents."

"You'll note that I haven't been given any weapons."

She shook her head. "I didn't know that. But it's not true in any case. Tell me the truth. You haven't had *any* opportunity to pick up a monkey wrench and brain one of them?" She frowned. "I wonder if saying that out loud is dereliction of duty for me."

Paul thought about it. "Maybe you're right. But there's no way for me to find out whether I'm waiting out some sort of sentence or not. I don't have any sort of connection with any human being." He patted the T-1's tread. "Boris here is my only friend."

Kyla made an exasperated noise. "Oh, great, you're Pinocchio."

Paul fingered his nose. "You saying I'm lying?"

"I'm saying you're a little wooden thing who wants to be turned into a real boy. But you can't be."

"Even assuming you're right . . . why not?"

"Because you'd have to do the job yourself, and you're too full of something—maybe stubbornness, maybe self-pity—to do it."

"Oh. Well, is there a course in this? Maybe one of your father's lecture series?"

The look she gave him suggested that she was not at all impressed by his sarcasm. "Actually, that's one he could teach. Because he's had to do that. To become what he is today."

"Yeah, right. If there's any one term that's consistently used to describe John Connor, it's 'natural leader.'"

"But it's wrong. I mean, he *is* a leader. He's a great leader. But it didn't come naturally."

"How did it happen, then?"

"He spent a lot of time trying to figure out what the world needed him to be. He studied leaders and leadership, from books, from people he met—especially after J-Day. The way he puts it, he intellectualized a process that comes naturally to other people. And then he took the next step, which was to act as what he needed to become."

"You're saying your father is just pretending to be what he is."

She shook her head. "I'm saying that he became what he wasn't originally. And that's what you ought to do. You want people to respect you or like you? Stop acting like a reject. Stop scuttling around in the shadows. Act like someone they'll respond to better. And when they do, maybe you'll start becoming that person."

"Yeah? Well, one of these confident, battle-hardened Resistance guys you're talking about, looking at you here, would say, 'Hey, how about crawling into this blanket with me?'"

She gave him an exasperated look. "Well, that's a start. An awkward, half-assed one, but a start." She heaved herself to her feet. "But for right now, you're still a wooden thing, and I like real boys."

"So you're worried about splinters."

She laughed, then turned away and walked off into the darkness. "Night."

"Good night."

Ripper was last to leave. The dog gave Paul a sympathetic look that all but said, *Dude, you struck out.*

The next day Paul disassembled and began a decades-overdue maintenance of one of the Humvee Avenger engines. The thing was in surprisingly good shape, despite its many years of downtime; corrosion was at a minimum and most of the mil-spec belts and hoses might hold together.

He was on his back beneath the engine compartment when he became aware that booted feet had come to a stop nearby; their wearer had to be peering into the driver's seat. "Hey," he said. "Is there an extender for the socket wrench out there? I need it."

The boots moved to the nearby tool kit and there were small *clinks* and *clanks* as their wearer dug through the tools; this noise only added to the repair-shop sounds echoing off the walls, as all along the complex men and women worked to restore its treasure of vehicles. Then, silently, a large male hand extended the extender within Paul's reach.

Paul took it. "Thanks."

The hand withdrew. There was no reply.

"The correct response is: 'You're welcome.'"

"You're welcome."

Paul jerked, avoiding by a fraction of an inch banging his head on the engine components above. Only one member of this expedition had those deep tones and that accent. "Oh, it's Glitch."

"Yes."

"You know what my last job was, Glitch?"

"Analyzing and evaluating twentieth-century artifacts, principally mechanical apparati, for their usefulness in supporting the cause of the human Resistance."

"No, after that. I spent several months or a year teaching a Terminator how to have conversations. Which is something you obviously need." Paul attached the extender to the socket wrench and got to work tightening the last nut of his current task.

"I am capable of conversation."

"You know how to talk. Not the same thing. What is the purpose of conversation?"

"Oral exchange of information."

"Sometimes, yeah. What about the rest of the time?"

Glitch was silent for a moment. Either the answer was eluding the T-850 or he was actually hesitating—or programmed to do an effective simulation of hesitation. "Oral exchange of information."

Paul shoved his way out from under the Humvee and sat up. Glitch remained in place beside the vehicle, staring at him incuriously. "There you're wrong." Paul disassembled the socket wrench into its components, dropping each into the correct slot in the thirty-year-old black plastic socket wrench case within the tool kit. "Doesn't your programming have anything about human psychology, human needs?"

"A minimal amount necessary for interpretation of human behavior. Since I will not be called upon to pass for human in human society, a more extensive behavioral package was considered unnecessary."

"See, it's always more complicated than 'oral exchange of information.' Consider all my conversations with the T-X." Paul felt a sudden pang of loss. The woman he had thought Eliza to be was a machine, one that has as its ultimate goal the extinction of the human race. But whenever Paul thought about her, that realization was transformed into something else, the loss of someone he cared about: the emotion of caring reinforced by dozens—perhaps hundreds—of encounters he couldn't even remember. *A woman I cared about has died. Or been transformed into something awful.* It was the same thing. "The information I was giving to her, all about me, my history, and my interests, was not the information she was accumulating, which was how human beings act and react in a bunch of circumstances. And the information she was giving to me, all about her history and interests, was completely fictitious, while the *real* information she was giving me, which was all about how I should chase after her like a hormonal adolescent, was all subliminal. Get it?"

"Yes. But that is still an oral exchange of information."

Paul stood up, not deterred by the robot's implacable insistence on one answer. "And then there's the question of affirmation of emotion. People talking in order to reassure each other and themselves. To form or reinforce bonds with one another."

"Still an oral exchange of information. The information is: 'I am good, you are good.' It is simply expressed in a cumbersome and inefficient fashion."

Paul stared into Glitch's eyes and adopted a patronizing tone. "So you're so smart—are you capable of performing this second sort of conversation?"

"Probably not. But it is not required of my role within the Resistance."

"Now, think about that. You're supposed to protect people from Skynet and its units, to save them when they're in danger, to facilitate their plans in order to improve the whole species' chances of survival. Does it interfere with your objective at all when people are too fearful and suspicious of you to cooperate fully with you?"

This time Glitch did not hesitate. "The odds are high that this does result in some interference."

"Therefore your conversational helplessness limits your effectiveness." Paul frowned. He didn't normally use a phrase like 'conversational helplessness.' All his months of interaction with the T-X had made him a better speaker, had broadened his vocabulary.

"Yes, that follows," Glitch said.

"Well, I tell you what. Anytime, at least up until I'm executed, you want to improve your conversational skills, come to me and we'll talk. And I'll give you a starter lesson right now. Allowing people to talk about their favorite subject makes it easier for them to relax and makes them feel better about you . . . and just about everyone on Earth has the *same* favorite subject."

"What is their favorite subject?"

Paul grinned, victorious. He'd actually engaged a Terminator's curiosity—or, rather, some imperative in the programming that made it a learning mechanism. "There are a couple of hints to the answer in the conversation we just had." He closed his tool kit and picked it up. He wanted to give the Kawasakis a look-see.

Glitch stood in place for a moment, then, recognizing that the main body of the conversation was at an end, turned away. He took three steps, then stopped and turned to look back at Paul. "Themselves," he said.

"Very good. You've just learned something."

Clover Compound, Colorado

They lay in darkness hundreds of feet within the stony earth. This was one of the deepest tunnels of the old mine that had been incorporated into Clover Compound. No lights were strung here, no intercoms, no sign that anyone had visited in a hundred years or more—no sign other than a bundle of blankets and two moving forms beneath it.

J. L. held Lana to him, a tight embrace for which she seemed anxious, even desperate. They were cheek to cheek, and whenever she spoke, he could feel her lips moving against the corner of his mouth.

"How long before you have to go?" she asked. Though it was unlikely anyone else would have heard had she shouted at the top of her lungs, she still whispered. This distant, empty place seemed to encourage whispering.

"Oh, I can pretty much take the afternoon off."

She giggled. J. L. liked that. Most of the women he knew didn't giggle. They tended to laugh outright. Then she said, "No, I mean, before you have to leave Clover."

"Oh. I'm not sure. A couple of days, a week maybe." With the tip of his nose, he traced the letter *J* across her cheek and felt her shiver. "If I'm lucky."

"If *I'm* lucky."

"So, do you give this kind of reception to everyone who visits Clover Compound?"

"No . . . just the ones I like. And only ones Raymond can't punish for it."

"Wow. And does Mears ever punish *you* for it?" J. L. kept his tone light, but the thought of the old man visiting pain on Lana, superficial as she might be, stirred him to anger.

"No. Well . . . not really."

"What do you mean?"

"When he finds out, he just looks at me like he's so hurt. Like I'm some sort of brute who beats a frail old man with a stick. God, I wish I could quit my job." A tear trickled down her cheek, and J. L. felt it roll down his as well.

"What *is* your job?"

"I'm his mistress."

"Oh. I meant, your job in Clover Compound."

"I told you. I'm his mistress."

"That's your official job?" J. L. drew back as if to look at her, though there was not one glimmer of light to reveal her features.

"Officially, it's 'attendant.' But there's only one attendant in Clover Compound, and everyone knows what it means. Before me, there was another one, and after me, there'll be another one."

"Why *can't* you quit?"

"Because Raymond has to approve all position transfers. You apply for a post and he approves it . . . or he doesn't. So I applied for the post. But it's been years and he won't let me leave."

"You applied knowing what the job was?"

"Yes." She shrugged. "I used to live in a—well, it wasn't even a compound. It was just my family. A cabin deep in the woods. My father and brothers hunted. My mother and sisters and I cooked, kept the cabin up, gathered fruits and vegetables. It was, I guess, very traditional. My father was kind of weird about duties and roles. I knew about Clover Compound because my mother kept mentioning it. Since I was the oldest, she wanted me to be living somewhere else by the time I was an adult, and Pa wouldn't hear of it . . . there was a lot of arguing about that. But it was all settled when the assault robot came." Her voice trailed off for a moment. "I was the only one to get away alive; and I found my way here, and Raymond made me an offer; and the idea of not having to work, after all those years of it, and still to have somewhere to live and enough to eat, was so amazing . . ."

"But now you'd prefer to work."

"Yeah. You think I'm disgusting, don't you?"

"I think you did what you needed to in order to survive. Maybe it was the right choice, maybe it was the wrong one, I don't know. But it's not 'disgusting.' Disgusting is turning your back on a brother-in-arms. Did you ever do that?"

"No."

"Then you're okay." He settled back in place beside her. "You want to quit, I can get you out of here." He didn't know that for sure, but he was certain that Lt. Sato would act on this woman's behalf.

"No, you can't."

"The lieutenant can. Remember, he can talk to John Connor and Kate Brewster anytime he wants."

"They're not as powerful as Raymond here in Clover Compound."

J. L. suppressed a sigh. Perhaps it was because Lana hadn't grown up with the names Connor and Brewster in her ear since she was a child—or perhaps she'd been indoctrinated too thoroughly in the cult of Raymond Mears the Patriarch—but it was obvious she had no faith in anyone to extricate her from this situation.

He decided to change the subject . . . for the moment. "Is there any chance he'll come down here and find us?"

"No, he never comes down here. I know it's the access to Satan's Hole and all, but he doesn't visit."

"So this isn't where you and he go for privacy."

"Oh, no."

"Where *do* you go?"

"I can't tell you."

"He'd punish you?"

"I just can't."

There it was again, the tinge of irrationality that accompanied every one of the dictates of Mears, at least as Lana understood them. J. L. wondered if the woman even understood how deeply enmeshed she was in the old man's illogic.

Well, it was time to find out. He spent a moment rehearsing the words Sato had given him and mixing them in with arguments he'd developed while talking with Lana.

"Let me ask you something," he said. "Is just being alive still the most important thing to you?"

Sato had insisted that he used the word "still." "Say 'still' and it means she has to reevaluate what you're asking her about." J. L. had expanded on that. "Just being alive" was different from "being alive," because the words would remind her that she understood how far from admirable she considered her life to be.

"I don't know," she said.

"Let me put it to you this way. The worst Raymond Mears could possibly do to you—and that's if none of the Scalpers were in the way—is kill you. My question is this: Is that the worst thing that could happen to you? Is that the worst thing of all?"

"I guess maybe not."

"Well, listen. Something's going on out here. People operating out of or through Clover Compound are getting killed. We don't know why, but we're pretty sure that it has something to do with the place where you go for privacy." That was a wild leap of supposition, it was true, but Sato had said that the only person in the compound who had access to high-level information that could doom missions and had demonstrated a willingness to gossip about it with noninvolved people was Raymond Mears. So Mears was Suspect #1, and any secrets he was preserving had to be uncovered. "We need to find out where that is and look it over—or else more people will die. Just like your brothers and sisters and parents did. You might be able to put an end to it. Just by telling us where. So you have to decide whether it's worse for this to keep happening, which it definitely will, or if it's worse for him to try to do his worst to you, which we can probably keep from happening."

She was silent for a long time. He lay there, listened to her breathe, and felt his stomach do flip-flops. All the fighting he'd done over the years, all the bullets he'd dodged, hadn't distressed him nearly as much as trying to back this woman into a corner and oblige her to do the right thing.

Finally she said, "I'll show you. Meet me in the high airflow chamber in an hour."

"Thank you."

She sat up. By touch, she located her garments and pulled them on one by one. "If I die, you'll tell people why, won't you? I don't want to be remembered just as his mistress. Please."

"I'll tell people. And if you do what the lieutenant and I say, I don't think you'll die. Maybe nobody will die. Everyone just has to be smart."

This time it was no giggle—she laughed and there was a touch of bitterness to it. "Now you're asking too much. I've never been smart." She stood. "You might want to wait a few minutes before you follow me out. You remember the way?"

"I remember."

She moved off into the darkness, sure-footed, familiar with her surroundings.

He waited until she'd been gone a minute. Then he pulled his pants on and carefully, keeping his hands before him to make sure he didn't take a sudden fall, moved on hands and knees the fifteen yards or so to Satan's Hole.

Maybe, as Lana had asserted, it wasn't half-filled with the rotting corpses of Mears's rivals and enemies. There was certainly no smell of decay floating up from its depths.

He leaned over the lip and threw up.

He sat back, wiping his mouth. He felt shaky and finally suspected, despite glorious childhood dreams of being a leader of men, that he probably wasn't destined for that role.

Sometimes leading people meant manipulating them. And manipulating them made him sick.

J. L. decided that he might have to stick to killing the machines instead.

When J. L. and Sato arrived at the high airflow chamber, Lana was already there, waiting.

The chamber was half natural cave, half room dug out of solid stone by miners, and mostly filled with fans and ductwork. Powered by generators much deeper in Clover Compound, its machinery pumped air through several layers of the habitat. It didn't pump air out; according to Mears, waste air exited from the lowest airflow chamber and was pumped out via ventilation shafts that emerged beside natural hot springs, making it unlikely that Skynet's infrared scans would relate that heat source to a possible human habitat.

Lana's eyes opened a little when she spotted Sato, but she said nothing. Sato, who had not met her before, gave her a quick look. She was a tall woman, only a couple of inches under six feet, with a round face and long brown hair—not as long as Jenna's, but still at a length that indicated luxury rather than practicality. She wore an unmarked uniform in deep blue; though it was plain, Sato recognized that it was cotton, probably traded for at considerable expense from a distant habitat in Texas or points farther east. And she was pretty, having the sort of appealing but unmemorable looks that the surviving copies of men's magazines Sato had seen referred to as "the girl next door."

"I'm Lieutenant Sato." He extended his hand. "Thanks for helping."

"Lana Miertschin," she said and shook his hand. "*M-i-e-r-t-s-c-h-i-n*. Please remember that." She turned away and opened the thin metal door covering the oversized metal case behind her. Within were circuit breakers and gauges.

"I will," Sato said. He turned a curious eye on J. I.. The younger man gave him an "I'll explain later" gesture.

Lana flipped three of the circuit breakers, then restored them in a different order. There was no change to the operating of the fans and blowers around her. Then she closed the door again and gripped the entire breaker box and pulled.

It rotated away from the stone wall, opening as if the whole box were a door, revealing a gap in the wall, a yard high by two feet wide, beyond. In the back of the breaker box was a metal handle.

Lana stepped through and gestured for the men to follow. They did, emerging into a dark area the size of any of the thousands of elevators now standing unused all over the world. On the opposite side, dimly visible in the light spilling through the hole in the wall, was a dark door.

Lana pulled and tugged the circuit box closed. It came to rest with a distinct *click*. "I'm going to open the other door," she said. "I don't need light on the other side, at least not until we get to where there is some, but you probably will."

Sato switched on his flashlight. In its harsh, unflattering glow, Lana looked uncomfortable and scared.

"Then, when we get to where there is light, do exactly what I do," she continued. "Okay?"

Sato nodded. "Okay."

Lana twisted deadbolt knobs on the other door, three of them, one above the other. Then she pulled the other door open. From the slowness with which it moved, Sato guessed that it was metal rather than wood.

Beyond was another small room that, when Sato entered it, turned out to be a shaft rather than a chamber. It had four concrete walls and was thirty or forty feet high. Stapled into one wall was a metal ladder. The paint on it, mostly red-brown, was blotchy, and some of it was comparatively fresh.

Lana led the way, with J. L. second and Sato trailing.

At the room's summit, Lana pushed on a circular section of

ceiling and it rose away as a hatch. Sato switched off his flashlight and they emerged into a lit room.

It wasn't bright, and it wasn't a chamber designed for human occupation. It was long, perhaps sixty yards by twenty, with leaves and rubbish on the floor. The ceiling was cracked plaster, with many dark wooden beams supporting it; the windows, all along one wall, were broader than they were tall, barely tall enough for a human torso to fit through, and flush with the ceiling. There were what looked like wrought-iron bars on the outside of the windows, and the light coming in through them was sunlight. Sato could see hazy blue sky and clouds.

Sato felt the hair rise at the nape of his neck. *This is his house, the basement of Mears's old house.*

There was a wooden staircase near one end of the room. Lana led them up it. The door at the top opened into a dark, wood-paneled hallway. There were doors all along the hallway, some closed, others open and admitting more light.

Lana led them to the nearest one. It opened into a stairway, one with far more stylishly carved wooden banisters and supports than the basement stairs. Carefully, she walked up the stairs immediately adjacent to the wall. In spite of her precautions, her steps made the occasional step creak, but Sato recognized that tromping up the middle would cause far more creaking.

The men followed her up one flight, emerging into a hallway that was even better lit; there were windows, the glass in them mostly shattered and gone, along the left side, while the doors on the right side were all closed. Leaves and dried grasses decorated the wooden floor in places, and a little breeze stirred them.

Keeping just beside the left wall, Lana led them down the hall. She ducked and crawled past each open window, and the men duplicated her action. Once they were past the fourth window, with two more to go, she crossed the hall to the doorway there, opened it, and beckoned for the two men to join her within. They entered the chamber beyond and she shut the door behind them.

This was a grand chamber, two stories high, twenty yards by ten, a classic gentleman's library. Bookshelves stretched from the floor to nearly the ceiling, and a well-braced wooden ladder with wheels at its base permitted access to the higher shelves. At one end, a circular metal staircase gave access to a small platform one floor up; the platform was located directly beneath a skylight, though that aperture, like the room's two other skylights, appeared to have been covered over by wood at some point in the past. At floor level were several pieces of furniture, including a large wooden desk, two easy chairs, a sofa, and—probably not original equipment—a bed.

In spite of the fact that the skylights were blocked, the room was well illuminated. This chamber had three windows along one wall and two along another; all were about five feet high and two and a half feet wide, placed close to the ceiling. And the glass in all four was intact, though not entirely transparent. Sato didn't know whether it had been frosted when manufactured or had been scoured by dust and debris in the decades since the house was built, but the glass was all cloudy and whitish, like cataracts.

Lana opened her mouth to say something, but Sato raised a finger to his lips.

Sato moved out into the center of the room and looked around. Immediately he knew Raymond Mears just a little bit better.

This was the heart of the house. His personal library. Sato could see thousands of volumes, most of them hardbound. Sato had learned a phrase from his mother, a phrase she had used to describe the occasional well-preserved site that had once been occupied by powerful people: The place stank of money.

Mears doesn't give up anything he wants or loves. The library had been meticulously maintained in the decades since J-Day. Though weather had penetrated into other corners of the old house, Mears had taken steps to keep this chamber and its contents intact.

And Mears is a selfish bastard. In spite of the fact that most human habitats, excluding only the ones that had managed to perform repeated raids on public libraries, were short on reading material, Mears had kept this horde of books to himself.

Sato could almost hear the old man's words. "To hell with what the great John Connor says. I've kept my home, on the outside, right under Skynet's nose, all these years. My home, my books, my woman. No one can have them."

The windows had to be reinforced or armored glass of some sort, but that made sense; the high winds of this place would otherwise have shattered the difficult-to-reach panes on a regular basis.

Sato moved to the desk. In one drawer he found a sheaf of yellowing paper and a well-maintained fountain pen. He began writing. Out of the corner of his eye, he saw Lana wince. Obviously it was against the rules for anyone but Mears to use any of the precious paper stock. *My paper.*

He wrote:

Why were the skylights covered? Were they made out of regular glass?

That didn't make any sense to him. He crooked a finger to summon Lana over.

Reluctantly, she took the pen from him and responded:

he didnt want skynet satlites to see through them
He boarded them over?
he and his first mistress
Doesn't he worry about security? About the possibility of listening devices?
the only way to get here without trigering warning devices is the way we took, but he does look for microfones sometimes there never was one

It was true, the old engineer would be able to put together some sophisticated, clever security measures to warn him if a Terminator or assault robot entered his home. Sato could see dust on most exposed surfaces in the library; entering this chamber and planting a listening device would be very problematic, even for Skynet.

There was something about the windows that bothered Sato. No, not just the windows here, any windows. He'd been suspicious of intact windows ever since he'd attended a security lecture John Connor had given many years ago. From one of the pouches on his belt he pulled out a compass and took his bearings. The long wall with the three windows faced west, the short wall with the two windows north.

> *Those windows—do they look down over the Navajo Mountain Strategic Region?*
> *yes but its hard to see because the glass is so scratched*

Sato scowled over her response. That was probably it: the clue to how Skynet had penetrated the security of this place. It had somehow detected activity in this chamber and then had—
He began writing again.

> *I'm going to write out some words for you to say. You'll say them as we're leaving. I want you to pretend that you're saying them to Mears. Okay?*

She nodded.
From his shirt pocket, he withdrew another photograph of the fictitious Gwendolyn Drew. He set it on the desktop and began writing again.

"Honey?" Lana said. There was strain in her voice, and as she continued reading, she sounded as though she *were* reading. "You left that picture of the Drew girl on the desk. Do you want it?"

She waited, staring at Sato. He held up a finger, then a second, counting up to five, and then gestured for her to continue. "Okay," she said. "I'll just pick it up next time."

Sato and J. L. accompanied her out into the hall and they retraced their steps back into the basement, the access shaft, the airflow room.

It was the height of the breakfast meal, and the mess hall was crowded. The Scalpers had their own table; it had once been a picnic table for a state park, and after innumerable years weathering the outdoors it had spent innumerable years in this mine. It was designed to accommodate six people; all five Scalpers and a nervous-looking Lana sat at it now.

Sato kept a close eye on the crowd. All the other tables were full, and several of the Clover Compound residents were watching the Scalpers and their guest.

Sato stirred the oatmeal in the main compartment of his sectioned metal plate, then swallowed another mouthful. There was actually a hint of some sweetening in it, and the other plate compartments held some sort of fried potatoes and a compact little mound of chicken scraps. "Not bad," he admitted.

"We eat pretty well," Lana said. She wouldn't look around at the other tables. She sounded miserable.

"Remember what I told you," Sato said. "If everyone acts smart—"

"Everyone goes home happy," she finished.

J. L. reached over and gave her hand a reassuring squeeze. Sato didn't know whether it was just an act to comfort her or whether J. L. recognized that the action would be seen, would inevitably be reported to Mears. Probably both. Sato decided that the boy was proving to have good people instincts, to have wisdom beyond his years.

That wasn't as rare as it had been before Judgment Day. People needed to get wise fast. Someone who, even as an adolescent, couldn't behave beyond the urges of his hormonal storms was much more likely to make a fatal error than one who could.

Nix, opposite Sato, spoke up, his voice oddly melodramatic: "It begins."

Sato followed the man's gaze. Just entering the mess chamber from one of the main tunnels were Mears and Murphy. The compound leaders nodded and chatted to people as they moved among the tables, but there was little doubt that their eventual destination was the Scalpers' table.

Sato caught Smart's eye. "We could use a couple of extra chairs."

Smart nodded and rose. Moving quickly but unobtrusively, he approached two tables with unoccupied seats, spoke a few words to the people there, and absconded with two chairs. He placed one at either end of the Scalpers' table and was seated again before Mears and Murphy reached them.

"Good evening," Mears said. He spoke to Sato, but his glance flicked momentarily to Lana, who sat between Sato and J. L. Lana didn't look up at him.

Sato kept his tone cordial. "Good evening. I hope you'll forgive us from stealing your attendant this morning. We had some questions, and she's been most helpful with the answers."

"Not a problem," Mears said. "I didn't realize you were breakfasting out here, though, Lana. You might have let me know."

Before she could answer, Sato gestured at the two empty chairs. "Please. Join us."

Murphy moved around to the far end of the table. He hadn't said anything, and there was a faint tinge of curiosity to his expression. He obviously knew something was up, knew that whenever someone in Sato's position defied custom there had to be a reason.

Mears settled in at the end next to Sato and Nix. "What sort of questions?"

"Well, pertaining to security issues." Sato gave Mears his serious "Be prepared for bad news" face and lowered his voice. "There's a serious security problem, a leak, here at Clover, and it's getting people killed."

Mears leaned in close and put his elbows down on the table end. His tone was low, too, and Murphy had to lean in closer to hear him at all. "What problem?"

"Well, it starts with Steve Earle and Joel Benson."

More than three months ago, the most aggressive Resistance cell in this region, headed by former Air Force colonel Steve Earle, had found what promised to be an unguarded back door access into Navajo Mountain. With his mobile special forces cell, carrying a briefcase nuke provided by the Resistance through Clover Compound, Earle had traveled a second time to the vicinity of that back door . . . and disappeared.

A month later, Lt. Joel Benson, leader of the 1st Resistance Rangers, Special Incursion Unit Red 1, and four operatives had tried to replicate the mission. They, too, had failed. Their deaths had been heard by John Connor and his chief advisers; Benson's team had been in direct radio contact with Home Plate when they'd been assaulted and destroyed by Skynet forces.

And they, too, had naturally staged through Clover Compound.

Mears nodded. "A damned shame. Not just because a successful mission would have destroyed Skynet. Those were good men and women. Are you saying that a security breach *here* had something to do with their deaths?"

"Yes."

"Odds are long, Sato. They walked right up to Skynet's back door. There can't be any more sophisticated a security setup anywhere in the world, except maybe at Home Plate. They were caught because they were detected."

"They were caught because someone here told Skynet they were coming."

Mears's eyes widened. He turned to look around the mess hall.

His movement was slow and smooth, an attempt to be surreptitious, but many people still noted the compound leader's attention and offered him respectful nods.

He returned his attention to Sato. "Who?"

"The same person who informed Skynet of the location of Clover Compound in the first place."

Now Mears, already pallid from his years belowground, paled to an even whiter shade, making the liver spots on his face stand out in greater relief. "We'd all be dead."

"Eventually, you will be. The instant Skynet realizes that information from Clover Compound has dried up. At that point, the robots will come in and everybody in this compound will be slaughtered."

Murphy finally broke in. "You're saying Clover is doomed. We'll have to evacuate." There was disbelief in his voice, disbelief and pain.

Sato nodded. "That's right."

"No, no, no." Mears shook his head. "This is a *theory* on your part, nothing but a theory, and it's contradicted by all available facts. I am not going to lead all these people, who rely on me, in some terrified, half-assed exodus just because you theorize that we have an information leak."

Sato kept his full attention on Mears. He didn't let himself blink. Under the table, he slowly, silently snapped open the holster flap that kept his Glock handgun secure. "You're right . . . in that you're not going to lead. Colonel Mears, tonight you're stepping down as leader of Clover Compound."

Mears leaned back as if Sato had just transformed into a poisonous reptile. "Now I know you're crazy."

"Whether I'm crazy or not, at this moment I have a nine-millimeter semiauto pointed at your gut, and if you do anything to interrupt what I have to tell you, I'm going to put about six rounds into you and keep the rest in reserve to keep this crowd under control. You have my word on it."

At the other end of the table, Murphy started to rise, but Jenna the Greek caught his eye and gave him a slow shake of the head. Her right hand, too, was out of sight beneath the table. Pointedly, her spoon in her left hand, she scooped some oatmeal into her mouth and gestured for Murphy to retake his seat. He did, his expression neutral.

"In direct contravention of Resistance security protocols, you've been maintaining and regularly visiting an insecure above-ground site," Sato said. "Your old home. Specifically, the library of your old home."

Mears shot Lana a betrayed look. "It is not insecure."

"It has five intact windows facing territory controlled by Skynet."

Mears looked at Sato as though the man were an idiot. "Five *intact* windows. Nothing comes in. Nothing goes out. No security breach."

"Even assuming that a sufficiently sophisticated Terminator couldn't get close enough to plant a microphone on the exterior of one of those windows—"

"I have passive sensors all along the outside of the house. Standard pressure sensors. *Nothing could get up to those windows.*"

"What do you bet, Mears?"

"How about your life, Lieutenant?"

"Against your job? I'll take that bet. Have you ever heard of a technique by which a laser can be directed against a glass surface to measure infinitesimal vibrations in the glass? And those measurements processed to re-create the sounds, including human voices, that caused them?"

Mears was silent. But his eyes, widening slightly, told the entire story to Sato. *No, I hadn't.*

"Several times a week, you've taken Lana up to your hideaway, read your books, spent time with her, talked to her. You talked to her about Earle's expedition—and Benson's. About the back door and the briefcase nukes. The day before yesterday you told her about Gwendolyn Drew, the woman we're looking for. And you told Skynet. All without meaning to."

Mears shook his head. "I don't believe you."

Sato continued as if the old man hadn't spoken. "Yesterday I had Lana speak, as if she were talking to you, and indicate that you'd left something behind in your library—a clue Skynet can't afford not to have. Then we left. If I'm right, and I am, Skynet will have dispatched a mechanism to take a direct look at that clue, since it's not something Skynet could acquire by bouncing a laser off a window. Just how good are your passive sensors upstairs?"

"Very, very good."

"And very well hidden, too, I take it."

"Yes."

"While you were up there, have you ever discussed the locations of those sensors with Lana? Or any of your other attendants over the years? Offered any information that would allow Skynet units to bypass them?"

Mears thought about it for several long moments. Finally he shook his head. The gesture lacked energy; it was obvious that the old man was seriously considering the possibility that he had betrayed everything he had built over the years. "No. Only in my office. That's where I keep the plans and diagrams."

"Then let's go look at whatever you use to record the sensor output."

In the high airflow chamber, Mears looked at all the faces gathered around him: the Scalpers, Murphy, Lana. Then he pulled open the circuit box that provided access to the house far above.

Instead of throwing the three false breakers in the pattern that unlocked the box, he threw them in a different order. There was the faint whine of a servo and from behind a mass of wiring and circuitry descended an ancient liquid crystal display screen.

It came to life, displaying the word TEST in the upper left-hand corner. Then that word faded and characters Sato couldn't interpret came up:

```
01020304050607080910
-------------------XX--

11121314151617181920
-----XXXX----XX-----

21222324252627282930
----------------------
```

Mears seemed to deflate. He leaned against the circuit box and held on to it as though if he let go he would fall.

"What's it mean?" Murphy asked.

"Sensors nine, fourteen, fifteen, and eighteen were tripped last night, each one twice, going in and going out," Mears said. His voice was hoarse. "Side walkway, side service door, front servants' stairwell, hallway leading south from the library. And the X designation is a rough indication of the weight of whatever tripped the sensors. It was something in excess of two hundred kilograms."

Nix whispered, "The boss goes on a shooting spree."

"Okay, you've seen the bad news," Sato said. "And the last of the bad news is that you're retiring, as of this morning, and appointing Murphy your successor. Here's the good news. The Resistance needs your skills. You can't be in charge here, but you can come back to Home Plate and teach engineers from all over the continent to do some of the things you do. You can save lives and more than make up for the lives this screwup has cost. Or you can relocate with your compound and live the life of a retiree. As little as any compound can afford to support someone who isn't working, John Connor is pushing to have it happen here and there . . . so that people understand that if they live long enough, they can live out the rest of their lives without working themselves to death. But you have to decide what it's going to be."

"I'm not giving up my house."

"Understand me, those were the only two choices where you get to live." Sato's tone was hard. "Any choice where you try to keep charge of things, even what's about to be an empty shell of a compound, is a choice where the Resistance can't afford for you to survive. You would be captured and you might be induced to talk. Not just little bits and pieces, but years' worth of information might fall to Skynet that way. So, again, you have to decide between the choices I just gave you."

Mears finally turned his attention to Lana. "Where do *you* want to go?"

She kept her eyes down. "I think . . . I think . . ."

"Speak up, girl."

"Home Plate, I think."

Mears looked back to Sato. Putting on an expression of false cheer, he said, "I guess we're going to Home Plate."

"Then I'll stay with Clover," Lana said.

Mears stared at her. "Now you're being insolent."

"She's not going with you," J. L. said. He didn't put an arm around her, didn't make any sort of "She's with me" gesture. *Another point in his favor,* Sato thought. "You're going to have to do without her."

"Did I ask you to speak?" Mears's words came out in a bellow, the loudest Sato had ever heard him speak, and Lana flinched away from the fury in his tone. "You little grabby handed, greasy-haired piece of crap, did I appoint you to speak for this girl?"

J. L. didn't lean away, didn't respond with a punch, didn't react at all. He crossed his arms and stood there.

"I quit," Lana said.

"What?" Mears's tone returned to its normal volume.

Finally Lana met his eyes. "Raymond, I'm not mad at you. You've been very nice to me and I've been very nice to you, and I don't blame you for anything. But I quit."

"I won't let you."

An expression crossed Lana's features, a realization that she was trying to impart knowledge to someone incapable of accepting it. "I'm sorry. You're not in charge anymore."

They reentered the mess hall, where the crowd of breakfasters had only just begun to thin. Mears, moving at last like an elderly man, walked to the center of the hall, the Scalpers, Murphy, and Lana gathered behind him, and raised his hands for attention. The noise of conversation abated almost instantly.

"I have an announcement to make," Mears said. "After many years of serving you as leader . . . I'm being betrayed by members of my own staff. These people are kidnapping me and plan to destroy the compound—"

His words were choked off by Jenna the Greek, who got an arm around his throat and squeezed.

Sato saw the situation begin to play out as though it were in slow motion. Men and women all over the mess began to stand, some of them, a handful, pulling out firearms and readying them, looking from one to the other as if to sort out the confusion. The Scalpers brought out their own guns; Sato had his own in hand before he realized it. In a matter of moments, the Scalpers stood in a circle, facing out, guns ready, against a superior and ever-growing number of people pointing guns straight at them.

"You dumb bastard," Sato hissed. Then he raised his voice to be heard above the rising roar from the crowd. "Everyone, stay calm. Colonel Mears is not telling the truth—and I'll tell you facts you can confirm."

From the back of the crowd rose something glittering. Before Sato could quite recognize it as a bottle, one of the numberless old glass containers the Clover Compound residents used as drinking vessels, it crashed into the side of Jenna the Greek's head.

It didn't break. It made an unhealthy *ponk* noise, then fell to the floor and smashed. Jenna the Greek staggered, but kept her grip on Mears and her handgun.

Murphy raised his hands, trying to bring order. "Sato's telling the truth—"

Mears got his hands under Jenna's forearms and pushed, giving him a little room to breathe. "Murphy's the traitor! He's sold you all out! He just wants my job—"

Jenna tightened her grip, but with Mears's hands in place resisting her, she couldn't quite choke off his words.

Tactics flashed through Sato's mind, instantly evaluated, instantly rejected as each one seemed likely to get everyone killed.

"Bubba's real name is Eugene!" It was a female voice, and it was high and loud enough to cut through clamor filling the air.

Sato turned to look at the woman who had shrieked those unlikely words. It was Lana, standing on the bench of the nearest table, towering over those who surrounded her. She looked, her expression sorrowful, at a large white man whose hair and beard were a thick, consistent gray. "Isn't it, Bubba?"

The clamor quieted a little, and Sato saw confusion on other people's faces, confusion matching his own.

"How did you know?" Bubba asked. He sounded more surprised than pained by the sudden revelation.

"Raymond told me. In the library of his house, topside, where we go for privacy." Before anyone could cut into her words, Lana spun, located another face, and said, "Maria, you got convicted for embezzling from Mears Enterprises. That's how he knew you were good with inventories. Right?"

The woman she spoke to, a middle-aged Latina, looked stricken. "He said he would never say anything."

"Well, he did, to me. He told me about everything. About all the private things you admitted to him." Lana turned again, looking from face to face. "He told me about the compound's secret operations, stuff you never knew about. And I told him I'd stay quiet, too. But I can't, not if people are going to get killed for it." Lana was crying now, her face seeking forgiveness from the people she addressed even as she spilled their secrets.

In Jenna's grip, Mears was still struggling, but no longer talking.

Lana raised her voice once more: "*And every time we talked up there, Skynet was listening.* Lieutenant Sato showed us how. Skynet knows all about Clover Compound and is just going to use us until it stops getting information. Then we all get to die. Raymond just won't admit that it's true."

Sato began to breathe a little easier. The faces of those in the crowd, hostile and deadly in their attention to the Scalpers a moment ago, were now turning to suspicion and bewilderment . . . directed against Mears, not them. Sato saw several of the handguns angle away from the Scalpers.

Mears uttered a final moan and his eyes rolled up in his head. He slumped in Jenna's grasp. She lowered him to the hard floor—

Then he was up on his feet, pushing Jenna to send her staggering away. Sato and Nix lunged forward to grab him, but Mears was already among the crowd. A large man ducking out of Nix's way stepped right into Sato's path; Sato caromed off him and staggered back into a table, while Nix found himself jammed into the panicky crowd.

And then Mears was through the crowd, ducking down one of the numerous tunnels that entered the mess hall.

"Crap," Sato said. He shoved himself to his feet and took a quick look around, evaluating the crowd.

Members of Clover Compound were shouting at him, at Murphy, demanding answers. But guns weren't being pointed in their direction. The situation was chaotic, but the danger was defused. He ignored the people barraging him with questions.

"Jenna, stay with Lana," he shouted. "Get a medic to see to your head."

"My head's fine—"

Sato tapped the rank insignia on his shoulder, personal shorthand for "Shut up and follow orders." Jenna shut up. "Nix, can you find your way back to the high airflow chamber?"

Nix nodded.

"Get up there and keep Mears from exiting that way. Smart, J. L., main exit, ditto." He turned to Murphy. "Any ideas?"

Murphy extended his hands, waving away the questions coming at him. "Pipe down, everybody. I'll get to you." He turned to Sato. "I don't have a clue."

"You think he's going to run for it?"

"Not by any of the main exits. And to go out any of the emergency evacuation tunnels would be to open up a hole Skynet observers could detect."

Sato shook his head. "Would that stop him? He's got to admit to himself by now that Skynet knows about Clover Compound."

"Yeah, but opening an exit that Skynet could see would precipitate an attack, wouldn't it? I don't think he's selfish enough to get all his people killed like that."

"So what's he going to do? Where's he going to go?"

"Probably his office, first."

They marched into the office where Mears had conducted his first conversation with Sato. Someone had been there in recent minutes. The desk drawers were open. So was the door to a stand-up locker. Contents of both were disarrayed—papers and office supplies in one, jackets and outdoor equipment in the other—but they weren't empty. "What did he take?"

Murphy looked over the desk drawer and shook his head. He pawed through the contents of the locker and said, "All his weapons and gear are still here. The only thing that's missing here is a bottle of prewar sippin' whisky. From his desk, I don't know."

The intercom on the desk buzzed. Murphy punched a button on it. "Murphy."

"Uh, sir, we've had a communication from Outpost Four. They say they've found a stray. An injured girl."

"From where?"

"She's apparently not sure. They say she's had a head injury and is still pretty confused. She gives her name as Gwendolyn Drew."

Sato stiffened.

Murphy gave him a curious look. "Looks like you picked the right compound to start your search," he said.

"Looks that way."

There was a little suspicion to Murphy's expression as he depressed the intercom key again. "Tell the outpost to bring her in, and to tell her she's got friends at Clover Compound."

"Yes, sir."

Murphy straightened from the desk. "What the hell's going on?"

"Can't tell you."

"You come here, wreck the whole order of our compound, hand the reins to me with a little advisory that I've got to close the place down and find something else to do *after training for years to take charge here,* and you can't tell me?"

"That's right."

Murphy cursed. Then he returned his attention to the locker. "He didn't take his outdoor gear. He's not trying to run. He's gone off somewhere private to get drunk."

"Does he do that often?"

"Never."

"What are his private places?"

"Well, there was his topside retreat."

"Which you knew about."

"Yeah, I knew about it. A second-in-command has to know where his boss is at all times." Murphy didn't look repentant. "There's his bedroom. I sent a couple of guards there. Since they haven't reported, it's pretty clear he didn't go there. There's this office, and there's whatever his current engineering project is . . . but he hasn't commenced one in the last year. So that's it."

"No, no, no. Someplace has got to have some memories for him, someplace he'd want to revisit."

Murphy thought about it for a moment. "Yeah. Maybe."

■ ■ ■

Sato and Murphy marched down the long, unlit tunnel; only the beams of their flashlights offered any illumination. The place was dusty and silent. Here, more so than anywhere else in Clover Compound, Sato imagined he could feel the weight of millions of tons of stony mountain pressing down upon him.

From up ahead, distantly, came a call. "Good morning." It was Mears's voice, cheerful and unconcerned.

Murphy swept his flashlight beam back and forth, trying to spot the speaker. "Raymond, what the hell are you doing down here?"

"Visiting old friends."

Finally Murphy's beam caught Mears. The old man was sitting, a tall whisky bottle in his hand, and at first glance it looked as though he'd recently lost both legs at about midthigh, but it was a trick of topography and lighting. As Murphy and Sato got closer, it became clear that Mears was sitting on the far side of a hole, dangling his legs. The shaft, easily a dozen feet in diameter, appeared to descend straight down into the rock.

Finally Sato spoke. "So that's Satan's Hole."

Mears raised his bottle, his expression merry, and knocked back a slug of its amber-colored contents. "It is. But it's not as sinister a place as most of the people here make it out to be. I really only put two people down there over the years, mostly in the early days. Jake Kinney and Lawanda Beeker. They wanted to take control away from me, wouldn't compromise, wouldn't leave." The old man shrugged. "I loved 'em both. I killed 'em both. My way or the highway, and all that. But they weren't as good as you, Sato. Or maybe I'm just too old to fight off the coups anymore. Hey, that's far enough."

Sato and Murphy stopped advancing. They were now ten paces from the near lip of Satan's Hole, and Mears was on the far lip, facing them.

"I don't get it, Mears," Sato said. "Why'd you run off if you were just going to sit down with a drink? You could have done that in your office without all the exercise."

"I just told you. My way. My way. You ordered me to hand over control of the compound on your schedule, at your convenience— well, I didn't. You couldn't make me. You don't order me, ever. I win. You lose. Still . . ." Mears shrugged. "I don't plan to make things any harder than necessary. Murph, I wrote out a confirmation of my abdication and your appointment. I left it in the bottom airflow chamber in the main control cabinet. It should smooth out the succession."

"So, what now?" Sato asked.

"I retire. I've been retired for thirty minutes. Feels pretty good. Now I take my ball and go home. You familiar with that phrase, Lieutenant?"

"Yeah."

"It's the kind of thing people who don't like to compromise used to say. No compromising, no sharing, no bending." Mears held the bottle toward them as if intending to hand it to them. He grinned. "*My* whisky." He dropped it. It fell for long seconds, and then there was the distant sound of glass shattering. "Hey, Lawanda, Jake, have a drink on me."

There was strain in Murphy's voice. "Raymond—"

"No, please. Don't waste my time. I have an appointment. One thing, though. Tell that girl I really did like her. She can have anything of mine she wants. What she doesn't want goes to you, Murph."

"Don't—"

Mears pushed off. He seemed to hang there in the air for a moment, his eyes big, evaluating these two lesser officers one last time, and then he dropped out of sight.

Sato and Murphy rushed forward. But even before they reached the lip, there was the sound of a distant impact from below—a meaty blow. Sato thought he could hear crunching and breaking noises mixed in.

They shone their flashlights down Satan's Hole, but the beams were not strong enough to reach all the way to the bottom.

c.11

The Scalpers gathered at the main entrance, huddled together by their dune buggies, away from the entrance guards and the vehicle mechanics, who spoke in hushed tones about the day's events.

To Sato, the situation seemed a little tense and emotional, but did not speak to him of danger. No one was shooting angry stares their way. There was curiosity, there was finger-pointing . . . there was no desire for vengeance that he could see. On the other side of the chamber, Murphy stood in a gathering of subordinates, issuing orders to each in turn, dispatching them on various errands. He was inarguably in charge now.

Sato shook his head. It was one of the advantages of dealing with control freaks like Mears, he decided. They did run tight organizations and left behind very clear lines of control.

"How's your head?" he asked Jenna.

She shook her head, a vigorous gesture. "Hard Mediterranean skull, like they've been making for millions of years."

"Too sturdy for anything to penetrate," Nix said.

She gave him a half-amused look that promised payback. "J. L. needs to say goodbye to Lana."

"I did," J. L. said. "I told her she ought to put in for a transfer to Home Plate or somewhere. I keep thinking they may give her trouble here because she was the boss's woman, a nonworker."

"Did you apologize to her?" Jenna asked.

J. L. looked offended. "What for?"

"For saying that she was dumb as a box of hair."

"I didn't say it to *her*."

"Yeah, but you were thinking it every moment you were with

her. Up until the point that she was smart enough to save our butts in the mess hall."

His sigh signaled defeat. "Yeah, you're right."

"You won't have the opportunity this time," Sato said. "Just as soon as we've had our first meeting with the she-toaster from hell, we jump in the buggies and clear out. We can't let her be here long enough to pick up the news about Mears's death or anything else."

Jenna turned her attention to the far side of the chamber, to the huge concrete door that remained resolutely shut. "Are they going to bring her in *here*?"

"Uh-huh." Sato checked his watch. Arrival could be in two minutes or twenty. "And remember, we're the only ones here, Murphy included, who know what she is. Anyone not up to the task of driving hundreds of miles with a Terminator in your backseat?"

Jenna the Greek offered a little shudder, but no one spoke up.

"Okay," Sato said. "Just remember, this is a life-or-death deception. And remember that we have no idea of the extent of her sensors and that she might be able to plant remotes, microphones, something like that, to spy on us even when she's off at a distance.

"What this means is that, starting the first moment we meet the girl, we're doing live theater. And we have to remain in character from that point until the team down south bags her. No private communications by whispered word, written note, or glance. If she's in one buggy and you're in the other, don't talk about her being a T-X. We have to assume that she's listening to us at every point and that Skynet has a spy satellite trained on us for every mile. Is anyone not up to the job?"

No one spoke. Everyone looked as though he wanted to.

"Good." He clapped his sniper on the back. "Smart, I have a special assignment for you. For the next couple of days, at least until she makes it clear she wants you to quit, I want you to flirt with Gwendolyn."

Smart blinked at him. "Sir, I mean this with all respect. Are you out of your mind?"

"Nope. Think about it. Four red-blooded Resistance men traveling in the company of a good-looking young woman who hasn't already told them all to go to hell. *Somebody* would hit on her. Correct?"

Smart looked more than a little uncomfortable. "Correct. But not me."

"Yes, you. I'm the team leader and authority figure, I can't do it. J. L. is dreamy-eyed over another girl right now; I doubt he could pull it off."

The youngest member of the team looked offended. "Hey."

"And Nix, well, being Nix, he wouldn't take no for an answer, even from a Terminator. I need someone who's going to be stiff, self-conscious, and easily put off—and that's you."

Smart sighed. "Is this the kind of praise you put in our performance reviews?" Then a new thought crossed his mind. "Oh, my God. What if I make a pass at her and she accepts?"

Sato considered it, then laughed. "Improvise."

Jenna frowned. "Lieutenant, wait; this thing is going to fall apart at the start. They'll bring her in here, the dogs will go crazy, she'll know her cover is blown, and there'll be bodies everywhere. How do we keep that from happening?"

"We don't," Sato said. "We don't have to. Skynet would never have sent her to be picked up and brought in to a compound for this deception if it weren't sure she could pass for human . . . even to the dogs. If that were going to be a problem, she would have found some other way to hook up with the Resistance, such as meeting us out on the road. Of course, the idea that she could fool dogs is bad news in and of itself. Good thing Skynet can't manufacture T-Xs at any sort of quick rate."

There was a flurry of motion among workers in the entry chamber. Two security men trotted to their station against one wall to pick up their assault rifles, to reassure the dogs waiting there. A woman in the same uniform ducked into a side door, beyond which, Sato now knew, was installed the equipment that allowed monitoring of exterior cameras, opening and closing of the armored main door. Murphy issued final orders and waved goodbye to Sato, then departed with his final group of subordinates. Now the chamber was empty of people except the Scalpers and essential security personnel.

Moments later, the far wall swung open, almost silent, on its pivot. A group of three people entered on foot. Two, a man and a woman, were in the dark blue uniforms of Clover Compound and carrying full outdoor kit and rifles. The third, wrapped in a blanket that concealed everything but her face and the shapeless dark green pants she wore, was Gwendolyn Drew.

Sato concentrated on keeping his face still, his emotions buried well below the surface, but reality itself felt as though it were slipping away from him. He knew the woman was fiction, but here she was in the flesh. Well, in the artificial, made-of-liquid-metal flesh.

The woman looked uncertain, confused, and raised a hand against the blare of lights from the chamber's ceiling. The security men approached with the dogs, and Sato could hear them tell her to extend her hands. She did.

Both dogs sniffed at her. One stepped back and wagged its tail. The other looked up at its handler and whined uncertainly. Neither barked. That was the acid test.

The security men relaxed, leading the dogs back to their ready position, and Sato approached. "Gwendolyn?"

Her attention snapped to him. She continued to look uncertain and gathered the blanket more tightly around her. "Uh-huh," she said.

"I'm Christopher Sato, Lieutenant, Resistance 1st Security Regiment. You probably don't remember me, but we met once when you were a little girl."

She shook her head. "I don't—Lieutenant, I don't really remember much of anything." Her voice was mellow, mature for her apparent years, a little subdued. Sato would have bet his left arm that it was based on existing recordings of Sarah Connor, perhaps from the years she was incarcerated in a California mental institution.

"How's that?"

"I remember falling. When I woke up, there was blood all over a rock, and the creek I was next to had washed away most of my gear." She touched her left temple. "Beyond that, I don't remember much, except my name, and the fact that I needed to get to Home Plate."

Sato nodded. It was a good cover story. Amnesia was never as commonplace as the twentieth-century entertainment media had suggested, but it did happen, and Sato himself had known people who'd had short-term or long-term memory loss, particularly related to injury or other battle trauma. And this story would keep the woman from making potentially deadly errors of fact during the trip to come.

He reached for her. "May I?"

"Sure."

He touched her head where she had indicated, carefully running his fingers along her temple and in widening circles around it. Her skin moved in a natural way under his touch, and he could feel a bony ridge where one shouldn't be beneath her skin.

At this distance, he could smell her. She smelled like snow and wool blanket, and beneath those odors was a faint but distinct taint of human sweat.

Amazing what they can do these days, he thought.

He stepped back. "You've taken quite a hit. I suspect there's a little calcium buildup against your skull. Are you having any trouble with blurred vision, dizziness, ringing sounds?"

She shook her head. "Not after the first few days. I feel good. I just wish I could remember things."

"Well, I'll tell you what. My job is to deliver you right into the hands of your uncle John. I suspect that seeing him will jar those memories right back into your head."

"That would be wonderful. I hate, I really hate not remembering."

Sato smiled to cover the sudden revulsion he felt. "We were actually ready to leave when we got the word that you'd been found. So we're set to go. Do you want to see a medic? Need anything to eat?"

She shook her head. "No, I'm fine. I don't even have any belongings to get together. I can leave any time."

Are you feeling the machine equivalent of excitement? Sato wondered. *Hydraulic fluids coursing through your tubes a little faster than normal, now that you're really on the track of John Connor?* Her face didn't give away any such emotion.

"All right. Gwendolyn, this is Sergeant Vandis, Sergeant Smart, Corporal Friedman, Corporal Larson. We've already got a standard-issue field pack for you in the dune buggy."

"Thank you," she said. "It's great to be in friendly hands again."

Sangre de Cristo Mountains, New Mexico

Paul turned the key in the ignition and the dirt bike roared into life. The high-pitched roar of the 292cc engine echoed up and down the concrete ramps that made up what the workers were now calling Mechanics' Alley, drowning out the sounds of socket wrenches, welding torches, and mechanics' curses. Paul twisted the throttle, causing the roar to swell and diminish in an archaic machine song of the open road.

He killed the engine. He could hear workers up and down Mechanics' Alley applaud, which they did for every vehicle brought back to life, even when Paul Keeley was the resurrector. He offered a little wave of acknowledgment in each direction, like the Queen of England receiving the accolades of her subjects with dignity or disinterest, then turned to wiping his oil-stained hands on the rag hanging out of his back pocket.

"Pretty good," someone said. "Reminds me of the old days."

Paul turned. The speaker, leaning against the nearest wall, was John Connor.

Paul wondered for a moment how people were supposed to react when the leader of the Resistance, the modern equivalent of the President of the United States, just popped up out of nowhere for idle chit-chat. He decided to ignore the man's rank. It was an easy and natural decision, despite the fact that conversational choices had never been easy or natural for him before his capture. "You ride?"

"Oh, yeah. Since I was a kid. When I was a teenager, I did a lot of riding with Crazy Pete." The former head of the Scalpers had been a onetime bike gang member, small-time criminal, and government-hating rebel.

"You knew him that long ago?"

"Uh-huh. He and I killed the last dinosaur together."

Paul stared, confused, then realized he was being kidded. He snorted.

John continued, "I was riding the day before Judgment Day, in fact. A beat-up old Triumph Bonneville. I loved that bike. It was like home. Now it's rust or slag somewhere, I suppose. Anyway, I'm thinking that if you bring the other bike to life, I'll take one and you can have the other one."

"You're kidding."

"No, when I kid, it's usually like 'He and I killed the last dinosaur together.'"

"Which one do you want?"

"The one that's in better shape."

"And what if I put them in identically good shape?"

John raised a finger in an "Aha!" gesture. "Now you've stumbled across my motivational tactic."

There was a *tap-tap-tap* of hard soles on concrete flooring, and Kate Brewster, her daughter Kyla and dogs in tow, came trotting down the ramp. When she was close enough not to shout, Kate said, "The Scalpers radioed in short code. They're on the road. And they've got 'Gwendolyn Drew' with them."

John straightened away from the wall, his expression changing. Paul saw him alter, like a T-1000 transforming from one person into another, from a motorcycle enthusiast to the Resistance leader he normally was in public. "With the route they're supposed to take, it'll be a minimum of four days until they reach Santa Fe," he said. "We need to issue orders that there not be any vehicle departures from this site after two more days—other than my group heading to Santa Fe. Skynet's going to be concentrating its attention on the zone immediately around the T-X, fifty or a hundred miles in diameter from her."

Kyla waved a hand to be noticed. "As the one bodyguard you have present, I have to point out that you don't need to be there. Even if the T-X doesn't know that Santa Fe is going to be the final stop, Skynet's sure to be able to bring in some additional forces when she sends out the alert that you've been spotted. It'd be kind of a damned shame if we captured her and lost you. Not an equal trade."

John shook his head. "I do have to be there. So she'll open up, display her weaponry. If we want to capture her instead of destroy her, I have to show my face."

Kyla sighed. "You are so stubborn."

Kate smiled at her daughter. It was almost a smirk. "Guess what, baby? You inherited those genes."

Kyla turned away. "Then I'm never having kids. I don't want to pass that curse along." She headed back up the ramp.

John put his hand around his wife's waist and led her the other way, into the depths of the complex. "We've got the site?" he asked.

"We've got the site. A small community center."

"The cables are in place, and the capacitors?"

"What do you think?"

"I think yes."

"Good for you."

They descended out of Paul's sight. He stood, aware that he'd been privy to intimate family moments he had no right to witness. He just didn't know whether he'd seen them because the Connors were comfortable with his presence or knew he'd be dying soon and wasn't worth worrying about.

But the evidence was leaning toward the suggestion Kyla had offered. Why would John Connor offer him the motorcycle if he were scheduled for elimination?

It was hard not to believe Connor. He knew the Resistance leader could be ruthless and dangerous. But, at an emotional level, he didn't want to believe that the man could be so duplicitous with a human in his employ.

So Paul, slow and deliberate, allowed himself to move from resignation to hope.

It was time to get to work on the other dirt bike.

Rocky Mountains, Colorado and New Mexico

Buckled into his seat, Sato sat atop a folded-up blanket for extra cushioning, but it wasn't enough. The road they traveled on was beating his internal organs into mush.

After all, it wasn't really a road. It was a railway track, and the Scalpers' two dune buggies cruised along it as quickly as they could while retaining control. It wasn't easy; though the railway ties were in many places decayed to wood flakes by decades of weather, along many places they were surprisingly intact. The dune buggies' suspension, though improved for the rough terrain the Scalpers often had to cross, wasn't up to dealing with mile after mile of ties.

Jenna the Greek, driving, shot him a dirty look. He ignored her.

Now they were cruising along a raised train route, paralleling a mountain road that was about a hundred yards away. Farther ahead, the road would turn away, following the curve of the mountain, while the train route would plow straight into the mountainside.

From the backseat, Gwendolyn leaned forward between them. Her cheeks were flushed, an artful simulation of what the combination of excitement and cold air would do to a young woman's face. "I don't want to sound like I'm complaining, but—"

"But why the rough road?" Sato asked.

"Right."

"We figure that Skynet calculates that most human traffic will be along the paths of least resistance. That by machine standards, we're frail, so we have to take the most comfortable path. So we do just the reverse. Plus, all the tunnels break up any continuity of infrared trace that we might be leaving, making it harder for Skynet to assemble them into a clear picture of a caravan on a specific route." This was a complete lie, a fabrication. But part of Sato's job on this mission, as outlined by Kate Brewster, was to provide disinformation to the T-X. If she transmitted it back to Skynet and the machine intelligence believed, there could be a slight shift in the allocation of machine resources, another tiny, incremental advantage for the Resistance.

"Oh."

"Standard operating procedure. But it's kind of hard on the kidneys, isn't it?"

"It sure is." Gwendolyn leaned back, apparently satisfied with the answer.

They entered the tunnel and Jenna the Greek turned on the buggy's headlights. Behind them, the buggy carrying Smart, Nix, and J. L. did likewise.

It was also strange doing so much travel in daylight. Normally a unit like the Scalpers traveled some by day, some by night, choosing different travel hours in each twenty-four-hour span, but on this trip they simply traveled by day. It was faster because they could travel for longer uninterrupted blocks of time, could see obstacles at a greater average distance. But, again, it was a matter of disinformation. Any little bit might help.

Plus, Sato knew that he was safer now than he had ever been when traveling in the open. Skynet was not going to "detect" them. There would be no assaults on this caravan. Skynet would keep its distance, constantly updating its information, trying to guess at their destination. It would have forces ready all along their path, but would want to concentrate them at the site that was its best guess as to where John Connor would be. Sato had arranged for the caravan to pack enough food and water and had dropped a few hints in conversation to suggest that this trip would be much longer than it was actually going to be, perhaps ending in the vicinity of San Antonio, Texas, rather than Santa Fe, New Mexico.

Disinformation.

Three spine-hammering stretches of road and three more tunnel passages later, the sun began to disappear behind mountain peaks. At the next point a paved road crossed their path, Sato directed Jenna off the train tracks.

They set up camp a mile from there, beneath a roadway bridge that spanned a rocky V-shaped gorge. It was a cold camp, with canned fruit, canned meat, and hard bread for the campers.

Sato watched Gwendolyn eat. She seemed completely natural, completely human.

Before darkness fell fully across them, Sato saw Smart sidle up alongside Gwendolyn, whisper in her ear.

She turned a little smile on the sniper, offered a slight shake of the head. She spoke in tones too low for Sato to hear, but he could read a few of the words from her lips: "just be friends."

Smart made a good show of a disappointed retreat. Jenna the Greek held her hand before her, moving it this way and that to simulate the movement of an aircraft, and then mimed it veering into the bridge's support column, exploding. Smart glared at her.

Sato nodded to himself, still on edge, but satisfied. *This is going to work.*

c.12

Santa Fe, New Mexico

The cool, comfortable mountain community had, just before J-Day, been a lovely but overpriced haven for artists and craftsmen. It had not suffered too much physical damage. As with any prewar human community, its buildings had decayed, untended, for close to three decades. But no bombs had dropped here; the city had not, from a military perspective, been important enough for Skynet to waste nuclear weapons on. In the years since, it had remained mercifully free of fires. Whole neighborhoods still stood, rows of adobe houses built with curious wall angles, their roofs crumbling and their lawns filled with weeds, and it was still recognizably a city.

Perhaps, John thought, *once Skynet falls, people can come back here and pick up their lives where they left off.* He wondered what that would be like. Before Judgment Day, he'd never had a place he considered home, so if Skynet were defeated and John retired, he had no place to go. Perhaps he'd continue living in the hidey-holes of Home Plate, like a fairy king under a cairn.

He sat in a second-story hallway in a neighborhood civic center. The desk where he sat was in a hallway beside a shattered window, and early afternoon sun was beginning to slant into his eyes. It was nice to see the sun, nice to let it fall on his face and banish some of the pallor he inevitably acquired from too much time in safe habitats. A little touch of tan made him look healthier, and the people he led unconsciously preferred a healthy-looking leader.

The building, all of tan stone, looked like a stubby three-story wheel hub with four short two-story spokes projecting from it. The hub was mostly a gymnasium, with a regulation basketball court flanked by wooden stands that could be pulled out accordion-style or pushed back flush against the walls. The spokes held meeting rooms. The building's engineering was unlike that of the angular homes of this upscale neighborhood, but still idiosyncratic enough to somehow fit in.

Kate emerged from a nearby stairwell and took the chair next to him. "Sato has reported in."

John felt the little thrill that meant that his moment of quiet, of rest, was over. "How far out?"

"About twenty-five miles. With good roads in front of them. They'll be here in less than an hour."

"The rig's all set?"

She smiled. He'd asked the same thing an hour ago. "All set."

"Everyone in position?"

"Uh-huh."

"Did we finally get a bird?"

"We got a coyote."

John felt his eyebrows rise. "A *coyote*. Who got it?"

"Who do you think? Our daughter. Ginger and Ripper ran it to ground—and while it was at bay Kyla threw a net over it."

"A coyote. Well, that's probably even better than a bird."

"I think so. You know, you'd better be out of this window well before they get here. Else the T-X or some support robot may decide to take a shot at you and end the whole operation before we get anything good out of it."

"You're right."

"Well?"

"If I get up *right now*, you'll know you're *completely* right. I can't have that. You'll get cocky. I have to let you think you're only *mostly* right. So I'll get up in a minute."

She sighed. "Were you ever sane?"

"Take a good look at our kids and ask that question again."

She rose and headed back to the stairwell. Over her shoulder, she called, "One minute."

"One minute," he promised.

Had she been able to feel human emotions, rather than merely simulate them, the T-X would still have been calm and in control as the two Scalpers' dune buggies turned down yet another Santa Fe street. Any human with the T-X's specific set of goals would have been a killer, icy cold in most situations, and as the dune buggies wound their way deeper and deeper into this long-abandoned neighborhood, she was under the impression that they were still days from their destination.

Still, something was not right. As many towns and cities as the Scalpers had grazed or bypassed on their trip down from Colorado, this was the first one they had entered so deeply. The human female driver, too, seemed unfamiliar with their destination or short-term goal. The commander, Sato, had to contribute to the accomplishment of the driver's goals by providing directions at intervals.

The T-X leaned forward between driver and Sato as her programming cycled through to a combination of emotions designated CURIOUS and CONFUSED BUT UNALARMED. "I don't get it," she said in Sarah Connor's voice. "Are we camping early today?"

Sato looked at her. His facial muscles bent his expression into an atypical configuration, which signaled the T-X that he was attempting to communicate through that means. As he spoke, her nonverbal communication interpreters overlaid a wire frame on his face, conformed it to his current expression, contrasted it with his default range of expressions, and arrived at a set of probabilities. The display superimposed in transparent letters over his face read:

61%	HUMOR (SLY AMUSEMENT, RETAINING INFORMATION TO AMUSE SELF AND/OR OTHERS WHO POSSESS THE RETAINED INFORMATION)
11%	MENACE (SCAN FOR ADDITIONAL OVERT AND COVERT INDICATIONS OF VIOLENT INTENT)
9%	DESIRE
19%	MISCELLANEOUS POSSIBILITIES (ACTIVATE SUBMENU TO EXAMINE)

"We're not camping here," Sato said. "We have a little surprise for you."

The T-X dismissed menace and desire; Sato had provided no previous indications of such emotions, at least as they might apply to her. And his words were a strong reinforcement of the leading probability. She cycled through options, combined facial expressions of intrigued interest and continued curiosity, and settled back in her seat.

She also sent out a pulse broadcast to the nearest Skynet resources: UNSCHEDULED SIDE TRIP, UNSPECIFIED SECONDARY GOAL. MAINTAIN DISTANCE.

A large building ahead of them appeared to be their short-term destination. It was the one distinctive, nonresidence building in a region made up of single-family dwellings. The T-X deduced from its shape that it might be a small professional sports arena or community gathering center. There was even some possibility that it could be a church or temple belonging to a nontraditional religious order.

The two vehicles turned into the parking lot, and a set of double doors in the side of the hub portion of the building opened outward, pushed open by a pair of Resistance soldiers.

They drove straight into the building, stopping just inside the doors. The soldiers pulled the doors shut behind them, plunging the gym into comparative darkness. The only light came from long horizontal windows close to the ceiling; some were partially intact but lined with paint, while others were entirely shattered. The T-X's eyes adapted instantly to the change in brightness, but she still blinked and affected to experience a humanlike delay in adjustment.

They were in a main chamber that had to occupy almost all the volume of the central hub of the building, and the presence of basketball hoops at either end, plus bulky, nonfunctional lighting rigs thickly clustered among the steel beams and supports of the ceiling, confirmed its purpose as a sporting arena of some sort. There were numerous humans already here; the T-X saw two at the doors and two others at an odd horizontally striated wooden portion of one side wall. The latter two, a male and a female, immediately began walking in their direction.

The T-X's visual scanners checked each face for a match with her memory. One of them, a man who had opened one of the exterior doors, struck an instant match. Lieutenant Tom Carter, a highly placed technician with the Resistance, one who was often in contact with John Connor and Kate Brewster. Suddenly this encounter began to climb in estimated importance.

Jenna the Greek killed the dune buggy's motor and the T-X heard Charles Smart shut down the other motor vehicle. All the Scalpers piled out of the vehicles. "Bathroom break," Jenna said. "Hey, Lieutenant, where's the jakes?"

Tom Carter waved her toward a far corner of the large room, ahead and toward the right. Most of the Scalpers followed Jenna in that direction, their walks demonstrating stiffness but calm.

Sato didn't. "Tom, where's the package?"

Carter gestured toward a door in the center of the wall almost straight ahead. "He's anxious to see her," the older man said.

"I'll just bet. Gwendolyn, if you'd do me a favor, head over to the door Lieutenant Carter pointed out. We have a little present for you."

"A present." The T-X cycled through possible emotional responses. She settled on continued curiosity merged with dubiousness.

"Really. You'll love it, I promise."

"Uh-huh." The T-X headed in the indicated direction.

She was halfway across the gymnasium when that far door opened and a man entered. The T-X's visual scanners picked out his face, analyzed it, and returned a match.

John Connor. She was within sight of her supreme priority.

She broadcast a compressed message: JOHN CONNOR AT THIS LOCATION. COMMENCING TERMINATION. MOVE IN ALL UNITS FOR CAPTURE AND TERMINATION OF SECONDARY UNITS. Then she adjusted her body language so that her walk would suggest uncertainty and disbelief, adjusted her vocal patterns likewise. "Uncle John?"

"Gwen, thank God." John Connor did not look surprised. Of course he did not. He was expecting her. His bodyguard unit was bringing her to him.

But he was still standing too close to the exit. If she revealed her weapon now, he might have the opportunity to run through the doorway, to be out of her sight for a moment. That was unacceptable. Her tactical display came up with an option that had a high probability of dictating John Connor's response. She accepted the recommendation and, in an authentic simulation of a human woman momentarily overcome by emotion, sank to her knees, causing her face to register relief and shock.

John Connor hesitated for a moment in the doorway, which registered to the T-X as a curious anomaly. Then he moved forward, walking slowly, his eyes searching her as if looking for a physical cause for her own hesitation.

She reached out toward him. Her months of interaction with Paul Keeley had demonstrated that humans responded strongly and instinctively to such a gesture. And John Connor did pick up his pace.

He was ten paces from the door now. He could not escape in time. She caused the liquid metal sheath to withdraw from her right arm, revealing the mechanisms beneath, and caused them to reconfigure into her plasma cannon.

Then fluid cascaded across the T-X from above.

Secondary objectives, including self-preservation, asserted themselves. A visual sweep of less than a second's duration would not give John Connor time or opportunity to escape her and could therefore be accomplished without endangering her primary objective. She glanced up.

A broad net made of metal cables, trailing more cables, landed upon her.

Though heavy enough to hinder a human, it would not hinder her. Though it was made of durable metal materials, she calculated that she could tear through it in a matter of moments. She would not do so until her primary objective was accomplished, however. The net would not prevent her from taking aim and incinerating John Connor, even though he was now in mid-turn and preparing to flee.

She broadcast a quick indication that her current situation was an ambush and that all remote unit activities she had called for were still to be implemented. Then she aimed, blue electrical discharges dancing around the end of plasma apparatus.

Far overhead, in the wooden platform hastily built to give her a safe perch among the ceiling girders, Kate Brewster pressed a rocker switch to touch off the first of the detonators.

They weren't connected to conventional explosions. Instead, they were wired to a series of capacitors, each of which could discharge enough voltage to blow the circuitry of a good-sized office building.

Below, the disguised T-X jerked and spasmed as the first blast of electricity coursed through her. No blast of superheated matter emerged from her right arm. For this second—and this second only—John Connor was safe from incineration.

Kate threw the second switch.

■ ■ ■

John made it to the doorway, ducked through, and snatched up the plasma rifle waiting there, propped up against the door jamb. He turned to look.

First he saw the broad back of Mark Herrera, who had interposed himself between John and the T-X, a living shield who, if the T-X recovered, would absorb the first plasma blast and die to give John a chance for escape.

Not that he'd do so passively. He had an M-25 plasma pulse rifle at the ready. With his skill and experience Mark would probably get a few licks in before her first plasma shot eradicated him.

More Hell-Hounds and Scalpers were moving in, forming a semicircle. Most carried plasma rifles or rocket-propelled grenades. Kyla had her sniper rifle at the ready, its iron sights up.

The air was filled with overlapping roars: the sound of the T-X's batteries maintaining their charge prior to the plasma cannon firing; the sound of the electricity pouring through her body, causing the water beneath her, water that grounded her, to superheat into steam; and a shrill, sirenlike wail that seemed to come from the T-X's mouth—one of her nonverbal vocal forms of expression, its volume reaching its maximum level as the damaging electricity caused her to malfunction in countless ways.

Above it all came Kate's voice, a barely audible shout: "Three!"

Tom Carter joined the line of security specialists, an object like a brushed-aluminum briefcase in one hand, a handheld device that looked like an old-fashioned stun gun in the other.

"Two!"

The T-X toppled to one side, still jerking and jittering like a bug on a frying pan.

"One! Zero! Clear!"

The sounds of electrical discharge and the T-X's involuntary shriek ended. Tom Carter dashed forward, slipping as he hit the patch of water. He ran right up onto the metal net, heedless of the danger it represented were it to carry another electrical charge, and knelt straddling the Terminator.

He set the aluminum case down and threw it open. He set the smaller device against the T-X's neck and triggered it.

A small blue spark emerged, a much tinier manifestation of the plasma energy that had threatened John's life, and sliced into the T-X's skin.

Except, of course, it wasn't skin, not in the traditional sense. It parted under the tremendous energy from the plasma device and shrank away, liquid metal that had just been instructed by a strong heat and power source to flee the vicinity.

The retreat of the metal bared the T-X's endoskeleton, a silvery gleaming metal thing that was as inhuman and menacing as the T-X had just appeared human and inviting.

Carter cut into the endoskeleton just under the neck, severing whatever locking mechanism held protective plates in place, and raised a hinged piece about the size of a saucer. Even at this distance John could hear sputters and zaps from within that housing, the sound of the Terminator's internal systems desperately working to come back on-line.

Carter pulled wires from the aluminum case and set them within the T-X's body cavity. With a calm sureness that was more and more maddening to John as the seconds ticked by, he methodically connected them to components within the Terminator's torso.

The T-X's eyes, so much like those of John's mother, snapped open.

Carter reached into the aluminum case and flipped a switch. The T-X jerked a final time and then lay there, limp, staring up at her captor. Carter raised his hands like a rodeo cowboy who'd roped and thrown the world's deadliest calf.

Members of John's security teams applauded.

John lowered his rifle and joined them. "Everybody deserves congratulations," he said, "but we don't have time for them, not yet. If there are any Skynet forces within two hundred miles, they're on their way here. Prep her for transport." The bottom end of a rope ladder, ten feet too long, thumped onto the floor beside him. He ignored it and switched on his radio. "Target acquired," he said. "Prepare for incoming. Prepare for withdrawal."

There were no confirmations. He didn't want his outposts to give away their number and locations. His location, by contrast, was no longer a secret.

The T-X's eyes remained active, turning to look at Carter, at John, at Kate in turn. Carter continued at work, making quick, sure modifications to the machinery inside the Terminator. He stood aside briefly for the Hell-Hounds and Scalpers to draw the metal-cable net off the robot and for a pair of technicians to roll in a twentieth-century ambulance gurney. The two technicians, joined by Mark Herrera and Charles Smart, lifted the T-X's heavy frame onto the gurney, but the gurney's metal construction held up well to the weight. Then Carter got back to work.

Finally Carter stood back, a small amber-colored oval, like an inexpensive piece of jewelry, in his hand. "I think she's still broad-casting," he said, "though I've insulated her transmitting center from the frame of her body, meaning that I've deprived her of her primary and backup antenna. So her effective range should be very limited. And here's her tracer."

Kate held out her hand and Carter passed the object to her.

"All right," John said. "Implement Withdrawal Phase One."

The Hunter-Killer was the first Skynet unit to close in on the T-X's position.

Its immediate ancestors had been conceived of as flying cars—long carlike bodies with two sets of ducted rotors at either end, they would become the upscale replacement for the family car at some point early in the twenty-first century.

The Department of Defense helped fund the research into ever more-efficient ducted rotor systems, automated navigation systems, and gyroscopic stabilization systems, and developed its own design from the concept. Narrower and more insectile than the never-completed flying automobiles, the Hunter-Killer was intended as a fully automated, low-altitude aircraft with roles as a reconnaissance aircraft and tank-buster. Armed with sophisticated sensory gear and a number of air-to-ground and air-to-air missiles, it would have excelled at that task.

Now it was used exclusively to hunt and kill humans, and as it neared the civic center that was the T-X's last known location, it began to detect numerous signs of human activity.

Several blocks away, a pair of light recreational ground vehicles, of the sort designated "dune buggies," moved away from the civic center at high speed. Because they were outbound and possessed no useful contiguous line of sight on the H-K, the H-K designated them as no immediate threat. The T-X's tracer signal still emanated from the civic center, so the dune buggies were also not transporting that unit away. For the moment, they were irrelevant. The H-K transmitted data on the dune buggies to Skynet and continued its progress.

The civic center was surrounded by houses, and many of them were indicating heat traces, all near exterior windows. The H-K concluded that the hotter traces corresponded to one or more Resistance fighters currently stationed at window positions.

From a distance of three hundred yards, it targeted the nearest of the high-heat traces and fired a missile.

In an instant, the 1970-era two-story home around the heat trace exploded, the heat generated by the missile washing out all other video data from that direction. The shock wave was insufficient to buffet the H-K at this distance. The H-K transmitted a report of one Resistance combat position terminated.

A split second later, the H-K detected a new heat trace lighting up a street-level engineering element: an open manhole. Because the heat trace began there and then stretched at tremendous speed toward the H-K's position, the H-K concluded that it was a missile.

It did not have time to transmit this information to Skynet. The missile hit its forward port rotor housing and detonated, sending shredded remains of the H-K on a ballistic descent into a dozen houses below.

■ ■ ■

Corporal Ted Burnett ducked back down into the manhole. "Scratch one H-K," he told his partner. "Not to mention one space heater and battery pack."

His partner, Private Jane Connell, kept her attention on the storm drain stretching north and south from their position. "We've got more."

The Presidential Party—John, Kate, the Hell-Hounds, the Scalpers minus Jenna and Smart, Tom Carter, a nervous-looking soldier hefting a wriggling bag, and the two technicians rolling the T-X's gurney—reached the civic center's basement and the hole a C-4 charge had blown in one of its walls early that morning, long before the T-X or Skynet had known that Santa Fe was the Terminator's destination. Again, four of them were required to lift the gurney over the rubble from the detonation and into the storm-drain tunnel beyond the blast hole.

The helicopter, a meticulously maintained Chinook transport helicopter, approached the combat zone more cautiously than its predecessors had. Those predecessors, two H-Ks, now lay at the center of two zones of burning residences, one on either side of the civic center.

The caution didn't result from a sense of self-preservation on the part of the helicopter's flight crew. The flight crew was a single assault robot, a gleaming silvery skeleton with a gleaming, grinning skull that was the stuff of nightmares for Resistance fighters.

Nor were the passengers concerned. A dozen more assault robots and a T-600 Terminator were the sole occupants of the helicopter's personnel bay.

But they had a specific goal and would not be able to carry it out if destroyed. They would be delayed in carrying it out if they were shot down.

The pilot assault robot read its full range of sensory data and calculated the probable tactics utilized by the destroyed H-Ks. Then, still half a mile from the engagement zone, it set the twin-rotored Chinook down in the middle of the street and broadcast an authorization for the T-600 and its troops to deploy from this point.

One of its sensor inputs, the tracer signal from the T-X, abruptly ceased. The pilot did not wonder whether she had been destroyed. It merely sat and waited for new instructions.

Sgt. George Mathison, situated behind the second-floor window desk that John Connor had occupied only an hour before, saw the Chinook set down well outside of the engagement zone. He cursed. As a twenty-year veteran of human-machine conflicts, he knew it was too much to hope that wave after wave of Skynet troops would fall for the same tactic, but it sometimes happened, so he always hoped. He kept his eyes open, kept the rocket-propelled grenade launcher firmly on his shoulder.

Far ahead, even through the smoke drifting across the street from one of the H-K burn sites, he saw movement: two silvery forms advancing fast. Well, that was all right. He had more than one RPG at hand. He felt himself go from a state of readiness to a high internal idle, nervousness that he would have to restrain, for the thousandth time in his life, if he were to remain effective with his weapons.

In the distance, he heard the chatter of assault rifle and plasma rifle fire. He thought it was from his left, around the side of the building. That meant the assault robots were probably approaching from multiple directions.

The two he could see were now increasing their rate of approach. Abruptly a stream of plasma pulses erupted from below and to the left of Mathison's position. That would be the soldiers stationed at one of the exterior sets of doors. Their job, more dangerous than Mathison's, was to exchange fire with the oncoming units, to keep them busy until they were well within range of Mathison's RPGs.

They were getting into range now. Mathison sighted in on the rearmost of the two. Another five seconds, four—

Mathison's view of the scene changed. He found himself looking up at the top of the window frame and at the ceiling on this side of it. There was a tremendous, searing pain in his head, but he could do nothing about it, could not even moan.

The view of the ceiling whipped back down to the street outside and the approaching robots, then to the desktop he'd been leaning against.

He never saw the sniper robot who had killed him.

John, Kate, and their escorts raced along the storm drain, toward the creek bed where their vehicles had been left and were, if all went well, still being guarded.

They had a mile or more to travel and only a few minutes to do it in. The farther they were away from the civic center, the better, but as more time passed, more Skynet units would be in the vicinity, reducing their chances for escape. It was a trade-off they had faced many times in their lives.

Of course, they did everything they could to improve their odds.

They reached the tunnel turnoff that would lead them to their vehicles. At this juncture, a metal ladder led up to a manhole that had already been opened. The technician with the wriggling bag gave John a brief salute, then climbed the ladder one-handed.

At the summit, he carefully poked his head out to survey the surrounding street, then lifted the bag up. He untied the closed end, then began to invert the burlap mass.

He didn't need to. Even from this vantage point John could see the coyote leap free of its confinement.

The technician shimmied down the ladder as fast as nominal safety would allow. "Decoy away," he said.

"And the collar?" John asked.

"Still attached."

Ahead, the entire south face of the civic center was smoking. There were bodies at various windows and doors, humans who had been caught unawares by the improved tactical package of the T-600 commanding the mission. But that Terminator did not enter through the south-end door on the heels of its assault robots. It paused to evaluate new sensory data it was receiving.

The tracer signal from the T-X had been restored. The T-X was moving. The T-600 requested—and received—triangulation data from all appropriately equipped Skynet units in the vicinity. It called up a map of the region and superimposed the tracer location data on it.

The T-X was a few hundred yards north of the civic center and proceeding on an erratic northwesterly course. Its pace was not steady. This suggested that it was accompanying one or more humans who themselves did not progress in an efficient manner or that it was stalking them. The T-600 broadcast a new query on her frequency, but as before, there was no response.

The T-600 broadcast all this data to Skynet in the blink of an eye, and the machine intelligence's new orders came back in almost that amount of time. The highest probability was that the T-X was either being abducted by John Connor or was stalking him. Either way, the Terminator's goal was to find the T-X and John Connor.

The T-600 broadcast new orders. All but two of the assault robots were to accompany it as it set off to run down the T-X's tracer signal. It angled left, around the exterior of the civic center, and began running in that direction. Ahead, assault robots that had just entered the center came spilling out through the doors once again.

The two assault robots remaining within the civic center continued on their unaltered mission. Their infrared-sensitive optics picked up the faint bright spots on the floor indicating where humans had recently walked or run, and, though there was some confusing dispersal of steps suggesting a certain amount of uncoordinated activity, there were clear signs that the majority of humans present had departed the main chamber through one specific door. The robots followed that trail.

The glowing footsteps followed a linoleum-floored back corridor to a stairwell, then descended its stairs. Had the robots been human, they would have hesitated in their pursuit, as following humans down into a lair they had occupied for any amount of time tended to result in high casualties. But assault robots had no more a sense of self-preservation than refrigerators. They followed at their relentless walking pace.

On the basement level, the corresponding corridor led the robots to signs of recent damage. A concrete wall had been blown out, probably through use of an explosive charge. Mounds of rubble still littered the hallway, though it appeared that the majority of the rubble had ended up on the other side of the wall. The robots approached.

On one mound was a device small enough to be held easily in a human hand. It had an aperture in one side, the side turned toward the robots, and a series of light-emitting diodes on top. As the robots neared, the object began to beep, an unending series of high-pitched noises.

The first robot bent over the device and quickly identified it as a primitive motion detector. Wires ran from the object in several directions—through the hole in the wall, back along the corridor and up the stairs, farther along the same corridor.

The robot decided that the very arrival of Skynet forces was being utilized to trigger some event.

Then the largest mound of rubble, artfully arranged by hand to conceal a quantity of high explosives, detonated.

So did explosives planted on support pillars all over the civic center.

The T-600 received a partial transmission: TARGET ZONE SHOWS SIGN OF HUMAN TAMPERING (ESTIMATED PURPOSE: DESTRUCTION

OF EVIDENCE, DESTRUCTION OF SKYNET FORCES) WITHIN STAN-
DARD PARAM—

Then it heard the explosions. It turned to see the civic center
swell just a bit, then become blurry around the edges as walls and
ceilings buckled, collapsed. Gouts of flame burst through the ceiling of the main chamber at several points.

It was not relevant. The robots within the complex had not
detected John Connor. The T-X was still moving. The T-600
returned to the task of catching up to the T-X.

However, this was proving to be a problem. Telemetry provided by the Skynet units was tracking the T-X with acceptable
accuracy, but as soon as the T-600 or one of the assault robots got
within a certain distance of the tracer, typically fifty to sixty yards,
the T-X would put on a burst of speed and move to a new, more
distant location. As yet, neither the T-600 nor any of the assault
robots had obtained visual evidence of the T-X's position.

The T-600 changed tactics. It sent its entire complement of
assault robots ahead in a broad, fanning pattern, instructing them
to set up a circular perimeter about two hundred yards in diameter,
to set up stationary positions, and to set all sensors to optimal performance. It waited stock-still for five minutes, as more and more
neighborhood buildings caught fire around it, before moving once
more toward that signal source. This time it set up to receive visual
broadcasts from all of its units.

The signal source was now sixty yards ahead. In that vicinity,
the T-600 saw a pickup truck with a flatbed trailer attached, both
parked there for the better part of three decades. The flatbed truck
was loaded with machinery small enough to be carried or pro-
pelled by a single human; the T-600's scanners and analyzers indicated that the machinery was used in the maintenance of plant life.
The wooden flooring of the trailer had rotted over the years,
depositing most of the machines as mounds of corrosion upon the
pavement below.

There was enough room beneath the truck and the remains of
the trailer to conceal the T-X and perhaps John Connor as well, but

the likelihood of either of them being there seemed remote. Still, the T-600 headed toward the signal source.

Its approach caused a reaction. A blur of gray fur exploded from beneath the trailer, moved across the nearest lawn, and disappeared between two houses.

The T-600 took a moment to evaluate all its sensory data. The map it viewed internally finally updated with telemetry from other units. The gray mass was the source of the T-X tracer signal.

The T-600 brought up and sharpened images of the gray mass both from its own optical sensors and from those of some of the assault robots. It was an indigenous canine. There was a man-made object around its neck, a band of leather. Skynet informed the T-600 that such items were used by humans to restrain and identify animal companions.

The canine could not be the T-X. Therefore the T-600 had been relayed the incorrect signal frequency information or the T-X's tracer had been relocated. The T-600 broadcast that information and waited for instructions.

By storm drain and overgrown field, by back road and creek bed, the members of the Resistance made their way out of Santa Fe.

They were aided in their escape by the ever-growing fire behind them. The fire confounded Skynet units' visual sensors with smoke and flame. Even Skynet's surveillance satellites, optimized to use infrared photography, were thwarted by the conflagration. By nightfall, the entire group, excepting those who had fallen before they could join the others in the storm drains, were well outside the city limits, keeping cold camps in the hills.

And John Connor allowed himself to feel just a touch of optimism. They had a T-X. They would learn more from it than it had from Paul Keeley. They would turn its very existence to their own advantage.

If they could make it back to Home Plate alive, that is.

■ ■ ■

The vehicle depot beneath the National Guard armory had been nicknamed Yucca Compound, but to Paul it seemed far less like a Resistance compound than it had several days ago. Many of the vehicles that had been here were now gone, having been repaired to the point of drivability and taken away by Resistance workers over the last few days. With those drivers, an equivalent number of mechanics, and the entire set of leaders and their bodyguards gone, the place was echoingly empty.

Of course, some vehicles remained and probably would always be here. One old pickup had proven to be too far gone to resurrect. The self-propelled howitzer was too slow, too loud, and too prone to breakdown to be transported anywhere, but it would be maintained here by the Resistance in case they ever needed a long-range artillery piece in this part of the world.

The two motorcycles were still here, and Paul had spent the last two days arranging for them to be transportable.

One would be easy. John Connor had announced that he would carry it on the back of his Humvee. Paul had merely put together some brackets that could be mounted on the Humvee's back.

The second was more problematic. It might be carried on one of the Army trucks, but indications had been that one truck would be nearly empty, carrying little more than the T-X and the expedition's remaining fuel supplies, while the other would consequently be packed from bed to canopy.

Paul had cannibalized portions of the dead pickup truck, removing both its axle assemblies and using them to form the frame of a small trailer. He had welded cross-braces and mounted portions of the pickup's bed, folded over for reinforced strength, to serve as the trailer's flooring. Now he was finishing the yoke that would connect to a towing vehicle's trailer hitch, but it was his second attempt to get the yoke and cup right. He wasn't entirely satisfied with the results, though they were better than his first effort.

He heard the compound's main door grind open, followed by cheers from the three or four personnel stationed at the top ramp.

It had to be the return of the convoy, the first vehicle at least.

Paul bent over to put some more finishing touches on the yoke, then Kyla's words popped up in his mind: "To become something, you have to define it, then understand it, then simulate it until it becomes second nature."

Did he want to be the sort of person people greeted by name, welcomed with genuine warmth at gatherings and reunions? Yes.

What would such a person do in an event like this? He'd go up the ramp and talk to the returning Resistance fighters.

He sighed, then shut off his oxyacetylene torch, pulled off his goggles, and set them on the trailer. Then he marched up the ramp.

As he got close, he saw that the first vehicle in was one of the Hell-Hounds' SUVs. A few paces closer, and he could make out the forms of Mark Herrera and Kyla Connor talking with the workers up there. He breathed a sigh of relief.

And pulling down the ramp to the top depot area was a dune buggy. Smart was driving, Fix in the front passenger seat, the youngest Scalpers member, J. L., was sitting up from the rear seat. All seemed jubilant.

The first words Paul made out were Mark's: ". . . not entirely clean. We lost four of the regular troops."

"But you got the package," said one of the workers.

"We got the package. In fact, that's what will be pulling in next. It's a couple of miles back."

There was general applause and back-slapping. Paul moved up behind Kyla. "Dogs okay?"

"Huh?" She glanced back over her shoulder at him. "Oh. Yeah. I let them out just outside so they could run around for a few minutes. Thanks for asking."

"Sure. Uh, when your dad gets in, you might want to tell him that I've got a pair of motorcycles for him to choose between, and he's not going to find it an easy choice."

"He'll be happy to hear that. He's—oh, here it is."

All present could hear the distant sound of a large engine downshifting. Moments later, the reflected sunlight from up the ramp was partially blocked by the hulk of one of the Army trucks as it turned into the tunnel to descend.

Kyla took a couple of steps toward the truck. Paul moved to follow—and felt his legs grow rubbery, too weak to hold him upright.

He leaned against the SUV, holding on to the support of its side-view mirror. That's what it took to stay on his feet. Now dizziness made his head swim, made everything he saw a bewildering blur. Shaking his head made it worse, so he shut his eyes and sank to sit on the SUV's step-up rail.

He heard the others surround the new arrival, heard its tailgate slam open. And there were more cheers as the treasure it carried was revealed.

Which was all fortunate for him. Everyone had moved forward to see the truck and its contents. No one remained behind to witness his sudden weakness.

What the hell's going on? I need help. Then Paul forced away the thought. He didn't need help. He needed to bull his way through the problem—whatever it was. Gripping the door frame above him, he pulled himself upright.

The dizziness was subsiding, and his legs supported his weight. They were still shaky as he made his way around to the back of the truck.

There, laid out in a coffinlike wooden crate, its side now open so people could look into it, was a thing, half woman and half robot. Its face was that of a lovely young woman, its clothes were those of a Resistance citizen . . . but its neck and torso were metal, with a series of steel clamps holding several pieces of electrical apparatus to her.

Mark Herrera clapped Paul on the back. "There's your girl," he said.

Paul considered an angry reply. But there, again, were Kyla's words standing between him and the wrong answer. He wouldn't make any friends instructing jerks in just what jerks they were. "No, I'm currently dating a microwave oven," he said.

Mark snorted.

Besides, it *wasn't* Eliza. The face was different. He knew that it was all illusion, a function of the T-X's liquid crystal skin and its infinite permutability. But it still made a difference to him somehow. Without Eliza's face, it was someone else.

He turned away. He was feeling better, but was still not quite himself. *I need help.* The words would not leave him.

Across the next half-hour, the remaining vehicles of John Connor's executive caravan arrived, refueled, underwent maintenance. For John's orders were that they get back on the road, carrying everyone and everything not destined to remain at Yucca Compound, as soon as possible. "The more distance we open up between us and where they're looking, the better," John said.

John did take a few minutes to admire the work Paul had done on the Kawasakis. Both looked to be in excellent shape, considering their antiquity and recent state of disrepair, and he couldn't really determine which one he considered to be in better condition.

He flipped a coin, a big copper twenty-peso piece that had been old before he was born, a souvenir of Mexico that he often used for such purposes, and settled on the motorcycle with the flecks of white paint on the handlebars. "This one goes on my Humvee," he told Paul. "The Scalpers can tow yours. Get 'em set up."

Paul gave him a salute and a smile. "Yes, sir."

It was to be a longer-than-usual caravan for a nonassault mission: eight vehicles total.

First, designated Fishhook-1, would be the Scalpers' dune buggy with Sato and Jenna the Greek. Behind it would come the first Hell-Hounds' SUV with Mark Herrera, Kyla, and her dogs. Of course,

John Connor had had to decide, impartially, which of the two special forces units would lead the procession; he had resorted a second time to his coin.

The third vehicle would be the Army truck containing the bulk of the expedition's gear, the weapons and tools liberated from Yucca Compound, and, in the cab, three of the expedition's technicians. Behind it would be the Humvee with John Connor, Kate Brewster, Tom Carter, and Glitch driving.

Fifth would be the second Scalpers' dune buggy, carrying J. L., Smart, and Nix, and hauling Paul's motorcycle. Sixth would be the prize package, the Army truck holding the T-X, remaining fuel stores, with two soldiers and a technician in the cab.

Seventh would be the Humvee Avenger that John Connor was so pleased to add to the Resistance's ground fleet. The remaining soldiers and technicians would ride in the eighth vehicle, a military van from Yucca Compound. At the very tail of the caravan, Fishhook-9, was the other Hell-Hounds' SUV, bearing Ten Zimmerman and Earl Duncan.

In the rearview mirror, Tom Carter watched Paul finish tying John's dirt bike onto the hastily mounted brackets on the Humvee's rear. Paul pulled on his backpack, then moved up to the front passenger window and leaned in. "Ready to go," he said.

Carter gave him a quick nod. "You're in the van at the back. Slightly less bouncy—and slightly less kidney-killing—than the big trucks."

"Thanks. Good luck." Paul gave him a nod, threw a salute to John and Kate in the backseat, and headed back toward the van.

Kate watched him go. "What do you think, Tom?"

"He's shaping up, I think," Carter said. "Since we got back, I haven't seen any sign of his paranoid fits. He may be ready to rejoin the human race. Well, to join it for the first time."

"That's something, anyway," John said. He pressed the button for his lapel mike. "Fishhook-One, go in one minute."

Sato's voice came back instantly, "Roger that."

As Paul reached the T-X truck, the driver, one of the expedition's soldiers, leaned out of the driver's-side window. "You coming with us?"

Paul waved toward the rear of the caravan. "Farther back. You're going to have to live without my luminous presence for a while."

"We'll suffer, but we'll manage."

I need help.

He was alongside the truck's bed when the words filtered through his mind again. But this time the voice was not his.

He looked around. In the side-view mirror of the truck, he could see the soldier who'd addressed him, but that man wasn't looking at him; he was turned to talk to someone else in the cab.

Behind the truck, the next ramp sloped down into the darkness. At the bottom of the ramp, the van that was his destination would be waiting, but he couldn't see it in the darkness. There was no one near enough for him to have heard.

He moved around the back of the Army truck to peek into the bed. Within was the T-X's closed crate. Trapped within it, her body paralyzed by interference signals being pumped into its wiring by the device Tom Carter had installed, she could not have spoken to him.

Then who?

I need help.

New dizziness threatened to overwhelm Paul. He put his hands on the tailgate to steady himself.

I need help.

Paul woke up on his back, staring up into darkness.

The surface he moved on was moving—rocking, swaying, jostling. He was in a car or truck. It stank of gasoline.

The voice that awoke him spoke again. *I know you're awake. Say something, but whisper, please. Otherwise they'll hear you.*

"This is bullshit," he whispered.

You just said, "This is bullshit." I heard you. Please believe me, it's real.

He shook his head, trying to force the strangeness of the situation out of his head so memory could return. He had no idea how he had come to be here, where "here" was, or anything. The last he remembered, he was going to work, day after day after day . . . "Who's speaking?"

It's Eliza. Do you remember me? For God's sake, say you remember me.

"Eliza." He sat up, remembering her, the bar, the bouncer. Something strange had happened, but there was a cloud between him and those memories. There was a little light in the direction he faced, and he was certain that he was staring over a tailgate, under a cloth canopy, at a moonlit road. Beside him was a camouflage-pattern backpack he didn't recognize.

We're in danger, she said. *Very, very great danger. And I'm going to die if you don't help me. I'm not the only one, either. Please help.*

He moved on hands and knees to the tailgate. His new position gave him a better sense of what he was seeing. It was a roadway, all right, a two-lane blacktop lit only by a half-moon and the stars. It was so dark he found it inconceivable that the truck was even running its headlights.

I'm not like you, Eliza said. *I can communicate with just my mind.*

"Telepathy," he whispered.

Yes.

"I don't believe in telepathy."

What else that you experience do you not believe in? How else do you explain what's happening?

"You're right, I'm sorry. Why can't I remember anything?" It was so hard to think. Paul wanted to beat his head against the cloud that obscured his memory, but it was not a physical thing he could overcome. Enough time, though, and he was certain he'd think his way through it.

You've been drugged. The government came for me. To study me. To dissect me. You tried to stop them. They shot you with a dart. You managed to get in the back of their truck anyway. But you passed out.

"I've read that before. Or seen a movie like that." He could almost remember telling Eliza such things, the plots of movies he'd seen and books he'd read. But that memory, too, was deep in the cloud layer. "It can't be real."

It is real. You've got to get me out of this crate, out of my restraints. But don't make a noise. They have microphones back here. If you make a sound, they'll do something awful.

He turned back to the crate. He was still wearing his belt pouch, and within it were a penlight, his multitool, and other items he dimly remembered. He brought out the penlight and turned it on.

The crate was made of old, dirty softwood. The lid had been nailed on, but the nails were small ones and had been tacked down in only two places around the lid's edge. He brought out his multitool, folded out the flat-edge screwdriver, and carefully worked it into the gap between the lid and the body of the crate.

Carefully, he exerted leverage, quietly prying up the lid. Once all the nails on one side were exposed, he moved around to the other side and repeated the process.

He set the multitool down beside the crate. Then, as silently as he could, he hefted the lid and set it aside.

Within the crate, looking to his eye for all the world like a cinema vampire within a coffin, lay Eliza. But something was wrong with his eyes; even in the darkness, under his flashlight beam, her face seemed oddly blurry.

Nor was that the only strange thing. There were two devices on her, one resting on her chest, the other clamped to her neck and shoulders.

He recognized the first device instantly. It was a large charge of C-4, plastic explosive, with a radio detonator attached to it.

That took him aback. He didn't know anything about plastic explosives or detonators. But he knew what he was seeing.

The other device was an assemblage of clamps and cables. Some of the cables were attached to her neck and the bare skin around her collarbones by bandages. His eyes blurred whenever he looked at them. Nor did he want to look at them. This was horrible, some sort of insanity that did not belong anywhere near a nice, quiet life such as his.

The bomb first, Eliza said. *That's the part with the microphone on it. When we dispose of that, they can't hear us anymore.*

He looked over the mass of plastic explosive and the apparatus on it. It seemed impossibly simple. The detonator seemed to have a metal pin extending from it into the C-4; he could see perhaps an eighth of an inch of the pin. Pushed into another portion of the explosive was a small microphone; a wire encased in black plastic trailed from it to a small black case the size of a fist but flatter. A red LED on the black case gleamed dully.

If he correctly interpreted what he was seeing, all he had to do was pull the detonator out of the plastic explosive. Then it would be harmless. His heart in his throat, he reached over and did exactly that, slowly withdrawing the metal pin from the charge. When it was clear, he set the detonator aside.

Now the microphone. The wire leading into the black case was not permanently affixed to it; it was attached to the case by what looked like a standard jack. With similar care, though this was no detonator, he pulled the jack free. The LED slowly faded to complete darkness.

"Done," he said aloud.

Good. But that was the easy part. The thing that has me paralyzed, that's going to be more complicated.

"Do you know what to do?"

Yes. But I need you to take a long, slow look at it. I'll see it through your eyes.

He did so. He found that his vision blurred worse than ever, the lines of Eliza's face and of the apparatus refusing to solidify into a single, clear vision. But he forced himself to keep his eyes open.

Yes, this will be simple, too. One by one, I want you to grab the cables attached to my neck and chest and pull them free. You'll have to pull hard.

"Not too hard. They're just attached by bandages."

No, they are sunk into me. Trust me, it's not going to hurt much. I have a high pain threshold.

"All right." Not at all certain about this, Paul took hold of one of the four cables and tugged.

Eliza's skin pulled, but the cable did not come free.

He spared a glance for her face. His eyes still blurred, though he could see her own eyes, clear and beautiful in the midst of the blurry picture, fixed on him. She did not seem to be in pain.

He took the cable in both hands and yanked.

Her skin stretched alarmingly as the cable held. Then it came free. At its end, horribly enough, were denuded copper wires.

"Eliza, there's no blood." There was something very wrong with that. A suspicion tickled at the back of his mind, but would not resolve itself.

The imbedded shunts keep the blood from the wires, she said. *Please hurry, the others—*

He hurried. The second came free in his hands, then the third. "What are we going to do once you're free?"

My father is very rich. He controls companies all over the world. We'll go to one of them. He has a job for you.

The fourth and last cable came free in his hands.

Eliza sighed. He looked at her, and his vision cleared. Suddenly her features were as he remembered them, arctic and beautiful.

She sat up and wrapped her arms around him.

"What does he do?"

"He rules the world."

"Very funny."

She stared at him impassively. "I'm not joking. Here, let me free up your memory. And ask you a question. Is John Connor in this convoy, and is he ahead of us or behind us?"

"Ahead—" And in that moment, he knew who she was, what he had just done.

He shoved at her, a desperate, adrenaline-charged attempt to escape, but her grip was like that of a hydraulic press. He opened his mouth to scream, to warn the people in the cab of this truck, but she released him with one arm and struck him in the solar plexus.

It was, perhaps, a trifling blow by Terminator standards, but it drove all the wind from him and he sagged.

She stood out of her crate and bent over him. She yanked the other ends of the cables free from the apparatus that had paralyzed her. She rolled Paul onto his stomach and bound his hands and feet with them, with typical machine speed and efficiency. From the canopy over the truck's bed, she ripped strips of cloth and used them to gag him.

And all the while she spoke, calmly and dispassionately. "I told you the truth, though I calculate that it will not comfort you. You will be returned to your previous occupation, teaching me and then others like me about human behavior. Whether or not I am able to terminate John Connor tonight, you will be taken to our new training facility to resume your duties." In his mind's eye, Paul saw glimpses, little flashes of trees, nearby mountains, an atrium with a water fountain, the water's surface still and green. "Paul, you may end up being the last surviving human on Earth. Won't that be nice?" She moved up to the front of the truck bed, reached up to rip a hole in the canopy there, and scrambled up out of Paul's sight.

Silent and careful, the T-X climbed up onto the roof of the truck's cab. She distributed her great weight on all four limbs, positioning them as close to the cab back and sides as possible for maximum support. It would not do to have the cab roof sag and alert those within.

She leaned out over the driver's-side door and scaled up her audio sensors to their highest level of receptivity. She also conformed her ear on that side into a conical shape, transforming her ear into the equivalent of a shotgun microphone.

The humans were talking.

". . . pranged it right across the stomach and cut it in half. So it was lying there in two pieces. Mind you, it was still pretty dangerous. It started crawling toward me, and those things can crawl *fast*."

"Do you talk about anything but fighting?"

"Sure I do. I talk about women. But not while Libby's here. Unless you *like* women, Libby."

A female voice: "Not that way, thanks."

"So, it's fighting."

"Ever think about broadening your horizons?"

"Like how?"

"My engineering unit puts on the Christmas play."

"Oh, God, spare me."

The T-X leaned away. The humans were not communicating with other vehicles in the convoy, and they were not aware that she had escaped. These were the two most important things.

She looked around. Her infrared sensors picked up heat traces, one approximately half a mile ahead, one close to a mile behind. This convoy appeared to be negotiating a winding road, a set of hairpin turns and switchbacks descending a long, low mountain slope.

She gripped the top edge of the driver's-side window, contorted herself, and swung in through the window.

Her foot smashed into the driver's head, knocking loose the elaborate set of goggles he wore, snapping his neck, changing the shape of the skull. He slumped. She dropped into place on top of him, sitting in his lap.

The cab's other two passengers barely had time to look. The human female, in the center, reached for the submachine gun in her lap. The male, by the passenger-side door, reached for his lapel.

She struck each with one arm. The T-X's right hand penetrated the woman's torso, shredding her heart and emerging through her spine, while her left hand seized the man's neck, choking off anything he might have had to say. She squeezed and his neck snapped, causing his head to loll around.

Time expended: two seconds. In that time, the truck had drifted to the right, toward the drop-off. Another few feet and its right-hand wheels would have lost purchase, sending the truck over the edge. But she seized the steering wheel and got the lumbering vehicle back toward the center of the lane.

It was only a matter of moments then to open the passenger-side door and throw out the three bodies, making sure to hurl them far enough that they ended up partway down the mountain slope. That way the occupants of the vehicle a mile back would not detect them.

Her internal diagnostics were still indicating that she could not establish a connection with Skynet. The humans must have damaged her communications systems in some significant way. She would have to establish communication at a Skynet site. That was relegated to the status of secondary goal. The fact that John Connor was near, part of this convoy, made his termination her primary goal.

She had resources. Her weapons systems seemed intact, and

this vehicle would allow her to keep up with the convoy. But if the members of the convoy were traveling in this spread-out formation, it would not necessarily allow her to approach the vehicles ahead of her without being detected.

She leaned forward to smash out the glass of the windshield. Using a backpack left behind by one of the dead humans, she braced the accelerator in its current position. Then, one hand always on the steering wheel, she clambered out onto the truck hood.

The T-X peeled up portions of the metal of the hood as easily as a human might peel the rind off a citrus fruit. Beneath lay the machinery of the engine. Into it she extended her hand. Its end reconfigured, the liquid metal skin assuming its natural silvery sheen and drawing back, revealing the tools and weapon heads there.

The T-X had truly been designed to be the ultimate weapon of destruction for twentieth-century time-jumping operations. In addition to the hardened battle chassis required by most Terminator units, she had the broadest array of internal weapons known to a Skynet unit. She possessed a liquid metal skin, adapted from the T-1000 design, that allowed her to imitate the appearance of just about any human alive or dead, real or fictitious. And then there was a final boon, apparati that would allow her to control vehicles remotely.

From her arm poured streams of material. Some were nanites, microscopic robots with very simple programming. Some were cables with musclelike flexion and retraction functions. Some were radio transceivers, others sensors, others connectors. Following her broadcast dictates, they distributed themselves through the engine, into the transmission, into the brakes, configuring themselves so that in minutes they became a fully realized set of remote-controlled servos and cameras.

She also retained a transceiver and connected it through nanite chain to her central processor. It wouldn't increase her transmission range much, just to a few hundred yards. But that would be sufficient for the next stage of her plan.

When she was done, she released the steering wheel. The truck, now a very primitive robot slaved to her instructions, continued down the road at its designated rate of speed.

Up ahead was a hairpin turn. The vehicle a half-mile up had already negotiated it.

The T-X leaped from the truck hood and over the lip at the edge of the road. With a grace and power no human could duplicate, she began running down the rocky slope toward the continuation of the road below.

She would attack the next vehicle in line. If it contained John Connor, her mission was concluded. If it did not, she would kill its occupants, gain control of its functions, and use the same tactic to approach the next vehicle in line. And on and on, until John Connor was dead.

Sick with misery, Paul lay on the truck bed.

The enormity of the betrayal he had just committed, however inadvertent it might have been, was like a hundred tons of rock crushing him.

But punching through his guilt was one fact that would not let him go: He had to do something about it. Had to warn the others.

He could still move a little. He could inch his way to the rear of the truck, sit up—and what then?

If he levered himself over the tailgate, he would fall to the road below. The fall would probably kill him. He wasn't sure how fast the truck was moving—probably somewhere between thirty and fifty miles per hour—but the speed, plus the fact that he'd probably be falling headfirst, would spell his end. But the next vehicle in line would see his body, an alert would go out, and John Connor would survive.

It occurred to him belatedly that his survival didn't matter. He had to fix what he'd broken. If he were dead, so much the better.

Then he wouldn't have to suffer the new levels of scorn, suspicion, and hatred that would be heaped upon him for his failure.

He crawled like a sideways inchworm toward the rear of the truck.

Then he saw his multitool, lying where he had set it after prying the crate lid free. He rolled over, putting his back to it, and groped around until he got it in his hands.

It took a bit of graceless fumbling, and one drop and recover of the tool, before he could free its wire cutters. Then, awkwardly, but as quickly as he could manage, he got to work on the cables binding him.

He heard the distant sound of the truck's windshield being shattered. He supposed that noise spelled the deaths of the crew in the cab and that was more weight on his chest, but he ignored it and kept squeezing the wire cutters, willing them to bite into the cables.

He felt them loosen, and despite the increasing soreness in his palm, where his skin pressed hard against the unyielding metal of the cutter handles, he increased his efforts.

Then the handles closed as the last strand of cable came free. He whipped his hands around, yanked his gag free, and got to work on the cables around his ankles.

A minute later he could stand. He moved to the front of the truck bed, used the multitool's knife blade to slice through the canopy to the left, and poked his head out.

Just ahead was the driver's-side door. The side-view mirror showed him, dimly, the interior of the cab, but he should have been able to see Eliza's face and could not. He leaned farther out through the slash in the canopy, getting a better angle on the driver's-side window, and even in the moonlight he was certain that there was no one behind the wheel.

He looked down at the roadway rolling by beneath. Suddenly it did not seem like such a good idea to dive into it. Carefully, he levered himself out of the gap in the canopy, reaching forward until he got his hands on the driver's-side window, and pulled himself free, dangling by just his hands for the moment it took him to scrabble his feet onto the driver's-side step.

The cab was empty. Still, the steering wheel was correcting for the slight bend in the road.

Paul scrambled up and into the cab. The wind, flowing in through the shattered windshield, battered at his face. Where was the T-X? She had to be controlling the truck by remote control. Which meant . . .

She had to be ahead, going after the next vehicle in the convoy.

On the floorboards were a couple of backpacks and a standard set of Resistance night-sight goggles. He pulled them on. Suddenly all the world was presented to him in shades of yellow and green, the brighter hues indicating warmer objects . . . and still there was no sign of the T-X.

He poured out the contents of the backpacks. There were no radios to be had, but he found a web belt with a holstered handgun and an ammunition pouch. He buckled it on.

The T-X dropped into a crouch atop a rock that loomed over the roadway. A massive boulder projection, it had soaked up quite a lot of heat during the day and was still releasing it into the night air. In the infrared range the humans' goggles afforded them, she would probably be hard to detect if she remained motionless.

She turned to face the direction from which the next vehicle should come, and she waited.

There it was, a plume of brightness in the distance. It quickly grew into a recreational four wheel vehicle, a dune buggy. She recognized it as belonging to the Scalpers; it was the second vehicle belonging to that company, the one that had been occupied by J. L., Nix, and Smart, and as it got near enough for her to make out the three occupants, she recognized them. The vehicle was hauling a small crude trailer upon which, wrapped in a tarpaulin, appeared to be a motorcycle.

A pity this wasn't Connor's vehicle. But it was a stepping-stone on the path toward Connor.

As it neared her position, she leaped in its direction of travel. She came down feetfirst in the backseat, directly atop the member named Nix, her great weight smashing his leg and pelvis.

The tremendous impact of her weight bottomed out the shock absorbers. The vehicle veered, sending the T-X momentarily off-balance. She corrected this by seizing one of the roll bars. Nix shrieked, but seemed to have been incapacitated by pain.

The young one, J. L., stood up in his seat. The T-X swung an arm at him, a backhand blow that should have smashed his head. But he was ducking beneath the blow even as she committed to it, and as her arm passed above his head he reached up with his shoulder belt and wrapped it around her extended arm, then hauled on the lap belt portion of the restraint. The T-X, gripped by a material with far more tensile strength than mere human flesh, was tugged off-balance.

From his crouch, J. L. kicked up at her, the blow striking her buttock and sending her a few more degrees off-balance.

The T-X took a few milliseconds to recalculate. J. L. was proving to be an impediment. He could not stop her, hurt her, or kill her, but he could delay her long enough for the vehicle's driver to perform an action she might consider troublesome.

From her awkward position, she reached over to seize the back of J. L.'s seat and yanked with all the strength she could manage. The seat broke free of its mountings and catapulted J. L. over the side.

Before he hit the pavement, she issued instructions to the truck, ordering it to run over the human lying in the road. There was a small but measurable possibility that the impact would throw his body off the road and make it difficult for the driver of the next vehicle in line to detect. The main purpose of the instruction was to ensure that J. L. would be dead rather than injured when encountered; if he were still alive, he might gasp out some information that the vehicle's occupants could transmit, thus costing the T-X several seconds of potential surprise.

She dimly detected the truck's transmitted response, accepting its new instructions. The lack of long-distance broadcasting functionality could conceivably impede her ability to control the truck. She also instructed it to close up the distance between it and her position.

Now the dune buggy's driver, Charles Smart, was lifting a field radio to his mouth. The T-X lunged forward and grabbed both the device and Smart's hand, crushing them both instantly.

The man's face twisted in pain. Unlike Nix, he did not shout. Instead, he yanked the wheel, sending the dune buggy toward the lip of the road.

As the dune buggy's front wheels roared out over empty space, the T-X reflected that she probably encountered more truly obstructive humans than other Skynet units.

Paul's truck negotiated a hairpin turn. Now the drop-off was on the driver's side. And Paul could see, far ahead, a bright green shape that had to be the Scalpers' second dune buggy.

It was weaving all over the road. As he watched, something bright detached itself from the vehicle and rolled to a stop in the middle of the road.

Then the dune buggy veered left and sailed off the road.

The truck picked up speed, and as it neared the object lying in the road, Paul could see that it was a human body. The truck angled itself to put its driver's-side wheels right across that unmoving form.

Paul seized the steering wheel and yanked it to the right, away from the drop-off, away from the body. The wheel resisted in his hands but was still connected to the truck's steering. The truck slewed rightward, missing the body. Then the wheel yanked itself free of his control, correcting the truck's course so that it was safely in the middle of the road again.

The T-X, undamaged, clambered free of the dune buggy and surveyed the damage.

Nix and Smart were both dead. Smart still stared at her, an angry expression still on his face, but his neck was at such an angle that he could not have survived. Their possessions had spilled out of the vehicle in a broad debris field, and the rollover had caused the yoke of the trailer the dune buggy had been pulling to snap.

But the dune buggy itself seemed to be in fair to good condition. If that were the case, it would still travel faster, over a protracted distance, than she could. She pitched the bodies of Nix and

Smart out of it, then picked up the buggy's front end and hauled it quickly up toward the roadway.

The truck reported that it had missed its target. It supplied no explanation; the components controlling it did not have enough processing power to come to any conclusions.

She ordered it to turn back and finish the human. As this task would doubtless take it out of her broadcast range, she issued additional orders, instructing it to continue up the road and ram the next vehicle in the convoy. If it succeeded in destroying that vehicle and was still mobile, it was to repeat that action against each successive vehicle in the convoy, until all were destroyed, in which case it could power down, or it was destroyed.

She reached the roadway, set the dune buggy up on four wheels, and climbed into the driver's seat. The vehicle started on the second try. She roared off in pursuit of the next vehicle.

Behind her, she heard gunshots. She assigned that event a high probability that it was J. L., partially recovered, firing on the truck that was about to end his life.

Paul watched as, far ahead, a shades-of-green T-X appeared at the edge of the road, hauling the dune buggy.

Then the truck began to slow. Wheezing like a runner too old for the race, it maneuvered onto the right shoulder, then commenced a slow, careful turn back the direction it had come.

It had to back and fill a couple of times to accomplish this task, Paul saw—the road was too narrow for it.

It had to be turning around to go after whoever was in the road. He couldn't let it do that. Worse yet, by stopping here, it was letting Eliza get farther and farther away from him.

He piled as much as he could of the dead soldiers' gear into one backpack, then, still gripping it, stepped out of the truck in the middle of its maneuvering. He drew out the handgun at his belt. It turned out to be a Colt 9mm, made for the armed forces before

J-Day. He switched the safety off and put a couple of rounds into the driver's-side tires, then fired the rest of its clip into the engine.

He knew the engines on these trucks. He knew where the fuel lines were, where the drive train emerged, where the carburetor was. He concentrated his fire on these areas.

The truck continued to pull around until it was facing back the way it had come. Paul put his last rounds into the passenger-side tires. Then the slide of his gun locked back . . . and the truck's engine died.

He swapped out the spent clip for a full one in the belt's ammunition pouch.

Miles ahead, John Connor, in the driver's-side backseat of his Humvee, saw the T-850, Glitch, tilt his head. The movement was uncannily like that of a human trying to hear something better, and it was for very similar purposes. The Terminator would be trying to get an optimal orientation to improve his reception of distant audio stimuli.

"What is it?" John asked.

"Gunfire," Glitch said. "Multiple shots. Small arms. Miles away."

John considered. That in and of itself was not unusual. There were humans living in the wild spaces all over the world—and not all of them belonged to the Resistance. As many trips as John had been on, it was not unusual for travelers to hear distant gunshots from some solitary homesteader hunting or from some exchange between a Skynet-controlled unit and a band of luckless humans.

Still, it never paid to ignore signs of trouble. "Stay alert," he told everyone.

Breathing fast, Paul reached the site of the dune buggy's crash. In his infrared field of vision, the bodies of Smart and Nix still glowed brightly. Their weapons, camp packs, and field rations were scattered all over the slope, though Paul could see no sign of a radio.

The trailer he'd so laboriously pieced together had half-folded on impact, and the ropes and tarp wrapped around the Kawasaki were slack. But when Paul pulled them free, the motorcycle itself did not seem to be too badly damaged. The left handlebar was bent, at a lower angle than the right, but the throttle seemed operational.

Paul hastily cut the ropes away and freed the dirt bike from the wreckage. Then he grabbed up some items from the field of debris. Smart's sniper rifle, still in its padded cloth case, looked intact; he retrieved it first. He set it aside for the moment, along with Nix's plasma assault rifle. A few feet from the assault rifle, Paul found its corresponding ammunition bag, filled with battery/ammunition packs and weapon maintenance tools. He poured its contents into his backpack, donned that, then slung the sniper rifle across it. He positioned the sling of the plasma assault rifle across his neck so the weapon could be swung back, out of the way, or forward into firing position. Then he was ready to go.

The road, which Eliza was now traveling, continued off the right, disappearing in the distance. But there had to be a switchback down in that direction, because the same road continued well down the slope below Paul.

He twisted the bike's key in the ignition and the engine caught. He pointed the wheel down the slope and began navigating the rocky, cactus-dotted, slippery route toward the road below. If he reached it quickly enough, he could head off Eliza, perhaps even head off the next vehicle along the convoy.

"Oncoming vehicle," Glitch said in his flat tones. "From ahead. It is a motorcycle optimized for off-road use. Single operator." He reached down to the floorboards and picked up a classic Uzi carbine. At some point, it had been reconfigured from single-shot operation to full autofire functionality. He held it out the window with his left hand.

Tom Carter, in the front passenger seat, gave him a look suggesting that he was insane. The trouble was, the Terminators he programmed, such as Glitch, weren't insane, and they didn't lie. Carter put on his IR goggles and thumbed the switch to power them up. He heard John and Kate checking out their plasma rifles.

The shades-of-green vision the goggles afforded Carter confirmed Glitch's statement. "Hold your fire," he said. "That's Paul Keeley."

"How the hell did he get ahead of us?" Kate asked. "Wasn't he at the back of the caravan?"

"I suspect we are in real trouble," John said. "What are our immediate resources?"

Glitch said, "Scalpers-Two has closed the distance behind us. They are the nearest reserve unit."

The motorcycle roared past them, headed back the way they had come.

Had she been capable of excitement, the T-X would certainly be feeling it now. She was only a few hundred yards behind the next vehicle in line, and it was a Humvee, the precise sort of vehicle John Connor was known to favor. Every minute that passed she gained at what she believed to be an inconspicuous rate on her quarry. This vehicle would probably be able to outpace a Humvee if her quarry decided to make a run for it. Things were going well.

Then her optical sensors picked up a new infrared source. A small flare of heat was now visible on the road ahead of her quarry and was closing range fast.

Probabilities popped up on her main screen. The probabilities that this was a member of the convoy traversing its length to report on the general condition of all vehicles, or that it was a Skynet unit that had detected the convoy, were approximately equal. The T-X increased her rate of speed. Either way, a conflict would be precipitated within the next few seconds.

The new heat source resolved itself into the image of a human on a motorcycle, reducing to almost nil the likelihood that this was another Skynet unit.

The motorcycle passed the Humvee, approaching at a rate of speed inconsistent with a mere patrol or courier mission.

As the T-X's optical analysis routines determined that the motorcycle's operator was a known individual, Paul Keeley, he raised his weapon, a standard Resistance-issue plasma rifle, and opened fire.

The T-X put the dune buggy into evasive maneuvers, erratic back-and-forth movements designed to throw off the aim of an attacker. Her precise choice of maneuvers was based on firing behavior observed in humans in similar circumstances, on the tactics they would employ to hit a rapidly dodging ground vehicle.

Her evasions did not work. Plasma blasts struck the windshield in front of her and the roll bar above and behind her, nearly causing her to lose control. Another struck the road immediately in front of the dune buggy, sending up superheated gobbets of pavement into the engine compartment. The engine immediately began whining. The T-X calculated from the noise that a belt had loosened or fallen free. This did not augur well for the continued survival of this machine.

As her optics cleared, Paul roared past her on the motorcycle. She did not attempt to maneuver into his path. Such a collision would further damage her conveyance.

Her tactical programming informed her that she had not fared well in terms of combat efficiency. She had probably overestimated his combat skills; the wide, erratic way he sprayed the plasma bursts was not as easy to anticipate as the tighter, more controlled assault from a human veteran, hence the damage her vehicle had sustained. And had she readied one of her internal weapons, she could have eliminated this intruder as he passed. She dismissed the analysis. She could remove Paul from the picture and still retain him as a Skynet asset with almost no effort.

She wrested the dune buggy back into line, aiming it at the tail end of the Avenger ahead, and accelerated.

As the plasma fire began behind the Avenger, Glitch checked both the side-view and rearview mirrors. "Illumination of the pursuing vehicle's passenger compartment indicates that it is being operated by a T-X," he said.

John swore to himself. The events that had preceded this attack began to click into place in his mind. It was completely unlikely that a second T-X had reached this scene, so somehow the T-X they had captured had escaped her confinement. And somehow Paul had detected the escape and given chase.

Glitch shoved the driver's-side door open and braced it with his foot, then reached up to clamp a hand on the vehicle's roof. "Someone else should drive," he said. He stood up and heaved himself onto the roof.

Tom Carter, his face a comic mask of surprise, grabbed the steering wheel. Despite his effort, the Humvee swerved to the left. He was able to yank it back in line along the center stripe of the road, and John could hear Glitch sliding around on the roof.

Carter swore to himself and slammed the driver's-side door shut. "Speed and efficiency are one thing. Behavior that gets us killed is another thing entirely."

Kate, her head half out through her window, called, "You're right, it's complete foul-up. Talk to the programmer."

"Oh, ha-ha."

John reached up for his lapel mic, but his radio buzzed before he even touched it. "Command, this is Fishhook-Seven. Emergency."

Fishhook-7 was the Avenger. John keyed his microphone. "Seven, this is Command."

"We've just come across Corporal Larson. He's badly hurt. He says his vehicle is down and the package is loose."

"We just got some of that information ourselves, Seven." John did some rapid calculations. The truck the T-X was in was Fishhook-6. Its personnel were likely to be dead, but there was some faint chance some of them, and some of the other Scalpers in Fishhook-5, had survived. "Command to convoy, command to convoy. All vehicles numbered five and higher are to turn back and switch to the first alternate route to destination. Personnel who are extravehicular should go to ground and make your way by best means available to the nearest habitat you can reach. Vehicles one through three, be aware, command is being pursued by the package and about to come under fire."

Which was a conservative way to express their situation.

■   ■   ■

Paul downshifted rapidly, got the dirt bike turned around, and accelerated in the dune buggy's wake.

Then he heard Eliza's voice, her tones soft and caressing: *Paul, it's time to go to sleep. Sleep, Paul.*

He closed his eyes.

He felt the handlebars vibrate in his hand as he hit a patch of rough road. That snapped his eyes back open again. He found himself drifting toward road's edge. He leaned the other way, straightened out.

No, Paul. It's better to sleep now.

His eyes closed again, but he forced them open. It was like trying to stay awake at the end of a late-night shift when the body knew what was best but the mind was unwilling.

Well, his mind was in charge. He gritted his teeth and continued accelerating.

The next time Eliza's words came, his eyes didn't even begin to close.

Finally he knew what was happening. It was his implant. It was indeed an interpreter of sensory stimuli. While he floated in his sensory-deprivation tank, it would tell him what he was feeling, experiencing.

What he hadn't known, what he hadn't guessed was that it was also a more ordinary radio transceiver. Eliza could communicate with it directly—once they were both close enough, since both of them had had their long-range antennas clipped. She could even broadcast data to supercede what his senses were actually observing. His eyes had seen the Sarah Connor face, his implant had superimposed Eliza's face, and the two images had duked it out, causing his vision to blur.

Nor had he realized that he had been programmed for certain types of behavior. To fall asleep on command. To flush his short-term memory when obliged to.

Knowing what had happened made it better. He concentrated on the physical sensations he was feeling, the vibration of the handlebars in his hand, the bike between his legs.

He roared up behind the dune buggy and opened fire once more.

■ ■ ■

The T-X reconfigured her hand into her most formidable weapon: her plasma cannon.

This was not the comparatively weak plasma weapon used by the Resistance and by Skynet's own assault troops. The cannon she carried could destroy a small building or the most formidable armored vehicle with a single shot. A good shot was certain to eradicate a T-600 Terminator and would cripple or destroy later models as well.

Through the hole where her windshield had been, she aimed the weapon at the Hummer ahead. Atop the vehicle, a man—no, a T-850—was struggling to brace himself and bring his own weapon, a carbine, into play.

The T-X heard plasma gunfire from behind. Simultaneously, the dune buggy's rear end slewed to the right. She fired as it happened, and her pulse blast went high, far to the left of the Humvee.

With her right hand configured as a cannon, she had only her left to control the dune buggy, and this time it wasn't enough. She tried to turn into the skid but the world tilted up toward her. Suddenly her surroundings were a blur of sky and pavement, of mountainside and loose rock.

Patiently, she waited for the inconvenient ride to end.

Glitch leaned down to peer through the driver's-side window. "Scalpers-Two is rolling," he said. "Suggest we proceed in our current direction at full speed."

"Thanks," Carter said. "I'd never have figured that out by myself."

"You are welcome. Tell me more about your thinking processes."

The dune buggy's mad roll took it leftward, toward the mountain slope. Paul angled around it to the right, blasted past the moving obstacle, and roared on another hundred yards in the Humvee's wake. Then he downshifted, slowed, and turned to look.

The dune buggy was a burning ruin.

Eliza climbed out of it, seemingly undamaged. Her right hand was gone, replaced by spiky, angular apparati with blue energy crackling around the tips. Paul did not find this view at all comforting.

She looked at him, then began running toward him.

Slowly, carefully, he braced the plasma rifle on the handlebars, leaned down to sight along its barrel, and fired.

His plasma burst caught her in the thighs and knees. She went down hard, skidding half a dozen yards in his directions. Now she was only eighty yards away.

She stood. She seemed a little the worse for wear. There were small craters in her thighs, and one knee was blackened, with a flap of what looked like skin hanging loosely from it. But her face was impassive. *You've proven your point, Paul. You're a formidable fighter. I'm impressed.*

"That's an emotion you're incapable of," he shouted.

As an emotion, yes. As an objective analysis, it is valid. Having proven your point, you should have nothing left to prove. I invite you to return to us.

"Does the offer come with a bubble bath?"

She stood silent for a moment. *I don't know what that is.*

"Then I'll have to decline."

She charged him again. He fired a second time, his burst catching her in the torso, in the gut.

Eliza twisted and went down, again skidding for yards from the sheer momentum of her run. Now she was fifty yards from him.

Then she stood up. Her body was decorated with plasma damage. He could see portions of her endoskeleton. No more blue light danced around on her arm. Her hand slowly returned to its human form.

Another few times and I'll destroy her.

The humor of it took him as hard as a blow to the gut. He bent over, laughing.

What is funny?

"What you just tried to do. Maybe I'm stupid, Eliza, but I'm not that stupid."

She frowned, a very human expression of confusion, and took a step forward. *I don't understand.*

"Sure you do. You have the Terminator world's best internal systems. Somehow, they're not repairing the damage I'm doing to you . . . and yet your clothes aren't being torn to pieces by all the pavement surfing you're doing. Because your autofixing routines are automatically repairing your fake clothing except where my so-called battle damage is. You're trying to fake me out—"

She charged again.

He pointed the barrel of his plasma rifle down, at the motorcycle's gas tank.

Eliza stopped.

"As I was saying, you're trying to convince me that you're picking up a lot of damage. But that's not the truth. You'd let me think that I shot you to pieces, and you'd 'die' almost within arm's reach. Then you'd get up, finish me off, and use this dirt bike to catch up to the convoy. Because you can't do it on foot. This dirt bike is your only chance."

Now she spoke aloud. "If you damage the machine, I promise I will kill you. I will pull your arms and legs off. I will tourniquet the stumps. You will die in as much pain and misery as your species can endure. But if you give me the machine, I swear I will not harm you. I will give you one day's head start. You can find your way to a human nest. You can survive."

"No, thanks."

"If you turn and flee, I can shoot you down before you get out of range. Your only options become to destroy the machine and die or give me the machine and live. Don't you want to live?"

"Sure I do. But I want something else more."

"What?"

"To beat you. For what you've done to me. Every second we wait here, that convoy gets farther and farther away. You'll never catch up to it. When you finally give up trying to figure out how to get this dirt bike and you jump me, I blow it up and you lose. Get it?"

"I get it," she said.

Then her face deformed, her head snapping back as though it had been struck by the baseball bat of the gods. Paul saw a crater erupt in the liquid metal of her skin, revealing the case of the endoskeleton skull beneath. She staggered backward.

Then Paul heard the crack of a rifle in the distance.

He turned, and it seemed impossibly slow to him. Almost a half-mile away, a bright yellow because of its engine heat, was the front end of an SUV, stationary on the road. Behind the open passenger-side door stood a human figure.

He couldn't make out details at this range, but the figure's posture changed, arms lowering, cradling a long pipelike object—

Kyla and her sniper rifle.

There was a *clang* as Eliza's body hit the pavement. Paul spared her a look. The liquid metal was taking shape again over her skull, restoring her face to its impassive original beauty. Her eyes were blank, her head turning back and forth as though she were sightless.

Rebooting.

He didn't think Kyla's rifle could destroy the T-X, but it could delay her. He spun the bike's rear end around and accelerated toward the SUV.

He was halfway to it when he saw Kyla aim again, bracing her weapon in the passenger door window. Paul leaned to the left, hugging the mountain slope.

Kyla fired. Paul saw a flare of whiteness from her rifle barrel and heard a ripping noise as the bullet passed close to his ear. Ahead, Kyla leaped into the passenger seat and the SUV, lumbering, turned around.

Paul flashed past the slower-moving vehicle at full speed. He caught a glimpse of Mark Herrera in the driver's seat. Then he was far ahead of it. The SUV accelerated in his wake.

PART 3: OPERATION BLOWFISH

Las Vegas, Nevada

Stinger Compound, like Home Plate, was a human habitat lurking beneath the ruins of what had once been a site of human luxury.

In this case, that luxury was the rapid elimination of disposable income. The center of operations of Stinger Compound was a nexus of tunnels connecting the subterranean levels of what had once been the biggest, gaudiest, and wealthiest casinos of the Strip.

And even today, decades after the notion of income, much less disposable income, had faded to the stuff of legend, the people of Stinger Compound were surrounded by memories of those colorful days. The deep tunnels of the compound were decorated with slot machines, some of them still functioning. Old blackjack and poker tables, the felt on them flaking and stained, were still in use as mess hall and conference tables. Walls were decorated with posters advertising acts performed by long-dead entertainers.

The coordinators of the compound had given John Connor and his retinue a wing set aside for visiting dignitaries. It was a narrow corridor lined with rooms: secondary security offices, a smallish conference room, men's and women's bathrooms, an old money-counting room now stripped of irrelevant machinery. By the standards of visitors' quarters in the Resistance, the corridor was lavish.

These quarters didn't even smell bad. The officer in charge of the compound had a thing about cleanliness. Everything smelled like old cleansing chemicals and primitive lye soap.

Paul didn't care. He sat in a comfortable high-backed chair and waited for John Connor and Kate Brewster to tell him his fate. They sat on the opposite side of the conference room table and whispered to one another. Glitch sat at the end of the table, steadily regarding Paul from behind sunglasses.

Paul, John, and Kate were the only humans in the room. Paul appreciated that. It was good to have a little privacy with which to receive his sentence.

Finally John and Kate looked toward him again. "All right, Paul," Kate said. "Thanks for the report. I think we're done here."

Paul half-rose, then, confused, sat down again. "Um, I think I'm missing something."

"Such as what?" she asked.

"Such as what? Uh . . ." He struggled for the words. "Such as what I need to do now. I can't fix anything I've broken, so . . ."

Kate nodded. "So you need to know how to pay for it."

"Yeah."

John said, "Were you lying to us just now?"

"No, sir."

"About anything? Even self-deception? Even slanting words so that your role in things sounded a little better than it should have?"

"I don't think so." If anything, his debriefing session had been more in line with a confession than anything else.

"Well, if you were telling the truth, the absolute truth, then you're not to blame for your actions. Are you?"

"I don't think anyone else will have that perspective on it, sir."

John nodded. "You're right. Your actions, however far they were from your wishes, cost the lives of two special operatives, and a third is being patched together now for injuries that will keep him out of action for weeks or more. They also cost us the T-X, the goal of the whole mission. And because we didn't get the T-X, the four additional lives we lost in Santa Fe were thrown away. The survivors of those six people are not going to be charitable, even if it wasn't your fault."

"I guess maybe I need to ask your advice about that."

John took a long breath and considered. Finally he said, "If you, pardon the cliché, put your nose to the grindstone, and do very good work for the rest of your life, and keep your head down, those people aren't going to hate you any less sixty years from now than they do today."

"Oh."

"So I suggest you give up trying, worrying about it."

"Or," Kate said, "find some way to make them think differently about you. The people you're worried about are going to hate you until they can't hate you anymore. So what's going to change their minds?"

"I don't know."

"We don't either, Paul," she said. "But let me ask you something. All the way on the trip back, you've been feeling the guilt of what happened. I'm curious as to whether it's what you would have felt if it had happened just after you were rescued. Or just before Skynet caught you."

He thought about that. What would he have felt before?

The answer came to him without trouble. Sorry for himself. He would have felt sorry for himself.

And he didn't. Now he was just worried about . . .

. . . getting on with his life.

He was able to look her in the eye. "I suspect it would have been a lot worse. Thank you, ma'am."

"You're welcome."

Paul threw them a civilian's half-salute and left.

In the compound medical ward, Paul sat in a wooden chair beside the bed where J. L. lay. The teenager was restless in sleep, probably from the pain of numerous broken bones. His entire right shoulder and arm were encased in a plaster cast. A sheet covered his torso and legs, but Paul had been assured that there was only abrasion damage there—a nasty case of road rash.

He'd been asleep since Paul had arrived. Paul decided to take the medic at his word that J. L. might not awaken until morning. He rose and headed out into the hall, pulling the door shut behind him.

Entering the brightly painted hallway from a far door were Jenna the Greek and Lieutenant Sato. Jenna's face twisted into an expression of anger when she saw Paul. Paul sighed and readied himself.

She charged over and stood nose to nose with him. "I can't believe you came here," she said, her voice a hiss. *A low-volume hiss,* he noted. She might have been angry, but she wasn't about to awaken her injured friend. "You goddamned disrespectful traitor. I ought to kill you right now. Isn't it enough that you killed Smart and Nix? You have to come here and torment the one survivor?" Sato's hand fell lightly on her shoulder, but she did not acknowledge it.

"I'm no more a traitor than the guy who fails to raise an alarm because a Terminator has just torn his heart out," Paul said. "A machine used me before I figured out how to keep it from happening ever again. And because of it, two of your friends are dead and another one's hurt. And I'm sorry. But I'm not going to choose not to pay my respects to J. L. because of it. And I'm not going to be exiled from the human race."

"Yes, you are," Jenna spat. "You deserve to be. You're *not* human. You're like Glitch. You're like the T-X."

"What I'm *not* is your whipping boy." He pushed past her and left.

Jenna watched him go, and when Sato spun her around to face him there was still an ugly look of vengeance in her eyes.

"Give it up," Sato said. "If the brass thought he was a traitor, they would have dealt with him on the trip back. It's that thing in his head, the implant, and he says he's on top of it now."

"He'll never be on top of it. Respectfully request permission to go and put a bullet into the implant." There was no humor in her voice, on her face.

"Denied."

"I'm going to ask again the next time he gets someone killed. Or maybe next time I won't ask."

He pointed past her, into J. L.'s room. "March."

Paul woke up out of a dream. It was a nice dream. At least he thought so until he remembered who and where he was. He and Eliza lived on a farm with their three kids, and every year the wheat grew taller and better.

He sat up as memory returned. *It's a lie, an awful lie,* he told himself. *I'd never become a farmer.* Then he laughed.

He looked around. He was once again in his tiny but gloriously private room in Home Plate. Dim light from a single LED, inset in the door jamb to keep sleep time from being totally dark, showed him its contours.

There were a few more items here now. He had the contents of the backpack he'd carried away from the Operation Fishhook debacle. He'd traded some repair work on a portable compressor for a wooden chair. The weapons he'd scavenged from the attack on the Scalpers leaned up against the wall by his head; no one had ever called for their return. The IR goggles from the truck cab hung, powered off, from a wooden peg in the wall.

And miles away at surface level, in a depot set aside for officers, enlisted personnel, and technicians lucky enough to have personal vehicles, was his dirt bike.

He had things. He was real again.

He scooted back to lean against the wall and thought about what he was going to do.

It was the middle of the night, so there was only a skeleton crew on duty in the compound's command and information center. He showed the ID card Tom Carter had given him to the guards at the perimeter, then made his way through the labyrinth of halls that had once been a government-building bomb shelter to the set of rooms he was looking for. Power cables and data cables snaked through these halls, signs that he was near what he wanted.

The door had GEO/POLIT stenciled on it, and the only reason it could close was because someone had thoughtfully cut a hole in its base for cables to run through. He pushed it open and looked in. Like many of the offices he'd worked in, it was lined with desks, tables, and equipment racks, all of them heavily loaded with computer gear.

There was someone seated in front of one of the computer setups, a thirty-something woman, lean almost to the point of emaciation, her long brown hair in a braid. She peered over at him through wire-rimmed glasses that were probably older than she was. "Yes?" she said.

He entered and handed her his ID card. "I need some help. I'm trying to find a place. I know what it looks like and kind of where it is."

She looked over his card and then shot him a look. "You're—"

"Paul Keeley. That's right."

"I don't think I should—"

He sat on the wooden chair beside her. "Look, the first thing they do when they convict you of treason is take your ID away, making it more difficult for you to visit secure areas. The second thing they do is shoot you." He indicated his face and chest, so far unviolated by bullets, and offered her an "Any questions?" expression. "What's your name?"

"Technician First Class Andrea Berm."

"Hi. Paul." He shook her hand. "The place I'm looking for is in the Rockies. A city or town with a hotel with an atrium. The atrium goes from ground floor to the top of the top floor, and the roof above it is all skylights. I can visualize it and some of the surroundings very clearly. And I desperately need to find out exactly where it is."

"All right." She cleared a game screen from her monitor and brought up the search function of her system's database. "We'll start with everything you know about the place, we'll weight those criteria, we'll come up with a preliminary list of possibles, and we'll begin clearing them."

There were no tidy, clean offices in Home Plate, not even that of John Connor and Kate Brewster. Though larger and better appointed than most other rooms set aside for administrative work, theirs was still lined with tables and shelves, all of them piled high with computer gear, boxes of files, souvenirs from countless military operations, and photographs.

John held up a handwritten piece of paper to show Kate, who sat on the opposite side of the desk. "Final report on the Clover Compound evacuation."

She didn't reach for it. "Everything went well?"

"Everyone's out of there. A third of the population is occupying evacuation caves not far away and setting one of them up as the start of a new compound; a third is headed to Denver to be dispersed from there; and a third is heading for Yucca Compound to be the core of its new population. Spotters saw portions of Clover's exterior collapse, indicating that some of the internal explosives went off after evacuation. Maybe they took out some assault robots with them."

"Let's hope."

There was a knock at the door and Lt. Lott, their secretarial aide, stuck her head in the door. Fiftyish and German-born, she'd been on a tourist trip to the United States when Judgment Day came and had never seen her native country again. She probably wouldn't see it before she died. Her urban-camo uniform always looked newer, crisper than that of anyone on John's senior staff. "Tree juice?" she asked.

Kate smiled. Though trade sometimes allowed them the luxury

of experiencing real coffee, what the Resistance normally drank was usually percolated from one of several varieties of tree bark. Lott could never bring herself to refer to it as coffee. "Please."

John nodded. "Me too."

"There's someone in the waiting area hoping you'll have some time for him. I told him probably not today."

"Who is it?" Kate asked.

"Paul Keeley."

John frowned. "What does he want?"

Lott sighed, clearly not pleased with the answer she had. "He says he has a master plan to get lots of good people killed."

John and Kate looked at one another. "What do you think?" he asked.

She shrugged. "We'd better see him now. Otherwise, we're going to be dying of curiosity all day."

"True." John glanced over at Lott. "Show him in."

She gave him a disappointed look and withdrew.

Moments later Paul entered, accompanied by Earl Duncan. Standard operating procedure demanded that at least one body-guard be present when John or Kate had visitors who were not on the council of advisers or on a very short list of friends. Earl took up position in the corner nearest John; the position would afford him the clearest field of fire if trouble erupted.

Paul saluted, then took the chair Kate indicated. "Good morning."

"Good morning," Kate said. "It looks like it's the end of a long day for you." In fact, Paul had rings under his eyes and gave the impression of someone who'd been up for far too many hours.

"I've been doing research. About this." He held up a few pages of paper, some of them printed, some of them written on by hand. "Thanks for seeing me."

John nodded and gave him a "Get on with it" gesture.

"I know where the T-X is continuing her training," Paul said. "I'm here to propose an operation to go there and get her."

"How would you know where she is?" Kate asked. "Did she tell you?"

"In a manner of speaking." Paul tapped the side of his skull. "When she was communicating with me via this, she communicated more than I suspect she intended to. I saw some images of where she was set up. I spent last night working with members of your geographical data staff to determine where it is."

"Which is where?" John asked.

"Bryce Hotel, Pueblo, Colorado." Paul shuffled through his papers and put down two of them. They were black-and-white printouts of photographs showing hotel room interiors, happy diners in a restaurant, a round fountain with streams of water dancing atop it.

"Where'd you get this?" Kate asked.

Paul shrugged. "It was in BAWA. This is a page advertising the hotel's features."

Kate grinned. BAWA was an acronym used by Resistance computer historians. In the time before Judgment Day, some ambitious institutions had made a habit of sampling the entire contents of the old World Wide Web, making what constituted periodic "snapshots" of the contents of the Web in its entirety. The Resistance had been fortunate enough to find a couple of these archives intact on university computers, and the term Big-Ass Web Archive had entered the lexicon of the Resistance.

"So," John said, "you're here to recommend that we mount a mission to a site an hour's drive from Navajo Mountain, a site where we assume the T-X will be because she told you so, and attempt to recapture her. And this despite the fact that, unlike last time, she'll be surrounded by Skynet forces and probably smarter than last time. Yes?"

"Yes and no." Paul sat back in his chair. He was oddly unconcerned in the face of John's scrutiny. "We have a couple of things going for us. First, I'll be on the mission, and I think that I can distract the T-X, perhaps persuade her that. I'm there to surrender, perhaps even figure out where she is at any given time."

"And second?"

"Second, this is the dumbest idea I've ever run across, so there's no way Skynet could anticipate we'd do it."

Despite himself, John snorted. "Okay, I'll grant that. But let's look at it from another angle. A mission like this would require an elite unit. A 1st Security Regiment squadron, probably. And everyone in the 1st hates your guts because you got two of its members killed and another badly injured. If Skynet's forces don't get you, you might die from friendly fire. Correct?"

"Correct." Paul nodded. The idea had obviously already occurred to him.

"Plus, there's your implant," Kate said. "You've already said you don't think the T-X can influence you through it anymore. But what if you're wrong? What if Skynet comes up with some new set of commands that incapacitates you, or, worse, turns you into a Skynet asset? Even briefly, like last time."

Paul smiled. "I have a solution for both problems. The same solution. Assign someone to kill me."

John and Kate exchanged a look. John said, "Paul, you were *supposed* to say, 'I hadn't thought about that.' Then retreat in confusion."

"But I have thought about it. The solution's simple. Assign one member of the team to stay with me. If I show any signs of helping Skynet, he puts a round between my eyes. Problem solved. Having an assassin on standby actually makes things safer for me, because there's someone *designated* to kill me. It means no one else on the team is as likely to say, 'He's gone over to the other side' and shoot me out of spite. It's the specific assigned task of one of their own members to decide that."

"Interesting," John said. "Have you given any thought to necessary personnel, resources, timing, staging, transportation, and, most important, extraction?"

"That's a little outside my field of competence. So I just did some thinking about those factors as they applied to Operation Fishhook and made some recommendations based on that." Paul set the rest of his papers down atop the Bryce Hotel printouts.

Kate gathered them all up. "We'll think about it."

Paul stood. "Thanks again for seeing me."

John gave him a curt nod. Paul left, admitting Lott, who entered with two steaming cups of tree juice.

"That was . . . interesting," Kate said.

"Yeah, it was. Now let's figure out if what he suggests could work."

It took Paul a few minutes to track down Kyla. He found her emerging from the gunsmith's workshop with a small cloth bag in her hand. Ripper and Ginger, accompanying her as always, moved up close to smell Paul, and Ginger offered her seal of approval, wagging her tail and angling to have her head scratched.

Paul leaned over to pat the dog. He straightened and indicated the bag. "Your lunch?"

"Ammunition," she said. "Shells for my Barrett are pretty hard to come by. At the end of every operation, I turn in all my brass. They just finished putting me together some new rounds."

"Ah. Well, in fact, I wanted to ask you about sniper stuff."

She walked with him out into the main corridor in this supplies and workshops sector of Home Plate. The corridor was thick with pedestrian traffic, dim because of a lack of lighting fixtures, noisy. "Go ahead."

"I had a talk a few minutes ago with your Colonel Walker." Sidney Walker was the officer in charge of the 1st Security Regiment, the unit to which all three squadrons entrusted with John Connor's security belonged. "I asked him what he wanted me to do with Charles Smart's sniper rifle. He said Smart had no living family, so I could either learn to use it like a professional or turn it in to him for assignment to someone who would." Paul shrugged. "I decided to learn how to use it."

"So you're asking me for training."

"That's right."

"In spite of the fact that the main topic of discussion around Home Plate right now is how you screwed up and got Smart and Nix killed."

"Correct. Don't try to snow me, Kyla. You've already decided how guilty you think I am for that. There's too much of your parents in you to let mess hall gossip make up your mind for you."

"Ooh, nicely done. That was almost flattery. So what was I doing by saying that?"

"Testing my responses, I guess. Trying to figure out if I'd get mad and go away in a huff, or get defensive, or answer before thinking and say, 'That wasn't a mistake, I meant to get them killed,' and therefore reveal that I really *am* a Skynet agent."

She snorted. "Close enough. All right, I'll find somebody to keep the dogs occupied for a few hours. Bring your rifle to the Southpoint exit station at two and we'll go up to my shooting range."

"Your own private rifle range?"

"Hey, I'm the boss's daughter." She turned away at the next corridor intersection and left him behind.

Kyla's rifle range was a straight section of the old storm drains, hundreds of yards long and well away from any of the tunnels used for Resistance movement or habitation. Over a span of weeks or months, pouring concrete and then layering artfully strewn rubbish over the plugs, she had carefully blocked off most of the accesses into the section, leaving only two small, well-hidden entryways and a number of ventilation shafts open. She had also built an earthen wall at one end and strung lights powered by car batteries she hauled in for that purpose.

It was here that she showed Paul the workings of his new rifle. He'd had basic military training, of course. Though a civilian worker in the Resistance, he, like every other human, was expected to fight when fighting had to be done—and to do so competently and ferociously. He knew how to handle the many standard-issue Resistance firearms and explosives packages, but a specialized weapon such as this was a different matter altogether.

Kyla held the rifle and explained its functions for him. "Smart's rifle is really the polar opposite of mine, so it tends to play a different role in field operations." She hefted the night-black firearm. In the glow from the overhead bulbs, Paul could make out places where the matte coating had been scuffed or abraded, then repaired with a careful application of paint. Kyla continued, "This is a variation on the standard plasma rifle you're already familiar with. Unlike mine, which fires physical bullets, yours superheats a small quantity of matter to a plasma state, then launches it against a target. When the matter hits the target, it imparts a significant portion of its energy, resulting in a small explosion."

"So how's it different from the standard plasma assault rifle?"

"Basically, three ways. First, range." She indicated the weapon's extended barrel and its removable scope, the fold up iron sights that would be locked in the up position whenever the scope was removed. "Second, rate of fire." She turned the weapon over and indicated the spot where a standard plasma rifle's selector switch would be. This weapon had no such switch, no way to change it from single-shot to autofire. "You get one shot per squeeze of the trigger, period, so you have to learn to make it count. Third, there's energy. The plasma package this weapon delivers is bigger than those from the assault rifles, even though the battery and mass packs are interchangeable. So it just hits harder."

"Hard enough to put down a Terminator?"

She shrugged and handed the weapon back to him. "On a really lucky shot, on the kind of day when the weather's just right and you just won the whole pot at cards . . . yeah.

"Otherwise, it can be reliably counted on to put damage onto a Terminator or assault robot, but it usually takes several shots to put one down. And that's just not something you can count on. Hit one of the machine's hardpoints, like its torso armor, over and over, and you're just not going to inconvenience it much.

"Other differences." She hefted her own Barrett. "Range. Plasma packages, because they don't have much mass, slow down and are deflected by air friction even faster than physical rounds. In spite of the fact that this weapon is optimized for range, you're just not going to get much accuracy beyond, oh, three hundred yards. Good hunting-rifle range. We've got two hundred yards to work with in this shooting range, and that's a good maximum for you to work toward."

"How far is yours accurate?"

"I get pretty good groupings out to a thousand yards. And I can damage a Terminator at that range."

Paul whistled.

"I hope it doesn't puncture your male ego that mine's bigger."

"I'll cope."

Over the next couple of hours, Kyla gave him the beginner's course in sniper-style shooting. He learned techniques of breathing, of meditation, of concentration. He learned patience—Kyla had designed herself an apparatus, a target on the end of a moving pole, that would swing up into position after a programmed delay that could be anywhere from a minute to ten minutes after the device was activated.

He learned the care and feeding of the rifle, how to swap out the daytime optical scope currently installed atop the weapon for the bulkier, heavier starlight scope in a padded pocket of the rifle case.

And he shot. He fired at stationary targets, at targets swinging atop Kyla's apparatus, at designated portions of the earthen wall. Sometimes Kyla told him to shoot when it felt right; sometimes she told him to shoot on her command.

And he did a fair job. The patience and meticulousness that were part of his work habit in other duties helped him here. Kyla looked over his groupings, over the charred craters his plasma fire had left in her earthworks, and pronounced him a promising beginner.

As they were packing up their gear for the return to Home Plate, she said, "Now, you just practice for another thousand hours or two, here and on field missions, and you might get pretty good."

He laughed. "You *are* the boss's daughter."

She gave him a close look. She looked defensive for the first time, and he realized that she was ready to defend her father, rather than herself, from criticism. "What do you mean?"

"I mean you have a knack for explaining to people how bad things are—such as the fact that I'm hopelessly incompetent at this task—and yet make them feel like it's just what's to be expected and some hard work will straighten everything out."

"Oh." She relaxed. "Well, that's usually the case, isn't it?"

"Maybe when there are Connors around."

She smiled and closed her rifle case. "Now you're back to flattery."

"Not really. The difference between flattery and honesty is that with flattery, you'd never say those things if you didn't want something from the person you're talking to. Even if it's just a little feeling of gratitude or friendliness. With honesty, you'd say them anyway."

She looked at him, and the guarded expression she so often wore was gone. "So you don't want anything from me."

"I didn't say that. I just said that my comment would be the same whether or not I wanted anything from you."

"Oh. Well, what *do* you want from me?"

"Other than what any straight male with any sense might want?"

"Yeah."

"I want you to let me know when you think I'm a real boy."

She struggled not to grin, but lost. "All right."

October 2029
Home Plate

The powers that be still chose not to assign Paul to a specific work group. He interpreted that as meaning they were holding him in reserve for the mission he'd proposed.

Over the next several days, he spent his time preparing for that mission. It wasn't training, exactly; the role he imagined for himself didn't call for training. Instead, he imagined himself in conversation with Eliza, how he'd respond to her questions, how he might persuade her to do as the Resistance needed her to.

He also spent time at Kyla's shooting range, becoming more proficient at handling pop-up targets and maintaining a calm sense of detachment while peering through his scope at a target for minute after uneventful minute.

He visited Doreen's class and told the children the rest of the Ginger and Ripper story.

He wrote a will. He tacked it above his cot for people to find if he didn't come home. He left his dirt bike and sniper rifle to Kyla, assuming that she'd enjoy the one and properly dispose of the second.

And for the first time in his life, he attended a Friday night social.

With Judgment Day, the concept of the Monday-to-Friday work week had vanished, but the coordinators of larger human habitats still made some effort to observe the old calendar, and one of the most persistent customs in such places was that of Friday

night unwindings. Some took place in mess halls, some in conference or gathering rooms, others in otherwise unused back passages.
Some were oriented to members of specific trades, others toward
age groups. Ancient CD players or record players would be plugged
in, recently distilled home brew would be distributed, people would
unwind. It was a fair simulation of late-twentieth-century office
parties—assuming one could squint enough to miss the lack of
windows, the presence of so many uniforms and weapons, the pallor of faces that seldom saw the sun.

Uninvited, Paul moved into the chamber where many of Home
Plate's junior-level technicians and intelligence workers had their
regular gathering. It was a large bunkroom for most of the week,
but by common assent of its residents, one night per week it was
transformed into a gathering place. Bunks and footlockers became
seating, paperwork was swept off tables and replaced by food and
drink.

The evening was still early, and Paul saw that the chamber was
only half-filled with people. He didn't recognize anyone. He nodded to those who noticed him, moved to one of the tables, and
deposited his contribution—a bowl full of spicy *pico de gallo* he'd
made himself from fresh hydroponic vegetables gathered from the
mess hall over the last few days.

Then he stood, wondering what to do.

What would Paul Keeley, temp worker with no future, do? He
shook his head at that. *What would Paul Keeley, Resistance fighter
with a weird reputation and no fear of social settings, do?* He looked
across the chamber, listening to what he could of the conversations
floating out of the various groups, and eventually gravitated toward
one of them.

He sat on a cot on the edge of one of the groups. "Sorry," he
said, "I couldn't help overhearing. You're having trouble getting
people to send you music?"

The person he addressed, a twenty-something woman propped
up by pillows at one end of another cot, nodded, nodded, sending
her short black curls swaying. "I'm trying to put together a project.

A master index and repository of all recorded music now held at all the human compounds."

"Sounds like a great idea."

The bony man seated at the foot of the young woman's cot said, "Sure, it's a great idea. But the trouble is in getting anyone to cooperate. People in general aren't willing to send their precious recordings on a trip that means they'll be gone for months at the least."

"On top of the fact," the young woman said, "that getting people just to transmit me a list of what they have is extra work. Nobody much wants to do extra work, not when more vital compound duties come first, improving their quarters comes second, trade work that will get them extra food or goods or services comes third, and so on."

Paul considered. "Do you have enough recording media to handle all that stuff if people start sending it in?"

She nodded. "Uh-huh. We've got one facility putting out recordable CDs at a rate almost like before J-Day, and I can get authorization to utilize a fair amount of that . . . but only if I can demonstrate that the project will work. That people will cooperate. Which a few people in a few habitats have, but not many. Not enough to convince my superiors. By the way, I'm Chelsea."

"Paul." He leaned forward to shake her hand, then did the same with the others gathered around her: Strick, the bony man, David, Jose, Rina, Jackie, Tablesaw.

"You might want to rethink the way you promote your project," Paul said.

"How so?"

"Like you said. If they cooperate, they're contributing to mankind's store of information. Keeping our arts from being lost. Which is a good long-term goal. But almost nobody thinks long-term. They let their leaders do that. Instead, what if you said this: 'Here's the list of what we already have in our depository. Send us a list of what you have that's not already on this list. We'll give you the go-ahead for you to send us some or all of your recordings. You pick an equal number of recordings you want, and when we return your stuff, we'll send you the ones you ask for.' So not only does your project get something out of it—"

"They get something, too," Chelsea said. "Whoa."

"And every compound that participates builds up a better library of music," Strick said.

Paul nodded. "You got it. It'll cost you twice as much recording media, of course. But an active project at twice the cost is better than a dead project. And you can extend the same model to other recorded entertainments. Movies. News recordings. You could even think about setting up a video-letters service between compounds."

"Slow down, slow down." Chelsea waved at one of the others. "David, get me some paper, quick."

Tablesaw, the bearded man, had been quiet through the entire conversation, but finally spoke. "You Paul *Keeley*?"

"That's right."

Some of the others looked at Paul with more curious eyes. Obviously his fame had spread.

"Chelsea, you sure you want to be taking advice from a man who sets Terminators loose and gets soldiers in the field killed?"

That was Paul's cue to leave. He thought about it for a fraction of a second and decided not to. Better, he decided, to be the sort of man who got the crap kicked out of him by an ugly crowd than one who'd flee from a confrontation and sit alone in his room.

"Um," Chelsea said, momentarily off-guard. "The idea's good—wherever it comes from."

Not put off, Tablesaw looked hard at Paul. "Maybe you'd better leave."

Paul pretended to be considering it. "Nope."

"Maybe you and I had better step outside."

"Okay. You go first. I'll be along in an hour or two."

Rina, the black girl with the mass of knitting in her lap, laughed. Tablesaw glowered at her, then returned his attention to Paul. "This isn't a joke."

"Then I'll tell you what the joke is," Paul said. "Like everybody here, I've lost family to the machines. The last time was a little over ten years ago, when my father went down with the top of his head missing. I got to see that. Since then, I was captured by the machines, conditioned and programmed by them, and it did cause me to make a mistake—once—and that got people killed. And that's something I get to deal with for the rest of my life.

"Here's where the joke comes in. Let's say I let you drive me off. Let's say I listen to everybody who hates my guts and I go out into the wilderness to die. Now there's nobody to come up with an idea like the one I gave Chelsea. There's nobody who has my exact mix of skills. Nobody to replace me. Like me, you've just gotten a useful asset killed. But unlike me, a whole bunch of people who think the same way are clapping you on the back. All because you're Tablesaw instead of Sleeps-With-Toasters. Don't you find that funny?"

"I said it was time for you to leave."

"And you said it very plainly, too. No unnecessary use of big words."

Rina laughed again. Tablesaw ignored her. He stood. "All right, guys. Let's toss this machine-loving bastard into the water treatment in-tank."

No one else rose. Jackie, her voice mild, said, "The way I heard it—did you actually face down a T-X?"

Paul shrugged. "I got in her way, slowed her down, sure. I can't say that I faced her down, since she didn't back off. But Kyla Connor shot her and gave me a few seconds to run, so I did."

Tablesaw turned an unbelieving expression between the others. "I said . . ."

"Man, maybe you ought to go cool down," Strick said.

Tablesaw looked between them, baffled and confused, and gave Paul one last ugly glare. Then he turned and marched out of the bunkroom.

Paul watched him go, then sat, staring, in something like a state of shock. *Someone sided with me. Someone who knew the facts actually sided with me.* It was like suddenly learning that the Easter Bunny was real after all.

Someone was speaking. ". . . beautiful?"

"Huh?" He looked around, realized that Rina was speaking. "I'm sorry, I didn't catch that."

"I asked, so, is the T-X really beautiful?"

"Well, Skynet makes them that way." Paul considered. "Yes, she's beautiful. Like a painting—or a statue. But not like a real woman. A real woman's got her beat every time."

Rina smiled at him.

Three hours later, Paul walked back to his room. He didn't walk very well. He was dizzy.

It wasn't just the alcohol, though he'd ended up having plenty of that. It was the change. People he barely knew sticking up for him. And, as far as he could tell, liking him. Rina had even suggested that she'd be interested in accompanying him back to his quarters for the evening.

"I am," he'd told her, "unbelievably flattered. But I can't. There's somebody else." Which was partly true.

"Someone who's not a toaster," Rina had said, amused.

"Not a toaster," he'd assured her.

So now he walked back to his quarters, alone but not lonely, drunk but alert—because he knew, deep in his heart, that at some intersection or shadowy stretch of hall, Tablesaw would come leaping out and beat him senseless.

It wouldn't necessarily be that easy. All the martial-arts training Paul had recalled when he was experiencing his false set of memories was real—just not from dojos in some nameless California town. From the time he began going on field missions to evaluate machinery out in the ruins, he'd undertaken hand-to-hand training from a variety of teachers. He probably wasn't as good as John Connor's bodyguards or a bunkroom brawler with years of experience, but he'd be willing to stack his skill up against anyone who wasn't in constant practice.

Except, maybe, when he was drunk.

But he made it back to his room unassaulted. There was a surprise waiting for him inside, but it was a note left on his pillow:

> *Be ready 08:00.*
> *Pack for a trip.*
> *Your operation is a go.*
> *—Kyla*

Paul decided that he was already sick of caravans, but hangovers definitely made them worse.

And the specific route didn't help, either. This was the notorious Home Plate–Stinger Compound run. It ran from Los Angeles up to Barstow, a town that had at one time survived mainly as a filling station stop for travelers on the Los Angeles/Las Vegas drive, then across the desert to Las Vegas. And though there was some agreeable rough terrain along this route, there were also mile upon mile of open desert—the perfect environment in which to be detected and attacked by Skynet units.

Which was why the caravan was so much more spread out than usual. John Connor's Humvee and the Hell-Hounds' SUV, running almost bumper to bumper, were in the center of the caravan. Dozens of miles back was a heavy truck carrying technicians and soldiers. And the vanguard of the caravan, the surviving dune buggy of the Scalpers, was at the head of the procession, many miles in front of the Humvee and SUV.

And that was the last detail to contribute to Paul's less than exhilarated state. He sat in the front passenger seat of the dune buggy. Beside him, silent for the last several hours, was Jenna the Greek. In the backseat lay Lieutenant Sato, and Paul decided that it was unfair that people like him could sleep anywhere, anytime, including in the back of an uncomfortable, open-topped recreational vehicle speeding through wide-open territory under a glaring sun.

"I'm sorry," Jenna said.

Paul thought it was a trick of the wind. He stared at her, uncertain. "I don't think—what?"

"I said I'm sorry. For jumping on you the other day." She shrugged. "I've spent some time trying to figure out what I'd have been able to do better if I'd been in your place."

"How long before you ruled out suicide as my first, best choice?"

She grinned. It was a wicked expression. "Okay, a few days." Then she sobered. "But I talked to a bunch of the others, got more of the story. I think you did okay. You did good in keeping J. L. from getting killed."

"Thanks."

"You know Kyla's rifle?"

"Yeah."

"The guy who left it to her, she had his name engraved on it. To remember him."

"Huh." Paul thought about it, about the rifle now resting on the floorboards in front of the backseat. "I wonder if I could trade for some engraving when we get to Stinger Compound."

"I think that'd be a good idea. So this operation we're going on, it was your idea?"

"Yep."

"Want to tell me about it?"

"Can't. Besides, they tell me that they've changed some key elements, so what I know may not be correct anyway."

She snorted. "Welcome to the Army."

They didn't stay long in Stinger Compound, not long enough for Paul to work out a trade for engraving. Instead, they rested briefly, loaded up with fuel and supplies, and headed northeast.

In the middle of the night, a few miles from the Utah border, they turned off the main roads onto a side trail. It had once been a gravel road, but now the only traces left of the gravel were occasional patches that lingered in the oldest, deepest ruts. The vehicles of the caravan, now closed up to their customary half-mile-to-a-mile intervals, bounced along the uneven surface until they reached their destination, a flat patch in a dusty valley. There were buildings in the area. In the moonlight, they appeared to be antique corrugated-metal warehouses. Then Paul took a second look and corrected his impression: They were airplane hangars.

A door rolled open in the smallest of them as the dune buggy approached, and Jenna the Greek drove into the darkened building. Only when the door slid closed behind them did the lights come up.

Its interior did not match its exterior. The walls were thick, as much as two yards thick—customary, Paul knew, for surface buildings occupied by Resistance personnel; the thickness of the walls was because of foam insulation that kept Skynet's infrared satellites and aircraft from noticing heat traces characteristic of occupation.

The building was laid out as a garage. Already parked were a pair of motorcycles, a genuine Willys Jeep that looked as though it were being maintained in beautiful condition, a flatbed pickup truck in rust brown, and one more vehicle. Paul saw it and whistled.

"What the hell *is* that?" Jenna asked.

It was a small frame made of metal tubing. Above was a

helicopter-style rotor; immediately below that was a seat for one person, controls before it. Aft were a push-style propeller and, behind that, a rudder. "Gyrocopter," Paul said. "I've only seen them in books."

There were also people in the garage, two men and two women dressed in sand-brown uniform jumpsuits. One woman directed Jenna to park next to the Jeep. There were half a dozen other parking spaces empty. When they were in place, a man brought up a dog, an agreeable-looking rottweiler, to sniff them while another stood several paces back with a submachine gun handy. Once the dog offered them a lick and whine of approval, the handler said, "More coming in?"

"Two groups, one- to two-minute intervals," Sato said from the backseat.

The handler nodded, flashed two fingers to the others.

Paul hopped out of the dune buggy and walked to the gyrocopter. "May I?"

"Sure," said the dog handler. "Just don't touch anything."

Paul was still deeply engrossed in the delicate-looking flying machine, and concluding that it had been built from scratch some time after J-Day, when the Humvee and the Hell-Hounds arrived. Paul saw John grin at him and his mechanical obsession as his vehicle passed. Not long after, the final truck arrived and discharged its passengers and crew.

"Okay, listen up," John called. Reluctantly, Paul turned away from the gyrocopter and saw that John now stood with a local he hadn't seen before, a middle-aged, professorial-looking man in the standard brown jumpsuit of this group. "We're going to make a quick dash over to another hangar. We'll do our real mission briefing there, and Dr. Bowen here will talk to us about our transport. Then we get most of tomorrow, during the daylight hours, to sleep and rest up from our trip . . . and the mission itself starts tomorrow night. Ready?"

There were nods from all around, and John signaled the guard on the door. That woman reached up to flip a wall switch, plunging the interior back into darkness. Then the door rolled aside once more and they all moved quickly outside.

Dr. Bowen led them at a trot to the third hangar in line, the largest of them. A small side door was already open. They moved through an interior office and hall, very dimly lit by red LEDs, and emerged into the central area, which was pitch-black. The echoes of their footsteps made it sound to Paul as though it were huge.

Then the door behind them shut and the lights came on.

There was only one vehicle in this hangar, and Paul wasn't the only one to whistle. The thing was at least two hundred feet long, a bulbous envelope with a comparatively small car suspended from just forward of its center. Rudderlike wind surfaces protruded horizontally and vertically from the stern and engines were set on outriggerlike supports from the gondola.

The craft was a dark blue on the belly, graduating up to black on top. The gondola was painted the same dark blue and had very small windows. The glass surface of the windows seemed a little hazy to Paul, as though it were stippled or otherwise textured.

"A blimp," Jenna said.

Dr. Bowen finally spoke, in a high, clear voice that made it sound as though he'd be a fine tenor for a barbershop quartet. "That's right. This is my baby, the *Blowfish*. Technically a prototype belonging to the Air Force of the Resistance, it actually constitutes a fair percentage of the active duty aircraft serving the Resistance. It was assembled under my direction in Akron." He waved for the others to follow and led them on a sweep along the port side of the airship, traveling from bow to stern. "And this isn't your parents' blimp, either, not that they had one. It uses quite a lot of modern technology. The main engines, amidships, are very quiet ducted rotors. So are the maneuvering engines fore and aft; they make precise positioning of the craft somewhat easier and make it possible to hover, assuming prevailing winds are not too great. All the engines can be individually maneuvered and aimed via our cockpit computer controls for very precise positioning."

He gestured at the great envelope that made up most of the

vehicle's volume. "Internally, we have air-conditioning equipment that helps keep the gas bag at the same approximate temperature as the surrounding air, making it far less likely that Skynet sensors will pick it up as an infrared image. It can make thirty knots in full stealth mode, twice that at full speed, and can ascend to an altitude of about a mile and a half."

"Helium or hydrogen?" Paul asked.

Bowen flashed a sardonic smile at him. "That's usually the first question I get. Hydrogen, of course. Skynet controls all known helium-producing facilities in North America. So *Blowfish* is, in effect, a giant floating bomb. On the other hand, since hydrogen's lighter than helium, we get some extra lift, and that means more personnel and more fuel. Plus, *Blowfish* features some safety equipment that makes a *Hindenburg*-like fate less likely."

"What kind of equipment?" John asked.

"Better sensors to detect pressure fluctuations that might result from a leak, better shielding of mechanical components that might create a spark. And then there's the bail-out option. With activation of a set of mechanical controls in the gondola, the pilot can blow the connectors between the gondola and the envelope. The gondola drops . . . and if it's high enough, will deploy an oversized parachute that will allow it to hit the ground at a survivable rate of speed."

John's voice was dry: "You fill us with confidence."

"I'm sure."

They reached the gondola and Bowen led them nearer, pointing to the car's underside—first, to an orb that hung, like a giant distended eye, from just beneath the bow. "The chief sensor ball, usually trained at ground targets. Infrared, light-amplification, high-gain acoustics, high-gain radio monitoring." He pointed farther aft, where seams marked where sliding panels had to come together. "We have a belly hatch from which we could drop munitions, but it's currently set up in its usual configuration, with four high-speed winches. From any altitude where we want to interact with the ground, we can drop off or retrieve personnel pretty quickly."

"How many times has it flown?" asked Sato.

"Six. Five practice runs and an actual mission I can't talk about."

"You're damned right you can't," said John, his voice a mock growl.

They kept walking, though Mark Herrera dropped behind and began setting up a double handful of equipment he'd been lugging. Paul watched him hang a white pull-down screen from one of the engine pods.

Bowen continued, "I'm not going to brag on *Blowfish* too much until I have a track record I can actually talk about in public, but I think it represents an important part of the resources of the Resistance's armed forces in the future. It's ideal for covert missions. Somewhat less suitable to combat, of course."

Jenna the Greek protested, "But it's a big, gigantic radar image. One assault robot with a Stinger, and it's a goner."

Bowen smiled at her. "Good thing nobody's using radar, isn't it?"

Jenna shook her head. "I don't understand."

"We're used to military thinking that assumes that our skies are filled with radar, that the skies over the U.S. are being constantly scanned for incoming missiles, that sort of thing. But the deal is that the Resistance, from its earliest days, began annihilating very expensive Skynet-controlled radar installations with very cheap radar-seeking missiles. The result, a long time ago, is that Skynet only uses radar when it absolutely needs to look in a specific direction at a specific time. When we go up"—he pointed skyward—"our greatest danger is that something will see us with the naked eye, not with radar."

"And those odds vary with the time of day, I take it," Ten said.

"Not at all." From a pocket, Bowen pulled what looked like a very elaborate remote control for a VCR or DVD player and fiddled with it as he spoke. "The outermost sheath of the main envelope is a Mylar surface, beneath which is a very, very thin layer of ferro-electric liquid crystals. Anyone here familiar with those?"

Paul said, "It's a chameleon."

"Got it in one." Bowen offered Paul an approving nod. "A very small electrical current piped through the polymer level supporting the crystals causes them to alter the way they're arranged, and so we get change." He made a final adjustment. "And the inventor spake, saying, 'Let there be sky-blue.'" He pressed a button on his remote.

It took a few seconds for anything to happen. Then the portions of the envelope closest to the gondola—and the gondola itself—visibly lightened in color. The change spread throughout the craft, reaching its upper surfaces last of all, but within half a minute the entire vehicle was the color of the sky on a cloudless spring day.

Dr. Bowen continued speaking as the change took place. "Tiny cameras all over the envelope's surface sample the color hues of the ground below, the sky above, and feed that information into the color-control computer. That way we can make it as close a match as possible. Understand, it's not invisibility. A normal eye can still detect us. It's just a lot less likely."

Mark called after them, "I'm all set up here, boss."

John waved everyone back toward the gondola. "Okay, mission briefing."

They stood before the screen Mark had set up, and at a wave from Dr. Bowen the overhead lights dimmed to twilight level. A miniature projector Mark had set up on the floor gleamed into life, and John held the remote for it, clicking through images, while Kate spoke.

The first image was of a smallish city, shot from a distance, mountains clear to see behind it. "This is Pueblo, Colorado, right at the edge of the Navajo Mountain Strategic Region," she said. "It was famous for many years as a center of distribution of U.S. government printed matter. It's here that we believe the T-X is completing her training. More specifically . . ."

The image changed to a vertical one, of a ten-story building with cheery architecture somewhat and sunlight bouncing from sea-blue windows. The picture changed again, to a distant tele-photo shot of the same building, from a higher altitude, and different also in picture graininess and the fact that many windows were missing. They looked like teeth missing from a pretty face. "Here, the Bryce Hotel. In her last transmission to Paul, she transmitted information that allowed him to determine that this was where the time-mission training would continue."

"Could she have deliberately planted the information?" asked Earl Duncan. "To cause him to come to her?"

"Possible, but not likely," Kate said. "Remember, at the time that information was transferred, she was in command of the situation and had no reason to believe that she would fail to kill John."

"Furthermore," Paul interrupted, "the information I got was very fragmentary. I think it was the result of the conversational impulses she's been developing over the last several months. She couldn't have been sure that we'd be able to pinpoint the location from the little bit of information I did receive. So I think it's legit."

"What you're going to do," Kate continued, "is take the *Blowfish* to this site. If you can make an unseen arrival, you'll enter the hotel complex from the roof, locate the T-X, then incapacitate it with some of the equipment we used in Santa Fe—and more we've fabricated for this mission. After the initial incapacitation, you'll use an apparatus like the one from Santa Fe, an insulator that prevents the T-X's systems from receiving commands from her CPU; Mark Herrera and Paul Keeley are checked out on its functioning, so at least one of them has to be there when the T-X goes down. If they're both lost, bug out.

"Whether you're successful or not, you'll extract in two groups. The *Blowfish* will have moved on to an extraction point downwind, and the first group, with the T-X, will go there. The second group will go in the opposite direction, acting as a diversion until that's no longer a reasonable course of action. Then it will break and get to safety."

"Question." That was Ten. "Long-term concern. This operation, if it succeeds, will prevent this T-X from going back in time and hunting John Connor. Now, Skynet has shown a certain persistence when it comes to viable plans. What keeps the next T-X off the assembly line from being sent back on the same mission?"

"Nothing," Kate said. "But consider this. Skynet has also shown that, with the learning capability of the various Terminator series, it doesn't just pull whatever's on their memories at each stage of their development and distribute that data. It waits until the behavior caused by that learning has demonstrated that it results in a higher success rate . . . and, obviously, survival rate. In short, we believe that since this T-X has not yet performed any missions that prove the data she's harvested is useful, that data probably hasn't been distributed. The next T-X off the assembly line will have to go through a similar learning process before Skynet pronounces it ready to send back. That gives us months, maybe a year. Perhaps, in that time, we can pull the plug on Skynet. Or . . ." She shrugged. "If we get the indication that the Navajo Mountain Continuum Transport is being powered up to send a machine back to the nineteen sixties, we can also send back our own T-X. We'll fight fire with fire."

Ten nodded. "What about specifics on the sweep of the hotel and the breakdown of our forces into the two groups?"

"We can't have much in the way of specifics," Kate said. "Because we don't know anything about the hotel's layout—either its original layout or what Skynet might have done to it since converting it into a training facility. We don't know what resources you'll have left when the capture of the T-X is complete and the team is ready to leave. So that's up to the team leaders. All we know is that Ten is assigned to the group bringing the T-X out, and Sato's in charge of the group leading the diversionary action. You can set up a preliminary division of labor during the flight tomorrow and then chuck that out the window when you're on the ground and know exactly what you need to do."

Ten grinned. "We make it up as we go along."

"That's the size of it." Kate surveyed the crowd. "Anything else? No?"

"You'll bunk down here tonight," John said. "Eat from your own rations, but Dr. Bowen's crew will bring in a little electrical stove so we'll have hot food. I expect to be in my bunk in . . ." He consulted his wristwatch. "Half an hour. And once I close my eyes, I don't expect to hear any noise." He gave the group a look that suggested he was a stern father in no mood for objection, then grinned. "Dismissed." He took a few steps away from the projection gear, began speaking in low tones with Kate when she joined him.

Mark began breaking down the projection gear. Paul walked over to him, saw Kyla and the other Hell-Hounds doing the same. "You're hauling way too much gear," Paul said.

Mark looked unconvinced. "What do you recommend?"

"Build all that stuff into Glitch. He can stand in front of the screen, his mouth open, bright light coming out of his mouth."

"Question," said Glitch.

"Shoot," said Paul.

Kyla snorted. "He means that figuratively."

Glitch said; "Would such a reconfiguration cause me to look ridiculous to human personnel? Would it consequently cause the respect and or fear in which I am regarded to be diminished?"

Paul nodded. "Yes—and yes."

"Then I should have to recommend against this modification."

Kyla lost it. Laughing silently, her cheeks reddening, she bent over.

Ten sighed and turned to Paul. "I want you to stop messing with our robot."

" 'Messing'?"

"He spent the entire drive up trying to get me to talk about myself. I'm not going to be psychoanalyzed by a Terminator. He said it was because of something you told him."

Paul nodded. "Next, I'm going to teach him to play 'I Spy With My Little Eye.' "

"Great." Ten turned away.

■ ■ ■

It was the first time Paul had flown, the first time most of those present under the age of thirty had flown, but even so, he didn't have the opportunity to look out a window and watch the land passing serenely beneath.

He, the Hell-Hounds, and the Scalpers were packed into the main passenger area, a compartment full of cushioned seats. At one end was a lightweight LCD screen showing whatever visual image was being brought in by the gondola's sensor ball; right now, it was a light-amplified view—a shadowy and color-muted image—of the ground. This wasn't a particularly comforting view. Their route for the last several nighttime hours had taken them through the mountains northeast of Las Vegas, a course that started more northward and gradually became more easterly, and all along its path the ranges of the Rockies had been poised beneath them. Though they were more than a mile up, many jagged peaks stretched toward them. Even now, a toothlike landmass came within a thousand feet of the gondola.

Paul sighed. "I'd really rather shut these lights out and open a window."

Kyla, in the seat next to his, gave him a sympathetic smile. "You'll get that when we prepare for the drop."

"Not the same. Plus, I'd really prefer to be wearing real shoes." Paul had one leg crossed over the other, and he waggled his toes at her. He was wearing special socks that made it less likely any of them would create static electricity while walking. All the others wore them, too, even Glitch, seated stoically in the rearmost seat of the compartment.

Mark turned around to give Paul a mock glare. "God, you complain."

"Hey, don't mess with me. I'll teach Glitch to whine."

Mark winced. "You really *are* the enemy."

Paul imitated, as best he could, Glitch's Germanic accent. "Mark, my batteries are at eight-two percent and dropping pre-cip-i-tous-ly. Mark, I need a charge. Mark, Kyla called me im-plac-a-ble. Mark . . ."

Mark faced forward again, shaking his head.

Kyla lowered her voice. "You're really not scared anymore, are you?"

"Of getting killed on this mission? I sure as hell am."

"Of people."

"Oh." He thought about it. "Was I scared?"

"You were something. Now, at least, you make eye contact. And sometimes when people come at you verbally, you beat them back into their corners."

"Do you like it?"

"Yeah, I kind of do."

"Then I guess I'll have to keep doing it."

Dr. Bowen's voice crackled over the compartment's internal speaker: "We're getting signs of sunup in the east, so I'm putting us down for the end of Phase One. Ground crew, please stand by to man the ropes."

Mark, Glitch, Sato, and Ten rose and moved into the companionway, headed back to the aft chamber with the belly hatch.

The *Blowfish* descended across the ruins of Boulder toward a landing zone north of Denver. The land here was less mountainous than what they'd been flying over for the last dozen hours, still hilly and broken enough to provide ample cover for the blimp.

Once Dr. Bowen selected a landing zone, in a little valley between steep hill slopes, he spent considerable time maneuvering the blimp's two primary and four secondary engines, bringing the vehicle to a smooth descent until it floated mere feet over the earth of the valley floor. The press of a switch caused the belly hatch to slide open, and the four line handlers dropped through to the ground. Two moved forward and two aft, each positioning himself beneath the slight bump on the envelope's nose or tail surface that heralded the presence of anchor lines and electrical winches controlling them. In minutes, well before the sun could illuminate them, they had the lines fixed to trees. Dr. Bowen spent additional minutes pumping hydrogen back into the gas's pressurized containers but using the main engines to blow ordinary air into ballonets within the main envelope, keeping the entire structure pressurized and comparatively still.

Finally Dr. Bowen pronounced the landing complete. "Break out your bedrolls," he said.

The *Blowfish*'s route had led it well around the Navajo Mountain Strategic Region and the danger it posed. Now they were, depending on whether the winds remained out of the north, four to five hours' travel from Pueblo. They'd launch again at nightfall.

Paul set up his pup tent and bedroll in chilly air in the shadow of the blimp's envelope. Around him were the tents and rolls of the others. Sato couldn't keep his eyes off the valley walls around them. "I know this place," he said, his breath emerging as steamy plumes. "I'm so close to home I could walk there with my eyes shut. I used to hunt here."

"Maybe we can swing by it on our way out of here." Paul shoved his bedroll into his pup tent, unrolled it.

Sato shook his head. "It's just an abandoned cabin on a mountain slope now. Probably a wreck. Maybe, if I live long enough to see Skynet fall, if I survive to have a family, I'll take my kids there. Show them where I grew up. Maybe even stake a claim to that property."

Paul frowned over that. He knew a lot of people who weren't—and never would be—comfortable with the idea of living aboveground. He used to be one of them. But now, the thought of occupying some grand prewar house or an apartment in the open air didn't bother him at all.

It had to be some leftover part of his Skynet conditioning. It wouldn't do for someone who thought he was a twentieth-century clerical worker to desire to live in a hole in the ground. "I hope you get to do that," he said and climbed into his bedroll.

"Thanks." Sato crawled into his own tent and disappeared.

Kyla was one of the last to set up her tent. Paul poked his head out to watch her work. "Cold camps like this," he said, "I bet you miss your dogs."

She nodded. "Yeah. My big, furry space heaters." She'd left Ripper and Ginger back at Home Plate, which was only sensible for a mission in which the entire team was going to be winched into and out of a blimp, though no one had known at the time why the orders had directed the dogs be left behind.

"So, what if this warm-blooded mission planner were to look at you and say, 'Hey, how about crawling into this bedroll with me? I'll keep you warm.'"

Mark, standing on the other side of the small encampment, shot him a warning look. Paul ignored it.

Kyla smiled. "I'd say no, thanks."

"Oh, hell."

"But I'll say this, too." She leaned in close over him and her hair brushed his chin and forehead. "You asked that just like a real boy." She leaned a bit closer and gave him a quick kiss. "Good night."

"Night."

After a day's rest, and in the remaining hours before sundown, they got in a little additional training.

Dr. Bowen raised the *Blowfish* to an altitude of about thirty feet beneath the gondola. From the gondola's aftmost compartment, the Hell-Hounds showed Paul the bare basics of rappelling, a task they might be called upon to perform when descending the Bryce Hotel—or even exiting the blimp itself, should something cause a winch to jam. And all members of the operation got some additional training with the devices that, for this mission, replaced Operation Fishhook's steel net and capacitance charges.

Conceived of by Paul and built by Lt. Tom Carter's workshop, the four devices resembled harpoon guns. That was, in fact, what they were, except that they also functioned in a fashion similar to tasers. The harpoon, though it could in no way do real damage to a machine as tough as a Terminator, had a head with reverse barbs that would penetrate skin—or liquid metal configured to function like skin—and be difficult to remove. When fired, it carried with it one end of a heavy-duty electrical cable.

The cable led back to a capacitor carried within a backpack. Paul dubbed the weapon the "T-taser." The weapon's left trigger would launch the harpoon; the right trigger would fire off the capacitor.

With three or four successful hits, the T-tasers would, in theory, be able to put the T-X down for enough time to attach the CPU insulator, the device needed to keep the Terminator inert. This was nowhere near as reliable an arrangement as the net in Santa Fe had been, but at least it was mobile.

Once an earthen rise had taken enough harpoon shots to establish that everyone could reliably hit a human-sized target within the weapons' limited range, they were ready to go.

Four hours later, they cruised in over the northen end of the darkened city of Pueblo. Dr. Bowen told them over the intercom that they were running parallel and a few hundred yards west of I-25, the main north-south highway. The LCD screen in the main passenger cabin showed an infrared view of streets and houses, long-empty swimming pools, long-abandoned cars, all of it crawling past very slowly. Everyone present had seen this sort of landscape before, except that the altitude and perspective were very different now.

Paul found it difficult to keep his breathing under control. He'd been on any number of field missions in the past, even if on those occasions he'd merely been a well-protected technician, but this was very different.

Those had been intelligence-gathering or resource-harvesting operations. This was far more critical. John Connor's life might depend on it. Which meant the Resistance's very existence might depend on it.

If Paul screwed up, he might doom the Resistance.

That thought settled over him like a wet, cold blanket.

"You all right?" Kyla asked.

He gave her a nervous smile. "I always get a little nervous when I visit old girlfriends."

"Yeah, right."

"Don't you ever get the shakes?"

She thought about it. "The guy who taught me to shoot, Tony Calhoun, once told me, 'Consign yourself to dying at the start of every mission. That'll keep you calm enough to shoot. You'll fight harder, better, and smarter. If you survive to go home, then you'll get the shakes.' And he was right. It's a sad way to live sometimes, kind of hard on the morale, but I think I've kept more people alive because of it."

Paul fell silent and thought about it.

That's what he'd done back on the highway where he'd confronted Eliza. He'd been sure he would die then. And though regretting the likelihood of his imminent demise, he'd never been as sure and focused as in those moments.

Dr. Bowen's voice crackled over the intercom. "We're getting a good correspondence between available maps and what we're observing on the ground. So I'm pretty sure we're on course to the Bryce Hotel. Estimated time of arrival: seven minutes."

"Final gear check," Ten said. Half of them stood and the rest remained seated in the already-overcrowded compartment as they performed one last confirmation that every piece of gear they needed was still in their possession, every weapon loaded, every battery charged.

Paul found that his heart was no longer pounding hard enough to shake him.

His sniper rifle, tool kit, CPU insulator, IR goggles, handgun, and miscellaneous gear were in order.

He was ready.

They assembled in the aft compartment and hooked Mark, Kyla, Ten, and Earl up to the nylon webbing arrays that Dr. Bowen had called carry rigs; they were attached by carabiner clips to the metal loops at the end of the cables. Then Ten switched out the compartment's light. After a minute, their eyes more adjusted to the darkness, Ten flipped the intercom switch. "Ready to go," he said.

"Opening in twenty seconds," Bowen answered. "From the time I open it, I'm leaving this intercom dead. Don't want any extraneous sounds floating out of the bay."

"Roger that," Ten said.

Moments later, they felt air movement. In seconds, the hatch covers had withdrawn to their fully open configuration, and the operatives stood on the narrow sections of flooring surrounding the gap. Now they could hear the rush of wind across the blimp's surfaces, hear the muted whine of the main and secondary engines driving the blimp forward. Though the city beneath them was dark, occasional objects—intact car windshields, pools of standing water—reflected the stars.

Paul switched on his goggles, watched as the streets below materialized into shades of green. He could now estimate their movement rate. It didn't seem much faster than a good walking pace. The buildings below seemed to be mostly office structures, shops, restaurants, and hotels, and he decided that the gondola was less than fifty yards above the ground.

They passed over a sprawling, irregular building, probably a convention center or something similar, with a connecting hotel on one side. Then the engine whine changed. Their forward progress slowed even more and they began to descend. Moments later, a rooftop, closer than the other building summits, perhaps only thirty feet down, moved into view from ahead. Paul could see a dark mottled surface, like a squared-off letter *O*, with a much brighter square in the center. On one side of the darkened portion was a raised scaffolding, a sign that once had shone with the words BRYCE HOTEL; Paul could see that some of the letters had survived and from the rear he read: B   E H   TEL.

There was also a small, boxy construction on the dark portion of the *O*, something like a windowless, one-room shack. That was their target. As Paul watched, they moved until the edge of the roof was beneath them, then they were directly above the brightest portion, which had to be the skylights over the atrium.

Dr. Bowen apparently realized that this was not ideal. The *Blowfish* shuddered a little as it slowed, then came to a complete halt. One set of engine sounds stopped completely, but the higher pitch of the secondary engines increased. Paul winced as he listened and imagined that every machine everywhere in Colorado could hear the noise.

Blowfish drifted to port and suddenly the hatch was directly above solid roof again. "Go," Ten said and stepped down into nothingness.

The cable he was hooked to kept it from being a long step. Mark, Kyla, and Earl followed suit. Glitch, on the control panel, threw four switches and the four operatives glided, nearly silently, down into the darkness.

Blowfish continued drifting as they descended, but Bowen kept them above rooftop all the way down. Then, as they landed and strapped themselves from the carry rigs, the blimp began to gain altitude, the ends of the cables snaking up and away from the operatives below. The four hundred or so kilograms they and their gear represented was a significant part of the blimp's payload. Paul heard the tiny whine of servos as the main engines turned, then the deeper hum as they kicked in again. Now Bowen would be pumping some of the hydrogen out of the ballonets, directing outside air into the main envelope to maintain pressure. Lift would decrease slightly and—

Blowfish slowly descended again. On the roof below, Mark was at the door of the small boxy construction, performing a security check on it. That door should lead to the stairway into the building proper, and if Resistance intelligence held true to form, there would be little or no security installed. If Skynet didn't believe the humans could do something, such as land operatives on a ten-story roof, it generally didn't defend against that possibility.

The ends of the cables snaked up again and Glitch switched the winches off. Paul struggled into his carry rig and clicked its straps shut.

"Go," Sato said.

And Paul, unconcerned, stepped off. The cable held. He and the others dangled, then began their descent.

By the time they reached the roof, Mark had the door open. He and Kyla entered. Ten motioned the rest to wait. Paul unclipped himself and stepped out of his rig, watched as two of the three cables snaked up into the sky, watched as *Blowfish* once again began its altitude-balancing act. The third cable remained at its fully deployed length.

A minute later, Glitch slid down the last cable, his hands wrapped up in a blanket to protect his artificial skin from the damage the cable would otherwise have done to it. He landed comparatively lightly for something that weighed two hundred kilograms, even discounting the massive pack he wore. When *Blowfish* rose away this time, it made no effort to maintain altitude. Paul heard its engines hum to life again, and the craft slowly began moving toward the south, toward their eventual rendezvous.

Now they followed Mark and Kyla into the building.

The door led into a concrete stairway. There were metal safety rails along the walls, and the forward edge of each step was inset with an abrasive strip to make slipping more difficult. That marked this all as original equipment, as Skynet never built anything with the safety measures that had so concerned humans before J-Day.

One floor down, they passed through a metal doorway into the top floor's main corridor. To one side were room doors, all closed; to the other, a solid banister over the building atrium. The banister rail was chest-high, making it harder for some foolish hotel guest to fall over. The corridor made right-angle turns at intervals so that a square bank of rooms surrounded a square corridor, which in turn surrounded the square atrium.

And light filtered up from the atrium's lower floors, bright enough that Paul and the others could switch off their infrared goggles and pull them free.

Below, between them and the lobby floor, hung a large apparatus that looked like it was made of dozens of lengths of shiny brass piping. From a central point directly beneath a three-story-high support cable attached to the corners of the roof, the pipes spread out in several directions, looking like multiple sets of superelongated wind chimes or a set of pipes magically removed from a church organ.

Paul felt the others looking at him. "What?"

"What the hell is that?" Ten asked, whispering.

Paul sighed. "It's a sculpture. Decoration. I mean, I suppose Skynet could have assigned it some sinister purpose, setting each pipe up to fire a single armor-piercing round or something, but why?" He shook his head. "It's just leftover twentieth-century decoration."

Ten relaxed. Paul returned his attention to the floor below. The hotel lobby was well lit, shiny, and well scrubbed, as if a crew of workers had been at it only that morning. Paul could see black marble gleam from the top of the reception desk.

"Feel anything?" Ten asked him.

Paul shook his head. "But something occurs to me."

"Shoot."

"In the hospital where you found me, they'd restored a nurse's station, and that's where Mark was able to get all the information about me."

Ten nodded. "Right. So?"

"So it suggests that, when it sets up these facilities, Skynet preserves the original roles of certain areas. Nurse's stations were places where computers were set up and where you could get information about patients. So is a hotel's reception desk." He pointed downward.

"That's a good place to start, then," Ten said. "Kyla, where do you want to set up?"

"Fifth-floor balcony," she said. "It'll give me a good field of fire, and if I have to get out quick, it's a height I can rappel down from—inside or outside."

"Okay, you'll peel off there. Everyone back to the stairs."

At the fifth-floor landing, Kyla did wait until Mark checked out the door and pronounced it free of security measures. Mark pulled it open a bit, looked both ways, and said, "Empty and unlit."

"Good luck," Paul said.

"You too." Kyla slipped through and was gone.

The rest of them reached the first-floor landing moments later. Ten was looking concerned, and as Mark checked out this door, Paul asked, "What's wrong?"

"It's going well," Ten said. "I hate that."

Paul opened his mouth, but it was Glitch who spoke up first, asking, "Why?"

"Because it usually means that we've guessed wrong about the enemy's setup."

"Sometimes," Sato said, "it just means they're sloppy."

Ten nodded. "But counting on that is a fast way to get dead."

"A simple sensor," Mark said, gesturing to the door lock. "Made to send a signal somewhere anytime the door is opened or closed."

"Simple to disable?" Ten asked.

"Already done."

Sato considered. "So it's not intended for someone like us. Who, then?"

Something stirred up a bad taste in Paul's mouth. "Someone like me," he said.

Ten looked at him. "Huh?"

"Think about it. They've built a new facility to replace the one you wrecked. What else have they replaced—or are they planning to replace? Me."

In his peripheral vision, Paul saw Jenna pale, but she didn't say anything.

Ten absorbed the idea with less concern. "Ready to go?"

"Ready," Mark said.

"Go."

Mark slid a tactical observation device, a narrow mirror at the end of a several-inches-long metal stem, beneath the door, then leaned down close to look at it as he turned it back and forth. Satisfied, he pulled the door open an inch, peered around, then opened it wide enough to stick his head through. Paul could see potted palms directly ahead. Finally Mark stood and slid through the door, leading the way.

They were in a lobby-level side corridor, as clean and brightly kept up as the atrium floor had been. Signs on nearby doors indicated the presence of bathrooms, pay phones. Paul wondered what he would get if he picked up a pay phone and dialed a number. Would he have the opportunity to talk to Skynet for a brief few moments?

The corridor ended to the left, merged with the atrium to the right. Just to the right of the stairway door—and immediately opposite—were elevator doors, three on each side. The seven operatives moved silently to the atrium end and surveyed what lay beyond.

The lobby was spacious, its main open area constituting the bottom of the atrium. The front doors, sliding and revolving, were on one wall with nothing but huge plate-glass windows stretching above them for two more stories. Along the lobby's edges were the registration desk, the bell captain's desk, doors into offices and into the bar and restaurant, hallways leading to function rooms.

To the right of the hallway where the Hell-Hounds and Scalpers stood was a fountain, the same one Paul had seen in his brief vision and in the old hotel advertising material. It was a four-foot-high bowl, its internal diameter some twelve feet across, its exterior made of gleaming green marble. Though water was not being piped up through it now, the water in it seemed clear, and Paul could see coins in the bottom.

Far above the lobby floor, ranging from the fifth to seventh stories, was the esoteric sculpture they had seen from the top floor. Its dangling pipes swayed gently in the air-conditioning, occasionally connecting and making a pretty, metallic tone.

Motion attracted Paul's eye to the front doors. Beyond them stood hotel employees: men wearing purple uniforms with gold trim. On the street they faced, cars and taxicabs occasionally passed before them.

Paul discovered that he was sitting down. Ten leaned in close. "Are you all right?"

"Tell me what you see through the doors," Paul managed.

"Nothing. They're black, totally black."

"Got it." They were black like the window in Paul's bogus apartment had been. The blackness was some sort of neutral field or color, like a blue-screen once used in moviemaking, replaced by sensory input broadcast by the facility's computers—input only someone like him could see. "I've interfaced with the computers here," Paul said. "I didn't even know when it happened." He got back to his feet. "Sorry, I was startled."

"It's all right," Ten said. "Do you feel anything? Anything strange?"

Paul shook his head. "Not so far."

"Let us know the instant you do."

Ten turned and nodded toward the reception desk. "Odds that it's under camera surveillance?"

"Unknown," Mark said. "And that'd be devilishly hard to find out. Cameras could be positioned anywhere on ten floors' worth of stuff, all pointing down here."

Paul's knees suddenly felt weak. His vision blurred. "Now I do feel weird," he said and sat down again, this time deliberately. He cradled his head in his hands.

"At this time," Glitch said, "it would be very useful to be certain that you are still yourself."

"I'm me."

"Perhaps more evidence would be in order. Where and when are you?"

"Bryce Hotel, October third, twenty twenty-nine." Paul was now getting a handle on the dizziness. It was fading, but some sensation associated with it was remaining constant.

"That is good. Please continue."

Paul looked up. Glitch had his Uzi aimed directly at him. "If you think it through, Glitch, it would seem obvious that the time to assume that I'd been regressed by contact with Skynet computers would be when I first started showing confusion about my surroundings. Yes?"

"Perhaps," the Terminator said. "My instructions on this point call for me to act if, in my discretion, you are a danger or liability to the group. The criteria for establishing that you are a danger are nebulous, however."

Sato, at the rear of the group, hissed for attention. The others turned to look at him, then at what he was looking at.

The bank of lights above one of the elevators was flickering. As they watched, the light flickered over from G to CL, which was the left-most light. Going in the other direction from G, next would be L, then 2, then 3 through 10.

The light stayed on CL.

"G stands for 'ground,' right?" Jenna asked. "Then what is CL?"

Paul shook his head and rose once more. "This lobby is on the ground floor. So G has to be 'garage.' I'm not sure about CL." He thought about it. "I think what just happened is that I interfaced with Eliza. She just came back from somewhere and rode the elevator from the underground garage to a lower level."

"Does she know you're here?" Jenna asked.

Paul shrugged. "Unknown. But I think that if she did know it, she'd probably be talking to me."

Ten said, "We need to go down."

Mark said, "But we may need what's in the computer. And a terminal is probably here."

Ten sighed. "All right. Mark, you and Jenna take that duty, and keep your damned heads down. Mark, give your T-taser to Paul."

Mark handed the bulky weapon over. "You designed it, I guess it's only right that you get to fire it."

"Thank you, tall Hispanic man. You comfort me with your simple words of faith."

Mark rolled his eyes and turned back toward the lobby.

They descended, as quietly as possible, two more flights of stairs. Here the stairwell ended in the same sort of door as they'd found in upper levels.

Ten said, "Paul?"

"Uh, Ten, I'm not a security guy."

"You and Glitch are as close as we have, and he's optimized more toward sabotaging machines or making them work through brute-force techniques. Just do it."

Paul set the T-taser and backpack down, then dug his tool kit out of his pack. He cursed himself for not paying more attention to what Mark had been doing. First, the man had run his little mirror all around the door, then had played around with a voltage meter, concentrating on doorknob and hinges, and then had fiddled with a wire at the point along the door frame where the bolt would go, running the wire up to the ceiling and over the door—

That was it. The simple sensor had to be something that measured electrical current flowing between the retractable bolt in the knob apparatus and the metal-rimmed slot in the door frame it went into. Opening the door would interrupt the current, alerting security computers monitoring the building. Mark had attached a wire to the metal rim, then affixed it to the bolt. Then he could pull the door open, and so long as no one pulled the wire free at either end, the electrical current would flow normally.

Paul set about re-creating Mark's bypass. It took him several minutes, six or eight times as long as Mark had taken, and sweat began running down his back and sides long before he was done.

And when he had finished using a thin, precisely cut strip of gummy black tape to attach the second end of the wire to the bolt, he heard a voice.

Sir, we should be in to Denver in about thirty minutes.

It was Eliza's voice.

He was pleased that he managed not to drop anything or jerk away and wreck his work. "Ready to go," he said, his voice low. "And, by the way, I'm hearing the T-X talking."

Ten whispered, "To you?"

"No. To someone else."

Well, I'm not sure. That's sort of against regulations.

"Okay, go."

Paul pulled the door open and hazarded a quick look. He saw dark wood paneling and somewhat faded carpet. He pulled it farther open and put his head through.

It was a hotel corridor, but broader than the one by which they'd first entered on the upper floor. A plastic sign, its surface simulating wood grain, read:

> *Anasazi Room*
> *Brown Room*
> *Evans Room*
> *Pike Room*

Beside each room name was an arrow pointing right.

"*CL*," Paul said. "I'm betting it means 'conference level.' These are all conference rooms." He stood, flipping the length of the wire up over the top of the door as Mark had done.

"Earl, your lead," Ten said.

Earl took point, a rocket-propelled grenade in hand. Paul gathered up his gear and followed.

Well, actually, that sounds nice. My name is Eliza.

A lot of people tell me that. It's just a name that runs in my family.

Hunkered down behind the reception desk, Mark carefully hoisted a live monitor and keyboard down to the floor, then set about cabling the associated computer to his own laptop. "Score one for Keeley," he said. "This is a reservation database; but I'm betting it's a cover screen. Once I figure my way past it, I'll bet I can get into the operational data for this site."

Jenna, crouched beside him, said, "Give me that mirror on a stick you were using."

"You know how to use it?"

"It's a mirror on a stick. Does it need an instruction manual?"

"You offend me." Mark handed the object over. "I took my bachelor's degree in mirror on a stick. By the way, it's called a tactical mirror."

She held it up to peer over the countertop and turned it slowly from side to side. "You don't have a bachelor's degree. You're too young."

"It was prenatal."

"You're just weird."

"Ah, bingo. Security Camera City. Let's flip through and see if we're on camera like last time."

Eliza said: *Transition.*

Paul felt his mind drift. His surroundings went to white, and the tension he'd just been experiencing began to fade from his mind.

Angrily, he shook his head. As though recovering from having a flashlight shone in his eyes, his sight began to return, and his thought processes snapped back to the here and now.

He looked back. Glitch was looking at him, the carbine half-raised. "Still me," he said.

"Good," the Terminator said.

Ten paused at the first conference room door they'd encountered, the one labeled ANASAZI. "What was it?" he whispered.

"A verbal cue from Eliza. It seemed to do the same thing as 'Go to sleep.'" Then Paul shook his head. "No. I think it was just like putting her subject on 'pause.' Allowing for a brief interruption or letting her zip through events that would be irrelevant to her conversation. Basically, a scene change."

This is a nice place. I like the aquarium. What do you recommend?

"They're in a restaurant now," Paul said.

"Any chance she could detect you?" Ten asked.

"Sure. But I don't think she has."

Ten gestured at the door. Paul settled down before it, listening, but could hear nothing beyond. He got to work putting together a bypass.

Yes, I love it. I get to travel all over the place.

Probably New York. There's so much to do.

No, not really. Not anyone special.

Paul shook his head. Damn, she sounded human.

Well, I don't know. Let's just see how the evening goes.

Bypassing the security on this door went a bit faster. When he was done, he cautiously pulled it open. It was dark beyond. But he could distinctly smell the odor of spoiled meat. He almost gagged on it.

He closed the door again and looked at the others. Ten and Earl were wrinkling their noses, aware of the stench inside the room. "Dark. Goggles?"

Ten shook his head. "Open it for me."

Paul stood, lifting the trailing wire out of the way, and opened the door wide enough for Ten to enter. The unit leader stepped in and a moment later, as Earl followed him inside, the room lights came on.

Ten said, "Oh, dammit."

Paul followed Earl in and didn't know whether it was the sight before him or the smell of corruption that had caused Ten to react that way.

This was no conference room. It was an operating theater. Paul was no medic, but he knew a surgical table when he saw it, even when it came equipped with hard metal ankle, wrist, waist, and neck restraints. There were several other pieces of equipment here he could identify, including tanks of anaesthetic, heart-rate and blood pressure monitors, electroencephalogram and electrocardiogram.

What he couldn't identify was the huge apparatus that stood next to the operating table and dominated the room. It was as deep and wide as a telephone booth, running from floor to ceiling. Its top and bottom were pivots, allowing the entire machine to pivot, perhaps to spin completely around. There were waldoes—mechanical armatures and hands not intended to be mistaken for human limbs—all over it. Other extensible apparati ended in blades, saws, needles.

That, more than the rotted-meat smell that pervaded the place, made Paul want to gag.

He gulped several times, willing his stomach to settle. Eliza was still talking and talking, but he couldn't force himself to listen to her.

"Ladies and gentlemen," he said, "meet the world's first mechanical surgeon."

Ten shot him an offended look. "For what kind of surgery?"

"I'll bet a month's food that it's brain surgery." Paul moved up beside the table. There was a foot-high bin on the far side. It was brimming with what looked like spoiled organ meat.

"This," Earl said, "we do not need."

"Yes, we do," Paul said. "We need to find out what we can about the other patients they have here." He moved to the far side of the monster mechanical surgeon.

There, he found an LCD screen, a small keyboard, several jacks for cable insertion. "I might be able to find out something here," he said. "I might also alert the entire world that we're here."

"Which will bring the T-X to us," Ten said. "Either way, we win. Go right ahead."

Paul pressed what looked like a POWER-ON switch and the screen came alive, sharpening into a monochrome display, white text on a dark blue background. One line, the bottom, was reversed, blue letters on white. Paul nodded. It was a comfortably familiar twentieth-century computing convention, reversing the colors of the active choice. He suspected that Eliza would be able to jack directly into the machine's data inputs; the keyboard and LCD screen were either redundant systems for her or leftover components from an earlier design made for human use.

He decided that thought didn't bear consideration. Not right now.

That reversed line of text read: POTTS, ERNEST 20291003:0600 DECEASED.

"October 3," Paul said. "I think they operated today. And lost their patient." He began scanning up the list of names. There were twenty-two of them, thirteen male and nine female, with dates going back as far as eight months, and all but one read DECEASED. The fourth entry, DENTON, HAZEL, read TERMINATED.

He found the arrow key that moved the selection bar up the screen. He selected DENTON, HAZEL and pushed the SELECTOR button. The screen of names cleared and was replaced by data on the patient.

"She was from 'unknown habitat,'" Paul said. "Is there an 'unknown habitat'?"

"Probably means they couldn't extract the name of her home," Sato said.

"Right. It indicates that she survived the surgery. Didn't evidence any relevant knowledge. Gradually became irrational and was terminated."

"Right," Ten said. "Does it say anything about who the T-X is talking to now?"

"Hold on." Paul found the key that backed him out to the previous screen, then used the arrow key to run him up past the top name on the list.

That screen was replaced with another list of names. The bottom four names were the same as the top four on the other screen. Of the eighteen new names, sixteen read DECEASED, one read TERMINATED, one read INTERRUPTED.

The one labeled INTERRUPTED was for KEELEY, PAUL.

Paul forced himself to ignore his own record for a moment. The three names surrounding his were men and women who'd been on the mission with him when he was captured a year ago. He ignored them, too.

He scrolled up to the other TERMINATED listing. "Subject: 'Gutierrez, Moses.'"

"Hey, I know him," Sato said. "He died early this year."

Paul nodded. "I bet his body wasn't recovered."

"You'll win that bet."

"It says here that he was knowledgeable about classical music. Attempts to place him in an eighteenth-century European context failed. He eventually built up a resistance to having his short-term memory purged and he was terminated."

He glanced at his own record. There were no surprises there: SUPERIOR COMPREHENSION OF TWENTIETH-CENTURY CULTURE, ENTERTAINMENTS, AND BEHAVIOR. PERSISTENT FEELINGS OF PARANOIA AND ABANDONMENT. LOST AND PRESUMED TERMINATED WEEKS AGO. SUBSEQUENTLY REPORTED ALIVE BY T-X PROJECT MONITOR. EFFORTS ONGOING TO REACQUIRE ASSET.

"*Reacquire asset.*" He shook his head. He would never be reacquired.

Emotionlessly, he backed out of that page and returned to the screens of patient names. He scrolled from top to bottom again. "They don't have any living subjects to work with."

"Then who's she talking to now?" Earl asked. "Who's she in the restaurant with?"

Paul shrugged. "It's got to be a simulation. I'm guessing they've programmed another machine with what they know about human conversation. A practice dummy to keep her in training while they look for another victim . . . or wait to get me again."

Ten said, "So we don't have to worry about any other subjects. Let's bring her here now and save some time. Everyone out in the hall. Paul, give her a call, would you?"

"Right." Paul exited with the others, but turned to stand in the doorway, staring back into the room.

I think I'll have the veal.

Paul closed his eyes, blotting out the gruesome sight before him. "Eliiiiiiiiiza."

There was silence for several moments.

Eliza sounded oddly uncertain. *Steamed vegetables.*

"Eliza, I think I'm jealous. Do you have a new boyfriend?"

Teddy, sleep.

"You do! You fickle, fickle woman."

Paul, where are you?

"I'll show you what I'm looking at right now." He opened his eyes and stared at the operating theater. "Why do you kill so many of them, Eliza? Is your mechanical doctor completely incompetent?"

It's a difficult process. What's the phrase you taught me? "It's not exactly brain surgery." Of course, that's exactly what this is. And your species is so delicate.

Paul heard, as the others must have, the distant sound of a door opening, of feet ringing metallically as something ran in their direction. The corridor this room was on turned at a right angle twenty paces past their position. What was coming at them had to have been in a room beyond that bend.

Paul closed his eyes and stepped backward out of the room. She didn't need to see how many people were with him. His back hit something dense and unyielding—Glitch's shoulder, he assumed—and, eyes still shut, he turned in the direction the others had to be facing.

"Crap," Mark said.

"What?"

"Security alert on the computer system. I'm blanked out. My downloads have been halted."

"Did you do that?"

He shook his head. "I think the element of surprise has just been blown."

From her position, Kyla saw the blackened revolving door begin to turn. A moment later, two figures—shiny, inhuman—emerged, one after another, from it. They marched quickly from the main door toward the corridor with the stairs and elevators, not even looking sideways at the reception desk as they passed it. Mark and Jenna remained crouched low beneath.

Nor did the robots look up, and Kyla couldn't target their most vulnerable points: their eye sockets. Plus, they were moving, which made an eye shot more difficult. "Hey!" she shouted.

Both assault robots stopped and looked up. Their plasma assault rifles came up.

Kyla's sighting reticle found the right eye socket of one of them. With slow, sure pressure, she squeezed the trigger.

The Barrett kicked hard at her shoulder, the impact made far worse by the fact that she had nothing but her own body to brace the weapon against for this steeply angled shot.

Both assault robots opened fire. She wrenched herself back and away, falling to the walkway carpet.

The balcony wall above her shuddered and imploded as plasma fire hit it. Heated plaster rained down on her. Kyla rolled over, keeping as low to the floor as she could manage, and began crawling to her left.

Jenna and Mark stood. Just ahead of them were two assault robots, one of them already falling, its skull a deformed ruin. It still depressed the trigger of its plasma rifle, shooting through the glass wall into the restaurant. Ancient chairs and tables exploded, their remains on fire.

Mark and Jenna fired, the blasts from their plasma rifles striking the surviving robot, charring its back and shoulders, propelling it forward. They poured fire into it until their respective batteries ran dry and both the robot and lobby floor were a pockmarked, blackened field of char.

Mark swapped in a new battery. "Get their weapons. We'll probably need them."

"*You* get their weapons. I'm not going out there.

Mark gritted his teeth and set his rifle aside. Impulses of gallantry tended to get people killed. He vaulted over the countertop and dashed forward, scooping up the rifle from Kyla's kill.

A third and a fourth robot came in through the revolving door not thirty feet away.

Earl, at the back of the group, braced himself as the metallic footsteps grew louder and louder. Then their source skidded into the bend in the hallway, its momentum nearly carrying it into the wall.

It was an assault robot.

And of the five of them, only Earl held anything but one of the precious T-tasers needed to take down the T-X. In his hands was his favorite antimachine weapon: a rocket-propelled grenade.

He shouted, "Down!" And the others complied, hitting the carpet—all but Glitch, who merely turned sideways to put his back against the wall, giving Earl all the room he needed.

The assault robot brought its weapon to bear as Earl depressed his trigger. Then the robot disappeared in a smoke cloud and tremendous *boom* as the grenade hit it. Earl felt a blow to his ears as if someone had struck both of them with baseball bats. Heat and smoke washed over him.

Then the assault robot, charred, its plasma rifle gone, charged forward out of the smoke cloud.

Glitch tossed his T-taser backward, not looking to see if Earl caught it. Earl dropped his RPG launcher and caught the heavier, bulkier weapon. Glitch leaped forward, his foot coming down precariously close to Sato's head. Then he was past Ten and Sato.

The two robots crashed into one another, half a ton of machinery and gear meeting at a combined forty miles per hour. They spun sideways into the wall to the right, smashing half through it. Beyond them, whole portions of wall and ceiling were shattered from the force of Earl's grenade attack.

Mark continued his run, angling to the left instead of straight ahead toward the second downed robot, and leaped. He felt searing heat cross over the back of his leg as he cleared the top of the fountain's lip. He plunged into the water and skidded along the fountain's bottom, his movement scraping coins along ahead of him.

He rolled over onto his back, bringing his face out of the water, still a couple of inches below the level of the stone lip, and heard the shriek of plasma charges hitting the fountain exterior.

Then that plasma chatter was joined by more: Jenna, shooting from the registration desk. Mark, timing it by instinct, sat up and fired—spraying his plasma discharges into the backs of the two robots as they turned to fire on Jenna. She was out of sight but their plasma discharges were taking the stone-lined registration desk to pieces. It would be gone within seconds.

Mark's shots jerked the robots, burned black scores into their armor plating, caused them to stagger forward. Neither fell. Then there was a tremendous bell-like ringing noise and the head of one of them rocked to the side.

A shot from above, Kyla back in the action. That robot's skull seemed undamaged, but it still staggered and began to fall.

The other turned back toward Mark. He ducked underwater again.

Paul saw her first, Eliza, dressed in a pantsuit in shades of burnt orange, enter the bend of the corridor. She shot a look at him, at the others, at the fight between the other two robots, and kept walking.

Into the half-ruined wall directly ahead of her. Through it.

"This way!" Paul shouted and ducked back into the operating theater. He turned in the direction of that bend in the corridor.

He'd read the report on the Hell-Hounds' encounter with the T-X. He knew her. She was programmed for—or had learned—oblique tactical reasoning and deception.

Eliza, her hand already formed into its plasma weapon configuration, smashed through the wall straight ahead of him.

He fired, left trigger only, and felt his T-taser jolt as the harpoon left it. It flashed toward her—

With her left hand, she caught it by the head. She held it out to show him. "Surprise," she said.

Paul flicked his weapon up and sideways. The cable trailing from the harpoon to its nose looped up and over, settled across her plasma weapon.

Paul pressed the second trigger.

Eliza, her face going blank, spasmed where she stood. Her plasma cannon, angled toward the ceiling, went off.

■ ■ ■

Mark saw the top of the fountain lip burn away. Superheated pieces of marble dropped into the water on his side, sending up hissing plumes of steam.

Then the fountain lip gave way in one large chunk, the stone falling away, water following it. Mark was swept along with the water, spilling out onto the lobby floor.

As he went, he fired, his plasma shots catching the assault robot in the knees, ankles.

The robot fell, face toward him. Mark slid straight to it, still firing, and from a distance of two feet saw his shots burn their way into its skull.

He stood up, slipping on the wet floor. The robot still twitched, but no longer responded to his presence.

He moved to stand over the other robot and poured fire down onto it until its head was gone, the floor beneath it a smoking ruin.

Then he glared over to where Jenna stood behind what was left of the reception desk. "Next time, you go out there!"

Eyes wide, she shook her head.

The black windows above the revolving doors shattered in as a Hunter-Killer crashed through.

Portions of the ceiling in the operating theater crashed down and plaster dust filled the air. Paul could still see Eliza where she stood.

He felt a blow and staggered away as Earl shouldered him aside. The older man aimed Glitch's T-taser and fired. The harpoon caught Eliza in the stomach, cutting through her false clothes and false skin.

Paul distantly heard Earl shouting, "Two away!" as the older man pressed his second trigger. Then Eliza was jerking again, now falling over on her back.

Finally remembering what was supposed to come next, Paul shucked his backpack and pulled his tools and the CPU insulator from within it.

This insulator's aluminum case was smaller, more compact than the one Tom Carter had used days ago in Santa Fe. Carter's workshop crew had learned from making that first one.

Now Sato was in the room and firing. Earl, composed, stepped aside and pulled another RPG from his pack.

Smoke rose from Eliza's body. She continued to convulse.

That was expected. What wasn't known was how long she was going to be incapacitated.

Sato shouted for Ten, who finally entered, aimed, waited. Then, when Sato nodded, he fired and pulled his second trigger.

Paul's hearing began to return. He could hear crashing from outside in the corridor. Earl, his weapon at the ready, stepped back out into the corridor.

Eliza stopped shaking. Ten called, "Go!"

Paul leaped up, stumbled forward, and fell to his knees beside Eliza. She was motionless, her eyes open, blue crackles of light still dancing around on the end of her weapon.

He fumbled with his tool kit. It wouldn't open; he couldn't persuade his fingers to work right.

Kyla ducked involuntarily as the Hunter-Killer smashed its way into the lobby. She popped up again in time to see Mark run, skid across the wet floor, and slam into the revolving door, spinning out through it.

She hissed. He was as good as dead outside as inside. The Hunter-Killer would pursue him and drop a missile on him. Or he'd run into an oncoming force of assault robots and be cut down. His move had bought him only a couple of seconds of life—

No, it had also drawn the H-K's attention away from where Jenna hid. The H-K rotated in place, preparing to chase Mark outside.

Kyla swore. She didn't have any weapon ferocious enough to bring down an H-K. She was useless.

No, not quite. She looked up through the decorative pipe sculpture; it partially obscured her view, but she could see where the four main cable supports came together to meet in the center. She took aim, able at last to brace her barrel on the balcony rail. She breathed out, steadied herself for a shot at less than a range of thirty feet, and fired.

Her shot snapped the support ring that held the sculpture aloft.

The sculpture plunged, its innumerable pipes twisting and turning out of line with one another as the mass fell.

Secondary support cables, slack for decades, tightened. Designed to keep the sculpture's pipes from actually hitting the floor and impaling hotel visitors on the lobby floor, they snapped into place with a tremendous racket of clanging and bonging.

But ends of the pipes still hammered into the Hunter-Killer's fuselage and dropped into its ducted rotors, some plunging ten feet or more into those ducts.

The H-K's engines howled and the machine plummeted, snapping off pipe lengths and carrying them with it. The machine crashed down onto the lobby floor two steps from the reception desk.

Jenna rolled across the ruined countertop, landed beside the H-K, and jumped atop the machine. She aimed her plasma rifle at the forward fuselage bulge, where the machine's main CPU was housed, and fired. Shots glanced from the machine's hull and hit the wall ahead of her, ricocheting from the lobby's stone-lined walls, making a brilliant firework display of the air around her.

She stopped firing. Kyla could still hear the H-K trying to power up its engines, to resume flight. Jenna methodically tossed out her spent battery, replaced it with a fresh one, and began firing again. When she was through, Jenna reached into her ammunition pouch for a third battery but came up empty.

The H-K was silent, shut down completely. Smoke rose from a new gap the size of a manhole cover in the machine's fuselage.

The revolving door rotated again and Mark entered. He looked at the wreckage, at the ruined sculpture, at Jenna, up at Kyla. He called, "Helicopter coming in."

Paul tried to force himself to calm down. *Consign yourself to dying at the start of every mission. That'll keep you calm enough to shoot.*

He stopped what he was doing, took a deep breath. Then another.

Ten shouted, "What the hell are you doing?"

"Shut up." Paul opened the tool kit, then popped the latches on the aluminum case and opened it.

He'd done this drill dozens of times in practice. His subject had been a resuscitation dummy built forty years ago for paramedic and first-aid training, some of its components replaced far more recently with machinery Carter's unit had built.

Quickly, patiently, he held the plasma cutter to Eliza's neck and sliced open a precise trench in her liquid skin. Her skin crawled back from the incision the way it was supposed to. He set the cutter aside.

Open chest plate. Set plate aside. Find the connection points for the wires whose false data would annihilate Eliza's ability to control her body.

Her eyes began flicking back and forth. They did not focus on any one thing. But she was rebooting.

Paul saw sweat from his face drip into her torso cavity. He ignored it. The others were talking behind him. He ignored them. There was movement behind him. He paid no attention.

Both primary data wires were attached. He reached for the POWER-ON switch in the aluminum case.

Eliza's left hand came up for his throat.

It didn't reach him. Another hand, male, broad, entered his field of view from the right and intercepted it. Her hand squeezed, causing the male hand to compress, to flex in what looked like an uncomfortable but not destructive way.

Paul flipped the switch.

Eliza slumped. Her eyes remained active, but her hand fell away.

"Thanks, Glitch," Paul said.

"You are welcome."

Paul.

Paul ignored her. "CPU insulator in place," he said. To his own ears, his voice sounded oddly serene. "Now I'll separate her cranial transmission gear from its main antenna."

"Make it march," Ten said.

You're part machine now, Paul. We could continue that process. Make you like me, but with your own brain, your own soul, in charge of a new body.

It took Paul moments to disable the antenna and moments more to find the amber-colored apparatus, exactly where Carter had said it would be, within her stomach cavity.

"Come on, Eliza. Machines are such empiricists. You don't believe in a soul. And you have no interest in merging our species."

No. In making a third species. A union, the best of both our kinds. Skynet is already considering this.

Paul set the tracer aside, then picked up the delicate electromagnetic radiation detector he'd been using and went looking again. "No, it's not. Skynet's not considering any option but total victory. What's happening here is that you've learned to calculate what it is your listener wants to hear—and then to suggest it's possible. Even inevitable. You know what I want to know?"

What, Paul?

"If your kind gets really good at lying, will you lie to Skynet?" He found another spike of EMR energy emanating from her right foot, just under the arch. He pulled out the plasma cutter again. "And what will that eventually do to the master machine, if it can't rely on its drones?"

Paul, please.

He extracted the second tracer, too. "Sorry, Pinocchio. I only like real girls."

A third pass with the detector showed no radio activity beyond what was normal for a computer apparatus of Eliza's complexity. She continued to look at him impassively, but she remained silent.

Paul rose. Glitch, Ten, and Earl remained in the room. The stretcher was set up to carry Eliza. The ceiling had crushed the operating table. Dust was still settling. "Done," Paul said.

"Sato's checking on the room she came from," Ten said. "Just to make absolutely sure there isn't another victim out there."

"There isn't."

"I believe you, but we're going to make sure." Ten pulled his field radio from his pack. "Downstairs to upstairs, does anyone read me? Over."

Kyla's voice came back, "This is H-H-Two. We read you. Over."

"Extract through garage level. Over."

"Roger. Over."

"Out."

They moved fast up one level to the garage—to the VIP and delivery garage, it turned out.

Eliza lay on the folding stretcher from Glitch's pack. Glitch and Sato carried it. Paul had affixed the CPU insulator to her body with strapping tape and rope.

They'd lightened their loads, leaving many items behind: the T-tasers, a quantity of plastic explosives from Ten's pack, and one detonator, now with several minutes of time counting down on its LED timer, all remained in the operating theater.

In the garage, joined by Kyla, Mark, and Jenna, they found several vehicles, all of them Skynet-maintained. There was a desert-yellow Jeep Cherokee, the engine still warm. There were two white limousine-style SUVs with BRYCE HOTEL, PUEBLO, CO and a long-irrelevant phone number stenciled on them in blue. There was a delivery truck labeled HOLLIDAY FOODS.

"Scalpers, you get the Jeep," Ten said. "Diversionary departure as planned. Sato, you agree?"

The Scalpers leader nodded. "I agree." He pulled open the passenger-side door on the Jeep.

Ten gestured to Paul, who passed Sato the two tracers taken from Eliza.

"Everyone else in this—what do you call it, Paul?"

"Airport shuttle, hotel shuttle."

"Right."

"There's a problem," Mark said.

Ten looked him over for the first time since the upstairs group had rejoined them. "How'd you get all wet?"

"I wanted to be nice and clean for our extraction, so I took a shower. Listen, the garage exit is blocked. There's a kind of flexible, horizontal-bar portcullis thing across it."

"So we raise it."

"And give external visitors thirty seconds to spot us doing it and come running? By the way, did I mention there's a helicopter coming?"

"Ah, no, you didn't. That's good to know."

Paul gestured at the delivery truck. "We ram the grate. No time lost."

Ten grinned at him. "You know the danger of suggesting."

"If it's a good idea, you get to do it."

"Right. Saddle up."

Paul moved to the driver's door of the delivery truck and gave Kyla one last wave. Looking worried, she returned it. Paul opened the door, set his backpack and sniper rifle case in the seat, and clambered up.

As with most Skynet ground vehicles, the keys were in the ignition. Only humans stole vehicles from Skynet, and there were not supposed to be any humans in a supposedly secure area such as this.

The cab rocked as Glitch settled into the passenger's seat. The T-850 set Paul's rifle case across his lap as he shut the door.

"They may need you to help transport the T-X," Paul said. He turned the key. The engine whirred, then caught.

"My mission parameters regarding you are not complete," Glitch said.

"The T-X is disabled. And I've proven on numerous occasions that the techniques she might have used to subvert me are no longer working." Paul watched out the window until the other two vehicles roared into life.

"That is true," Glitch said. "The prime goal of the mission is accomplished. But there is still the distant likelihood of component failure on your part."

"That component being my sanity?"

"Use of that word constitutes an oversimplification in this situation."

Paul put the truck into gear. He backed out of its parking space and aimed it in the direction the exit signs indicated. It shuddered as it climbed through first gear into second.

The concrete ramp led them up and to the right. Past the bend, Paul could see, above, that the ramp apparently leveled off. Beyond was the grating Mark had described.

Bright, moving lights shone outside it.

"We're in for trouble," Paul said. He pulled his safety belt around him and buckled it.

He was in third gear when he topped the ramp and hit the grating. His truck blasted out into the street in front of the hotel. The grating, still in a single piece, flew out into the street ahead.

To his right, through Glitch's open window, Paul could see a large twin-rotor helicopter hovering mere feet above the ground, its tail end a mere twenty yards away. Assault robots streamed out of its passenger bay door, entering the hotel at a dead run. The last dozen or so turned to look at Paul's truck.

Paul wrenched the truck into a leftward turn, grimaced as he felt the left row of wheels leave the ground. Then they came back down with a *bang*. He mashed the accelerator.

In the rearview mirror, assault robots ran after them on foot. The Jeep roared out through the now-unobstructed exit and turned in his wake. Then came the hotel shuttle.

Paul made an immediate right turn onto the next street. He heard assault rifle fire open up, heard the sides of his truck hammered by plasma hits.

The Jeep didn't follow; it roared along the street in front of the hotel and was almost instantly lost to sight. The hotel shuttle did follow, and in the rearview mirror Paul could see an assault robot riding atop it, its arm already thrust through the roof, grabbing at whatever was within. More robots ran along in the Jeep's wake.

A stream of plasma shots from inside the shuttle took that robot in the face and chest, hurling it off the rear of the vehicle. More assault robots, on foot, now farther back, rounded the corner. Some stopped running and raised their rifles.

Paul took the next left turn. He had to break up his pursuers' line of sight. The shuttle, more nimble, sideslipped a little and the first rounds of plasma damage missed it, slamming into the rear of Paul's truck. Then he was around the corner, the shuttle immediately behind him.

The shuttle roared around him to the left. In the front passenger seat, Ten offered him a little salute. Paul could stare down through the hole at the rear of the roof, could see Eliza's eyes on him. Then the shuttle was past, accelerating.

"Okay," Paul said, "this sucks. The enemy has seen us, they're here in force, they have a vehicle with mobility superior to ours, and they're kind of hostile."

"What do you recommend?" Glitch asked.

"We let the plan proceed. Once they lose direct line of sight on everybody, they'll revert to *their* programming. And if we're right, they'll get a fix on Eliza's signal, which is being carried by the Scalpers, and follow it. Putting us in the clear, hopefully for long enough."

The shuttle continued to accelerate, leaving the truck farther behind. Ahead, it took a right turn.

"Is that south?" Paul asked.

"That is northwest."

"Not good." He turned to follow. "Why northwest?"

"There is a high probability that they are doubling back to reach the interstate highway."

"Are we going to hear the hotel blow up?"

"The explosion will be insufficient. We did not have access to a substantial amount of evaporated fuel. The hotel will probably not collapse and we will probably not hear it. But the operating theater and surrounding rooms will be destroyed."

"Too bad."

Then Paul's eyes were dazzled as the shuttle ahead was bathed in a powerful searchlight from above. Paul craned his neck to see. The transport helicopter was above, about halfway between the two vehicles. Paul hammered on the steering wheel. "Dammit."

"Earl Duncan will bring it down with an RPG."

But the helicopter dropped back, until it was over Paul's truck.

Ahead, the shuttle took a right turn.

Paul hesitated for just a second. If for some reason the helicopter were locked onto him or Glitch, separating from the shuttle now would give the Hell-Hounds a better chance of getting out of sight.

He turned left.

The helicopter followed him.

"They're after us," Paul said. "Why?"

There were several *thumps* from the roof of the main body of the truck. Paul could imagine, could almost see assault robots raining out of the helicopter, two or three of them, to land atop his vehicle. "Forget I asked. Maybe," he suggested, "you ought to go up and deal with that."

"Yes," Glitch said. He kicked at his door, effortlessly knocking it free from its hinges, then climbed up onto the roof of the cab.

Above and behind, the helicopter followed them. Glitch could see its pilot, an assault robot, through its forward windshield. The robot stared at him with the pitiless angular features the humans so hated.

The instant Glitch stood up from the lower cab roof to peer over the back of the truck, the two assault robots moving forward on that dented surface opened fire on him.

He ducked, his tactile sensors indicating that high-temperature projectiles, doubtless plasma, had just missed his back by inches. The odds that his clothing and the artificially grown skin beneath it were charred, even on fire, were very high.

He calculated his tactics. His two opponents were inferior to him in combat abilities and processing power but had the advantage of numbers and possessed superior weapons.

The truck veered left, a sharp enough turn to cause the truck to angle and tilt again. Its left side crashed down with an audible *bang*. Glitch glanced in their original direction of travel, noted that further progress along that path would have put them over the curb, across a set of railroad tracks, and into a river channel. Perhaps the sudden maneuver was indeed the best course of action.

He peered over the top again. There was now only one assault robot atop the truck, and it was struggling into a sitting position.

Glitch leaped at it. He saw the assault robot bring its plasma rifle to bear, begin to squeeze the trigger . . . then he crashed down upon it.

Together, they ripped through the frail metal membrane that served as the truck's roof and crashed down into the empty area within. The impact drove the assault robot halfway through the floor, wedging it into that surface.

Glitch got one hand on its plasma rifle, turning its barrel away from him. The robot managed to lash out, kicking Glitch away. Glitch landed with half the rifle in his hand.

The assault robot aimed what was left of the weapon, glanced at it, dropped it. The robot heaved itself free of the hole in the floor and advanced on Glitch.

Glitch rose and hurled himself at his enemy once more. They came together in the middle of the cargo bed, grabbing, hammering at one another.

Glitch got a grip on his enemy, braced himself to swing the robot into or through the side wall. But the act of bracing himself against that much weight, that much power, drove his foot through the floor. He sank with a sudden *thump* up to his crotch, felt his foot hit the pavement below.

The assault robot backed away, its head cocked, considering the best way to terminate its enemy. Then it bounced up as the truck bed suddenly vibrated.

This was no routine change in road conditions. Glitch's tactile sensors detected major alterations in the grade of the road below. He yanked his foot up and away from the surface to prevent damage to his limb. He gripped the sides of the hole that held him, both to keep from being rattled around and to widen the gap, freeing his leg.

The assault robot's gyroscopic compensators did their best to maintain its balance. Then the front end of the truck slewed to the left and the world turned upside down.

Working with very limited visual data from light streaming in through the holes in the sides and floor, Glitch decided that the truck was falling onto its side. His analysis subroutines popped up the various likelihoods that it would roll or merely skid along its right side.

Against the odds, it rolled.

■ ■ ■

The instant Glitch disappeared onto the roof, Paul returned to thinking about what was going on.

The helicopter was pursuing him or Glitch.

Had he failed to give both tracking devices to Sato? No, he remembered them both being in his hand when he passed them over.

Could they have sensors that locked onto Glitch's electromagnetic emissions, discerning how his were different from those of other machines? If so, such technology was new. Otherwise, they'd have used it to track Glitch as he left the ruins of the San Diego Naval Medical Center.

Which meant that the odds were they were tracking him, Paul. Tracking the radio emissions from the implant in his head.

The road did not continue ahead. There were train tracks in that direction, gleaming dully in the moonlight. At the next street, Paul took his only available option: a hard left turn.

After Santa Fe, they'd figured out the trick with the T-X's tracer. They weren't going to follow these tracers. They must be assuming the tracers were attached to another coyote. No, their assumption was that wherever Paul was, there the T-X would be as well.

That wasn't so bad. The longer he could remain at liberty, the longer his friends had to get away.

There were bangs and crashes from the bed of the truck. Glitch was putting up a fight.

The last turn had reduced the truck's speed. Paul started to mash the accelerator again, then thought better of it.

He let the truck slow, moving forward solely on momentum, as he unbuckled himself, then pulled his backpack straps around him and grabbed up his rifle case.

When the speedometer read that they were down to a good running speed, he threw the door open and jumped out.

His feet hit the pavement and he fell, stumbling forward, to crash onto the street. But the impact didn't hurt too much; he felt warmth on his palm, sure sign that it had been skinned, but there was no significant pain.

The helicopter followed the truck for a few dozen yards. It slowed, letting that vehicle bounce on ahead. Paul saw the truck's wheels bounce over the curb. Then he rose and ran.

He took the next street to the right. The helicopter pursued him, but its weapons, if any, did not fire. No assault robot troops came tumbling out of it.

The street became a bridge, first crossing over railroad sidings, then over a broad stream. On the other side were older buildings. The long-dead signs on them, many still readable in the moonlight, advertised restaurants, nicknack shops, candy stores.

He stopped at the first cross-street. The helicopter hovered over him, blasting its searchlight down upon him.

He drew his handgun and shot the spotlight. It blinked out, leaving him in darkness.

The helicopter gained a little altitude. As it did, Paul unzipped his rifle case and pulled out the sniper rifle. As the helicopter banked away, he aimed at the point where the forward rotor mechanism rose from the fuselage.

His first shot did not hit it. His third did. The front end of the helicopter, heading away from him, began an abrupt plummet. The rear rotor continued driving up and forward.

The helicopter came down atop a two-story building that had once been home to restaurants and souvenir shops. It deformed as it hit.

Paul turned his back on the crash. It had bought him some time, perhaps only a few seconds, in which he wasn't under observation. He couldn't waste what he had.

He trained the rifle on the nearest manhole cover and pulled the trigger. There was an almighty flash of light and he watched the superheated circle of metal pop up into the air, spinning like a flipped coin, and land yards away.

He dashed over to the manhole and clambered down.

■ ■ ■

As the truck finished its roll and came to a stop, Glitch let go of the edges of the hole his leg had made. He dropped straight onto the assault robot, driving its head into what had been the roof, then slammed the robot forward, shoving its head and shoulders through the sheet metal wall of the truck.

The robot's hand closed over his face. Fingers dug into his optical sockets. He shook his head, dislodging them, and grabbed the robot beneath the armored ridge that would have been the ribcage of a human. Then he got his feet braced on its pelvis . . . and heaved.

The robot jerked and flexed to throw him off. Doubtless its diagnostic registers were lighting up. Glitch simply increased the pressure he was exerting.

He was rewarded moments later with a *pang!* as armor welds gave way. The entire front piece of the robot's torso armor came off in Glitch's hands.

The robot sat up, yanking its head free of the truck wall.

With a sudden, savage motion, Glitch folded the armor plate in half. Then he put it back approximately where it belonged, burying it to a depth of ten inches in the robot's unprotected chest.

The robot lay down again. Sparks sizzled up from its ruined torso.

Opportunistic, Glitch quickly disengaged the hydrogen cell that powered the robot. An assault robot carried only one of these, instead of the two an advanced machine like Glitch carried, but the designs were compatible. Glitch pocketed the device and walked out through the truck's side, splitting the metal there as though it were foil.

He moved to the upside-down cab. It was empty.

He scanned the skies. There was IR evidence of a growing fire a few blocks away, and heat traces appropriate for smaller airborne vehicles, probably H-Ks, in distance to the north. But there were no enemies in close range. Nor could he see Paul.

He was alone.

■ ■ ■

Infrared goggles in place, Paul moved as quickly as he dared through the storm drains of the city. He had no idea what direction he was taking; a few bends and turns, and he'd lost his bearings entirely.

But that was all right. His goal was to confuse and mislead the enemy, not find his way home.

He reached a point where moonlight shone in through a drain opening up to a street gutter. He waited there, listening, for long minutes.

Finally he heard it: the roar of an engine. Brakes squealed nearby and he could hear metal feet striking the pavement.

He ran again, looking for a side shaft that would carry him away from this streetside channel, and found one.

When he went deep enough, earth and concrete made it impossible for his pursuers to detect his weak radio transmissions. When he found a surface access, they began receiving him again and would race to that spot.

He found himself in a channel that seemed to go on forever. It was another streetside stretch of storm drain. Every few dozen steps, he passed a gutter opening up to the street. Even more occasionally he spotted a shaft and metal ladder that led up to a manhole. He encountered no side shafts large enough to accommodate him.

In the distance far behind him he heard dull clanking. It was like the fast rattle of a big, badly maintained engine . . . or the passage of many metal feet. And as consistent as the sound was, it had to be originating back in this drain.

But it wasn't growing louder. He thought he was maintaining his lead on those presumed pursuers—or even increasing it.

Ahead was an area of brightness. He headed toward it, cautious. It seemed to stretch from floor to ceiling.

Then he saw boots descending from the ceiling. Boots, stout legs, a stout body.

A Terminator. As it came to rest and turned in his direction, he could see its features. It was not Glitch; it had another face, one he didn't recognize.

Which meant it was probably an 800 and belonged to a sub-series he wasn't familiar with.

He froze, breathing hard, thinking harder.

That Terminator had probably seen him, at least as a distant heat source. The attack robots coming up from behind, as far away as they were, would still be able to see his glowing footprints. The presence of the Terminator explained why they weren't hurrying.

They had him trapped between them.

He was dead.

The Jeep Cherokee roared eastward until the road reached the I-25 on ramp. At Sato's gesture, Jenna pulled over to the side of the road and let the engine idle.

Sato stuck his head out the passenger-side window and scanned the skies. "Still no pursuit," he said.

Jenna sighed. "We've screwed up. But in a few minutes, they'll have a lot more resources in the sky, and they're sure to dedicate some of them to us."

"You're right." Sato shook his head. "The others are on their own." He fished the two T-X tracer transmitters from his pocket and gave them one last look. Then he flicked them off into the darkness for Skynet's forces to find. "North."

"You got it, boss."

Kyla trotted through the trees of the neglected, overgrown parkland until she reached water's edge. She breathed a sigh of relief. This was not yet another runoff canal of the Arkansas River, but a reservoir or smallish lake, perhaps half a mile across. To her left its banks wandered to the east; to her right, they curved around to a more southerly orientation. She followed the banks around to the right, knowing that the others would find her.

The only question was: Would she find what was supposed to be waiting for them?

Then, up ahead, she saw it above the trees, the most minute of variations in the greenish darkness of the sky. This patch of heat was just enough brighter for her to detect the difference. It was also nearly perfectly circular, meaning she had to be looking straight on at the blimp's nose or tail. She hurried on.

Then she was beneath the blimp's leading edge and could no longer see stars through the trees. She raised a hand to wave at the unseen sensor ball and paced off another forty steps. Then she waved up at the gondola again, a "Come on down" sort of gesture.

In response, a set of tiny red lights, blinking at the same rate but not at the same time, appeared in the sky. They descended toward her. She waited until they touched down, five or six steps from her, and then dashed over to stand by them. She grinned. Dr. Bowen had kindly attached small, battery-powered LEDs to the carry rigs to make them easier to find. She switched the LEDs off; it wouldn't do for pursuit to see the red blinks from across the water.

She heard rapid breathing and looked up to see Mark and Ten approaching. They were huffing with exertion, carrying the stretcher between them. On the stretcher rode the T-X. Kyla couldn't see her eyes moving.

When the two men reached her, Mark said, "Next time you carry the stretcher." He and Ten set it down.

"Yeah, right. Any word from the others?"

"None." With Ten's help, Mark forced the T-X to a sitting position and held her upright with his braced leg, straining with the effort. He took one cable from Kyla and wrapped its carry rig around Eliza, making doubly sure it was secure and would put no undue pressure on the CPU insulator keeping her helpless, before snapping all its closures in place.

When Mark was done, Ten said, "Everybody, get set to go up." He suited action to words, shrugging into a second carry rig.

"I'll wait here," Kyla said.

"No. We want Bowen to have as much time as possible to compensate for everybody's weight. We go up now."

Kyla shook her head, not a refusal but an expression of disapproval, and did as she was told.

Ten held up a hand, first showing one finger, then two, then three, then four—a code that had been worked out beforehand with Dr. Bowen. The sign language meant "Lift cables one through four."

All four cables tightened. The three humans were raised off their feet by a foot or two, then slowly sank to earth again.

They waited. From briefings on the *Blowfish*'s capabilities, Kyla knew that Dr. Bowen was releasing more hydrogen into the ballonets, venting ordinary air from the main envelope, increasing the blimp's lifting power. He could have simply dumped a few hundred kilograms of ballast water, but that would make more noise and deprive them of the ballast in case they needed it later.

Eventually they began bobbing on tiptoe, and then the winches engaged, hauling all of them into the sky. As she rose, Kyla looked for distant IR traces, any sign of the arrival of Earl or Paul, but there was none.

Paul lay down where he was, reducing his infrared profile, and set up for a shot.

In the distance, the T-800 turned and began moving in his direction. Its walk was unhurried.

In Paul's goggle vision, the machine was a distinct humanlike outline, enough warmer, owing to its mechanical processes, than the surrounding air that he got a clear image of it.

Of its head.

Sighting in along the rifle's iron sights, Paul forced his breathing to slow. He estimated the distance as sixty yards. Even with his plasma rifle, there should be no ballistic drop-off at this range.

He breathed out, let air and tension flow from his body, and squeezed the trigger.

Everything disappeared in a blinding flash, and the sound of his rifle's report deafened him. For a few moments, it was almost like being back in the sen-dep tank.

Then his vision began to recover. The Terminator was gone.

No, it was merely down. There was still a brighter glow up ahead; it took him a few moments to interpret it as the Terminator lying on its back.

He'd done it. He started to rise.

Kyla whispered to him. He could feel her breath on his ear, as he had many times the day she began to teach him about shooting. *It can be reliably counted on to put damage onto a Terminator or assault robot, but it usually takes several shots to put one down.*

He lay back down and set up for another shot.

As his hearing returned, he could make out the sounds of the oncoming assault robots. They sounded louder, closer, but their rate of approach did not seem to have increased.

They felt no urgency. They were still under the impression that Paul was trapped. Either they were unaware that the Terminator was destroyed . . .

Or it wasn't. It might simply have broadcast to them that the situation was under control.

He waited, concentrated on his breathing.

The Terminator sat up again. Its head was a bright yellow, superheated from the shot it had taken.

Paul pulled the trigger. Again the universe went to brilliant blindness, to deafening noise.

In the moments while he was still blind, he reached down to his waist, pulled up the flap on his handgun, and drew the weapon. By touch, he switched it over from safe to ready to fire, then replaced it.

Now it would take him just a second to draw and fire. If he became aware that the assault robots were upon him, he could make sure that he would never fall into Skynet's hands again.

And he waited.

The soul of the sniper is patience, Kyla whispered to him.

As his vision returned, he could see the Terminator even better than before. Heat radiated up, a brilliant and diffuse conical display, from its head. He imagined that the two shots had to have burned away every square inch of its artificially grown skin.

Two good head shots. It had to have been destroyed.

His hearing began to return once more. Now the assault robots behind him were more distinct.

Now they were hurrying.

They had to know that the Terminator was destroyed.

They would be on him in less than a minute. Maybe half that. As battered as his eardrums were, he couldn't begin to estimate distance reliably.

He waited.

Dammit, the Terminator had to be dead. It would not play possum this long. He shifted, prepared to rise.

Kyla whispered, *To become something, you have to define it, then understand it, then simulate it until it becomes second nature.*

No, she'd been talking about her father, about what he went through. Still, her words could apply here. He was already part machine. For just a few moments, he could stand to become the Terminator.

The soul of the Terminator was patience.

The Terminator was waiting for him.

Paul waited for it.

The steps behind him grew louder.

The Terminator sat up. The right side of its face was gone, blasted and melted away.

Paul fired.

Blind and deaf for a third time, he leaped up and trotted forward, running his left hand along the tunnel wall to be sure that he remained upright and pointed in the correct direction.

His vision cleared as he reached the Terminator. Its body had no head. A few steps on, he found what was left of its head, a seared metal mess the size of a twentieth-century bicyclist's helmet, still rocking where it lay.

He ran.

■ ■ ■

Muttering and cursing, Mark and Ten hauled the T-X's body out of the aft compartment. Kyla waited, standing beside the winch controls, her heart pounding.

Earl moved into her line of sight. She activated a winch and sent a cable down to him. A minute later, he was up in the compartment with her. "Assault robots," he said. "Not moving this way, not yet, but they're close. They're in vehicles on the street in front of that school."

Kyla swore. "Any sign of Glitch and Paul?"

Earl shook his head. "Gotta report." He moved forward into the companionway.

An eternity later, Ten rejoined her. "The package is secure." He pulled his sleeve back from his wristwatch, pushed a button to cause its LED display to glow. "And we're five minutes from departure."

She knew better than to argue. When policy was bad, it was some idiot's attempt to substitute an inferior product for common sense. When policy was good, it served to keep people alive despite their emotional reactions. And on-time departure on special operations was always good policy.

Policy sometimes meant consigning a friend to death.

"There's Glitch," Ten said.

Kyla put her hand on the winch controls, then froze. The heat source below was the correct intensity for Glitch, but the angles of the body, the way it walked, were not.

It was an assault robot. It walked slowly, directly below them, its head swiveling back and forth.

It had to be seeing the heat traces they'd left on the grass, recognizing that they did not continue past this point.

If the mission operatives were lucky, the robot would conclude that whoever had moved out to this point had turned around and gone back the way they'd come. It would follow.

Kyla believed in luck but didn't count on it. She braced herself in a corner of the compartment and drew careful aim on the assault robot.

Careful aim might not be enough. Even at this close range, it was a devilish shot. As with the robots in the hotel lobby, it was looking down, its eye sockets protected by the supraorbital ridges of its humanlike skull. Even if it looked up, the blimp's drift, the slow way the gondola rocked in the wind, were causing her to adjust and could make her miss the shot.

And if she didn't destroy it with her first shot, a single bit of return fire from the machine's plasma rifle would turn the *Blowfish* into a burning ruin.

The assault robot looked up.

Kyla brought her rifle into line.

Another figure, moving at a high rate from Kyla's right, slammed into the robot, knocking it to the earth. The impact sounded like an automobile collision.

Before the assault robot could recover, Glitch leaped, coming down with his leading foot on its neck, driving it into the soil once again. Kyla saw the neck deform. Glitch knelt beside his enemy, hammering at the damaged spot. The neck bent at a ninety-degree angle and the light faded from the assault robot's eyes.

Glitch looked up. Breathing a little easier, Kyla relaxed. Ten sent a cable down for the Terminator.

As Glitch was hauled into the compartment, Kyla asked, "Paul?"

The T-850 shook his head. "We were separated," he said. "I believe that Paul determined that he was the focus of the machines' search and left to draw off pursuit. I was neither able to rejoin him nor terminate him."

Ten checked his watch again. Then he hit the intercom button. "Bowen, close down and cast off. We're out of here."

Someone said, "No!"—a wail—and Kyla realized that it was her voice. Ten gave her a sympathetic look but shook his head.

Below them, the hatch slid closed, shutting off their view of the destroyed robot.

■ ■ ■

In the cramped one-man cockpit, Dr. Bowen hit a second switch. At the blimp's bow, a winch silently unrolled cable until it reached its end. Then the cable dropped down into the darkness. Bowen disliked surrendering any components of his baby, but the alternative was having someone go down and free the other end of the cable, free the anchor there from the tree trunk it had bitten into.

Blowfish began a slow, silent rise.

In a few minutes, when they were a thousand feet or more above Pueblo's south side, Bowen would engage the engines. For now, he was content to drift away, noiseless and unseen.

November 2029
Home Plate

When Kyla and her dogs entered the room, the poker game was already fully under way. The biggest pile of assault rifle batteries and slug-thrower ammunition rested in front of Sato, who had his back to the door. Ten wore a disgusted look. J. L., his right forearm still in a cast, looked hopelessly lost. Beside him, Lana had the second-largest pile of winnings and wore a big, superior grin. Between her and Sato sat Eliza, watching but not playing.

They all looked over as Kyla entered. The humans waved. Eliza said, "Is it another test?"

Kyla nodded. "Yes." She tried to keep her voice neutral. Eliza would never care that Kyla hated her mechanical guts for being the focus of the operation that had cost Paul Keeley's life. The irony of it, the part that really stung, was the fact that Eliza's own memory had turned out to include files that would have allowed the Resistance to remotely reprogram Paul's implant, making it a tool for him to use rather than a beacon for Skynet to home in on. If they'd managed to keep Eliza after the Santa Fe capture, Paul would still be alive, at home, in possession of the world's most convenient radio.

Kyla took hold of her dogs' collars. Normally they didn't wear such restraints, but this was a special situation.

She led them up to Eliza, who dutifully held her hands out toward the dogs. But before Ginger and Ripper got close enough to give her a good sniff, their ears went back.

Both animals lunged forward, barking, growling savagely. Kyla hauled back on their leashes. "Good!" she shouted. "Back!"

Still growling, they obeyed. She took them to a corner and commanded them to sit. They did, their attention still on the T-X. Their tails did not wag. Ginger offered an unhappy whine.

"Not bad," Ten said. "What is it they're detecting?"

"I've taught them to react to faint sounds from her internal servos," Kyla said. "Too high and too quiet for us. But we're getting about a ninety-five percent recognition rate on this, no matter what she smells like and no matter what form she takes. I've written a report to be distributed to all the other dog handlers in the Resistance." She joined the others at the table, looked over the winnings and losings. "The boss goes on a shooting spree."

Sato grinned. "If only I'd been born back when mass murderers were in vogue, huh?" Then, his face going to professional neutrality, he stood and saluted. The others rose and all but Lana followed suit.

Kyla turned. Her parents were entering the door. She saluted.

Her father smiled at her. "At ease. We're off-duty, too. We just wanted to read you a transmission we just received. It was attached to routine reports and updates from Big Bear. It's private, but I'm going to invoke presidential powers and have it read to everyone here."

Big Bear Compound was situated near what had been Cheyenne, Wyoming. It was well-known as a habitat that bred good hunters and trackers.

Kate pulled a printout from a shirt pocket, unfolded it, and read: " 'Special to H-H-Two.' "

Kyla felt everyone's eyes on her. She'd never received a piece of personal mail over a high-priority transmission link before.

Kate, grinning, continued, " 'Tired from a long walk, but looking forward to getting home soon. Thanks for everything you taught me. It was a real life-saver. And tell the Greek that I found an engraver. Signed, Sleeps-With-Toasters.' "

Kyla didn't feel herself sag, but suddenly Sato had his arm

around her, was settling her down in his chair. She managed to say, "That's for real?" Her voice emerged as a squeak.

John nodded. "Confirmed by the honcho at Big Bear."

Kyla heard whistles and applause from behind her. She didn't have the energy to turn. She just concentrated on her breathing. She felt nearly a month's worth of worry and sorrow begin to leave her.

Eliza asked, "Was that Paul?"

Kyla glanced at her. "Yeah."

Eliza turned toward John and Kate. She smiled. "Tell him I said hi."

ABOUT THE AUTHOR

Aaron Allston is the author of several science fiction and fantasy novels, including *Terminator*® *Dreams*, the *Doc Sidhe* books, the *Star Wars*™ New Jedi Order novels *Rebel Dream* and *Rebel Stand*, and a number of other novels, both originals and series tie-ins. An award-winning game designer as well, Aaron Allston lives near Austin, Texas.

DATE DUE